JANE AUSTEN
MADE ME DO IT

Ballantine Books Trade Paperbacks / New York

JANE AUSTEN MADE ME DO IT

Original Stories Inspired by Literature's
Most Astute Observer of the Human Heart

EDITED BY

Laurel Ann Nattress

A Ballantine Books Trade Paperback Original

Copyright © 2011 by Laurel Ann Nattress
Reading group guide copyright © 2011 by Random House, Inc.

Published in the United States by Ballantine Books, an imprint of The Random House Publishing Group, a division of Random House, Inc., New York.

BALLANTINE BOOKS and colophon are registered trademarks of Random House, Inc. RANDOM HOUSE READER'S CIRCLE & Design is a registered trademark of Random House, Inc.

Story credits can be found on page 446.

LIBRARY OF CONGRESS CATALOGING-IN-PUBLICATION DATA
Jane Austen made me do it: original stories inspired by literature's most astute observer of the human heart/edited by Laurel Ann Nattress.
p. cm.
ISBN 978-0-345-52496-6
eBook ISBN 978-0-345-52497-3
1. Love stories, American. 2. Love stories, English. 3. Man-woman relationships—Fiction. 4. Austen, Jane, 1775–1817—Fiction.
I. Nattress, Laurel Ann.
PS648.L6J36 2011
813'.010806—dc23 2011024613

Printed in the United States of America

www.randomhousereaderscircle.com

2 4 6 8 9 7 5 3 1

Book design by Casey Hampton

To my mother Carolyn,
who always encouraged me to reach for my dreams . . .

and to Jane Austen,
the "gilder of every pleasure, the soother of every sorrow."

—LAUREL ANN NATTRESS

CONTENTS

INTRODUCTION

*That the Miss Lucases and the Miss Bennets should meet to talk over a
ball was absolutely necessary.*

—*Pride and Prejudice*

There are few authors whose name alone personifies wit, style,
and social reproof as brilliantly as that of English novelist Jane
Austen. Her six major works, published between 1811 and 1817,
have been embraced as masterpieces of world literature by scholars and pleasure readers alike, evoking images of the landed gentry engaged in drawing-room comedies of manners and social
machinations during the Regency era. Renowned for her percep-
tive characterizations, beautiful language, and engaging plots,
Austen was not only the witty muse of the nineteenth-century
novel, she continues to inspire writers today, fostering the flourishing Austenesque-sequel genre. For those who greatly admire
Austen and the unique world she created, there are now hundreds
of books continuing her stories, characters, and outlook on life
and love, written by creative and talented authors. This short-
story anthology contains twenty-two contributions exclusively

commissioned from popular and bestselling authors who have excelled in fiction inspired by Austen or other genres and who greatly admire her talent. Each will readily admit, "Jane Austen made me do it!"

> *"We have all a better guide in ourselves, if we would attend to it, than any other person can be."*
>
> —Fanny Price, *Mansfield Park*

Editing this anthology has been a lifetime in the making, and I, too, freely admit that "Jane Austen made me do it!" In 1980, I was a young college student studying landscape design at Cal Poly, San Luis Obispo, secretly taking elective units in British history and literature to fuel my interest for all things English. I was a closet Anglophile in a sea of agriculture and engineering students when the PBS television series *Masterpiece Theatre* aired Fay Weldon's adaptation of *Pride and Prejudice*. It was a seminal moment. A fan had been born. I was now a Janeite, though at the time I did not know the term existed, let alone that there were other acolytes out there as passionate as I was. Inspired by the miniseries, I read all of Austen's novels and worshiped in silence.

> *If adventures will not befall a young lady in her own village, she must seek them abroad.*
>
> —*Northanger Abbey*

I was familiar with Jane Austen and the story of *Pride and Prejudice* in a peripheral way through an early introduction by my mother to the 1940 MGM movie starring Laurence Olivier and Greer Garson. However, that creative Hollywoodization of one of literature's glistening jewels did not ignite an iota of interest beyond a quick perusal of an edition of *The Complete Novels of*

Jane Austen in the family library. It did, however, plant a seed. By the time I saw actors Elizabeth Garvie's and David Rintoul's captivating portrayals of Elizabeth Bennet and Mr. Darcy in the 1980 adaptation, I was primed for a revelation. Five hours of visual splendor—including plenty of footage of English drawing rooms filled with period frocks and breeches—combined with Austen's beautiful nineteenth-century language and an enchanting love story, hooked me like an intoxicating drug. In 2007, after years of reading, study, and online discussion, I created Austenprose.com, a blog dedicated to the brilliance of Jane Austen's writing and the many books and movies that she has inspired. To the unindoctrinated, devoting an entire website to one author may seem a bit excessive. For me it was as logical as dancing being "a certain step toward falling in love," leading me to connections and a career that I never anticipated.

> *"One man's ways may be as good as another's, but we all like our own best."*
>
> —Admiral Croft, *Persuasion*

Thirty years after I first discovered Austen, "my Jane" is everywhere. In the last two hundred years, there have been many novels that qualify as masterpieces of world literature, but none have inspired the creative output that Austen's have. From books to movies to websites—not even the eminent Charles Dickens or the venerable William Shakespeare can touch our Incomparable Jane. Why do her stories so entrance and delight us? What is it about her haughty Mr. Darcy that makes him an iconic romantic hero? How does she cleverly play with our emotions, making us laugh out loud while reading *Emma* for the tenth time? And why has she inspired a whole new book genre?

Perhaps the most curious question is: How did an English author of only six major novels written anonymously "by a lady" close to two centuries ago become an international sensation, media darling, and pop culture icon?

> *I am very much flattered by your commendation of my last letter, for I write only for fame, and without any view to pecuniary emolument.*
>
> —Jane Austen, in a letter to her sister Cassandra,
>
> 16 January 1796

Austen's rise to fame has been steady since her nephew James Edward Austen-Leigh's biography, *A Memoir of Jane Austen,* introduced "dear Aunt Jane" to broader readership in 1869, but recently, two elements have been her strongest catalyst: the Internet and a wet shirt. In 1995 a new five-hour mini-series of *Pride and Prejudice* adapted by British screenwriter Andrew Davies would expose Austen to a wider audience with his new, more energized interpretation, including a provocative plunge into the Pemberley pond by Austen's hero Mr. Darcy, who emerged not only dripping wet, but a romantic icon of Nonpareil. Moreover, add to that the notion that both Regency-era and twentieth-century ladies thought it absolutely necessary that they "should meet to talk over a ball," and Jane Austen on the Internet was born at Pemberley.com. With the further production of movie adaptations of each of her novels in the mid 1990s and into the 2000s, Austen's celebrity had reached far beyond its author's ironic boast of "writing only for fame" to megastar status.

> *"But, Lizzy, you look as if you did not enjoy it. You are not going to be missish, I hope, and pretend to be affronted at an idle report. For what do we live, but to make sport for our neighbours, and laugh at them in our turn?"*
>
> —Mr. Bennet, *Pride and Prejudice*

Prior to the landmark airing of *Pride and Prejudice* in 1995, only a few dozen Austen-inspired sequels had been published, and even fewer still remained in print. Jane Austen's own nieces were the first to take up the banner. In the 1830s, Anna Lefroy, daughter of her eldest brother, James, was the first to attempt completing *Sanditon,* Austen's last unfinished work, written in 1817 while she was in failing health. Ironically, Lefroy did not complete Austen's story either. I can't say I blame her. Aunt Jane was a hard act to follow, and the pressure must have been overwhelming. Two decades later the novel *The Younger Sister* by Catherine-Anne Hubback, daughter of Austen's brother Frank, was published in 1850. Freely incorporating characters and plot from Austen's unfinished and unpublished fragment *The Watsons,* it can now be classified as a completion of Austen's story, though at the time of publication, the only credit given to her Aunt Jane was Hubback's dedication to her in the book. Fifty years later the first Austen sequel to be published would be Sybil G. Brinton's 1913 *Old Friends and New Fancies,* a clever amalgamation of characters from each of Austen's novels worked into Brinton's own unique plot. One could say that it was the first Austen "mash-up," published close to a century before *Pride and Prejudice and Zombies* would make the bestseller lists in 2009. Each of these novels, though vastly different in style and concept, share their success through their unique creativity and connection to Austen fans who crave more of the world and characters that Jane Austen created.

"Silly things do cease to be silly if they are done by sensible people in an impudent way."

—Emma Woodhouse, *Emma*

Since 1995, the Jane Austen sequel industry has evolved into its own niche-genre in publishing. As a professional bookseller, I do not remember a month in the last ten years that an Austen-esque novel or two has not been featured on the new-release table. With so many titles readily available from your local bookstore or online retailer, there are prequels, sequels, retellings, and continuations to suit every reading style. We all have our favorites, and one of the joys of editing this anthology was composing a list of my "dream authors" who write in the genre, and others whom I greatly admire who have been influenced by Austen's style, and asking them to contribute a short story. My only request was that they stay within the theme of exploring Austen's philosophies of life and love by reacquainting readers with characters from her novels or introducing original stories inspired by her ideals. From historical to contemporary to young-adult fiction to paranormal, five of the six major novels and Austen's life are featured in this anthology, covering "every possible flight which the subject will afford." I hope you will be as pleased and delighted as I am by the variety of amusing and poignant stories created for this collection.

"Oh! It is only a novel . . . or in short, only some work in which the greatest powers of the mind are displayed."

—*Northanger Abbey*

In an era when women had few opportunities beyond marriage and motherhood, Jane Austen chose another path—she became a writer. In keeping with Austen's passion for her craft, it seemed only fitting to encourage new writers to do the same. The *Jane Austen Made Me Do It* Short Story Contest was held online this past winter at Pemberley.com. One new voice in the Austen-esque genre would be chosen from the entrants. Eighty-eight previously unpublished writers submitted their Austen-inspired short stories. The variety and talent exhibited was amazing. Selecting only one was quite a challenge, but I'm elated to include "The Love Letter" by Brenna Aubrey, a story that embraced both the spirit of the contest and Austen's enduring legacy, in this anthology.

> *"It is not time or opportunity that is to determine intimacy;—it is disposition alone. Seven years would be insufficient to make some people acquainted with each other, and seven days are more than enough for others."*
>
> —Marianne Dashwood, *Sense and Sensibility*

As 2011 marks the bicentenary of *Sense and Sensibility,* Jane Austen's first published novel, please join me and the twenty-four contributing authors of *Jane Austen Made Me Do It* in applauding literature's wittiest muse and astute observer of the human heart with this celebratory collection of short stories, created to honor and to entertain.

Laurel Ann Nattress
Austenprose.com

JANE AUSTEN
MADE ME DO IT

JANE AUSTEN'S NIGHTMARE

Syrie James

Chawton, Wednesday 2 August 1815

An extraordinary adventure which I only just experienced proved to be so vivid and distressing—and yet ultimately so illuminating—that I feel I must record it in its entirety.

It was a gloomy, grey, frigid afternoon, and I found myself traversing a strangely quiet and deserted street in Bath. (Bath! It is indeed the most tiresome place in the world, a visit there surely akin to a descent into Hades.) A low fog hung in the air, dampening the pavements and obscuring the heights of the long rows of limestone townhouses on either side of me.

I wondered how I had come to be there, and why I was alone. Should I not be snug at home at Chawton Cottage? Where were all the residents of Bath—a city generally so filled with crowds, noise, and confusion? Where did I get the (very smart) pale blue muslin gown in which I was attired, and the grey wool cloak with its beautiful lace collar, both too handsome to be seen much less worn? As I shivered and wrapped my cloak more tightly about me, I observed a pretty young woman of about seventeen years of age emerge from the fog and venture in my direction. I could not prevent a little start of surprise, for the newcomer looked exactly like Marianne Dashwood—at least the Marianne that I had envisioned while writing *Sense and Sensibility*.

How wonderful it was, I thought, that a real-life woman and a complete stranger should so closely resemble the character whom I had created entirely in my mind! I was about to politely avert my gaze when, of a sudden, the young woman's eyes widened and she marched determinedly up to me.

"Miss Jane Austen, is it not?" exclaimed she, stopping directly before me.

"Yes," replied I, uncertain how it was possible that this young woman should be acquainted with me.

"Surely you recognise me!" persisted she in an impassioned tone.

"Should I? I am very sorry. I do not believe we have ever met."

"Of course we have! You created me. I am Marianne."

I was at a loss for words. Had I imbibed too much wine at dinner? Was this exchange simply another one of my imaginative flights of fancy? Or could it be that, by some remarkable twist of fate, it was truly occurring? Whatever the cause, I did not wish to appear rude. "Of course," said I, smiling as I extended my hand to her, "I *did* think you looked familiar. How lovely to make your acquaintance in person at last. How have you been?"

"Not well. Not well at all!" cried she with a vigorous shake of her curls as she ignored my proffered hand. "I have wanted to converse with you for *such* a long time, I am grateful to at last have the opportunity." Her eyes flashed as she demanded, "What could you have been thinking, Jane—I *may* call you Jane, may I not?—when you wrote all that about me?"

"When I wrote what?" responded I uncertainly.

"In every scene throughout that entire, horrid novel," answered Marianne, "you presented me as the most selfish and self-involved creature on the face of the earth. I was always waxing rhapsodic about poetry or dead leaves, harshly critiquing somebody or something, or crying my eyes out in the depths of despair! Could not you have given me even one scene where I might have behaved with equanimity?"

This verbal assault, so entirely unexpected and delivered with such depth of emotion, took me utterly aback. "I—I was simply attempting to make you different from your sister," explained I, my voice faltering, "to portray two opposite temperaments."

"By my example then, do you mean to imply that having passionate feelings is a great evil?" cried Marianne.

"No—not at all. My aim was to illustrate the injurious nature of *wallowing* in excessive emotion and the importance of self-restraint."

"If that is so, was it truly necessary to enforce such suffering upon me to get across your point? You made me look ridiculous and pathetic! You humiliated me at a party! You nearly had me die—*literally die!* And the most cruel offence of all, Jane: you broke my heart. You had me fall madly, passionately in love with a man who was akin to my second self, and then you deliberately and remorselessly snatched him away!" Marianne choked back a sob as she dabbed at her eyes with a handkerchief from her reticule. "*All* the other heroines in *every one of your novels* end up with the man they love, *except me.* You married *me* off to a man nearly twice my age! How could you do it?"

A paroxysm of guilt pierced through me with the speed of an arrow. Every word she spoke was true. Had I indeed sacrificed Marianne's happiness to convey a lesson? But no—no.

"I am sorry, Marianne," murmured I with sincere compassion. "I did indeed put you through a great many trials in my novel—but in the end, everything turns out well. I hope you and Colonel Brandon are very happy?"

"Colonel Brandon is the most loyal, amiable, and good-hearted of gentlemen," retorted Marianne testily. "He loves me, of that I am well aware, and I suppose I love him back. Every day I try to remind myself how fortunate I am to be his wife. But every day is just as quiet, spiritless, and dull as the last! We read. We take walks. We ride horses. We dine. He cleans his rifle and hunts. I do needle-work and play the pianoforte. Oh! Were it not for my mother's and sisters' visits, I think I should go mad! Where is the heart-pounding excitement I felt in every encounter with Willoughby? Am I never to feel that way again?"

"Marianne," answered I solemnly, "the excitement you describe might be thrilling for a moment, but it is not the preferred way to live. A marriage based on affection, respect, and companionship is a more desirable union, and will make you far happier."

"Happier? What do you know of happiness, Jane? Upon what do you base these assumptions? You, who have never married!"

Her brutal and tactless remarks made me gasp—yet I reminded myself that *I* had created her—*I* had made her what she was. "I base them upon my observations of other married couples. I could not in good conscience allow you to marry Willoughby. He was greedy, selfish, and fickle, and would have made you miserable. I thought you understood that at the end."

"You put words in my mouth to show what I had learned—but they were *your* words, Jane, not mine. I know the truth. I know why you stole my Willoughby away: it was because *you* could not have Mr. Ashford. You suffered, so you made certain that *I* suffered, as well!"

At the mention of Mr. Ashford's name, my heart seized and I let out a little gasp. Not a day passed that I did not think of Mr.

Ashford. He was the one, true love of my life, but for good reason, I had told no one about our relationship—no one except Henry and my sister. How could Marianne know about him?

"It was most unfair of you, Jane! Most unfair!" Tears streamed down Marianne's cheeks now and she took a quivering breath. "Could not you have given me and Willoughby a second chance? You might have redeemed him at any time had you chosen to, but you did not. I declare, I will never forgive you!" With this last, heated remark, she turned and darted away.

"Marianne, come back!" cried I, running after her. "Have you forgotten Eliza, whom Willoughby seduced, disgraced, and abandoned? I *saved* you from Willoughby! He was one of the worst offenders I ever created! Colonel Brandon is worth a hundred Willoughbys! He is the true hero of the novel!"

But the fog enveloped Marianne's retreating form and she disappeared from my view.

I stopped, catching my breath, remorse and confusion coursing through me. If only she had given me more time to explain! But even if she had, how could I defend what I had done? *Should* I have redeemed Willoughby? I had barely the briefest interval, however, to contemplate these misgivings when, from a tea shop but a few yards ahead of me, emerged two young ladies deeply engaged in conversation.

I recognised them at once: it was Marianne's sister Elinor, walking arm in arm with Fanny Price. I was astounded. How was it possible that these two women from entirely different novels should be acquainted with each other? Moreover, what were they doing in Bath? They looked up, exchanged a brief, surprised glance, and hurried up to me.

"Good afternoon, Miss Austen," said Elinor with a graceful curtsey. "How lovely to see you."

"This is an extraordinary coincidence," murmured Fanny with a shy curtsey of her own. "Mrs. Ferrars and I were just talking about you."

"We only just met an hour ago," explained Elinor, nodding towards the establishment behind them, "and already we have become fast friends. We discovered that we have a great deal in common."

"You are indeed very much alike," agreed I with a smile, pleased by the notion of their new friendship. "I have dearly loved you both since the moment of your inception."

"You see?" said Fanny quietly, darting a meaningful look at her companion.

Elinor nodded gravely but remained silent.

A foreboding feeling came over me. "Is any thing the matter?" asked I.

"Not a thing," said Elinor.

"The weather is very cold and damp," observed Fanny, "do not you think?"

I knew them both too well to be taken in by the polite composure on their faces. "You need not keep any secrets from me. If there is something you wish to say, please speak freely."

"Well," said Fanny reluctantly, "we do not mean to complain. It is just that—" She could not go on.

"It is about our characters," interjected Elinor quickly.

"Your characters?" answered I. "But what is wrong with your characters? You are both excellent, intelligent women, with sincere and affectionate dispositions, strength of understanding, calmness of manner, and coolness of judgment."

"Precisely," stated Fanny.

"You made us *too* perfect," said Elinor.

"Too perfect?" cried I. "How can any one be too perfect?"

"I always behaved with the utmost of propriety," said Elinor, "no matter how difficult or oppressive the circumstance. At only nineteen years of age, I was required to be the model of patience, perseverance, and fortitude, obliged to keep my entire family financially and emotionally afloat, and to conceal my pain beneath a façade of complete composure, even when my heart was breaking."

"Yes, and you are *admired* for your strength of character, Elinor," insisted I.

"Admired perhaps, but not *liked*. No one likes a character who is flawless, Miss Austen."

"It was the same for me," remarked Fanny. "How I succeeded in maintaining even a modicum of self-respect in such a hostile, belittling, and unfeeling environment as Mansfield Park is purely due to God's grace and your pen. You made me sit timidly by while the man I loved chased after another woman, had me refuse a charming man because you deemed him insincere, and would not even allow me to participate in a private play, insisting that it was indelicate and wrong! How I disliked myself! No one is fond of a shy, priggish, and passive character, Miss Austen. No one!"

"*I* am very fond of you," returned I emphatically. "Henry and Mary liked you. And Edmund *loves* you."

"Only because you made him just as good and virtuous as I."

"The book has oft been praised for its morality and sound treatment of the clergy!" insisted I a little desperately.

"That may be so," said Fanny, "and please correct me if I am wrong, but your own mother finds me insipid, your niece Anna cannot bear me, and the reading public at large finds Edmund and I both annoying and as dull as dishwater."

To my mortification, I could not refute her statement.

"People love strong, outspoken characters," said Elinor, "who will not allow themselves to be trampled on by others—characters who have flaws but overcome them. Yet in *our* books, you imply that by being consistently patient, good, and silent, a woman can rise above difficult circumstances."

"Surely this message controverts everything you told us about life in that *other* book," said Fanny.

"What other book?" asked I.

"Why, the book that is everyone's favorite," answered Elinor with a tight little smile. She then said good-day, and after Fanny made a final comment about the weather, the pair linked arms, turned, and made their way down the damp, grey pavement.

My thoughts were in such a state of disarray that I hardly knew what to think or feel. I strode off in the opposite direction, crossing the road, when a carriage suddenly appeared out of the fog and nearly ran me down. It was some time before my heart returned to its natural pace. How long I walked on in this distracted manner along the nearly deserted streets I cannot say, but at length I passed the Abbey Church and found myself standing outside the Pump-room. A cacophony of voices issued from within, proof that not all the inhabitants of Bath had stayed at home.

As I was cold and thirsty, I hurried inside the Pump-room, where a crowd milled about in spacious elegance, and musicians in the west apse performed a pleasant air. A cursory glance revealed that I had no acquaintance there. Appreciative of the heat emanating from two large fireplaces, I made my way to the fountain, where I paid the attendant for a glass of water and drank it down. As I turned, I nearly collided with a handsome young man smartly dressed in the uniform of a naval officer, exactly like that of my brothers Frank and Charles.

"Forgive me," said he with a bow, before purchasing his own glass and moving on. The naval captain made a most arresting figure, and I wondered what lay behind the sad look in his eyes.

My attention was soon diverted, however, by the sight of an attractive, fashionably dressed young woman who was intently studying all the passersby, as if seeking out some one in particular. She looked strangely familiar. All at once I knew why: it was Emma Woodhouse.

Emma! In my view, one of the most delightful creatures I had ever conceived! Upon catching sight of me, Emma started with recognition, a look that quickly turned to worry as she glided to my side.

"There you are! I have been looking every where for you, Miss Austen. Have the others found you?"

"The others?"

"Word has got out that you are in town. There are quite a few people who are—" (she hesitated) "—most *anxious* to speak with you."

Oh dear, I thought, my heart sinking. This could prove to be a most exhausting day. "Thank you. I will keep an eye out for the others, whoever they may be. But how is it that *you* are here, Emma? My book about you is only just completed. It has yet to be sold or published."

She shrugged. "I suppose since it is written, I therefore exist?"

"I see." I smiled hopefully, praying that, unlike my previous encounters, *she* might have some kind words for me. My hopes on that score, however, were soon dashed.

"I admit, Miss Austen, that I too have been hoping to have a word with you. You know it is not in my nature to criticise. And far be it from me to give *advice*—Mr. Knightley is for ever counseling me on that subject, and he is never wrong—but I believe it my duty as a friend to share certain thoughts which I feel might prove to be of benefit to you."

"Do go on."

"You must be the judge of what is best to write, of course—I would not *dream* of interfering—but I cannot help but think that you presented me in a very disagreeable light in your novel."

"Disagreeable?" I sighed, knowing full well what was coming. "How so?"

"It started out so well. You called me handsome, clever, and rich, and you gave me a happy disposition. You placed me in a comfortable home, I was original in my thinking, and admired by all who knew me. But then you went off in such an unacceptable direction! You made me oblivious to every real thing going on around me. I spent the entire novel completely blind to the truth of my affections, while trying in vain to elevate Harriet's status and procure her a husband. I was dense, obtuse, manipulative—yet all the while firm in my belief that I knew what was best for every body!"

"Yes, but Emma: every thing you said and did, you did from the fullness of your heart and with the best of intentions."

"Not everything," insisted Emma. "I gossiped wickedly about Jane Fairfax, I flirted outrageously with Frank Churchill, and I was unpardonably rude to Miss Bates at Box Hill."

"That is true, but in each instance, you learned from your mistakes—and this ability to learn and change is the very definition of a heroine. Consider your many positive and attractive qualities. Your temperament is cheerful, patient, and resilient. You are not given to self-pity. You are intelligent and have an excellent sense of humour. Your errors are the result not of stupidity but of a quick mind—a mind so necessitous of stimulation that you were obliged to invent interesting diversions for yourself. You are an *imaginist,* Emma—like me."

Emma puzzled briefly over all that I had said, then charged, "Nevertheless, there is one offence so egregious, it negates all the positive qualities you mentioned: you portrayed me as a *snob*."

"Dearest Emma," returned I quietly and with affection, "compare yourself to Mr. and Mrs. Elton. *They* are my shining examples of true vulgarity, self-importance, and boorishness. You, by contrast, are a charming and amusing creature—a *loveable* snob."

"How can a snob be loveable?" retorted Emma sharply. "That is a contradiction in terms. Even *you* admitted that you were writing a heroine whom no one but yourself would much like."

"Perhaps I will be proven wrong. My sister read the manuscript, and she loves you as you are."

"She is hardly the most impartial judge, is she?" cried Emma. Lowering her voice now and speaking with great feeling, she added, "I must depart, but please allow me to leave you with two vital pieces of information. First: tell your cook to try gooseberry jam in her Bakewell Pudding, it is quite delicious. Second: I have just been speaking with a Mr. Thurston, a most *interesting,* unattached clergyman with good teeth and a nice living in the parish of Snitterfield. Do you see him standing over there by the great clock?" With a slight inclination of her head, Emma gestured towards a stout, red-faced, nearly bald-headed clergyman who was smiling at me. "I made all your charms known to him and he is hoping to speak to you. No, no, do not even think of thanking me," said she, turning to go. "Just to know that my actions *might* bring you some future happiness gives me great joy. Good-day, Miss Austen, and good luck."

"Wait!" cried I, darting after Emma, as anxious to continue our conversation as I was to avoid the man in question, "may we not return to the earlier topic of our discussion? You are the second person to-day who has alleged that I gave her too many faults, while two others insist that I made them too perfect. How am I to reconcile these opposing points of view?"

Emma glanced back at me and shrugged prettily. "That is for you to decide. I cannot give you an opinion. If you prefer to go on writing flawed heroines who must continually humiliate themselves on the road to learning life's lessons, then be my guest—do not hesitate. You are the author, not I. Not for the world would I think of influencing you either way." With a parting smile, she whirled round and vanished into the crowd.

In a state of great agitation, I hurriedly navigated my way out of the Pump-room and into the yard beyond. How could it be, I asked myself, that all the characters whom I loved and had created with such care should prove to be so unsatisfied with themselves? Had I erred in their conception? Was it better to be good or flawed? If neither option was acceptable, what was an author to do?

Half a minute conducted me through the empty Pump-yard to the archway opposite Union-passage, where I paused in great surprise. Even Cheap-street—which was normally so congested with the confluence of carriages, horsemen, and carts entering the city from the great London and Oxford roads that a lady was in danger of losing her life in attempting to cross it—was entirely devoid of traffic. The bleak, eerie stillness was not even broken by the advent of a single female window shopper or a gentleman in search of tea and pastry. Where was every body? The only evidence of life in Bath had been the congregation in the Pump-room. The late afternoon light was quickly fading into early evening. Perhaps, I thought, there was a ball taking place in the Upper Rooms.

I had only just conceived this notion when, to my astonishment, I suddenly found myself halfway across the city, standing immediately outside those very Assembly Rooms, enveloped by an eager, jostling crowd making its way in through the open doors.

I had no wish to go within. In my youth, I had greatly enjoyed a ball—I loved music and dancing, and had welcomed the opportunity it afforded for animated association with friends and neighbours or, at times, new faces—but I had never cared for such diversions at Bath, a city of peripatetic visitors of little sense and even lesser education, where young ladies made overt displays of themselves in search of husbands.

Nevertheless, I was pulled along by the crush of people into the hall and the adjoining ball-room. At length the bustle subsided, depositing me at a vantage point from whence I was able to obtain a good view of the dancers. I felt very out of sorts, and was mortified to be standing amongst this well-dressed crowd clad in my day gown and bonnet (although a brief glance in a nearby looking-glass revealed that the bonnet *was* trimmed with the loveliest blue satin ribbon and a very fine spray of forget-me-nots).

I was fanning my face from my exertion when my gaze fell upon two couples dancing nearby, at the end of a line. Did my eyes deceive me? Could it possibly be? The first couple looked for all the world like Elizabeth and Mr. Darcy. Dancing directly beside them—I was absolutely certain of it—were Jane and Mr. Bingley. The music ended and I watched in wonder as Elizabeth slipped her hand into the bend of Mr. Darcy's arm and, smiling and chatting, they made their way across the floor. Jane and Mr. Bingley followed behind at a leisurely pace, engaged in a similarly affectionate tête-à-tête.

A great thrill coursed through me. Was it possible that I was actually going to meet those four dear souls with whom, for so many long years, I had been acquainted only in my mind? My initial exhilaration, however, turned to alarm at the thought of another demoralising scene such as the ones to which I had just been subjected. Hot tears threatened behind my eyes. Oh! I could not bear it! Despite my desperate wish to leave, I was frozen to the spot. In moments the first couple stood before me.

"Good-afternoon, Miss Austen," said Elizabeth, beaming.

"What a pleasure it is to see you!" exclaimed Mr. Darcy.

Their manner was so friendly and congenial, I could scarcely believe my ears—but I knew better than to expect it to last. "Please," returned I anxiously, "if you have complaints—if you are angry with me or have found fault with any thing I have done—I would truly rather you did not voice it."

"Complaints?" repeated Elizabeth in surprise.

"Faults?" reiterated Mr. Darcy. "We could not in good conscience find fault with you, Miss Austen. And we are hardly angry."

"In fact, it is quite the reverse," said Elizabeth. "We would like to express our most fervent gratitude."

"Gratitude?" said I, astonished.

Elizabeth and Mr. Darcy exchanged a very loving look and then a happy laugh, as he gently clasped her gloved hand in his. "Everything you devised for us was so cleverly thought out," said Elizabeth.

"I shudder to think what kind of man I would have been, had you not thrown my darling Elizabeth in my way," said Mr. Darcy with a warm smile.

"I believe we are the happiest two creatures on earth," added Elizabeth with the liveliest emotion.

"No, you must reserve that honour to us," interjected Mr. Bingley, joining us with a bright grin and Jane on his arm. "I thank you, Miss Austen. You have done us all proud."

"Truly, I do not deserve such happiness!" cried Jane, her adoring gaze meeting Bingley's, where it found an identical response. "Miss Austen, you are a heroine in our eyes. And thank you for giving me your name."

So fraught with emotion and relief was I at this discourse that I was unable to utter a single syllable. All four shook my hand enthusiastically in turn and said their good-byes. When I had at last sufficiently regained my composure to make my way out of the rooms, I was still so consumed with delight that I barely noticed the coldness of the evening air or the grimness of the ever-present fog.

What felicity was this! I thought as I wandered along, heedless of the direction in which I was heading. After such a litany of heartbreaking indictments, to find that I had at least done *something* right! It was in this exultant frame of mind that I approached the wide green lawn of the Royal Crescent, where I suddenly felt a hand on my arm and my musings were interrupted by a feminine voice.

"Miss Austen! Oh! I have been quite wild to speak to you!"

I stopped and looked at the young lady in astonishment. It was Susan Morland! It must be, for she was pretty, seventeen at most, and dressed just as I had imagined her, in a sprigged muslin gown with blue trimmings (which was bound to fray upon the first washing). Well, I thought—at least it makes sense that *she* is in Bath, for I did put her here before sending her off to Northanger Abbey.

"I must be quick," exclaimed she, looking about with an anxious expression. "I fear for your safety, Miss Austen."

"My safety?"

"Yes! I will explain in a moment. But first—oh!" (studying my expression) "I dare say you have forgotten all about me. I would not blame you if you had—I have been sitting so long on the shelf!"

"How could I forget *you*, Susan? You were my very first sale."

"It is that very subject which I long to discuss with you. Oh! Miss Austen—it has been twelve years that I have languished in obscurity at Richard Crosby and Company—twelve years and still I have not seen the light of day! Clearly that gentleman does not intend to publish my story. I understand that ten pounds is a great deal of money—but you are a successful author to-day. Surely you have the means to buy back the manuscript *now*. Would it be asking too much—could you find it in your heart— please, please, will you rescue me?"

I took a moment to consider her request. I, too, had long ago-nised over that book's fate—but I had written it so long ago, and much had changed during the interval. Would another bookseller—not to mention the public—still find *Susan* to be of interest? Or would they think it obsolete? Yet how could I voice aloud these thoughts to the sweet, innocent girl who stood trem-bling so violently before me, gazing at me with such hope and trust in her eyes?

In a tone softened by compassion, I said, "Dear Miss Morland. If I am fortunate enough to sell *Emma,* I will use a portion of the funds to buy back your book. You may depend upon it."

"Thank you, Miss Austen. Thank you so much!"

"However, I must warn you, Miss Morland—should I succeed in this effort, there is another problem which I fear may cause you additional distress."

"What is that?"

"It has come to my attention that an anonymous, two-volume novel called *Susan* was published by John Booth some six years ago. Therefore, even if I *do* recover my own manuscript, its title— and your very *name*—will necessarily have to be altered."

"Oh! I would not mind that a bit," replied Susan earnestly. "In truth, I have never much cared for my name. Please feel free to change it. Although I do hope you will not call me Milicent or Lavinia or Eunice—that would be too, too horrid!"

"I promise to give you only the most delightful name."

"You fill me with relief, Miss Austen. And now—" She looked

about us with an expression of renewed dread and apprehension. "To that other matter of which I must speak without further delay. I am very concerned about you. You must leave Bath this instant!"

"Leave Bath? Why?"

"A little while ago," confided Susan with rising agitation, "I was strolling through Sydney Gardens when I observed Mr. Wickham engaged in a heated discussion with Mr. Willoughby, William Walter Elliot, and John Thorpe. All four appeared to be very angry about something."

My heart leapt in sudden alarm. I had already witnessed the wrath and disdain of several of my creations whom I *thought* I had portrayed in a most becoming light. What manner of reception could I expect to receive from those characters whom I had represented in a *less* than favourable manner? Indeed, I could not deny that with the most deliberate of intentions, I had conceived a great many characters who were truly selfish, vain, vulgar, greedy, wicked, stupid, thoughtless, or senseless—or, as in the case of the four scoundrels Susan had described, a combination of most of those traits.

"You say that all four of those men are in Bath to-day?" replied I with unease.

"They are! While strolling by, I overheard some of their conversation. It was dreadful!" She moved closer. "I heard Mr. Wickham and Mr. Willoughby mention *your name,* Miss Austen, in the same sentence as the word *murder.*"

"Murder? Pray, Susan, do not let your imagination run away with you. Did you learn nothing from your own story?" Despite my brave words, in truth I was growing quite afraid.

All at once I heard the ominous sound of approaching footsteps. Appearing out of the dark fog on the rise of lawn before me came the very four male figures Miss Morland had just named, steadily advancing with torches in hand and no kind looks on their countenances.

I swallowed hard and stepped backward. "Miss Morland—" I began, but strangely, Miss Morland had vanished. I was alone, quite alone, except for the men who were bearing down upon me. The heavy trampling of feet began to grow into an ever-louder, thundering din. To my dismay, just behind the angry four, I saw another group of people coming at me through the fog: Mr. Collins, Mrs. Bennet, Lydia and Mary Bennet, Louisa Bingley Hurst, Caroline Bingley, and Lady Catherine de Bourgh.

I gasped in terror. From a different direction, an additional, furious assemblage was descending: Mr. and Mrs. Elton, Sir Walter and Elizabeth Elliot, Mary Musgrove, Isabella Thorpe, and General Tilney. Behind them strode Fanny and John Dashwood, Lucy Steele, Mr. Price, Mr. Rushworth, Maria Bertram Rushworth, Lady Bertram, Mrs. Ferrars, and Robert Ferrars. Many of them carried pitchforks and flaming torches. Some had guns. All of them were staring at me. The hatred and malice in their eyes is beyond my power to describe.

Panic surged through me. I screamed in horror, but no sound escaped my lips. I turned sharply in an attempt to flee, when I heard Lady Catherine de Bourgh call out in fury:

"Not so hasty, if you please. Unfeeling, selfish girl! I am most seriously displeased!"

Her piercing tone so paralysed me that my feet were rooted to the ground. The fuming horde drew closer and closer. They were chanting now: "Jane! Jane! Jane!" Again, I tried to scream.

"Jane! Jane! Jane! Wake up!"

Cassandra's voice broke through my consciousness, hurtling me out of that terrifying reality and back to the warm cocoon of my own bed. I awoke to find myself bathed in perspiration, my heart pounding, my sister's gentle hand upon my arm as she looked at me through the moonlit darkness from the next pillow.

"Oh! Cassandra!" I struggled to catch my breath. "I have just had the most horrible dream."

"What was it about?" asked Cassandra softly.

I told her everything, as I always did.

"Well," said she after I had finished my story, "your dream does not surprise me. Your characters have become very real to you—as real as life itself. It is only natural that you should hear their thoughts and feel their emotions as they do."

"Yes, but what does it signify? I can understand why many of my lesser characters would despise me. But my heroines? I love them all! To think that four of them are so unhappy makes me absolutely miserable. Have I done a terrible thing? Am I the most vile and ignorant authoress who ever dared to put pen to paper?"

"Of course not, dearest," replied Cassandra soothingly, as she found and tenderly squeezed my hand. "If all writers were obliged to atone for the portrayals or fates of their creations, think what Shakespeare owes to Romeo and Juliet or Iago and Richard III. Should Defoe and Richardson feel remorse for the trials and tribulations they inflicted on poor Mr. Crusoe, Clarissa, or Pamela?"

"Of course not. Their work has afforded me and the public untold hours of reading pleasure."

"So it is with your books, Jane. You have told me time and again that a perfectly smooth course never makes a satisfying story, that it is an author's job to make his or her characters suffer so that they might learn something at the end."

"True. Although after hearing Fanny Price's complaints, I believe I may have erred in her creation. I ignored my own model! Her suffering did not culminate in a lesson."

"I did *try* to persuade you to let her marry Henry Crawford."

"I know." I sighed. "I have learned *my* lesson. People do not appreciate pure goodness in a character in a novel. Even Fanny does not like herself! Given the complaints of the others, perhaps I ought to strive for a more happy medium in my next effort."

"A happy medium? What do you mean?"

I thought for a moment. "Next time, I will create a heroine who is modest and good, but not *entirely* perfect. She will have made mistakes that she regrets." My mind fixed on one of my greatest regrets in life: the day I was obliged to say good-bye to Mr. Ashford. "Marianne asked for a second chance. Well then—I will fill this new character with longing and regret for a lover she was persuaded to refuse many years past, and I will give her a second chance to make things right."

"A lovely idea. Who will this lover be? A clergyman or a landed gentleman?"

"Neither." New ideas spilled into my brain with lightning speed. "In my dream, I saw a young officer in the Pump-room—a naval captain with sad eyes. Perhaps he was regretting his lost love. I will write about *him,* and thus honor Frank and Charles and all men of that worthy profession."

"A naval captain! I approve of this notion."

"I think I shall set the book primarily in Bath."

"Bath? But Jane, you hate Bath."

"That is precisely why it is the ideal location." I sat up, hugging my pillow to my chest, my heart pounding with rising excitement. "My heroine will be obliged to quit her beloved home in the country and remove with her family to Bath—just as we did when papa retired—and she will despise it as much as I did. Think of the drama! Imagine all the intriguing circumstances which may ensue! And to make up for the odiousness of Bath, I will include a visit to a place I love—" (recalling the precise spot where I met Mr. Ashford) "Lyme, perhaps. Yes, Lyme."

"I declare, Jane, this *must* be the book you are supposed to write next. I have not seen you this impassioned about any thing in months."

"Speaking of passion," said I with enthusiasm, "do you recall how Marianne accused me of giving passionate feelings a bad name? This time, I will allow my characters to better express their emotions. And something else occurs to me. In my dream, all my female heroines seemed so incredibly *young*. I would prefer to write about someone a bit closer to my own age and experience now."

"What age do you have in mind?"

"I don't know, seven-and-twenty perhaps."

"A heroine of seven-and-twenty is very old indeed," returned Cassandra dubiously. "Has such a thing ever been attempted before?"

"Not to my knowledge, but I could be the first to do it. And what would you think if I named her after our dear friend Anne Sharpe?"

"I should think Anne would be flattered."

"Then it is done! Anne she shall be." I leapt from the bed and threw on my shawl, ignoring the brief, painful twinge in my back which I had been experiencing infrequently of late, clearly a sign of my advancing age.

"Jane, what are you doing?"

"I am getting up."

"It is the middle of the night."

"Do you imagine that I could sleep, with all these ideas spinning in my head?" I lit a candle and strode to the door. "No, I must go downstairs at once, write out the dream I had, and then jot down my plans for this novel, before all these thoughts scatter to the wind."

"Of course you must," said Cassandra with a smile as she lay back upon her pillow. "Do not stay up *too* long, dearest."

"I will not," replied I, although we both knew very well that I would be up until my fingers were stained black with ink and the first light of dawn was creeping in beneath the shutters.

SYRIE JAMES, hailed as the "queen of nineteenth-century re-imaginings" by *Los Angeles* magazine, is the author of *The Lost Memoirs of Jane Austen* (the untold story of Jane Austen's love affair), an international bestseller named Best First Novel by *Library Journal*; *The Secret Diaries of Charlotte Brontë*, the Audie-nominated story of Charlotte's life and romance, selected by the Women's National Book Association as a Great Group Read; and the critically acclaimed *Dracula, My Love*, Mina Harker's passionate love affair with the most famous vampire of them all. Syrie insists that her very romantic Dracula is inspired by a combination of the most swoon-inducing traits of Mr. Darcy, Mr. Knightley, Mr. Rochester, and Heathcliff—as is the hero of her most recent novel, *Nocturne*. A lifetime member of WGA and JASNA, Syrie is an admitted Anglophile and is obsessed with all things Austen, although she lives in Los Angeles.

www.syriejames.com
@syriejames on Twitter

WAITING

A STORY INSPIRED BY JANE AUSTEN'S *PERSUASION*

Jane Odiwe

Captain Wentworth was awake early to witness the greyness of the day, mists rising in a smoking pall above the city along with the icy rain which lashed at the windows of his lodgings in a manner fit for any storm at sea. His spirits were high, though truth to be told, he was more than a little nervous at the prospect of the interview he was about to face. As he adjusted the cuffs at his wrists, he glanced out of the window to observe the dash of carriages rolling round the square depositing new arrivals in Bath.

Had it only been yesterday when the unimaginable had happened at last? Frederick recalled every second of the encounter, revived every feeling. They'd met in Union Street. He'd been almost afraid to witness her reaction to the heartfelt letter he'd sent. But he needn't have worried. Her eyes had spoken the sentiments she could not immediately express. Anne Elliot had taken his arm, and he'd sheltered her from the rain with his umbrella.

From his viewpoint past the railings on the other side of Queen Square, Gay Street effortlessly progressed up its steep incline, elegant façades on either side ascending to the Circus much as he and Anne had advanced before turning off to find the relative quiet of the Gravel Walk. Heedless of the sauntering politicians, bustling housekeepers, and flirting girls around them, they had confessed all their hidden, secret feelings, buried for so long.

"She loves me, as I love her," he said out loud to confirm the truth to himself. He wanted to open the window and shout it out to the muffin man below. *"Anne Elliot never stopped loving me from the day we parted. Oh, that my stubborn pride had not prevented me from seeking her out sooner. I've wasted almost nine precious years when we could have been together! I admit; I felt very differently all those years ago when she rejected me. I held her in contempt then, although sweet Anne, I now believe, was perfectly justified in withdrawing from our engagement. I was proud, made to feel that I was not good enough for a baronet's daughter, and the truth of it stung me to my very soul. But there is little point in grieving over the past; I must look to the future with the girl I love most in the world by my side. My only fear, nay dread, concerns the interview I am to have with her father this morning. Not that his consent really matters. Anne will not be persuaded against her wishes this time, not like the first time. We are older, and, I hope, much wiser, both secure in the knowledge that our love is ever true and constant. But, this will not do, I have an appointment with Sir Walter, and I must not be late!"*

In the most imposing house on Camden Place, Captain Wentworth's beloved Anne Elliot was looking out anxiously through the window in the drawing room, though she tried to give an air of calm. Her thoughts and ideas ran on similar lines to the gentleman whose attendance she expected. Half elation, half dejection, her mind veered from the images of yesterday, which had her spirits dancing in private rapture to the imagined scene of what was about to take place. That is, if he kept his promise and came. She could not help but smile at her own fleeting misgivings, because if she truly examined her heart, of one thing she was certain. He would come. Captain Wentworth would ask for her hand. Anne did not think he would be refused, but she knew that her father and the rest of her family would be shocked by their news.

Anne heard snatches of her sister Elizabeth's conversation with her friend Mrs. Clay, as they discussed the previous evening's party, taking delight in discussing the faults and shortcomings of the guests present. Sir Walter attended to his newspaper, occasionally interjecting with news of some entertainment to be given at the Assembly Rooms. Anne's attention was suddenly caught at the sound of his dear name.

"I think Captain Wentworth improves on acquaintance, do not you, Miss Elliot?" enquired Mrs. Clay.

"Indeed, Penelope. One would never mistake him for a lowly sailor now. He is certainly a gentleman by his appearance; what a difference money can make."

"And in agreeable manners and conversation, he is altogether a perfect companion," replied Mrs. Clay.

Elizabeth studied her friend intently. "I was not aware that you spoke to Captain Wentworth last night."

"I did not, but I saw you engaged in conversation with him several times. Indeed, Miss Elliot, it seemed to me as if he were particularly seeking you out. It quite put your cousin's nose out of joint. Elizabeth is gathering admirers by the dozens, is she not, Sir Walter?"

Elizabeth smirked at the hints Mrs. Clay was making even though she was not quite so sure herself that she had gained such admiration from either the Captain or her cousin, Mr. William Elliot. Her sister Anne put herself forward far too often to talk to those gentlemen, she thought.

Sir Walter put down his paper upon the chaise longue. "Captain Wentworth is a well-looking man, one whom I would not be ashamed to be seen with anywhere. A degree lower or two than I would usually tolerate, but his style is good, and he is less weather beaten than his sister, Mrs. Croft, whom I declare has the complexion to outstrip a mail coach. I daresay the Admiral sees something to esteem in such a square, upright sort, but I like a woman to be less vigorous in her appearance."

"At least we have been able to escape their acquaintance here in Bath, Father," said Elizabeth. "They've found their own level amongst those odd-looking sailors, I am glad to say. Thank heaven, for I'm certain our cousin Lady Dalrymple would be embarrassed by such a connection."

"Quite so!" Sir Walter exclaimed. "Still, it is something of a disappointment, I confess, that the Crofts, as my tenants who have all the advantages of presently residing in our family home, should not have a better appearance. A lady's complexion should be as pale as porcelain, and as fine."

Anne heard this in dismay. "Mrs. Croft is tanned because she has been at sea with her husband. They are devoted to one another, and share their life together like no other couple I know."

"Well, I should hate to see a daughter of mine succumb to such abuse," Sir Walter declared, "though perhaps a catch of twenty-five thousand pounds might be well worth going to sea for, wouldn't you say so, Mrs. Clay?" He paused in order for them to laugh at his joke before returning to his newspaper.

"Though Captain Wentworth may have made his fortune, we must remember 'new money' does not allow for the same privileges that we are afforded," Elizabeth remarked, "or permit society's doors to open. He must be aware that he will never be fully admitted to the upper echelons. And the Crofts hardly assist him in both manner and mode. Such hideous fashions I never did see in my life. Do, however, send them my best regards, Anne, next time you see them."

"Oh yes, I know what's due to my tenant," said Sir Walter.

"Say I shall call soon, though I am sure they will not expect more than my card."

Anne's anxiety increased, but she could not help thinking that if her father had not been such a spendthrift, Captain Wentworth's amiable sister and her worthy husband, Admiral Croft, would not be ensconced at Kellynch Hall and paying them rent. In the circumstances they had been utterly thoughtful and discreet, a fact her father did not even consider.

Anne promptly turned away to cover her discomfiture. There was a knock at the door; she sat down, her heart in her mouth. When the servant entered she held her breath to hear the announcement she'd been longing for.

"Mr. Elliot," were the words she heard instead, and to her consternation, her cousin came into the room to greet them all cordially and take the seat next to hers. Anne remonstrated with herself, for she considered her behaviour quite ridiculous. She must remain calm. After all, another five minutes or even an hour in the scheme of things would hardly count. She had managed to wait for nearly nine years. If she had to, she could wait another nine!

"I've brought that book of poems I was telling you about," Mr. Elliot said, proffering a leather bound volume. "I have marked one in particular I think you will enjoy."

Anne's spirits sank on reading the love poem, only recalling how much Lady Russell had hoped for a match between herself and Mr. Elliot.

"Do let us have our share in the poem," demanded Elizabeth. "Anne, read it aloud."

"Allow me," Mr. Elliot insisted, and with looks only for the girl at his side, he started to read with feeling.

Anne only heard the rain drumming against the long floor-length windows. She folded her hands in her lap, resisting the urge to pleat the fine white muslin of her gown under her fingers as she waited.

Another knock on the front door was heard. Anne was trapped with Mr. Elliot; it was impossible to move. She listened. Voices were distinguished, a man's deep tones. Elizabeth was talking, Anne could not be sure. The click of heels rapidly ascending the stone staircase heralded their visitor. And then all of a sudden Captain Wentworth was there waiting for her father. Anne felt the flicker of Frederick's eyes upon hers for just a moment.

When Sir Walter and Captain Wentworth left the room, it was impossible to avoid the enquiring looks of Elizabeth, Mrs. Clay, and Mr. Elliot, who had not missed Captain Wentworth's request or the way he'd looked at Anne.

"Do you know why the Captain wishes to speak to my father, Anne?" barked Elizabeth, her foot tapping impatiently. "He seemed very particular in his address."

Anne heard the hostility in her sister's voice, and felt the charge of all that she implied. All three straightened in their seats; the only sound came from the ticking of the elegant clock on the mantelshelf.

Anne dared to say the words she had only dreamed of uttering out loud. "We are to be married. Captain Wentworth and I are engaged."

"Engaged!" Elizabeth's laugh tinkled like the little brass bell upon the Pembroke table at her side. "Anne, you always leap to the wildest imaginings. Besides, he's already promised to another!"

Anne noted the amused expressions of her accusers, glimpsed the spiteful gleam in their eyes.

"Why, you must know that he's in love with one of the Musgrove girls," continued Elizabeth. "What's her name, that girl who fell off the Cobb at Lyme? She laughs too much, and her hair is too outré for words. Anne, she is a good deal younger and prettier than you; it's common knowledge that Captain Wentworth is to marry her!"

For an instant, Anne's old fears revived until sense finally prevailed. "You mean Louisa, I suppose, but I can assure you that there is no love in the case, whatever might formerly have been presumed."

As she calmly repeated her news, Anne watched their faces change from stupefied astonishment to a realisation of the truth. The air vibrated with seething emotion kept under regulation. Elizabeth's face turned white with anger, her eyes narrowing as her mouth twitched with indignation, but not another word was spoken.

Congratulation, she had not expected, but this silence, the sense of resentment, was unforeseen. In the next moment, Elizabeth turned away with cold unconcern to resume her conversation as if Anne did not exist. And when Mr. Elliot and Mrs. Clay exchanged glances, his disappointment etched plainly on his features, she could not bear it a moment longer. It was too much to stay in the room. Making her escape, Anne waited, listening to the murmur of voices coming from the library.

"*Frederick, is it true you are really here at last?*" mused Anne, hoping that all was going well behind the closed doors. "*There have been so many misunderstandings. The expectation that you were to marry Louisa truly broke my heart. But, in the end, your beautiful letter changed everything. Your heartfelt words I will treasure forever. 'You pierce my soul,' you declared; 'I have loved none but you.' After waiting for so long, I cannot believe I deserve such happiness.*"

After their marriage they planned to stay a while with Frederick's brother and his wife in Shropshire. Just thinking of Edward Wentworth took Anne back to the time she'd become acquainted with his sailor brother. It was summer when they had first met. Anne was nineteen, extremely pretty, gentle and modest. At an age when she was beginning to go out into society, Monkford, a market town within walking distance of Anne's home at Kellynch, provided much entertainment in the way of shopping, the monthly balls at the Assembly Rooms, and attendance at the parish church.

Anne first spied Lieutenant Wentworth across the aisle. He commanded her attention by his dark, good looks, framed as he was against a vase of country flowers, and by his air that was striking in its confidence. She knew immediately he must be the curate's brother, and on being introduced, her first impressions were confirmed. He was a most cordial gentleman with pleasing manners and address.

At the Assembly Ball on the following Wednesday, Lieutenant Wentworth wasted no time in presenting himself. Anne stood with her friend Lady Russell, watching her sister Elizabeth surrounded by gentlemen.

"May I have the next dance, Miss Elliot?"

Anne readily assented, but she couldn't have been more surprised. Elizabeth was regarded as the beauty, and she couldn't think why he had singled her out. It wasn't that Anne was never asked to dance. Indeed, Charles Musgrove from Uppercross seemed to increasingly enjoy her company. It was just that Frederick Wentworth was so extraordinarily different, quite unlike anyone Anne had ever met before. She felt overawed by his intelligence, spirit, and brilliance, but sensing her unease, he took pains to draw her out.

"It is so kind of you to take pity on a fellow who has not had a dance these last twelve months. I confess being at sea for so long has made me forget how much I've missed a ball."

"The pleasure is all mine, Lieutenant Wentworth, but I assure you there are young ladies enough here this evening who will only be too glad to take pity on you. There is no one quite like an unknown gentleman coming into a neighbourhood to inspire fellow feeling."

Lieutenant Wentworth smiled. "But, I should not be so grateful to them as I am to you, Miss Elliot. Your pity is the only compassion I wish for, your commiseration the only kindness I desire."

Anne did not know how to reply, and was thankful when new partners separated them. She knew that he would not ask her again especially when she observed him dancing with Amy Parfitt. Anne felt she had not been lively enough or said anything witty, she'd only blushed like a schoolgirl.

A garden party at the rectory brought them together again. The curate liked providing opportunities for his parishioners to mingle, and besides, he'd observed the way his brother had been taken with Miss Elliot, hearing him drop her name more than once into the conversation. Anne made an early appearance to see if she could help, and to bring a basket of roses from Kellynch. She could see the marquee but there was no one about when she walked into the walled garden. It promised to be a beautiful day. Lances of sunlight speared through the canopies of boughs, highlighting pink brick and rambling honeysuckle but making violet shadows on the green lawn still wet with dew. A few cloth-covered tables were already set out. Anne was placing her basket when she heard a voice call out behind her.

"Miss Elliot, forgive me for not greeting you sooner, but I'm afraid I've rather had my hands full."

Lieutenant Wentworth advanced bearing plates of cake and thinly sliced bread and butter.

"Oh, do let me help," cried Anne, rushing forth to relieve him, glad to do something to cover her confusion. Just seeing him again overset all her feelings.

"We're all hands on deck in the kitchen," he continued. "Mrs. Badcock's fairly cooked herself out with a battery of buns and cakes, and though I can slice a loaf to within a sail's breadth, I must admit to being all at sea with their display."

Anne laughed. "I'd be happy to arrange slices of cake, or anything at all! Show me the way."

The curate was rather shocked to find the baronet's daughter in his kitchen but she protested against being shooed out. Anne took pleasure in selecting the prettiest floral china and deciding what must go where, and then she and Lieutenant Wentworth took everything out into the garden to cover it all carefully with snowy cloths before the guests arrived.

"I was rather hoping you might help me with something else later on," he said, as they both took the ends of a tablecloth between them. "I have a feeling that your particular talents will be needed."

Anne couldn't imagine what he meant, though she expressed her willingness to be of help.

"I noticed when we were in church last Sunday how you kept some of the noisier children amused with pencils and paper. I confess; it was your gentle way with them that impressed me. You seem able to make them do as you wish with the smallest effort."

"Idle hands are often mischievous ones. I find if the children are occupied, it follows they are no trouble. Their contentment had little to do with me."

"You are too modest, Miss Elliot. I've seen how your particular methods work on the most troublesome case. I am certain you could persuade anyone to anything. Indeed, no one could be safe from the charms of Miss Anne Elliot."

Anne could not decide what he meant nor did she know how to answer. Smoothing the corner of the cloth with her fingers, she avoided looking up directly at the face she knew was scrutinising hers. "Lieutenant Wentworth, I fear you greatly exaggerate my abilities, and I own, I do not quite know what to say."

"Just promise that you will assist me. The fact is that my brother has put me in charge of the running races for the children this afternoon. I admit, I'd rather face a whole fleet of the French Navy than a gaggle of small children."

Anne laughed. "I haven't much experience at organising races, but for my own part, I must say that the thought is not such a terrifying one compared to fighting old Boney."

"Thank you, Miss Elliot, I knew you'd come to my rescue."

Anne was thankful that she spied her basket of roses just then, giving her an opportunity to be busy. She set about snipping the stems and arranging them in a vase under the watchful eye of her friend. They were alone, but the garden was alive with the music of soft air murmuring in the trees. Birds chirruped in a larkspur sky, and the sun's warmth drew the fragrance from the petals blushed with pink to match her cheeks.

"I love to watch someone else working," said Lieutenant Wentworth, coming closer to observe Anne's movements.

He enjoyed watching her dainty fingers fly. The scissors flashed, a snip here, a tweak there; Miss Elliot was most accomplished. A stirring breeze snatched at her sprigged muslin, outlining her pretty figure and playfully shaking her dark curls.

Anne fixed her eyes on the base of the silver vase where the sun winked in a bright star. Her mind was not entirely on the task. She knew that he was staring, and when she looked up his penetrating expression was entirely her own.

"Ouch!" she exclaimed, as the thorn pierced her flesh, at once wishing she'd been paying attention. And when he rushed to her side, she was mortified. He would think she'd pricked her finger on purpose.

He took her tiny hand. Anne felt the warmth and strength of

his long fingers pressed against her own. Her breath quickened. A bead, like a ruby red jewel, spurted to the surface of her skin. She eased her hand from his grip to bring her finger to her lips knowing that his eyes were on her mouth. Just a small scratch, the flow of blood was easily stemmed, but not before Lieutenant Wentworth took her hand again to inspect the wound. Anne regarded the eyes fringed in black lashes deep in concentration. He seemed to be holding her hand forever. Nevertheless, she was sorry when he finally released it.

"I hope it's not too painful. I'm sorry, Miss Elliot, I wished you to enjoy today so much."

"It does not hurt. In any case, nothing could spoil the pleasure I'm having. I thank you kindly." Anne felt she'd said too much, and, blushing again, made a move to walk back towards the house.

At that precise moment, the curate, accompanied by his first guests, Elizabeth and Lady Russell, came bustling in through the gate. Anne turned, immediately hiding her hand behind her back almost as if she imagined they could see the imprints of Lieutenant Wentworth's fingers upon her own.

"Lady Russell, Miss Elliot, here is the delightful Miss Anne and my brother to keep you company. Miss Anne has been working all morning, above and beyond the call of duty, I might add," said Edward Wentworth.

"I can quite imagine!" Elizabeth cast her eye knowingly over the pair. Their close proximity did not escape her observation. "I don't doubt that my sister makes herself agreeable at every opportunity. And, she has always been very much at home in the kitchen."

The curate moved away to greet the procession of villagers now straggling through the gate, and Anne was grateful for the flurry of activity. Neighbours, friends, and children started to fill the garden. Maids bearing pitchers of cool ginger beer or orange wine proffered liquid refreshment.

"Thank goodness, there are the Musgroves arriving. At least there will be one respectable family I can talk to even if they are only farmers," Elizabeth declared as she watched the gate. "I cannot imagine what my father will have to say when he witnesses the rabble all making for the tea tent with indecent haste."

"Anne, you will accompany us to greet the Musgroves." Lady Russell issued her request as a command. Anne felt her cool reserve, sensing her disapproval of the young lieutenant.

Anne saw Lieutenant Wentworth watching them both, and saw the look of disgust cross his face before he turned away with the excuse of going to help his brother. She was embarrassed by her sister's words and Lady Russell's behaviour. The idea that Lieutenant Wentworth might think she shared similar views and manners distressed Miss Elliot greatly. When she heard that the races were due to commence in five minutes, she excused herself to find a quiet part of the garden where she could hide. She was sure he would never ask her now. Sitting down upon a stone seat, Anne could not bear the idea that he would not seek her help. When she saw him moments later, she could not have been more surprised.

"You've forgotten your promise to me, Miss Elliot," Lieutenant Wentworth said as he regarded her, his head on one side. "I've been waiting for you."

Anne felt her cheeks grow warmer. "I did not think." It was impossible to continue.

He came to sit by her side. "How is your finger?"

"Oh, perfectly mended. It is of no consequence, I thank you." Anne wanted to say something, to explain her sister's outburst, and the bad manners of her friend, but how could she possibly justify their behaviour?

"Please, Miss Elliot," he said gently, "if you feel well enough, the children are waiting."

Anne recalled the gleeful faces of the children, remembered those first feelings of happiness as she and Lieutenant Wentworth had truly taken the first steps to falling in love on that sunny, sparkling day against the backdrop of the green garden, the red-roofed rectory with its barley-twist chimneys, and the golden tower of the church rising above the cheerful scene, framed in her memory like a beautiful painting.

Summer had run its course blazing in light and life as they'd rapidly and deeply fallen in love. Such joy and felicity when Frederick proposed Anne had never known before, and such pain and heartache when she'd withdrawn were emotions she recalled with aching clarity. Persuaded by Sir Walter and Lady Russell that to become involved with a young man who had no money and no connections would be an action of folly had been the reason and their undoing. Anne had broken off the engagement. Acting with a sense of duty and obedience to her friend and father, nevertheless, Anne consequently believed that she'd been right to fall in love with Frederick Wentworth and wrong to deny their future together. When her friend Charles Musgrove proposed later on, she refused him, and when he turned to her younger sister Mary, she knew her instincts and her feelings had been right. Anne was sure she would never have found happiness with Charles. She had only ever loved Frederick Wentworth.

Waiting. Anne considered the years of waiting. For almost nine years she had waited, believing all hope was gone. Anne heard the creak of the door, saw the handle turning, and there at last stood her very own Captain. The sounds that greeted her ears were amicable enough. At least her father was addressing Frederick civilly, but she supposed that would be inevitable whatever the outcome. Anne came forward, but Sir Walter did not. A vivid flash of burgundy sleeve, a crisply starched stock, and the discomposed face above it, florid and severe, did not reassure her. Her father withdrew and the door shut fast. Again, Anne had not expected congratulation. No doubt, her father's pride had suffered during the interview, for even he would have recognised the reversal in their fortunes as Captain Wentworth divulged all the particulars of his newly acquired wealth that now gave him the undoubted right to offer for Anne's hand.

But there was something more. Captain Wentworth looked quite as grave as her father had done. His cheeks were suffused with pink. Frederick wore an expression Anne would never forget; the very same countenance she had witnessed when her father had given the young lieutenant short shrift all those years ago. Perhaps all was now lost, after all. Had the Captain changed his mind? Anne's heartbeat quickened, she felt the threat of tears prick behind her eyelids. Waiting to hear the worst, a million thoughts rushed through her mind.

Captain Wentworth tried his best to compose himself. He had known exactly how Sir Walter would react, so why did he feel so upset? Anne's father was hardly going to welcome him or his proposal with open arms, but his manner had still been very condescending. Frederick Wentworth had repressed every nerve in his body, had concealed every urge to behave in a manner unbecoming to a gentleman in order to maintain the equilibrium. He did not know how he'd managed it under the provocation, but he'd maintained a calm and collected disposition.

Anne could bear it no longer. Rushing forward, instinctively clasping her hands together as if in silent prayer, her eyes beseeched him to speak even if she could not utter a word.

"I am in need of fresh air and a change of scene." Miss Elliot heard the clipped tones, his voice strained with emotion. Captain Wentworth gestured towards the staircase. Anne descended, each step feeling more uncertain. By the time she'd fetched her bonnet and pelisse she dreaded knowing her fate. At the front door he snapped open his umbrella and led Anne out onto the wide pavement. Only conscious of the thundering water dripping off the umbrella and gurgling in the gutters, she struggled with thoughts too unpleasant to bear. As they walked towards Belmont, where they began the descent into town, Anne observed the Captain's struggle expressed in every feature.

They walked in silence amid Bath's noisy din of rumbling carts, roaring tradesmen, and the clink of pattens on wet pavements.

"Please do not keep me further in suspense, Captain Wentworth," burst out Anne at last. "I must know what you said to my father, and how he behaved."

It was a moment before he spoke. "I thought I had forgotten the brusqueness of your father's manner, and his undisguised contempt, or at least, I did not think it mattered to me anymore. However, I felt very differently when we came face-to-face. I felt as if I were that very young man again, a poor sailor with no fortune and no prospects. I kept remembering how he'd listened that first time with a sneer curling his lip, followed firstly by cold astonishment, then a stern declaration that a more degrading alliance he could not imagine; words to wound my pride, which have haunted me ever since."

Anne looked up into Frederick's eyes, trying to find some comfort from his countenance, but he looked straight ahead determinedly. Then he stopped, pausing to regard her, and she saw his mouth begin to twitch. There was a hint of amusement just dancing behind those dark eyes, and then to her utter relief he was smiling.

"There was a delicious moment when he pretended he did not know why I had come to see him, although there was a look of genuine surprise when I mentioned your name. Perhaps he thought I'd come to ask him if I could marry Elizabeth!"

"Oh, Frederick, you delight in taunting me," Anne cried, with relief that Captain Wentworth had not entirely lost his sense of humour. "Will I ever hear the truth of the matter?"

He took her hand and tucked it into the crook of his arm. "And then I had a moment when I wished to tell him everything I was truly feeling, especially when he hardly noticed me for observing his own reflection in the looking glass opposite. How I wished to gloat, to boast of my luck and good fortune. I wanted to make him suffer for the way he'd treated us, for the years we were forced apart, but in the end, I could not."

"You would never do anything that wasn't right in your heart. You've proved that to me."

"I could not do or say anything to hurt you or any member of your family, whatever I might feel was a justified grievance. I was suitably humble, and simply asked if we might have his blessing to marry."

"So, you did not ask his permission."

"I thought about that, but I was not willing to risk a negative answer, even if I knew that ultimately it would not stop us from marrying. At least, I hoped it would not. If he had said no, what then, Miss Anne?"

She loved to hear him say her name. "You know the answer."

"But, I want to hear you say it."

"I would still marry you. No one will ever part us again."

"And that is precisely why I love you."

"Do you love me, Captain Wentworth?"

"I love you, Anne, more than I ever have before. My heart is entirely your own, and with your permission, I wish to spend the rest of my life with you."

The moment she'd been waiting for was here at last. Captain

Wentworth took her hand to his lips. "So, we have your father's professed approval, and I propose, Miss Elliot, that the ceremony will take place just as soon as we can get a special licence."

They were soon in town and just coming upon the White Hart Inn when Anne's sister Mary walked out on her husband Charles Musgrove's arm. Their astonished faces when they saw Anne arm in arm with Captain Wentworth were nothing but a delight to the betrothed couple, and Mary insisted that they come in to see her relations just as soon as they'd shared their news.

Charles's parents, Mr. and Mrs. Musgrove, were initially speechless, especially when they privately considered how a few months before they thought the Captain might marry one of their daughters. Henrietta and Louisa had been quite smitten for a while. Yet they were delighted for Anne, who was always a favourite with them. Mary couldn't wait to tell them everything they didn't know about the past.

"Well, it was never divulged, you know, Mrs. Musgrove, but some years ago when I was still at school, Anne and the Captain were engaged once before."

Anne felt herself blush. Mary never did know when to be quiet. Mr. and Mrs. Musgrove tried not to look too curious, Anne observed.

Charles came to her rescue. "May we offer our heartiest congratulations? On behalf of us all, we hope you'll be very happy!"

Captain Wentworth and his fiancée beamed with pleasure. It was wonderful to feel that someone else rejoiced in their good news.

"It will be very creditable to have a sister married," Mary declared. "And I flatter myself; it is entirely due to my invitation to Uppercross last October that they are reunited. Just think; if Anne had not come, things might have turned out very differently."

Wincing again, as Anne realised the reference Mary was making to Frederick's passing interest in Charles's sisters, she recognised that there were bound to be many embarrassing moments like these yet to be endured.

"And you will be married from Kellynch, of course," Mary continued without a pause for breath. "I'm sure a word to your sister and Admiral Croft, Captain Wentworth, will suffice. Anne must be married from home, however settled they have become. It is not as if it is really their home. People who rent other folks' houses must always be used to moving on, and I daresay they could go at a moment's notice!"

"Mary," Anne interrupted quietly, "there will be no need of anyone moving out. Besides, Captain Wentworth and I are to be married in Bath just as soon as we can."

"Such haste! Goodness me, can you possibly mean it? You will be married before the Musgrove girls have had time to shop for their wedding clothes. What does Father think of that? There will be three rushed weddings, one after another, and then we shall be left to shift for ourselves whilst you're all off enjoying the pleasures of some seaside place, I've no doubt. I'm sure I never heard anything like it, but I have my usual luck. I am never considered when any thing desirable is going on; always the last of my family to be noticed."

It was time to say goodbye, but not before Mary swept out before them. "I suppose when you are married, you shall take precedence once more, and I shall have to give way to you."

Anne did not reply; the thought had not even occurred to her, but it very clearly mattered to Mary whose curiosity about the rest of their plans got the better of her as she saw them to the door.

"I do not suppose you will settle near Uppercross, though of course I should like it above all things if you were close to me. But, I cannot think that there is a suitable house in the village.

Henstridge House is a significant residence, but you will not need such a large manor. No, a cottage like ours with scope for improvement, and a green verandah, will suit your needs well enough. Charles, isn't the lease on Cossington Cottage available? I'm sure it is; I shall make enquiries forthwith, and with such a location so close to Crewkerne you will have no need for a carriage either. I do quite well enough without such a conveyance; and I am fortunate to have Mr. Musgrove's carriage at my disposal, though I always say that if only I had the strength, I should enjoy a walk more often."

Captain Wentworth heard all of this with a good deal of amusement. He knew that Mary could never truly be pleased for her sister Anne, who would soon become the owner of a pretty landaulette that he'd already picked out as a wedding present, and be established in her own substantial home, with all the riches that Mary had ever dreamed about. It occurred to him that in marrying Anne he had also married her family, with all the consequences that entailed, but it had given him the idea that when looking for a permanent home, they might find somewhere at a suitable distance where the ordeals of family life might not encroach upon the Wentworths too often. And, there was always the additional hope that in time he might yet win them over, and come to regard them all with something nearing affection.

Anne knew there were yet many trials to overcome, but nothing could dim her happiness, no mortification could prove too much. And as they walked towards Rivers Street where Lady Russell lodged, she knew the worst was not yet over. Anne was convinced that it would still be some time before Lady Russell would take the Captain to her heart. But everything could be accomplished in time, and she more than anyone else knew that to be true. Waiting had been the story of her life, and she could wait for her friend to love Captain Wentworth. They paused before the door. He took her hand; his eyes told her of his true attachment and constancy.

Frederick Wentworth gazed at the girl of his dreams, thinking she had never before looked so beautiful or been so precious to him. He wanted to preserve the moment, to capture it like an exquisite fragrance in a bottle, to be enjoyed forevermore in cherished droplets relinquished in sweet reminiscences. "Just think," he said, his voice filled with love and longing, "that the very next time we'll cross this threshold, we shall do so as Captain and Mrs. Frederick Wentworth."

Anne Elliot returned his sentiments in a look of her own and a squeeze of his hand whilst she rejoiced in the old proverb that, "good things come to those who wait."

JANE ODIWE lives in North London and Bath with her husband, family, and two cats. More than anything she loves a house full of people, music, and good books, which is just as well, because that's the norm! She is the author of *Effusions of Fancy, Lydia Bennet's Story, Willoughby's Return,* and *Mr. Darcy's Secret.* When she isn't writing, she loves painting watercolors, especially of Jane Austen and the world in which she lived.

www.austeneffusions.com
www.janeaustensequels.blogspot.com
@janeodiwe on Twitter

A NIGHT AT NORTHANGER

Lauren Willig

"Northanger Abbey stands low in a valley, sheltered from the north and east by rising woods of oak. But"—Fred's voice dropped to a thrilling whisper—"what lies within?"

Straightening, Fred brushed his hands off against his gray cords. "All good?"

"I thought it was excellent!" gushed Erin. "Your best work yet!"

Cate threw up a little in her mouth. "Gag me with a spork," she muttered to Lenny, the cameraman.

"What's a spork?" asked Lenny.

"It's a—never mind," said Cate. If it wasn't electronic, Lenny wasn't interested.

Lenny peered fretfully at the clouds gathering over the low stone roof of Northanger Abbey. "We'd better finish up here before the sky opens. Rain isn't good for old Bessie." He dealt his camera an affectionate pat. "Is it, old girl?"

"I'll just leave you two alone, shall I?" said Cate.

How in the hell had she gotten here? Not to Northanger per

se (answer: by van), but here in the larger sense. Here in England, here with Lenny and Fred, here doing investigative reports for that hard-hitting, cutting-edge miracle of modern scientific journalism, *Ghost Trekkers*.

Ah, *Ghost Trekkers*. Cate even had the parka to prove it. Black with white lettering. Very snazzy. There was always a shot at the beginning of the show where Lenny zeroed in on the logo on the back of their jackets, panning to follow them as they all clambered into their big, black *Ghost Trekkers* van, ready to take on another gang of hardened ghouls.

Ghost Trekkers was Fred's baby. As lead investigator (read: prime tool), Fred scouted out locations and schmoozed up the owners, convincing the gullible to open their houses for the team's dubious paranormal ministrations. His brother, Hal, lovely, kind Hal, with the M.Phil. in history from Oxford and a perpetually perplexed expression, was head researcher, cobbling together the historical bits and pieces that formed the ostensible background of their "reports."

The day Cate stopped using inverted commas to describe what they did would be the day that she knew she'd officially lost it.

The rest of the team consisted of Lenny, tech geek extraordinaire, and Erin, the program's femme fatale, whose primary qualification for the job appeared to have been spilling her Cosmo on Fred at a West End watering hole. And Cate? She was a lowly assistant investigator, which meant, generally, that she swished her hair in the right places and squealed on cue.

This wasn't the way it was meant to be. She had left Columbia J-School with all sorts of bright and shiny dreams about a career in investigative journalism. She was going to ask probing questions of prime ministers, parachute into Afghanistan, exchange professional courtesies with Barbara Walters. Everyone had to put in an apprenticeship; she was okay with that. A few years with CNN in London or maybe one of the larger news networks in New York, and then, ten years down the road . . .

Cate Cartwright Presents!

Instead, two years out, it was *Cate Kartowsky Babbles Psycho-Rubbish, Cate Kartowsky Fetches Coffee,* or, on an exciting day, *Cate Kartowsky Trips over Stray Wires* because Lenny couldn't be bothered to pick up his electromagnetic whatchamacallit. Fred was saving that one for the show's annual bloopers tape. Just the thought of it made Cate want to slink beneath the van.

"Okay, folks!" Fred clapped his hands together. "Inside! Chop chop! We have a Pictish poltergeist and a specter at Sainsbury's tomorrow, so let's get Northanger in the bag tonight, yeah?" He snapped his fingers under Cate's nose. "Any year now, Cate!"

Fred turned to Erin, gesturing to Lenny to follow them with the camera, then leaned solicitously forward. "What can you tell us about the abbey, Erin?"

Erin swept her long red hair over one shoulder, hunching forward in the approved style, with the dual effect of creating dramatic tension and showing off the cleavage displayed by the deep vee of her shirt.

Tits 'n ghouls, thought Cate glumly. That's us.

"Well, Fred, Northanger Abbey was once an abbey, you know, with monks and stuff. We've had reports that on stormy nights you can still hear the monks wandering around the place, chanting their monkish chants." Erin consulted her clipboard, a prop that Fred fondly believed lent them a professional air. "There's also a White Lady, believed to be the wife of a general who lived here in the late eighteenth century. Was it . . . murder?"

"Dark deeds will out," said Fred sententiously. "What else do you have?"

Erin rustled importantly through her papers. "There's an unidentified female ghost who haunts one of the bedrooms. She's associated with a roll of paper that reappears and disappears in a lacquered chest. Could it be the record of her untimely death?"

"Cut!" called Fred. He turned to Erin. "Love the White Lady, could do without the paper woman. Probably just a laundry list."

Waving Erin away, Fred beckoned to a man bundled into a shabby tweed jacket layered over a sweater vest, layered over a sweater, which, Cate suspected, was layered over yet more sweaters. During her two years with *Ghost Trekkers,* Cate had learned that the size and age of the house was generally inversely proportionate to the quality of the heating apparatus. This did not bode well for a cozy and comfortable night.

On the other hand, at least she wouldn't have to fake the shivers.

Fred spoke directly into the camera. "We have with us the owner of Northanger Abbey, Mr. Morland Tilney-Tilney. Mr. Tilney-Tilney, your family has lived in Northanger Abbey for how long now?"

Mr. Tilney-Tilney tucked his nonexistent chin into the opening of his sweater vest. "Well, you see, there was a spot of bother about Henry VIII and the monks a few hundred years back—"

"Fascinating, Mr. Tilney-Tilney! But what about the paranormal appearances?"

"The whatsits?"

Erin oozed into the frame. "Ghosts, Mr. Tilney-Tilney. Specters, ghouls . . ."

"The shades of the not-so-departed departed," contributed Hal, from safely out of range of the camera. He shared a wry smile with Cate.

What was a bright man like Hal doing in an operation like this? At least Hal had the excuse of filial affection. Whereas Cate was here out of cowardice and habit, too afraid to leave the security of the familiar to actually go after what she wanted. What did that make her?

She decided she'd rather not think about it. She'd gotten very good at not thinking about it.

"Ghosts?" Mr. Tilney-Tilney cocked his head in confusion. "Oh, you mean that rubbish by the lady novelist! Frightfully famous, too, can't think of her name at the moment. Crashing bore, all this dance and that aunt and who's going to marry whom. Don't go in for that sort of thing myself."

"Who would?" The only thing Fred read was *Hello!* and, occasionally, *OK!* If it didn't have an exclamation mark in the title, he wasn't interested. "Now, Mr. Tilney-Tilney, what about—"

"Slept here once, you know," Tilney-Tilney carried on, oblivious. "More trouble than they're worth, those writing folk. Frightful cheek, putting all those lies in print. Aged housekeepers, secret passageways, murdered wives. Nonsense!"

"Nonsense . . . or truths too terrible to be contemplated?" Fred jumped once more into the breach. "Tell me about the White Lady. Was she the murdered wife of General Tilney? Or yet another lost soul haunting the ancient grounds of Northanger? A novice, perhaps, seduced by a renegade monk and shamed into an early grave, leaving a phantom infant behind?"

Tilney-Tilney crushed his hopes with a decisive, "Lies, the lot of it! Never had a speck of trouble until *she* got here."

Fred pasted on a big, fake smile. "Excellent, Mr. Tilney-Tilney! Beautifully done!" Leaning towards Lenny, Fred murmured, "We'll edit that out later."

Lenny sketched a brief thumbs-up. They'd played this game before.

The team trailed along after Fred as he led them into a spacious hall, well furnished in cobwebs but conspicuously lacking in pennants, baronial fireplaces, dark paneling, and the other indicia of a good haunted manor. The room had obviously been remodeled in the eighteenth century. Neoclassicism made for poor haunting grounds.

"This," said Fred into the camera, "is the Great Hall."

"Er, just call it the hall, actually," said Mr. Tilney-Tilney, popping into the camera frame.

Fred shouldered him out. "*Thank* you, Mr. Tilney-Tilney. Now, if you look here, you'll see— What's that, Hal?"

Hal rubbed the back of his neck. His lips were blue. "Is it just me, or is it colder in here than out?"

It was one of their standard lines, but this time, Hal actually looked as though he meant it. Cate felt a shiver travel up her spine. Hal was right. It *was* cold. Not that that was unusual—old building, poor heating, limited sunlight. All logical.

Even so, she couldn't help but look uneasily over her shoulder. Crap, this job was beginning to get to her. Next thing you knew, she'd be gibbering on about White Ladies.

Or just gibbering. "Ouch!"

Fred had jabbed her in the ribs with an elbow, hard.

"Did you see that, Cate? Cate! Sod it, Cate!" Fred stamped a foot, grinding mud into the old Turkish carpet. "Now we have to re-tape that. Look alive, will you? We don't pay you to daydream."

"Sorry!" CNN. MSNBC. Even Bloomberg. How had it all gone so wrong? "Shall we do it again?"

"We're going to have to, won't we?" Fred mugged a quick turn towards the door, burlesquing shock and surprise. "Why, what's— Cate! Did you see that?"

"See what?" she asked obediently.

In the final version, it would be rendered in grainy black-and-white, shot in the quick, jerky movements for which Lenny was known. Cate wasn't entirely sure they were intentional, but the result made Fred happy, and if Fred was happy, her bank account was happy.

As Lenny prowled the room with the EMI, aka the electro-magnetic indicator, making the occasional beeping noise, Erin stepped out into the center of the room, head flung back.

"Are you there? We can feel your presence. . . ." Erin wandered in a circle, hands out, palms up, eyes raised soulfully to the ceiling. Cate waited for her to trip over the edge of the carpet, but she traipsed neatly over it in her high-heeled boots. "We know you don't want to be here. We know you haven't done anything wrong. . . ."

"Of course I haven't!" said an indignant voice in Cate's ear.

Cate slapped a hand to her ear. "What was that?"

She whirled in a circle, but there was no one there.

Fred winced. He moved the mike away from his mouth. "Nice try, but a bit much, hot stuff. Bring it down a peg."

"But I—never mind."

Erin jumped in. "Oooh! Oooh! I'm getting something!"

An STD at a guess. It was an open secret that Erin was sharing Fred's bed.

"What are you feeling, Erin?" Fred asked, in the deep, low voice he used for the camera. It made him sound a bit like Alistair Cooke after a few sleeping pills, but the audience seemed to like it.

"I feel . . . I feel . . ."

"Not so fresh?" murmured Cate.

Hal stifled a snicker.

Erin dropped pose long enough to shoot them both a nasty look. "*If* you would?" Throwing back her head, she returned to trance mode. "I feel . . . a presence!"

Outside, lightning crashed. The chandelier overhead sputtered and sparked out. The EMI gave one last despairing beep before it, too, whined into somnolence. Even the red light on the camera had gone out.

The sounds of the storm seemed closer, clearer. Cate could hear the tap, tap, tap of branches against the windows, the hard patter of rain on the stone sills, the strained breathing of her crewmates as they all stood frozen, listening. There was a strange, whispering noise, like the sound of a long dress sweeping across the wool of the carpet.

The wind, of course. It had to be the wind. These old houses were riddled with drafts. Cate could feel it trailing across the back of her neck, stirring the painstakingly straightened strands of her hair.

She shivered, wrapping her arms around herself, cold with a fear she couldn't even name.

"Oh, bugger," said Lenny prosaically. "I've stubbed my toe."

His words broke the spell. Cate let out the breath she hadn't realized she'd been holding. Fred cursed. Erin giggled nervously.

"How long do you think it will take to get the power back?" Hal asked.

"God knows," said Fred crossly. "Old house like this—I doubt the old boy has a generator. It's a fucking nightmare."

"Don't you mean a fucking Northanger?" Erin giggled at her own cleverness.

Someone let out a sharp gasp of disapproval. "Really!"

There it was. That voice again. The breeze. The cold. The hairs on the back of Cate's neck prickled.

"Let's tell ghost stories!" Cate could hear the muted thump of Erin's heels against carpet as she blundered across the room, looking for Fred. "Won't that be fun?"

"Er . . . Erin?" said Hal, in a slightly strangled voice. "Is that you?"

From the other side of the room, Fred exclaimed, "Christ, Erin! Your hand's like ice."

"Okay," said Cate, in a low voice, "this is getting seriously weird."

"Maybe you're weird," said Erin crossly. "Sorry, Ha—Ahhhh!"

Her voice spiraled into the sort of shriek that generally went with showers and ax murderers as an apparition appeared in the doorway, a hideous, deformed creature glowing with an unnatural orange light.

Cate's breath came out with a rush. "Mr. Tilney-Tilney!"

Their host lowered his torch, returning his features to their normal proportions. In the sudden glare of the flashlight, Cate could see her teammates scattered around the room, looking like something out of *Scooby Doo*—Erin clinging to Hal, Lenny clinging to his camera, Fred standing with his arms folded across his chest and a scowl on his handsome face.

Did she look as white and scared as they did? Cate hoped not, but she rather suspected she did.

"Wanted to let you all know, there's cold beans on toast in the pantry if anyone is hungry," Mr. Tilney-Tilney said helpfully. "Might have the odd herring on hand as well."

"Red herrings?" blustered Fred.

Erin tittered, rocking on her rickety heels.

"Er, no," said Tilney-Tilney apologetically. "Quite the usual sort, I'm afraid. Sort of a pinky-gray."

"I think I'll pass." Cate started abruptly towards the door. "If it's all the same with you guys, I'm going to bed."

"Dorothy will show you the way," said Tilney-Tilney. "M'housekeeper, don't you know. Dorothy!"

Dressed in rusty black pants and a tentlike black shirt, Dorothy led Cate up a broad staircase and down a narrow hall flanked on one side by doors, on another by windows, the glass shivering and shimmering in the rain. A musty scent rose from the carpet runner beneath their feet, the smell of slow decay and long-held secrets.

It's just an old house, Cate reminded herself. Just like any other. So it was an abbey once. No biggie.

"Thanks so much for showing me to my room," she said politely. "I'm sorry to be dragging you out of your way."

"You thank me now," said Dorothy darkly. "But will you be thanking me later?"

In the narrow beam of the flashlight, portraits leered down at them from the walls.

Dorothy lowered her voice to a whisper and lifted the torch to just below her chin. "They say that it's on rainy nights that she comes."

"Who?" asked Cate.

Dorothy paused with her handle on the latch. "There's some as sees her and there's some as don't," she intoned.

"I can't really see much of anything right now," said Cate apologetically. "It's kind of dark."

Dorothy was determined to channel Mrs. Danvers. Fred should have interviewed her instead of Mr. Tilney-Tilney. "Ah, you'll be grateful for the dark! Grateful for the shadows that hide . . . the things that hide in shadows."

"Well, thanks," said Cate with determined cheer, as Dorothy flung open the door. In the feeble rays of the single flashlight, the panes of the windows glittered wetly. "Good night!"

The words echoed hollowly down the corridor. Dorothy was already gone.

All righty then.

Cate ventured into the room, easing the door closed behind her. The ray of the flashlight illuminated the hulking form of a tester bed, mercifully not canopied. Cate wasn't sure she could take a canopy, not after Dorothy. A cedar chest, curiously and intricately carved, brooded in an alcove by the fireplace. The light glinted off the yellow decoration on an old black lacquer cabinet, now peeling a bit with age. There was a key protruding from the keyhole, hinting at secrets within.

"What secrets lurk within the chests and cabinets of Northanger?" Cate demanded of the empty air, and flinched a bit at the sound of her own voice, too loud and too American in the waiting silence of the empty room.

It really was a gloomy old place—and about as haunted as a New Jersey shopping mall, Cate reminded herself resolutely. The only hauntings they ever encountered on *Ghost Trekkers* were those they produced themselves, via low lighting, suggestive music, and the collaborative imagination of the credulous.

She really had to find another job.

A sharp cracking noise made her jump. The wind, only the wind again, which had ripped the ancient casement from its frame and banged it back again. Hurrying to the window, Cate leaned out over the edge and wrestled it shut, jamming the catch closed as, outside, the leafless branches gibbered and shook at her, venting their helpless fury.

Bedtime. Cate yanked her shirt over her head—and froze, in every sense of the word, as a voice demanded, "What are you doing in my room?"

Dorothy might have mentioned that there were other guests in the house. Hell, Cate wouldn't put it past her to have put two people in the same room, just to make trouble. The woman needed a hobby.

Clutching her shirt to her chest, Cate turned, apologies on her tongue. "I'm so sorry, Dorothy told me they'd put me— Oh."

"Dorothy?" said the other woman. She was roughly Cate's

height, and dressed in a long gown made of a pale material, with short puffed sleeves woefully unsuited to the November weather.

She did not, however, appear to be suffering from the cold.

"The housekeeper," said Cate numbly.

Goose pimples broke out across Cate's chest, over the incongruously bright pink band of her eco-friendly Fruit of the Loom bra.

Her visitor was transparent. Cate could see the gold and black of the ebony cabinet quite clearly through the other woman's white dress.

Oh no. Oh no no. She was not falling for this.

"Very funny, Fred," Cate said loudly. She didn't know how he'd gotten upstairs to set it up, but this was so his sort of prank. She'd bet Erin was in on it, too. "Fred?"

The apparition wrinkled its brow. She looked young, younger than Cate, her skin smooth and unlined. Unlined and seethrough. "Fred?"

Discarding the shirt, Cate dropped to her knees and began fumbling around along the carpet. "All right. Where are they?"

"Miss—Miss—are you quite all right?" The projection followed her progress, drifting along after her as Cate crawled across the room.

"The wires," said Cate distractedly. "The wires. There must be wires. Unless . . . is it a battery-operated projector?"

"Battery?" repeated the apparition delicately. "A battery of cannon? In a bedchamber? My dear Miss—er, do let me ring for the maid. You are not well."

Cate hadn't thought she could feel any colder, but suddenly she did. She settled back on her haunches, moving joint by joint, her body as sluggish as her brain. "You repeated what I said back to me. You responded."

"I could hardly be so rude as to do otherwise," said the apparition. She was carrying a candle, which she set down on the heavily carved chest. "Even if you have invaded my chamber in a very strange mode of dress."

The flickering light of the phantom candle made Cate's head hurt. Fred might be reasonably technically competent, but he couldn't—at least, she didn't think he could—create a program designed to respond coherently to outside stimulus. She wasn't willing to rule out the possibility that such things existed, but if they did, they were out of *Ghost Trekkers'* purview. Even Lenny couldn't pull that off.

But if this wasn't a prank . . . No. That didn't even bear considering.

An unidentified female ghost who haunts one of the bedrooms, Erin had said. *Associated with a roll of paper that reappears and disappears in a lacquered chest.*

"Who are you?" asked Cate hoarsely.

"This is all highly irregular," the apparition said critically.

"I couldn't agree more." Speaking with people who weren't there definitely came under Cate's definition of irregular. "Are you . . . ?"

She couldn't make herself say the word "dead."

"A guest," supplied the apparition.

Guest . . . ghost . . . It was just a twist of the tongue away. Cate swallowed a spurt of hysterical laughter.

This wasn't happening. This couldn't be happening. She worked on *Ghost Trekkers,* for the love of God. She, of all people, knew that such things were purely the product of smoke and lenses.

She hadn't even eaten the herrings. She had known better than that. Herrings were worse than bits of underdone potato when it came to conjuring specters.

"And you?" The ghost was looking at her keenly. "Are you a guest of General Tilney?"

"In a manner of speaking," hedged Cate.

If this was a dream, why conjure up an inquisitive female? Why not a strapping male in knee breeches? Or a Roman centurion in one of those cute little leather kilts? Her imagination clearly needed help.

"Who are those uncouth people in the hall?" asked the apparition, settling in for a good gossip. Her see-through skirts lapped around her ankles.

"Um, they're . . . I work with them. We're on a—" *TV show* really didn't seem like something her transparent visitor would understand. Cate hastily cobbled together the closest possible translation. "We're a sort of acting troupe."

"Theatricals." The apparition's face lit with interest. "Shall you perform for us?"

"Er," said Cate. "I think it's more that they'd hoped you'd perform for us."

Not that Fred would know what to do with a real ghost if he tripped over one.

Wait. When had she decided this was a real ghost? "Just ignore them," she said hastily. "If they come after you, pretend they're not there. Even if they make beeping noises."

"Beeping noises?"

"It's the most ramshackle operation," Cate said. "I mean, I don't know what I'm still doing here. I really only meant to stay for a few months, just for the experience—and, oh, hell, so I had sort of a crush on Hal, but the man is never going to do anything, about me or anything else. He's under his brother's thumb like you wouldn't believe. He'd probably have to ask Fred's permission before getting up the nerve to make a move."

"Like that, is it?" said the ghost sympathetically. "Is this Hal the younger brother?"

"Yes. Fred's older. He's the one who owns the whole kit and caboodle."

The ghost nodded sagely. Cate's slang might have been lost on her, but the general concept was one she understood.

"Nothing's going to change while Fred's in charge," Cate said glumly. There was something oddly soothing about speaking with someone who wasn't there. "Hal will never have the guts to do anything about it. It's a complete dead end." She looked at the ghost—or, rather, through the ghost—and clapped a hand over her mouth. "Oh, crap! I'm sorry. I mean, it's not going anywhere. Just forget I said 'dead,' okay?"

"Then why do you stay?" asked the apparition.

Cate found herself getting defensive. "I have a salary, I have benefits—"

"Benefits?"

"Never mind that." What would a nineteenth-century ghost understand? "The point is, thanks to this, I have enough to live comfortably on my own."

"An independence," mused the apparition. "Not something at which one would sneer. Even so . . ." She seated herself on a chair that wasn't there and looked thoughtfully at a fire that wasn't lit. "Poverty is a great evil, but to a woman of education and feeling, it ought not, it cannot be, the greatest."

"What do you mean?" Cate asked.

"We have all a better guide in ourselves, if we would attend to it, than any other person can be. If your mind mislikes this current employment, trust it." She looked earnestly at Cate. "There will be little rubs and disappointments everywhere, and we are all apt to expect too much; but then, if one scheme of happiness fails, human nature turns to another; if the first calculation is wrong, we make a second better."

"Um, what?" said Cate.

"There will be better," translated the ghost. "Do not resign yourself too soon."

Maybe there was some truth to that. Sure, she whined a lot, but when was the last time she had made any attempt to take an actual hand in her own destiny?

"I won't," said Cate decidedly. "I'll talk to Fred. Either he gives me something of real substance to do, or I'm out."

The apparition looked as though she only understood about half of that, but she gamely nodded her encouragement. "And what of your—forgive me, I've forgot the gentleman's name."

"Hal," said Cate absently. "Hal."

Did she still want Hal? She had, she realized, gotten into the habit of having a crush on him, like having her hair parted on the left side or carrying her bag on her right shoulder.

"You find him not what you believed him to be," the apparition deduced sagely.

This was all getting a little too close to home. And from a ghost. For a moment, Cate had almost forgotten she was a ghost.

"I'm sorry," Cate said apologetically, "I've been talking and talking at you and I don't even know who you are."

The ghost smiled pleasantly. "No matter. Close quarters make for quick friends. I am Miss Austen. And you are?"

"Miss . . . did you say 'Austen'?"

"Yes," said the specter. "Miss Jane Austen."

What was it Mr. Morland Tilney-Tilney had said? Something about a lady novelist coming to Northanger and spreading lies. Something beginning with a vowel . . .

Cate remembered the one picture she had seen of Jane Austen, on a Barnes & Noble bag. It had been strangely out of proportion, awkwardly drawn. The authoress's eyes had seemed to squint— although that might have been a fold in the bag—her lips had been pressed tightly together, and there had been a frilly cap covering her dark hair. She had looked, in Cate's opinion, more disgruntled than anything else, as though miffed at finding herself rendered in green and beige and used to convey other people's books.

This woman, on the other hand, was young and vibrant, with shiny hair and a sparkle in her eye. Or maybe that was just the gold from the cabinet showing through her transparent face.

"And you are?" asked the ghost who claimed to be Jane Austen.

Why? Why her? Cate was sure there were plenty of people who would be delighted to be visited by the ghost of Jane Austen. Cate had been a poli sci major. She had read Rawls and Nozick, not . . . what else had Austen written? Five hundred pounds and a room of one's own; no, that was that depressing woman who'd drowned herself. Cate wished she had paid more attention in Intro to English Lit.

Did watching that miniseries with Colin Firth in it count?

"I'm Cate," she blundered. "I mean Catherine. You can call me Catherine."

The apparition gave her a look, but dipped a tiny curtsy any-way. Oh, crap, they didn't use first names back then, did they? Damn, damn, damn. She was so not prepared for this.

Cate curtsied clumsily back, her jeans protesting against the movement. Her midriff felt very bare. She ought to have been freezing, but adrenaline pumped heat through her veins. Was this how deepwater divers felt or those crazy people who jumped off bridges on a bungee cord? Warm, with a desperate heat like a fever burning one up from the inside out? Or perhaps it was just because in real life, the real Cate was under the covers, burrowed in warmth, dreaming of an authoress she ought to have read.

"Forgive me," said Cate. "I know I should know this . . . But do you write ghost stories?"

"I write stories, yes," said the ghost firmly, "but not what you call a *ghost story*. I leave those to Mrs. Radcliffe and the heirs of *Otranto*."

"Oh?" Cate didn't like to ask who Mrs. Radcliffe was.

"I have no patience with such trumpery horrors—except in satire. I have," she added blandly, "written just such a story about Northanger. You can find it here, in this chest. I've left it as a gift for my host in exchange for the fine entertainment he afforded me during my visit."

There was a lively gleam in the authoress's dead eye that made Cate wonder just what sort of gift it was intended to be. And what sort of entertainment she had been afforded.

Hell hath no fury like an authoress bored?

"I think I may have heard of it." Cate conjured up Mr. Tilney-Tilney's ravings about aged housekeepers, secret passageways, and murdered wives. "What is it about? Your Northanger story, I mean."

The apparition gave the lacquer chest a fond pat. "My heroine, a great reader of Mrs. Radcliffe, visits Northanger. Overcome at staying under the roof of a genuine abbey—and one of such antiquity!—she imagines herself surrounded by every sort of ghost and ghoul. Naturally, she finds it to be nothing of the sort."

"Why naturally?" asked Cate.

"Silly Catherine," said the ghost of Jane Austen indulgently. "There are no such things as ghosts."

LAUREN WILLIG is the author of the *New York Times* bestselling Pink Carnation series, which follows the adventures of a series of Napoleonic-era spies in their attempts to thwart Bonaparte and avoid Almack's As-

sembly Rooms. A graduate of Yale, Willig has a graduate degree in
English history from Harvard and a JD from Harvard Law. After receiving her first book contract during her first month of law school, she
juggled the legal life and Napoleonic spies for several years before deciding that doc review and book deadlines don't mix. Now a full-time
writer, she recently taught a class at Yale on "Reading the Historical
Romance," an examination of the Regency romance novel as literature
from Jane Austen (especially *Northanger Abbey*!) through Julia Quinn.

www.laurenwillig.com

JANE AND THE GENTLEMAN ROGUE

BEING A FRAGMENT OF A JANE AUSTEN MYSTERY

Stephanie Barron

Editor's Note: The following journal entry, spanning a few days in the spring of 1805, was recently discovered tucked into Jane Austen's 1813 diary.

25 Gay Street, Bath
Wednesday, 17 April 1805

"By the by, Jane," my mother observed from her comfortable chair by the fire, "your disreputable Lord Harold has *again* brought disgrace upon all his noble family."

"Indeed, ma'am?"

"From this account in the *Morning Gazette,* I conclude that he has met a man in a duel—and been wounded for his folly! It is conjectured that his lordship's opponent is already fled to the Continent, in expectation of Lord Harold's death." She peered at me over the edge of her newspaper. "You do not seem excessively cut up at the intelligence! Have you given over your *tendre* for the villain?"

"My respect for his lordship is undiminished," I replied. "I have merely learnt not to credit every *on-dit* the papers may chuse to publish."

My mother's eyes narrowed. Tho' a woman blessed with a fund of absurdity, she is capable of exercising considerable wit when one least desires it—and our enforced tête-à-tête of recent weeks has redoubled her attentions to myself. My father having passed from this life in January, and my sister being absent nearly two months on an errand of mercy to our friend Martha Lloyd, I have enjoyed little society beyond Mrs. Austen's. Such a picture of female devotion ought to prove inspiring—but has been cause for exasperation.

"Fighting over a lightskirt, I daresay," my mother sniffed; "some brazen Cytherean the papers could not mention. Ah, well—it is all as I predicted. His lordship is a rogue not fit to darken the threshold; and I suppose there's not the *least* chance of you getting him now. When I consider, too, of the opportunities that have been thrown in your way! And so recently as last week! Every possible attention paid you in Laura Place—the most *distinguishing* notice—and it shall all be for naught, once his lordship is dead!"

"Forgive me, ma'am." I set down my needlework and pressed my hand to my eyes. "I have the headache—and believe I shall take a turn in the Gravel Walk. The fresh air will do me no end of good."

Impossible to explain that I could put a name to both the duelist and the Cytherean; nor to admit that I had witnessed the affair of honour, in the early hours of yesterday morning.

A walk was certainly in order, if I were to preserve my sanity; but my steps turned toward Laura Place, and the man who hung between life and death, in the great curtained bed of the ducal household.

.   .   .

The mad episode began with a gilt-edged card of invitation, bearing the Dowager Duchess of Wilborough's direction. The honour of my presence was begged in Laura Place Sunday evening—to celebrate the betrothal of Her Grace's granddaughter, Lady Desdemona Trowbridge, to the Earl of Swithin.

Lord Harold Trowbridge, that notable Corinthian, Admiralty spy, despoiler of maiden hearts, and general Rogue-About-Town, is Lady Desdemona's uncle and the Dowager Duchess's second son. He has honoured me with his acquaintance, and with his confidence in several affairs of a mysterious and deadly nature. I will confess to a decided partiality for Lord Harold's society—he may be dangerous, but he is never *dull*—and in such a season of enforced boredom, I leapt at the opportunity to meet with him again—in a suitable gown of dove grey sarcenet, trimmed with black velvet bands about the sleeves and bodice, as befitted my mourning state.

Torn between gratification and disapprobation—convinced that all gaiety must be foresworn in respect of my father's death—my mother very nearly forbade my attendance in Laura Place. Wild horses, however, should not have kept me away; I should have been forced to dose Mrs. Austen's soup with laudanum, and slip out of our lodgings while she snored unawares. In the end, however, hopes of the Gentleman Rogue triumphed over my mother's anxiety for my reputation; and to Laura Place I was to go.

"Only do not be drinking too much of Her Grace's claret, Jane," she warned, "for it heightens your colour unbecomingly. You are in only passable looks as it is. *Lemonade* will stand your friend."

I had been in Laura Place on several occasions—for a rout, a game of charades, and the unmasking of a murderer—and expected to find a crush in respect of Lady Desdemona's impending nuptials. Her Grace had collected a genteel party of but thirty persons, however, most of them members of the Trowbridge and Swithin families. It was with an unaccustomed shyness, therefore, that I dropt my deepest curtsey to Eugènie, Dowager Duchess of Wilborough; felt Lady Desdemona's arm slip about my waist; and turned to find the Gentleman Rogue performing his most elegant bow.

"My dear Miss Austen," he murmured. "You can have no idea how much pleasure this meeting brings. I have a thousand things to say to you! But they will keep until you have greeted your friends, and taken a glass of wine."

I had not had a glimpse of Lord Harold since the turn of the year; had received only a kind letter of condolence at my father's death—and then, silence. Word of his exploits occasionally reached the London papers, in the most veiled terms. I caught wind of him at Gibraltar, consulting with Nelson; knew that he had dropt down to Portugal, at the request of the Emperor; and read that he had danced at Devonshire House with Desirée de la Neuve, a celebrated French soprano who had taken the *ton* by storm.

I paid my respects to the Earl of Swithin, happy possessor of Desdemona's heart; enjoyed a bit of raillery with her brother, the Marquis of Kinsfell, whose neck I had saved from the noose; and observed at a respectful distance no less a prince than the Duke of Clarence, his jovial Royal face already shining with heat and good will. Fortified by Her Grace's excellent wine and even more amusing conversation—for there is nothing like an actress for all that is engaging, whether she be seventy years or no—I found Lord Harold once more at my side.

"Miss Austen—may I present Mademoiselle Desirée de la Neuve to your acquaintance?"

She was exceedingly lovely—just the sort of black-haired beauty the Gentleman Rogue cannot resist, with a queenly carriage, a stunning décolleté, and a damask complexion. None of your insipid blond beauties for his lordship, I thought with resignation; only a diamond of the first water should do. I managed a smile as I performed my courtesy, and said, "This is indeed an honour! I hope we may have the pleasure of hearing you sing this evening?"

Mademoiselle de la Neuve was plainly indifferent to my pleasantries, however; she merely inclined her head and saved her charms for Lord Harold.

"*Mon dieu!*" she breathed, so low as to draw him near. "Dear Aunt Eugènie keeps her rooms so very hot, is it not? I am always on the point of fainting. If you would be so good, 'Arry, as to procure me a glass of lemonade—"

So the toast of the *ton* called the Dowager her aunt, did she?—And was on such terms with the Rogue as to call him *Harry*?

I will confess to a swelling in my bosom that ill-became one so recently bereaved. My eyes followed Lord Harold as he sought the supper tables; watched the elegant figure vanish into the dining room—and turned with effort to the Incomparable before me. But she had long since dismissed the little dab of a female in fusty mourning, in favour of a gentleman better worth pursuing—whose air and address proclaimed the man of Fashion. He was a stranger to me, perhaps thirty years of age and exceedingly handsome; but something in the inclination of his head, the quirk of his lips, and the way his eyes roamed over the figure of Mademoiselle, proclaimed the accomplished rake. *Heat* was once more the subject of conversation.

"Her Grace lives in a veritable furnace, winter and summer," he said smilingly. "A rheumatic complaint, I believe. Allow me to escort you to the balcony, *ma chère,* before you swoon."

I stared after them, utterly unconscious of Lord Harold's return, until he said into my ear—"A glass of lemonade, Jane? For I perceive that it is no longer of Desirée's desiring. If you will forgive the pun."

"Thank you, my lord, but I detest lemonade."

"Well done." He set the offending glass upon a side-table. "When the ducal cellars are opened, drink nothing but the most noble vintage. And now I think you should pretend to feel the flames my mother has so obligingly fanned. Flutter your eyelashes a little and stagger, Jane, if you will."

Puzzled, I obliged. His lordship supported me—his long, elegant fingers burned unwittingly into my arm. I cannot deny the effect his touch has upon me; it is perpetually electric.

"Observe," he murmured. "There are *two* sets of French doors giving out onto the balcony; and we might be profitably disguised by the draperies shielding the nearest. The Witch, I believe, has disappeared with Harcourt through the farther set of doors. What did you make of her, by the by?"

"The Witch?" I repeated. "If you would refer to Mademoiselle—she is all that is lovely, my lord. And . . . forgive me if I wound you . . . *calculating*."

"You perceived, then, that she sent me off on my errand, the more readily to slip away with Lord Cecil?"

"Then you should not be following them. It is hardly gallant in you, my lord. She is young, and must be forgiven for . . . for . . ."

"Finding a vicious gamester more appealing than an elderly roué?"

"I should never describe you thus!" I whispered fiercely. "Acquit me of such an insult!"

"Your good opinion—and your better sense—are the very reasons you are with me tonight, my dear."

I wondered if Lord Harold intended me to witness his

shame—his sacrifice upon the altar of unrequited passion—from some perverse desire to mortify himself. A leaden band tightened below my heart.

"My lord—let us go into supper. There is no need—"

"There is every need," he whispered. "For if I do not mistake, Jane, we are about to witness an act of treason."

The Duchess's balcony gave onto the garden, and despite the torches set into niches at intervals, was quite dark. It was also distinctly chilly, April in Bath being like every month in Bath—much given to rain. Hardly the time or place for a romantic assignation, therefore; yet here on the balcony the ravishing Frenchwoman and her amorous rake were established, oblivious to discomfort as well as convention.

Lord Cecil Harcourt crushed the lady in his arms; from my position in the sheltering draperies, I could just discern the white shape of her dress and darker silhouette of his head—could discern, as well, his hand slipping inside her bodice. . . .

Lord Harold advanced, as lightly and soundlessly as a cat; and despite my conviction I should far rather be elsewhere—I followed. It was impossible to do otherwise; his lordship held my hand firmly in his grasp.

"Desirée," the Rogue said, "pray give me that interesting missive Harcourt has just thrust down your dress."

The pair of lovers nearly jumped out of their skins; Mademoiselle uttered a strangled cry of "*Salaud!*" and the gentleman stepped backwards, his eyes shifting from Lord Harold to myself.

"What the Devil do you mean by this, Trowbridge?" he demanded. "Would you expose Mademoiselle de la Neuve to the censure of the entire party?"

"Apparently *you* would not hesitate," his lordship returned easily. "If you must behave like a scrub, Harcourt, do so in an Abbess's house, rather than my mother's. The missive, Desirée darling—the *billet-doux* this shocking court-card has seen fit to tuck into your bodice. Give it to me at once."

Tho' he spoke in an undertone calculated to pass for pleasant conversation, should any of the Dowager's guests stumble upon our picturesque, there was an edge of steel to his tone that was unmistakable.

Mademoiselle clasped her hands protectively over her bosom, her dark eyes flashing. "You are jealous, *hein?* You play the fool, 'Arry. I do not like these rages! They are not *English.*"

"The paper, Desirée. Or must I summon the Duke of Clarence to fish it out of your stays?"

With a movement so swift I barely saw it, Mademoiselle de la Neuve raised her hand and struck Lord Harold a stinging blow to the cheek. He remained immovable; he did not deign to acknowledge the hit; but Lord Cecil Harcourt was galvanised to activity. He thrust himself between the Frenchwoman and the Rogue.

"Sir, you trespass too far!" he muttered between his teeth. "Honour and reason will not bear such an insult. I beg you will name your Seconds."

Lord Harold smiled. For an instant, his glittering gaze met mine. "I should never betray such shockingly bad *ton* at my niece's betrothal party, Harcourt. I shall wait upon you tomorrow. If you are still in Bath."

"You may find me at the White Hart. I breakfast at nine."

Mademoiselle de la Neuve grasped Harcourt's jacket furiously. *"No!"* she cried. "You will *not* fight him! He will of a certainty kill you!"

"Do not worry your pretty head, my sweet." The rake bowed with exquisite grace. "The man has not yet been born who may put Harcourt underground."

A rustle of silk in the doorway brought all our heads around; Eugènie, Dowager Duchess of Wilborough.

"Desirée, *ma chère,*" she called gaily, "we long to hear you! Will you not sing a little?"

The Witch drew a single breath, squared her shoulders, and stepped into the torchlight with a smile upon her face.

"But of course, *ma tante*. Anything you would ask—for you, who have been so good to me!"

"I think," Lord Harold muttered in my ear, "we should repair to the library, Jane. Would you care for a few lobster patties and champagne?"

"Is she *really* your mother's niece?" I asked, as Lord Harold closed the library door upon the sound of Mademoiselle de la Neuve's glorious singing, and set a plate of supper before me. I was established on a sopha in front of the blazing fire, surrounded by the rich leather binding of books; the room glowed from the numerous branches of candles the Dowager had caused to be lit. Rain had begun to tap at the windowpanes, and I was alone with the Gentleman Rogue; I was deliciously conscious of behaving in a manner Mamma should not approve at all.

"She is the granddaughter of my mother's oldest friend—who perished in the Terror, along with her parents and brothers," Lord Harold said. "Desirée was in Switzerland at the time, enrolled in a convent school; she should not have survived else."

"How does she come to be in London?"

The grey eyes glanced up at me; the Rogue was preoccupied with opening a bottle of champagne. "On a visit to my mother—who, despite fifty years' residence in England, preserves a fondness for all things French. Tho' I must believe the fair Desirée was despatched on an errand of espionage," he said calmly. "A ravishing girl with a beautiful voice and friends highly-placed among the *ton* . . . such opportunities do not often fall in Buonaparte's way! She has been going on exceedingly well, too, until this evening. I have observed her progress these many weeks—and aside from a trifling few articles I have managed to intercept, I should judge that Desirée has set the entire Admiralty by the ears!"

"But how is this?" I wondered. "A girl whose family was murdered by the mob—and she would dedicate herself to Buonaparte's cause?"

"To the *Emperor's* cause," Lord Harold corrected. "He is quite the darling of the younger set in Paris, you know, and becomes more aristocratic with every successful battle. After quitting her convent, Desirée was raised in the home of Admiral Villeneuve, who was once a friend of her father's. Hence her stage name—*de la Neuve*. She has taken it in gratitude to her foster parents."

"—And offered to spy for Villeneuve as well?"

"Certainly. That bit of amorous nonsense you observed on the balcony was but a deft manner of passing information." Lord Harold handed me a cup of champagne.

"The paper Harcourt thrust into her bodice? It was no love-note?"

"I should dearly love to have secured it—but I dare swear it was the latest disposition of Nelson's fleet. Harcourt is secretary to the Duke of Clarence, Jane, who is privy to Naval secrets; and they have been spilling rather frequently to the Enemy of late. Admiral Villeneuve broke the Blockade and slipped out of Toulon as recently as the thirtieth of March; and no one may say in which direction he sails, or what he intends. The great sea is a vast and utter blank. Nelson fears some assault is planned—the invasion, perhaps, of England in the offing."

He spoke with bleak simplicity; but his words could not fail of a listener. I knew that Lord Harold had recently been consulting with Nelson at Gibraltar; my brother Frank, in command of the *Canopus,* sailed with Nelson on the Blockade. Our nation's peril was, more intimately, my family's peril.

"She must be stopped!" I cried.

"Hush," he soothed. "What else were we about this evening?"

"A lover's quarrel," I retorted. "Your jealous rages."

"She is a clever minx, is she not?" He tasted the wine and sighed. "But not so clever as Harcourt. That was a piece of brilliance, challenging me to a duel. If he kills me, my suspicions of treason die with me—and he will have no recourse but to flee to France, to avoid being taken up for murder. As France is undoubtedly his object in any case, he cannot have devised a better plan."

"You will not *meet* him, of course," I said in horror. "You will turn him over to the Admiralty!"

"—And reveal that a certain fatuous Royal duke has been robbed of Nelson's secrets, by his trusted aide?" Lord Harold's lip curled. "Clarence will not thank me, if I air his dirty linen in publick. Harcourt counted upon *that,* too, when he challenged me tonight."

I cordially hated the man. "What can be Lord Harcourt's motive for such infamy?"

"He is a gamester," the Rogue replied indifferently. "Run off his legs with debt, Jane. His is a tragic folly—a once honourable son of an honourable house, who sold his soul at the faro-table. You may be sure Villeneuve pays him well."

"Have you considered, my lord," I said slowly, "that killing *himself,* and not *you,* may be Harcourt's object in seeking this duel? The Great World reckons you a deadly shot. A single ball at Lord Harold's hand may be infinitely preferable to a traitor's death on Tower Hill."

Lord Harold's brows lifted coolly. "I should never do the blackguard the honour of killing him, Jane. I should have to quit England, else. Naturally, I shall aim wide."

I do not think I closed my eyes the whole of that night; and as I appeared at the breakfast-table looking hagged to death, I won a lecture from my mother—who perceived at an instant that I had *not* partaken solely of lemonade in Laura Place. I ate a little dry toast and tea, and begged leave to throw off my fit of the sullens in an arduous walk up Beechen Cliff—where my mother was certain never to follow me.

In point of fact, I made immediately for Laura Place, despite the appalling earliness of the hour. Lord Harold had expressed the intention of waiting upon Harcourt at breakfast—and if luck was with me, might still be abroad on his errand. I did not wish to meet the Rogue; it was the Witch I was after.

I sent up my card to Mademoiselle; on the obverse, I had written—*Regarding Lord Cecil.* I was not surprised when she received me—in dishabille, before her dressing table, her hair undone and a brush in her hand. She was exceedingly lovely.

"Who are you," she demanded, when she had sent away her maid, "and what would you dare to say to me of Lord Cecil?"

If I felt a strong desire to shatter her mirror, I may perhaps be forgiven.

"I shall come straight to the point," I returned. "Harcourt intends to kill Lord Harold Trowbridge tomorrow at dawn—to save himself from the scandal and ruin necessarily involved in the charge of *traitor.* You, mademoiselle, have ensnared the fellow in this web of despicable deceit, and now fear for his life. Am I wrong?"

"You are not wrong," she said in a voice aching and low; "I did my best, me, to shield him—I did not give up the paper—but it was as nothing! He was *enragé*—he would throw his life away to defend my honour! He does not know that 'Arry will of a certainty kill him!"

"Is Harcourt accounted a good shot?"

She shrugged with Gallic eloquence. "I do not know this. I only know that 'Arry has shot scores of men in duels! He is famous for killing, that one!"

The Rogue's reputation in France far exceeded even his exploits, it seemed; he would be no end gratified to learn of it. But I saw no reason to improve the lady's faulty understanding.

"There might be a way you may save Harcourt," I said. "Give up that paper he stole from the Admiralty. Tell Lord Harold what his lordship most wishes to learn—the movements of the French fleet."

She frowned at me warily. "Are you mad? You would trap me! You would see me hanged!"

I sank down beside her and took her hand—the very soft, white article that had slapped Lord Harold so fiercely. "Do you love Harcourt very much?" I enquired.

"To the point of madness!" she cried.

"—And would do anything to save him?"

"*Mon dieu*—but anything!" She turned streaming eyes to mine. "Can it be that you will help me? But *why?*—Why should I trust you, *hein?*"

"Because *I* would do anything to save Lord Harold," I retorted drily. "Now listen, mademoiselle. Here is what we must do."

When the two men met on a flat stretch of ground adjacent to the Kennet & Avon canal, at precisely six o'clock yesterday morning, with their Seconds soberly pacing the ground and examining the pistols; with good Mr. Bowen, the surgeon, waiting to turn his back upon the opponents in expectation of an act his medical oath should not countenance; with a swift curricle-and-four standing ominously in readiness, to bear Harcourt away to the port of Bristol—Mademoiselle de la Neuve and I were there.

The duelists did not see us, of course; Desirée was too adept an Adventuress for self-betrayal, and I was something of a Student of Deception myself. She had paid off the boot-boy at the White Hart to overlisten the Seconds' conversation, establishing the hour and place of meeting; and after that, it was mere child's play. We hired our hacks at the livery-stable in Milsom Street, and rode out to the ground before dawn; tethered our mounts in a coppice, with feed-bags to their noses; and awaited the gentlemen's pleasure. By the time they arrived, both Mademoiselle and I were shivering to the bone—from apprehension as much as the raw Spring weather.

We lay flat on our stomachs, our gowns fearfully crushed beneath us, the cold seeping through our stout pelisses. We were invisible to the combatants; but our view of the ground was admirable.

Lord Harold and Harcourt stood with their backs together, and their pistols raised; at a word from one of the Seconds, they began to pace carefully apart. Lord Harold wore black; his coat was buttoned to his neck; he would offer no obvious target to his killer. Harcourt was more careless; an expanse of cravat was exposed by his broad lapels; and a sudden fear assailed me. *How could he be so sure of taking his man?*

I rose up on my knees, and Desirée rose with me. In an instant she was off at a run toward the dueling ground, reaching its edge just as the two men turned.

Their pistols were leveled—the count begun—

Desirée intended to hurl herself at Harcourt on the count of *two,* in the hope of pushing him off balance and out of harm's way. It was her only hope, she believed, of thwarting Lord Harold's deadly aim and saving the life of her Beloved.

It was *my* hope she would foil Harcourt's shot—which I suspected would be straight for his lordship's heart.

I had not calculated on a gamester's risks; upon a man determined to win at any cost. I had not thought a *gentleman* should so demean himself as to *fire in advance of his opponent*.

But on the count of *two,* Lord Cecil fired.

I saw Lord Harold thrown back—saw him spin, and fall to the ground—saw Bowen the surgeon leap forward to tend his patient—and saw Harcourt raise his second pistol.

He meant to despatch Lord Harold like a dog.

Even as I ran toward the Rogue in a fever of despair, Desirée hurtled into her Beloved—and the pistol discharged harmlessly into air.

I confess I did *not* take a turn on the Gravel Walk this morning.

The quelling personage who served as butler in Laura Place informed me that Her Grace was not at home to visitors; and when I enquired for Lady Desdemona, the reply was the same. I must be content with sending in my card; but as I turned away, the door was flung wide, and I perceived Desdemona's anxious face.

"Miss Austen!" she cried. "Come in at once—Uncle is asking for you!"

I hurried up the stairs in her wake. "How is he?"

"Better—the fever has broken, and he is able to rest a little. The doctors do not now despair of his life. But only think of it— *Uncle* fighting a duel over Mademoiselle de la Neuve, whom I did not believe he cared a particle for! It is beyond everything! And

Kinsfell is certain she is gone to the Continent with Lord Cecil—Kinny was Uncle's Second, you know, and witnessed the whole! My poor grandmother has taken to her bed!"

"She has had a great deal to bear," I murmured.

Lady Desdemona scratched at a bedchamber door, and peeped around it carefully. "Uncle! Are you awake? I have brought Miss Austen to you! Do not overtire him," she warned me. "It is vital that he rest."

I nodded, and heard the door close behind me.

The Rogue was propped up on a wealth of pillows, his left shoulder bound in a bandage. His pallor was considerable, and the lines on his face had deepened overnight—but when his eyes fell upon me, they were as cool and clear as ever. He held out his right hand imperatively. I went to him.

"I have some memory of you on the dueling ground," he said, "tho' you cannot have been there, Jane. Was I dreaming?"

"You were not, my lord."

"A lamentable contest, I fear."

"Harcourt fired before the count!"

"Blackguard," his lordship said carelessly. "And so they are off, then? To the Continent?"

"—Far beyond the reach of King and Country."

"And I never secured Nelson's plans. *Damn.*"

"Hush," I soothed. "What else were we about, yesterday morning?"

He stared at me, brows knitted.

Slowly, I drew off my gloves, and with infinite care, slipped my fingers into the bodice of my black muslin gown.

"You devil," Lord Harold murmured.

I placed the incriminating sheet of Admiralty plans into his outstretched hand.

"Villeneuve," I said, "passed Gibraltar three days ago. He is bound for the Caribbean."

The Rogue gripped my fingers painfully, Nelson's paper crumpling between them. "Desirée told you so much—she *gave* you this . . . in God's name, *why?*"

"Out of gratitude," I said, "for a worthless man's life."

STEPHANIE BARRON is the author of eleven bestselling Jane Austen mysteries, including *Jane and the Canterbury Tale*. She has also written the stand-alone historical suspense novels *A Flaw in the Blood* and *The White Garden*. As Francine Mathews, she is the author of several thrillers, including *The Alibi Club*. She lives near Denver, Colorado.

www.stephaniebarron.com

FAUX JANE

F. J. Meier

Nicola Scott crashed into her husband's restaurant.

"Charlie? Can you get me out of this thing? The damn pin is caught."

"Oops," he said.

"Be careful. It's Loro Piana."

"Poor Loro."

"Be serious. It's pulling at my jacket. My arm is caught too."

Charles Scott waved a flattened "calm down" hand until Nicola stood before him, patient as a dog on a grooming bench. She knew how to stand still; she asked people to do it all day. Her husband, with careful method in every finger, worked backwards. He found the point; the catch on the vintage brooch had snared a tangle of cashmere threads.

"Easy. That's my David Webb."

"Well, he's lost this battle, poor old Davey . . . ye-es, I think he has. . . . Nobody hurt."

He tapped her cheek. There it was again; the calm on which she so depended, the natural authority that she loved. She stood on high tiptoe and kissed his cheek.

"Why," he said, "do you wear things that imprison you?"

"I know." She heaved off the shawl. "I don't know what to do. I've limited my colors to black, white, gray, and navy. I've no extraneous pockets—no flaps, no ruffles—and I still sabotage myself. The other day at the Tiffany meeting, I looked down and I had on one black and one navy Belgian loafer. Mortifying."

"This is a grave matter."

"You're mocking me."

"This needs a Freudian. Five days a week."

"Well, it needs my camera bag to be lighter, for one thing."

He took the bag from her and winced.

"What in God's name is in here? Furniture? A spare toilet?"

"The crew always load me with extra lenses. And then we forget to take them out."

"Yell at them."

"I don't yell at my crew—I allow them to be creative. That's why they love me."

"I love to yell at my crew," he laughed. "They allow me to be creative." He changed the subject. "So how was 'The Star'?"

"Surprising."

"She knew how to use a knife and fork?"

"I didn't realize she'd be so nice. And so rich. My God, Charlie."

"Come on, Nic, you knew she was rich."

"Not this rich. I mean—planes and yachts. She owns a train in Hungary. A train, Charlie."

"Why didn't you bring her here?"

"I needed to meet her before the shoot. And you have nothing nice to say about her."

He let it pass. "You look excellent. Coffee? Dessert?"

Nicola Scott shook her head. "Nope. I've got to get home. It's"—she raised a brow at him—"Tuesday."

"I know what day it is," Charles looked bleak. "You should have let me bring Nora here."

"And the health inspectors?"

"I'd keep her in the office."

"Wouldn't it be smarter if we could find a houseman who would take off weekends instead of Tuesdays?"

"But it wouldn't be Uncle Julius. And Tuesday's his lucky day."

"Oh, right." Nicola, like all who handle clients, had developed the gift of heavy sarcasm. "So how much lucky money did he make last Tuesday?"

"You don't make money at Belmont if it rains."

"He never makes money. Charlie, we employ someone who doesn't iron, and doesn't cook, and can't even order in. Unless it's liquor." Nicola was building steam. "He can't get a phone message straight, he has stinky friends in at weekends when we're not there. And he doesn't work Tuesdays."

"Change the tape. He was there when I needed him. How did La Diva like your plans for Arden?"

Nicola beamed.

"Oh, Pop—do I have a story for you."

He leaned back and folded his arms. "I'm a blank page, write on me."

"Big secret. Not even the bloggers know. She's in love."

"Whose husband is it this time?"

"You'll have tears in your eyes. He's even posher than you. And ten years younger. She says he looks like a young Rupert Everett."

"Rupert Everett looks like a young Rupert Everett."

"And his father's just died, so he's Lord Something-or-other. Complete with ancestral pile."

"It is a fact universally acknowledged that a single female in possession of a vast amount of money must be in want of an English lord."

"That's such a cheap shot." She changed her tone to sharp inquisitiveness. "But why did you say that?"

"I like cheap shots."

"No. That particular mangled quote?"

"Because it's true, kid." He shook his head to rid himself of the nonsense.

"That's not what I'm asking. Why that particular quote?"

Charles Scott smiled a measuring look at his wife. He reached out and took her hand. "Come on. Shell it."

"You know something, Charlie, don't you?"

"I know many things, I'm a gnome, I'm a wizard." He pinched her hand.

"But you know something"—she began to whisper—"about my star and Jane Austen?"

"I know that the Austen movie made her a star . . ."

"Well . . ." Nicola paused, delighting in her secret. "Get this. She's just paid one million dollars for a signed first edition of *Pride and Prejudice*."

Charles hooted. "Then she's an idiot!"

"Because she overpaid?"

"Because there's no such thing!"

"Of course there is."

"No. *Absolument non. Nyet.*"

"Charlie, don't be silly. There must be."

"Nope, nope, no-diddly-ope."

"But Jane Austen's books were printed, weren't they? By printers? And bound? By binders. And they're on paper. They're not illuminated manuscripts."

"Look, Nic. I'm telling you. There is no such thing as a Jane Austen signed first edition. They didn't do that in Jane's day. The books were badly made. Not valuable. And most of all—*she* didn't do it."

"You don't know that, Charlie."

"Your actress has bought a pup. She's been royally taken."

"You're just being negative," Nicola said, confused and building a pout. "She says she's also been offered a signed first edition of *Persuasion*."

Charles snorted this time.

"That's not nice, Charlie."

"Sweetmeat, *Persuasion* was published posthumously. When Janey was dead. When she was an ex-author. A former novelist. Dead, don't you know. Dead women sign no books."

"I'm going home to walk Nora."

"I'm telling you, kid. Your *artiste* has been set up."

"Don't gloat." Nicola punched his arm. "You're not a nice man."

"Okay. Where did she get it? Who sold it to her? Because it couldn't have been anyone with credentials."

"Oh, Charlie, I might have missed something. She talks so fast and she's so—you know, dramatic. If you're so sure about it, we should tell her."

"No."

"What do you mean, 'no'?"

"She's a trailer-trash movie star who wouldn't know Jane Austen from Austin, Texas, if she hadn't been cast in that film."

"Charlie, she's in love. Love brings out the best in people. She bought it for this Lord—Lord Pigpen or something."

"And she was conned because of her greed. She wants the one thing her money can't buy—a title and a manor house in England. I'll bet you anything that she wasn't the least bit interested in little Lord Thingymajig until she saw his house. Very Elizabeth Bennet, by the way."

"No, it's not."

"Yes, it is. Our Lizzie had no interest in Mister Stiff-Britches Darcy until she saw the estate in Derbyshire. The world and his auntie know that."

"Come on, Pop—we can't just stand by."

"What is it they say? *'Yes, we can.'*"

"Charlie, we help people, don't we?"

Charles straightened up. "People, yes. But not spoiled little actresses."

"But are we going to sit here and let someone we know fork over a million dollars for a fake?"

"As Mamma would say, she's not someone we know."

"She's someone I know. And I'm telling you—there's something very genuine about her."

"Yes, kid, and—there's such a thing as a genuine fake. And that is something Jane Austen knew so well."

"Oh, blast. Look at the time. Nora will be crossing her little legs. Pop, will you bring my bag home with you?"

"Uncle Julius said he might be home early."

"Yeah, yeah," she waved the air with her hand. "Who hires an uncle, Charlie?"

No other New York restaurateur, safe bet, had such a knowledge of eighteenth- and nineteenth-century English literature. Charles Berkeley Scott, of Hotchkiss, Vassar, and Balliol College, Oxford, could quote Defoe, had memorized chunks of Smollett, knew what passages to jump over in Richardson—"Always skip in *Pamela,* never in *Clarissa*"—and did a passable imitation of the Great Bear, Dr. Samuel Johnson. But if those gentlemen of letters occupied his imagination, Jane Austen owned his heart.

"Would I?" he had answered Nicola on their first date. "You bet I would. She was so hot I don't even have to think about it.

The brain's the most erogenous zone. She was smart. Like you. Yeah, I'd have given her one."

"Yech," said his wife. "I hate that expression." But she loved his passion for the woman Samuel Beckett called "the divine Jane."

Not even their closest friends, though, knew a deeper reason why Charles Scott and Nicola Foreman so suited each other—lowlife. He mixed with them, and she fell in thrall to the dichotomy—a man whom everyone saw as "posh," yet who knew how to navigate the sewers and occasionally swim in them.

Charles Scott had been considered a "catch" most of his adult life. Adored by the Zagateers for the refined contemporary cuisine of his high-end-ambience restaurant, ASTA, he had a Gramercy Park townhouse profiled in *Architectural Digest,* a restored American Empire farmhouse in Connecticut, and a flat in London overlooking Saint James's Park.

His English grande-dame mother had pampered but not spoiled him, and he'd returned the favor, acting as her escort since he was eighteen years old. Her many admirers schooled Charlie in the best sartorials—the suits, the shoes, the stunning long overcoats—and when Nicola was sent to photograph him for a Movers 'n Shakers spread in *Vanity Fair,* they went to bed that night and forever after.

He'd have been a superb father—baseball stats coming out of his ears; a mountain biker; stroke oar for his school; playful as a puppy. Then Life kicked these gilded people in the stomach—one, two, three pregnancies that failed, among them a difficult stillbirth, ensuring that Nicola would not conceive again. And Charlie wouldn't adopt, summing up his refusal by saying, "I know what people are like." Nicola went back to work each time, and then for good. Nora became their baby, a sweet but neurotic dachshund with allergies and the silkiest ears on earth.

On the night he heard about what he called "Faux Jane," Charles Scott strolled home from ASTA around ten o'clock. From the hall, he heard Uncle Julius talking to Nicola.

"They don't call 'em forgers," Julius said. "They're 'spoofers.' Ask Charlie about Prickles—Charlie's dad gave him that name. D'ja actually see this book—with your own two eyes?"

Nicola shook her head.

Uncle Julius, excited now, surged onward. "If it looks good enough to be worth a million bucks, I'm telling ya, Prickles did it."

Uncle Julius petted Nora on his lap, and leaned back in a kind of reverie, remembering something beautiful.

"He's a Picasso. His special gift was the autograph. Churchill, Roosevelt. Jefferson was real special to him. And, yeah, he did English writers too; he did that fella, what was his name, Oliver Twist. Jeez, they oughta cost a million. The guy's a genius."

Nicola sat wide-eyed. Nora heard Charles arriving. A squealing, squirming sausage, she wriggled out of Julius's embrace, dropped like a pod from a tree and skidded across the black and white marble floor. She tried to jump into Charles's arms, but once again, not a chance. He bent to pick her up.

"Ooooh, you think you're a Jack Russell, don't you? But you are a hotdog, you little frankfurter. Yes—you're a leetle hot dog, aren't you? You weren't meant to jump in the air—you were meant to be tucked into a lovely, cozy bun. And. Just. Eaten. Up."

Charles held Nora close and tickled her pink dog tummy with his free hand, his face awash with her kisses.

Nicola called out, "I was telling Uncle Julius about the Jane Austen. And he's been telling me about his friend Prickles, the best forger—"

"Spoofer," corrected Uncle Julius. "I told her your dad knew him."

In a chopped voice, Charles said, "Is he still out?"

"Don't know," shrugged Uncle Julius. "Your father'll know—"

Charles interrupted with a curt question, "Anyone want food?"

A plate of crisped bacon sat next to the stove near a bowl of waiting eggs.

"I still can't get over how nice she is," said Nicola.

"Nic, this is none of our business," said Charlie, tying his apron with vicious knots. "There's no thanks in this. Let Miz Elliott pursue her lord."

"Elliott? Anne Elliott?" asked Uncle Julius. "Wowee zowee. That's some tomato."

Charles, clearly annoyed that he had to explain, said, "She's being conned. Nic wants us to step in and save the day—and we're not going to lift a finger. End of story."

Too little too late, because Uncle Julius said, gleaming with interest, "I wonder who the con is?"

"Julius—no!" said Charles.

And Nicola said, "Come on, Charlie, we can't just do nothing, can we?"

"No?" asked Charles. "Watch me." He fed Nora some defiant bacon.

On Friday, with the ASTA phone ringing off the hook, Nicola's assistant called from the studio to hold a table for eight o'clock. Number 42, the round table in the far right corner, was held for VIPs—socialites and pop stars, who rarely called ahead of time, assuming that there would always be room for them. Charles Scott turned them away if he didn't like them, thereby rendering ASTA even more desirable.

Anne Elliott arrived first, fresh from the set, still in Elizabeth Arden's hair and makeup. The glamorous Jackie O dark glasses, worn even at night, made her even more recognizable. In a world where celebrity had been reduced to the fodder of smartphones, she was holding up well. Oklahoma trailer trash she might have been, but she now had an image as powerful and fragile as the anklebone of a thoroughbred. And protected accordingly; many futures depended on that image's ability to win, place, or show.

Charles watched as she slipped off her glasses and eyed the banquette and then went arrow-straight for the spot where the light fell. When she sat down, she seemed to collect all the wattage in the room, and when she laughed, it cut like a diamond through the creamy din.

The restaurant began to behave as it always did when a star alit. No one wanted to talk or laugh too loud. No one wanted to miss a thing. Every moment was harvested, to be fed to the world as a personal trophy.

Like most movie stars, she had a large face on a head fractionally too big for her long, thin body. Her neck, though, worked as perfectly as a swan's; the shoulders were small and delicate; the ivory hands beautifully groomed. Teeth large and unnaturally white, lips plumped and rosy, nose sculpted to a perfect little point—Charles's surprise hit him with a sudden intake of breath.

Nicola, arriving minutes later, sat down and gasped—for a different reason: *Charlie's sitting at the table,* she thought. *My God! She's nailed him. He's smitten.* Eyelashes fluttering in the breeze, the actress was touching Charlie's arm, making eye contact closer than an oculist.

"Why is it so difficult to find great bread? I mean, it's just flour and water. And—yeast, isn't it? I mean, where is the magic that happens in France? Is it the water? I hear it's the water, Mr.

Scott—but of course, you must have these gorgeous little rolls flown in from—where? Dijon? I bet I know just the *boulangerie*."

"Please. It's Charles."

Of course it is, and you're dead, sister. Out loud, though, Nicola said with a clip, "They're made downstairs. In the basement. The cellar, actually." Her previous sympathy for the star of the show vanished like a wrinkle under an airbrush.

The diva barely acknowledged Nicola's presence; she didn't need the photographer's attention this evening. They'd had a good day. The pictures would be glorious; even the clients said so. Science and surgery, diet and pampering—and great good fortune—had given Anne Elliott, at forty-three, a face any twenty-something might have envied. If the world believed that Elizabeth Arden's products played a part in all that, then Ms. Elliott had earned her two million. Making forty look twenty—Nicola had thought about spoofers more than once through the day.

Nicola's irritation surged. She could foresee difficulties in bringing up the subject of "the book." The waitstaff were waiting in groups. Diners who had never spoken to him before began stopping by to greet Charles, so they could say tomorrow, "Guess who I met last night?"

Anne reclaimed his attention. She flicked the pouf of silk foaming from Charles's jacket.

"Tell me about your pocket square."

Nicola watched him blush: *He never blushes. Never. Only around his mother.* Charles, usually silvery of speech, stumbled and coughed. "It's, ah'm, you know, evening. The restaurant, I mean. Well, if not quite tuxedo, then—well, you have to put on a show. You know about these things."

Nicola watched: *What's the matter with him? Oh, brother!* But she chipped in, "Charlie's worn pocket squares since he was eighteen. But I've been collecting vintage squares for him for a few years now, and they've really become *fun*." The word "fun" sounded hollow, and anything but fun, as it came through her lips.

Anne Elliott turned slowly and reluctantly away from Charles, and looked at Nicola.

"How sweet," she said. "Aren't you just so—creative?"

"Charlie," Nicola started, "we wanted to say something to Anne about the book—"

Charlie said, "We don't want to talk about that now. Let's enjoy ourselves! You girls have had a hard day."

Nicola bridled but hid it: *You girls. He better not say that again.*

"Yes, let's enjoy ourselves. And each other," said the actress.

The sommelier hovered like a hummingbird. Charles inspected the bottle.

"Now, here's some true fun," he said. Nicola rolled her eyes.

A waiter began to set out a little forest of glasses. At which precise moment, as though called by a bell, Uncle Julius arrived at the table and pulled up a chair. Charles looked less than charmed, but Nicola thought of Pavlov's dogs and began to laugh. *He heard the damn cork pop. Five blocks away, he heard it. Perfect, Uncle Julius.*

Anne Elliott wore a pavé diamond airplane pendant suspended above her cleavage, toward which Uncle Julius thrust his finger, pointing none too subtly.

"From Marty," she said, a polished hand to her throat, nearly appearing to blush. "He tried to get me for the Ava Gardner part in *The Aviator*. He sent this as a lure. I didn't take the part, but I did keep the plane."

Uncle Julius said, "I like the landing field."

"This," said Charles, in a voice as dull as dust, "is Uncle Julius. He helps us."

To which Nicola, delighted to have the distraction, added, "Uncle Julius is our most indispensable person."

The food came and, unexpected by all, the actress chose a robust selection—crab cakes, followed by short ribs Roquefort; Uncle Julius had the same, and some calamari. Nicola ordered a salad, and Charles chose nothing.

"Oh, Mr. Scott! Won't you be so very hungry?"

At which Nicola thought: *He might, my dear, but not for you.*

Charles replied, "Really, call me Charles. . . . I'm sort of 'on,' if you know what I mean."

On? Excuse me? He's here every night. The voice in Nicola's head was so loud she feared it might be heard at the table.

Throughout the meal, when no one could speak for long to either the *patron* or his new admirer, Charles kept up a stream of whispers to the maître d', who brought tasting after tasting to the table, offering them first to Anne.

He's feeding her the way he feeds Nora, Nicola thought, but said out loud, "Anne, how on earth do you keep your figure? Every woman here tonight will want to know." To herself she remarked, *They've already read about the bulimia.*

"Sweet of you, Nikki."

Nikki? Euuuwww. Nicola thought that she saw Charles wrestle back a smile. When the chef appeared with his signature key lime sundae, the actress squealed in delight.

"How did you know?"

Charles smiled his Cheshire-cat, all-powerful smile. Nicola kicked Uncle Julius, now cutting a road through a second bottle of wine.

"Do something," she hissed.

Quick as a starter's pistol, Uncle Julius said, "Tell us about the book."

"I'm in love," said the actress, who turned to Charles as she answered Uncle Julius, and said, "It's all about timing, isn't it?"

Julius asked, "Was your dealer in New York?" He didn't wait for a reply. "I used to deal in antique books," and Charles Scott was far too much of a gentleman to add, "Yes, you and my father once tried to fence a Kelmscott Chaucer lifted from the Morgan."

"Boston," said Anne Elliott with huge eyes. "But—shhhh. I'm not supposed to tell where it's from. The war and all that?"

Uncle Julius nodded and murmured, "Nazi loot. Gotcha."

"Exactly," said the actress. "Tim, my new best boyfriend—it's for his mother. Restore the family library," and she put a finger to her lips. "Dignity. Their great name. I am so glad to help. He's just so wonderful."

"I used to deal in Boston," said Uncle Julius (not caring to add that he went to jail there too). "Who exackly d'ja work with there?" but Anne Elliott gracefully sidestepped his questions and, minutes later, made her exit, pleading early morning hair and makeup for a television appearance on *Today*. She nodded to those diners who stood in light applause, kissed Charles on both cheeks at the doorstep, and again as he handed her into her limo—and she was gone.

When he came back to the table, Nicola said, "We have news for you, don't we, Uncle Julius?"

"Manny Walsh," crowed Uncle Julius. "He's in Boston!"

Minutes later, a young man, tall as a tree, walked into ASTA, dropped his long leather duffel bag at the desk, and the maître d' led him to their table. Dark, immaculate, and lithe as a dancer, he looked like central casting's idea of the Handsome Prince. His hair was long and romantic; his clothes were graceful and romantic; his eyes were heavy-lidded, black-fringed, and definitely romantic. He wore his shirt open a few buttons deep, his collar up, with a long lavender scarf looped around his neck a few times. On his left hand he wore a large gold signet ring.

"Charles Scott?" He held out his hand. "Tim Pemberley. A friend of Anne Elliott."

Charles stood, and even at six foot two, was inches shorter than his guest.

"You've just missed her."

"Damn."

"I believe she's gone straight home. She has an early television call."

"Then she's also gone straight to bed and I shan't disturb her."

"Sit down," Nicola insisted, patting the place on the banquette next to her, and nurturing already. "Have you eaten?"

Uncle Julius decided to eat again, pasta this time, a pesto tagliatelle, and a second dessert. Charles glared at Nicola's encouraging: "You should both try the *pot de crème*. Shouldn't they, Charlie?"

"Where did you go to school?" asked Charles, the irony in his voice acknowledging the English discovery route.

"We're Bedfordshire. Did I read that you were Cambridge or something?"

"Balliol," said Charles.

Uncle Julius interrupted. "Whassa lord do, anyway?"

"I hear that Anne's found quite a surprise for your mother," said Nicola, testing the waters.

"Oh, the damned book," said the young dream, who ate as though he'd been fasting a week.

"Didn't *you* want it?" Nicola shifted to get his eyeline.

Charles watched: *Is she going to drool from her mouth over this guy?*—but he asked, "Where are you staying?"

"I'm here for the Sotheby's bash tomorrow. Do either of you go for antique porcelain?"

Uncle Julius apparently disapproved. "Breakage," was all he said. "Hard to shift."

"You've just landed, have you?" said Nicola, moving a bit closer.

Charles eyed his wife. *Yes, that's drooling, that's definitely drooling, that isn't eye contact, that's invasion.*

"Second time in a week," Lord P. said. "My jet lag has jet lag."

"Why don't you stay with us tonight?" said Nicola. "We have plenty of room"—which is how they came to be sitting in the kitchen at the townhouse until half past two in the morning, with Charles now trying to get the full story.

Good port thawed Tim Pemberley.

"I met Anne in Goa. They all go there, these days. Their authorities discourage the tabloids. She latched on to me, I suppose. Then I came home to London, after stopping in Delft and Antwerp, and there she was, sitting in our living room with my mamm-aah"—that famous English upper-class drawl, dragging out the word. "A little surprising, to say the least."

"Oh my," said Nicola, visibly reconsidering the story of Anne falling in love. "Do we have to save you from her?"

"Tell us about the book," said Uncle Julius, and Tim Pemberley flinched in discomfort.

"The book thing. Yes." He faced Julius. "I like nothing about this whole thing."

"You mean the Nazi connection and all that?" asked Nicola.

Lord Tim looked perplexed. "No," he said. "I mean, it's so awkward."

"No kidding," said Charles. Nicola looked at Charles with an expression that pleaded for candor, but Charles did not bite.

"So," said Uncle Julius, "did your mom like her?"

"Mamm-aah's iffy, you know how it is. The class thing. But Anne, she's an amazing woman. Let's face it."

Nicola was not sure that Tim meant "amazing" in a good way, but Charles—at last—was hooked. He dove into the ocean of controversy and asked directly, "Who bought the book? Where did it come from? Who actually paid for it?"

Lord Pemberley shrugged. "I did. In a way. That's what I mean by it being awkward"—and saying no more, he went to bed.

The next afternoon, Nicola dropped in to ASTA's.

"Look what I have. She's so proud of it, Charlie, it's heartbreaking. I asked her to let me show you."

Charles took the book and turned it every which way in his large hands.

"Well, it certainly is somebody's idea of her signature." He opened the cover with practiced delicacy and peeled back the first few left-hand pages. "It's probably a first edition, that's the ironic thing. See—1813. And now it's been defaced." Charles handed it back. "What do you think all this is about, kid?"

"I saw her this morning. We had to review the contact sheets and we have to cover one more setup."

"Tomorrow?"

"No. Day after."

"Is he staying with us again tonight?"

"Sadly, no," said Nicola. "The little lord was gone at seven. Didn't you hear him?"

"You make him sound like Jesus," Charles said.

"I wasn't thinking of sanctity." Nicola dreamed for a moment and then said, "Stop scowling, Charlie. You look harassed." She straightened his tie.

He opened the door into the restaurant to a sound dense and mellow—one of New York's favorite melodies, a full dining room. The crowd looked dressed to kill, pushing their top-dollar food from one side of their plates to the other. People waited in the foyer to get near the bar. It was after two o'clock and the place still hummed.

"A Page Six blind item claimed that André Talley had his own table at ASTA's. So the whole would-be fashion crowd is in again. Phones started ringing at eight."

"I didn't know that André was a regular, Charlie."

"He's not," admitted Charles. "It's chum, darling. Brings all the fishies. Keeps us in caviar."

"There's a pitchman lurking in you, Charlie."

"Go to Sotheby's, kid. Cast your own net and pull in some facts."

She saw him in an instant, leaning against a wall, speaking to two other men dressed in the English uniform of striped suit and striped shirt. He saw her too, but seemed embarrassed and looked away. Nicola stood at the rear of the auction room and waited. Tiles and murals came, urns and figurines went; gavels pounded, adrenaline surged, and money flowed.

Let's see what he'll do. But the young Lord Pemberley did nothing—until she waved her hand. *He has to respond,* she thought. *It could be anything, a bid I want to make.* She judged it well; as they loaded some new sale items, he nodded toward the door and moved to meet her.

"Nicola, what a nice surprise. Can I bid on something for you?"

"We have to know about the book, Tim," she said. "We can't allow Anne to think it's real. She'll feel humiliated."

"I couldn't let it happen. God's sake, I'm on a Sotheby's salary. I've borrowed against everything."

"Tim, what's going on?"

He stopped. "What did Anne tell you?"

"That she'd fallen in love with you. That she bought a book.
That your mother had sold her beloved Jane Austen first editions
when your father died. Not much more than that."

He hesitated. "You should talk to her."

"I'm talking to you." She leveled her gaze. Nicola's talent lay
in getting everyone on a set to sign on to her vision. She'd built a
career on that skill.

Tim Pemberley led her out of the auction room, into the polished beige foyer of Sotheby's, down the staircase and out onto
York Avenue. In sunlight bright and startling, he told his story
without temperament or guise.

When he'd finished, Nicola advised, "Say nothing to Anne.
Give us a couple of days."

That night, Charles and Julius listened to Nicola as Charles
worked a garlic scampi. According to Tim, the "rare books dealer"
from Boston had arranged to meet Anne at the Pierpont Morgan
Library, where, to prove his book's authenticity, they looked at a
facsimile of Austen's writing in the manuscript *Lady Susan*.

When Tim first arrived from England, Anne couldn't contain
her excitement, sure that this would cheer his mother, left so low
by her husband's death. Tim made some excuse about checking
provenance, and said that he'd want to ask the dealer a few more
questions before the checks were exchanged—but he raised no
alarm. When, instead of Anne, he went to the Morgan for the
closing of the deal, he threatened to tell the police. The "dealer"
said that Anne Elliott would buy the book for a million dollars,
authentic or not. Nonnegotiable, he said. Anne had been a very
ambitious girl. She'd done whatever it took to get out of Oklahoma and into orbit as a star. He had proof. Pictures and videos.

Tim couldn't countenance Anne's money being used on such
a swindle, especially—as he saw it—one connected to a gesture of
kindness intended for his own family. He went back to London

to raise his own cash. And he'd paid it just before he'd gotten into the restaurant the day before. It was gone. Paid and gone.

"So he was the mark all along?" asked Julius.

Nicola raised her eyebrows. "What do you mean?"

"The passerby," said Julius.

"The what?" Nicola looked bewildered. "Don't give Nora shrimp, Charlie—she gets hives from shrimp."

Charles rushed to change the subject. "They also call them spectators."

"Your father—he called 'em ticket holders," Uncle Julius explained, ignoring Charlie's frown. "The innocent third party," he said slowly, letting Nicola take in the concept.

"So—what do you mean? Now you think that Anne is up to something?" Charles, in an obvious about-face, simply didn't want to believe it.

Uncle Julius amassed a second helping of scampi.

"Dunno. She got out awful fast from dinner when I axed my question."

"It's 'asked,' Uncle Julius," said Nicola, whose eyes were distant with thought. Charles held Nora in his lap. She begged and squirmed and put her stubby little legs near his plate as he let her lick his fingers.

Nicola's eyes returned from her reflections. "I see you, Charlie Scott," she warned.

Uncle Julius rolled his own eyes.

"Dog's life," he said. "You know where we're goin' tomorrow, buddy?"

Charles shook his head.

With the waters of Long Island Sound flashing outside the train's windows, Uncle Julius said to Charles, "I'll do the talking. Manny's touchy."

"Julius, listen. How often do I have to tell you? Don't talk about my father in front of Nicola. Or anyone."

"Heard from him?"

"No, thank God."

"I had a card. He's in Moscow. So he says. I couldn't read the postmark."

"Sent to our house? Goddammit!" Charles pushed away his Amtrak cheese and crackers, which Uncle Julius grabbed.

"Anyway. Manny's tricky. Jewish mother, Irish father. He could be schizoid. But he's the best trader there is."

"You mean 'fence,' don't you?" Charles said dismissively. And when the driver pulled up in front of Manny's house, Charles Scott looked at the portico and its columns and said, "Jesus wept."

"Yeah, he makes a few shekels," said Uncle Julius.

A red-haired, large-breasted maid answered the doorbell. "He's in the library," she said, nodding toward the door at the right and toddling off on heels high as a footstool.

The room was deep with floor-to-ceiling bookcases. Charles could tell that few of the books had been opened—this was "library as movie set"—carved pilasters and pediments of inlaid, quality veneers. Manny saw Charles eye the marquetry.

"To be posh, you gotta look posh." He opened his arms in welcome. "How are you, Julie, my friend?"

Uncle Julius waved a hand to take in the entire property. "The Picassos?" he asked.

"You got it," said Manny, and laughed again.

"They go to Switzerland?"

"Where else?"

"And it's books now, is it?" Uncle Julius fingered the leather on Manny's pristine desk.

"Follow the money." Manny turned to Charles. "How's your dad? Now, there's a gentleman."

Charles shrugged ambiguously. Uncle Julius sat down.

"So, Manny, tell us," Julius said gravely, "about Jean Austen."

"Jane," corrected Charles.

Manny laughed, but seemed immediately uncomfortable.

Charles picked up the discomfort and went for the jugular. "Give it back."

"Was it Prickles?" asked Julius, ignoring Charles.

"Yeah." Manny, keen to recover, couldn't hide his admiration. "And a great binder. Out west. Does mostly family Bibles and stuff. He used two-hundred-year-old glue. That's talent. Two hundred years."

"You mean the whole book is fake?"

"Please. I hate that word," said Manny, as hurt as a maiden aunt.

Charles pressed. "There's more to this, isn't there?"

Manny said, "It's only business."

"Look, Manny," said Uncle Julius, folding his arms like a well-considered hero. "We can get the book back for you. We can make this just go away."

Manny opened the drawer and took out Tim's check. All he could say was, "Julie, I shoulda called you."

"Yeah-yeah." Julius said, smiling and patting Manny's shoulder.

Charles remained annoyed. "There's a little matter of the pictures," he said with some bite.

"Right!" said Uncle Julius, a little too enthusiastically. "Can we see 'em?"

"Down, boy," said Charles.

Manny said, "I got no pictures."

"What?!" Charles and Uncle Julius exclaimed together.

Charles asked, "A bluff?"

Manny nodded. "A bluff."

"What made you think he'd bite?"

"Gal like that?" said Manny. "You think there's no pictures?"

Julius took Manny's hand like a priest and kissed the top of his head.

"Manny, you're beautiful. What a pro."

On the train, Charles ordered doubles.

"I'm still not sure I know what's happened," he said.

Handing Charles the check, Uncle Julius said, "See, it's in Manny's interest for that book to disappear for a while. This dame, she tainted it by talkin' it up. If we keep a lid on it, he'll unload it next year. To someone quieter. A Swiss cheese or someone. He'll be fine. Don't you worry about Manny."

"Believe it or not, Uncle Julius," Charles said, dripping irony on the floor, "I'm not really worried about Manny."

Anne Elliott and Tim Pemberton announced their engagement the following weekend during a luncheon party at ASTA. All Tim would tell her was that the book wasn't what it was supposed to be. But he knew about a book that had just been sold, inscribed by Austen's publishers to a family friend.

"It's as close as we'll get to the holy grail," Tim told her. "As I see it, if you want to give me a wedding present, you could get that—or a new roof for the house."

"Why not both?" Anne laughed, looking as happy as a movie queen in the last reel.

They kissed for the cameras. Off to one side, watching the circus, Charles nudged Nicola.

"In *Pride and Prejudice,* what does Darcy do?"

"He pisses off Lizzie."

"No, kid, after that. What's the key thing he does?"

"You tell me, Charlie. You're the one who fancies Janey."

"He pays off somebody's debts. He proves he can protect someone. That's why Lizzie melts toward him."

Nicola, Charles, and Uncle Julius left the restaurant together. In the hall, they heard Nora's welcome and the tapping of her nails on the marble floor. Charles picked up his silky dog and Nicola stroked Nora's satin ears. Nora rolled her head back and closed her eyes—dog heaven.

"Well," said Charles, "she won't be the first commoner marrying into the English aristocracy. But she might be the most beautiful."

Nicola said, "You haven't seen her without the façade."

Uncle Julius went to bed. Charles opened the cognac, their late-night nip. He carried their glasses upstairs.

"Love," sighed Nicola, "it always brings out the best in people. Always makes them nicer."

"So I was the one with the prejudice?"

"You're always the one with the prejudice, Charlie."

"And the pride?"

She laughed. "I'm proud of the fact that Jane Austen can't have you. Nor can Miz E."

"Get over, Nora. Can you move her?"

Nicola picked up the dachshund, repositioned Nora at the foot of the bed, and made herself comfortable against her husband's shoulder.

"If Jane Austen were alive today—"

"You mean Jean Austen—"

Nicola laughed and continued. "What would she be writing about?"

"I dunno. She'd be writing about, I guess, a girl of humble origins who fancies a lord, and there's a lot of trickery with aristocrats and doubtful characters. And I'd still think she's hot."

"Would she write about us?"

"Yes." He hooked his arm around her. "She was very good on fine gentlemen. And on busybody girls with hearts of gold."

F. J. Meier is the nom de plume of husband-and-wife authors Diane Meier and Frank Delaney.

She: Author of the acclaimed novel *The Season of Second Chances* and the nonfiction cultural commentary on the changing styles of ceremonies and celebration, *The New American Wedding: Ritual and Style in a Changing Culture*. For the past thirty years Diane has been the president of MEIER, a NYC-based luxury marketing firm.

He: Irish-born Frank Delaney is the author of more than twenty books of fiction and nonfiction, including the *New York Times* bestselling novels *Ireland* and *Tipperary*. A veteran BBC broadcaster, his weekly podcast *Re:Joyce,* deconstructing James Joyce's *Ulysses* in five-minute episodes, is enjoyed by tens of thousands of listeners each week.

www.dianemeier.com
www.frankdelaney.com
@dianemeiernyc on Twitter
@fdbytheword on Twitter

NOTHING LESS THAN FAIRY-LAND

Monica Fairview

A wedding must always be an occasion for joy, except when the husband is unwise enough to come under his wife's influence. Mrs. Elton, married to the vicar of Highbury, had made good use of the newly-wed couple's two-week absence to persuade everyone in their circle of acquaintances that no good could possibly come of it.

"Poor Knightley. To think that he has been so taken in that he would be willing to give up his home—so comfortable an estate, so charming and superior—to satisfy the whim of a young girl determined not to leave her father! And to be obliged to move to a house so much inferior—sad business for him."

Few took such a grim view of the affair, since Emma Woodhouse and Mr. Knightley had a long history in the village, while Mrs. Elton had joined them only recently, and had already lost her position—and consequently part of her appeal—as the newly wedded bride. Nevertheless, the villagers of Highbury awaited the move with some measure of anxiety and a great deal of anticipation. No one, however, could be more sensible of the enormity of the event than the very reason behind it, Mr. Woodhouse himself.

Mr. Woodhouse had long tried to postpone what could only be an unwelcome source of disturbance, pointing out that it would be far better if Emma—poor Emma, for it was all so very inconvenient—could wait for Mr. Knightley to come and live with her until at least spring, or even summer, when the weather could be relied upon to be far more favourable. Storms were a regular occurrence in November, and depend upon it, someone was bound to contract a terrible chill as a result.

Mr. Woodhouse's gloomy predictions proved unfounded. Despite its being November, the weather was unseasonably warm, and seemed determined to contribute everything possible to support Mr. Knightley's decision to leave Donwell Abbey and reside in Hartfield. Even the sun resolved to give its blessing to the day. Emma was able to open an upstairs window without fearing a draught, and to look down upon Mr. Knightley as he conferred with Mr. Abdy, who was head man at the Crown. Mr. Abdy was overseeing the men as they loaded and unloaded the carts.

Mr. Woodhouse sat huddled next to the fire, his knees and shoulders wrapped in blankets. Anyone who set eyes on him could be forgiven for thinking that Mr. Knightley was forcing himself abominably on them in Hartfield, rather than performing an extraordinary sacrifice.

"If only Mr. Knightley could have managed to come and live with us without all this fuss," said Mr. Woodhouse, as soon as Emma came downstairs. "Doors opening and closing all the time, leaving us exposed to the elements. Men all over the house, bringing dirt unto the carpets. One cannot go anywhere without worrying about boxes and all manner of objects. Emma, you must not set foot outside the drawing room. I am certain you will trip and suffer a fatal injury."

"But Papa, surely you wish me to help Mr. Knightley arrange where to put his things?"

"You must not take too much upon yourself, Emma. You will get very tired. You and Mr. Knightley must leave the men to get on with their work and come and warm yourselves by the fire. He will grow quite ill, standing about in the passageways. You must ask Mr. Knightley to join us. I am convinced he is doing injury to his lungs."

Emma knew that nothing would calm her father's agitation until he assured himself that Mr. Knightley was in no danger. Accordingly, she left the drawing room to seek him.

"Dear Mr. K.," she said, sneaking up to him from behind after waiting for a moment when no-one was in sight and touching a hand to his cheek. "Will you do us the honour of joining us in the living room?"

Mr. Knightley drew her closer, and after favouring her with a few tokens of his affection, pinched her on the nose.

"If you persist on calling me Mr. K. in imitation of certain vulgar acquaintances of ours, I shall start calling you Mrs. K., and we shall see how well you will receive *that*."

"I have no intention of emulating your favourite, Mrs. Elton," said Emma, laughing. "But do come and sit by Papa a little. You know how perturbed he is by all these changes."

"I have sat by your father several times already this morning, Emma," he said. "I cannot continue to oblige him. At this rate, the move will take several weeks to accomplish. I am quite sure you cannot wish for such a thing."

Any reply she would have made was interrupted by the entrance of a man bearing several bundles of papers wrapped in string, who wished to discover where he would take the papers.

"To the library," said Mr. Knightley, briskly. Once the man was out of sight, however, he succumbed to Emma as she playfully pulled him towards the drawing room, where her father was.

"Did I hear Mr. Knightley say 'the library,' Emma?" said Mr. Woodhouse as they entered, his distress apparent.

"You did indeed hear me say so, Mr. Woodhouse," said Mr. Knightley, agreeably. "If I am to save myself several trips to Donwell Abbey daily, I must have somewhere where I can keep my papers, somewhere where there will be no danger of anyone coming upon them, or a sudden wind blowing them away."

The prospect of a wind should have proved deterrent enough, but it had no effect on Mr. Woodhouse, who had fixed his thoughts on something else entirely.

"You must know that I never use the library in the morning, Mr. Knightley," said Mr. Woodhouse. "Mr. Perry has said the room is damp in the mornings, since it has no sun, and he has recommended me to sit there only on such afternoons when the sun can dispel the damp."

"Precisely," said Mr. Knightley. "Since you will not be using the library in the morning, it will suit me very well. I will be able to use it to go over my accounts with no fear of interruptions, or of causing you any inconvenience."

"You must by no means use the library in the morning, Mr. Knightley. Mr. Perry—"

"I am sure Mr. Perry's recommendations are very appropriate for you, Mr. Woodhouse," said Mr. Knightley, "but as my health is robust, I have no fear of dampness. I must deposit my things where I think best, without regard to Mr. Perry. If you will forgive me?" His voice was more than a little sharp. Emma now regretted bringing him into the drawing room. Her father was looking even more downcast than he had been before.

Mr. Knightley left the room and could presently be heard giving instructions to carry a portmanteau of his clothing to the west room.

Mr. Woodhouse's alarm in hearing this was so great that it overcame his fear of draughts. In an instant he was in the passageway, protesting loudly.

"No, no, Mr. Knightley!" He voiced his objections so vehemently that the workman dropped the portmanteau onto the ground. "You could not possibly wish to sleep in that bedchamber. It faces north, and is extremely cold in the winter. No, no. You *must* take the bedchamber adjacent to mine. I insist on it."

Mr. Knightley stopped and turned to stare at Mr. Woodhouse.

"You cannot possibly mean that you wish me to take the bedchamber that belonged to your late *wife*?"

"It is by far the best room in the house, after my own, of course."

"But it has no adjoining room for Emma to sleep in," said Mr. Knightley, driven beyond patience. "I have come to Hartfield to be with *Emma*."

Emma looked from one to the other of the two men in her life and wondered how she could possibly have expected that this could work. Mr. Woodhouse was bewildered at Mr. Knightley's sudden anger.

"Come, Papa," she said. "You must not be away from the fire for too long."

"But I must speak to Mr. Knightley," said Mr. Woodhouse.

"You can speak to him later," she said, leading him away. Her voice fell to a whisper. "You would not wish to speak to him in front of the servants for everyone to hear, Papa, surely?"

Mr. Woodhouse allowed himself to be coaxed back to the fireplace.

"Why couldn't things have remained just as they were?" said

Mr. Woodhouse, mournfully, as she endeavoured to settle him down once again. "You would have been a great deal happier if things had stayed the same. You should not have married, Emma."

Emma was inclined to agree with him. She bitterly regretted acquiescing to such a scheme. She saw now it was not at all what she had first envisioned when Mr. Knightley had proposed coming to live with them at Hartfield. She had thought matters would remain very much the same. She now discovered that there was a great deal of difference between Mr. Knightley visiting them whenever he chose, enduring her father's humours when he pleased and leaving at his convenience, and being forced to live in close proximity all the time.

Her father was growing more nervous, but she felt it imperative to speak to her husband. She tore herself from her father's side and went to find Mr. Knightley. He stood outside on the steps, looking over the fields towards the direction of Donwell Abbey, his home.

"You must be patient with my father, George. You knew how it would be with him. He cannot endure change."

"I am very willing to be patient. I hope I have always been sensitive to his wishes. But there are things that cannot be endured. I can understand that he will not give up his chamber for us, even though, with its adjoining room, it is most suitable for a married couple. I cannot expect him to do so. But how can he even suggest that I sleep in the adjacent room? Does he not realize that I wish to be adjacent to you, not to him?"

"He does not think of these matters."

"Then he has not yet begun to understand that I am *married* to you," said Mr. Knightley, pacing back and forth. "It is quite impossible. Two men cannot be heads of the same household. We have done this all wrong. We ought to have waited until he was truly willing to accept that I was to be your husband." He stood with his back to her. "*I* am to blame for my impatience," he said in a choked voice. "I did not comprehend that your father would never see me as anything more than an intruder in his home. I thought myself more prepared to humour him, and I thought him more ready to receive me as his son-in-law. But I was mistaken." He stared into the distance for minutes more. By and by, he came to a conclusion. "Perhaps for the time being I should stay in Donwell Abbey until we have sorted everything out."

Without further ado, he hurried down the stairs and set out in the direction of his estate.

Emma made to go after him. She could not let him return to his estate. It boded ill for their marriage, if he was to think of Donwell Abbey as an escape from *her*.

"Emma, where are you?" called her father from within the house. "I must move my chair closer to the fire. The front door is open, I am sure. I can feel the draught most clearly."

Emma, torn between one and the other, decided to appease neither. Two weeks of time alone with Mr. Knightley had not prepared her for strife. At the seaside, surrounded by the trappings of love, free of all demands, she had thought herself in a fairy-land. Now she had tumbled out of fairy-land into the world of mere mortals. She could not believe she could be so wretched. Was it possible she had traded her single state for a lifetime of discord?

"Miss Woodhouse—I am sorry, I meant Mrs. Knightley," said Mr. Abdy, approaching her, his kindly face breaking into a smile. "Mr. Knightley is nowhere to be found. I am afraid I cannot give my men any further instructions without Mr. Knightley's recommendations."

Emma—as mistress of Hartfield—was long accustomed to assuming charge. She was on the verge of providing the men with instructions when it occurred to her that Mr. Knightley would not appreciate *her* intervention in his possessions any more than he would her father's.

"Mr. Knightley has been called to his estate to deal with an urgent matter," said Emma, trying to give the appearance of calm rather than the impression that matters were moving beyond her control. "I think it best that you disperse your men and return later. Since there is no danger of rain, Mr. Knightley's things may remain in the carts for the moment."

Mr. Abdy had business of his own to attend to, and looked relieved that she did not expect him to stay. Certainly she did not wish to hold him up if Mr. Knightley did not return. She was aware that he had offered the services of his men as a favour to Mr. Knightley.

"Then you will send round to tell me when Mr. Knightley returns?"

"Most certainly, Mr. Abdy," she replied.

But she had no idea if he would even return today. Perhaps he intended to spend the night at Donwell. Perhaps he would not even come for several days. Oh, what had he meant by saying he should stay at Donwell Abbey until they sorted matters out?

"Emma!" came the voice of her father.

Emma marched down the pathway, through the gate, and down the road to Highbury. She would occupy herself with other things; buying provisions or even a new pair of gloves. It might improve her spirits and she would be less inclined to blame Papa for causing a rift between her and her new husband.

Haberdashery, she discovered soon, held little appeal, despite the helpful suggestions of Mr. Ford. She could not distract her thoughts from the sight of Mr. Knightley striding away across the green verdure towards his home. Was this the end of their felicity together? It was not unheard of in wealthy families for wife and husband to live apart for some months of the year—during the London Season, for example—though no one of her acquaintance did so. Yet she knew it was not unusual. Would that be her fate with Mr. Knightley?

She excused herself from Mr. Ford and left the shop empty-handed, too restless to settle on any one thing. She had not the slightest desire to return home. She lingered.

At that moment Miss Bates opened her window and leaned out to invite Emma to visit her.

Emma had no wish to see Miss Bates, not now, certainly, but Miss Bates so clearly wished to question her on her expedition to the seaside that Emma could not refuse, though remembering her golden days alone with Mr. Knightley brought her pain. Oh, how could she have been so foolish as to agree to the marriage while her father was alive?

"It is so very obliging of you to come to see us and enquire after us, Mrs. Knightley," said Miss Bates. "We are very well indeed, so happy that Jane is soon to be settled in Enscombe and that things have come out so well—so anxious about her being a governess—such an uncertain future—such a wonderful surprise that she and Frank Churchill were engaged!—surely the happiest day in my life."

Emma felt a headache coming on, but she ignored it, determined to occupy herself with anything at hand.

"Have you received a letter from Jane?" said Emma, for once hoping that a letter might prove a distraction.

A brief moment of silence met her query. Emma was so accustomed to hearing of Jane's letters from Miss Bates that she could hardly credit the expression of pain that crossed Miss Bates's perennially cheerful face. It did not last long. Miss Bates rallied quickly.

"She wrote to us when she first met up again with the Camp-

bells in London," said Miss Bates, "did she not, Mama? I believe
you were kind enough to hear me read her letter then. Yes, you
are always so considerate—we have received nothing since
then—she has been too occupied to write to us since—all the excitement of the engagement—distracted by the preparations—
meeting with Mr. Frank Churchill—all the entertainment town
has to offer. So very kind of you to wish to hear her letter—but
we have not had news from her—"

Miss Bates's speech came to an abrupt halt. She looked around
her as if searching for something to speak about. Never in all the
years Emma had known Miss Bates had she been at a loss for
words, except perhaps on Box Hill, after Emma's own shabby
behaviour—but she did not wish to remember that.

Indignation at Jane's heartlessness rose up inside her. How
could Jane Fairfax spurn her aunt simply because she was on the
verge of contracting an eligible match? Jane knew full well how
much Miss Bates lived and breathed for news of her niece. It was
Frank's negligence to blame, certainly, his indifference to the
comfort of others, but could Jane be so weak-willed as to follow
his lead? No, it could not be so, not when Frank himself corre-
sponded quite frequently with his father. It was Jane, she was
sure, who had forgotten her aunt, absorbed in her own felicity.
Emma would never do such a thing. Jane may perhaps be
more accomplished, more well travelled, but *she* would never
abandon dear Papa for Mr. Knightley. In *this* she was Jane Fairfax's superior.

Her consciousness of her own superiority lifted her from the
cloud of oppression that had surrounded her. Secure in her own
virtue, she turned her attention fully to Miss Bates, who still sat
looking around her, grasping for a topic of conversation.

"Mrs. Bates's health is much the same?" said Emma, coming
to Miss Bates's rescue, unable to endure the unaccustomed silence.

"So very considerate of you to ask, Mrs. Knightley," said Miss Bates, making a great effort to appear lively. "As you can see, Mother is well—much the same as always, are you not, Mother? The same as always."

A small shaft of sunlight found its way through the window and settled on Mrs. Bates. Mrs. Bates did not appear to Emma the same as always. Perhaps she had not really looked at her for a long time now, or perhaps because she had been away—though it had not been that long. Mrs. Bates was so silent, so always out of the light, in the corner, and now was exposed under full sunlight—but it seemed to Emma that Mrs. Bates was very thin and frail, her face shadowed, her frame shrunken. Emma was shaken to see her thus.

"We are so happy that Jane's future has been settled," said Miss Bates, "it was a source of anxiety to us, you can be sure—never expected such good fortune—though Jane of course deserves the best—does not Jane deserve the best, Mother?"

Miss Bates continued to discourse in this manner, but her words were halting. Emma looked at Miss Bates, truly seeing her for the first time. She saw darkness under her eyes, lines of worry around her mouth. She wondered who would listen to Miss Bates when her mother was taken from them. She questioned who would supply Miss Bates's conversation, once Jane ceased to send her letters.

Emma had been very busy arranging everyone's lives, but she had never given any thought to Miss Bates. She had been contrite after Mr. Knightley had taken her to task for her abominable treatment of Miss Bates. She had sought to make amends through her willingness to *pretend* an interest. But she had deceived herself as well as Mr. Knightley. She had never really perceived Miss Bates as anything but a spinster who prattled endlessly, a source of irritation she must endure.

The very recollection of her past feelings filled her with mortification. Today would be the beginning, on her side, of a regular, equal, and kindly interaction.

She recalled Miss Bates's reaction when she had attended the ball at the Crown. Miss Bates had proclaimed in wonder that she had felt herself "quite in fairy-land." Miss Bates had been beside herself with happiness. She had not known that day that Frank Churchill would take her beloved niece from her.

Emma felt her own unhappiness pale beside this picture of Miss Bates's present sufferings. She imagined her—for Emma was good at imagining—sitting alone in their small apartments, chattering to herself, with no one to listen, and growing older by the day. She must not allow it to happen. She, Emma Woodhouse, had it in her power to do something for Miss Bates, beyond gifts of pork leg and arrow-root. She may not be able to reconcile Mr. Knightley with her father, but it was in her power to bring some happiness into Miss Bates's life.

"There was a reason for my calling on you, Miss Bates," said Emma brightly, spurred by an urgent need to make amends for years of neglect. "We require your assistance in Mr. Knightley's removal to Hartfield. You were so kind as to give your opinion to Frank Churchill about the dance at the Crown, as I recall. Perhaps you may also be able to give us the benefit of your advice—Mr. Knightley sees things his way, my father another, and I cannot arbitrate between them."

The look of genuine joy on Miss Bates's face was its own reward. Emma did not regret inviting her to Hartfield, though what contribution she could possibly make, Emma could not imagine. But then the joyful look faded as Miss Bates glanced at Mrs. Bates in the corner.

"It is difficult—I would love to help more than anything, you understand—but it is hard for Mother to leave the house—hard to leave the house, isn't it, Mother?—too many stairs—can't really leave her too long in case she falls—though very honored for being asked to be sure."

"I will send one of the maids to take care of her," said Emma, and that was that.

The smile returned to Miss Bates's face. Eager to be of use, she fetched her bonnet and prepared to walk to Hartfield.

As they walked through the high street, Emma's gaze landed on the Crown, and a scheme hatched in her mind. She had often heard Miss Bates speak with affection of old Mr. John Abdy. His son was a widower, had never remarried, and at the age of fifty was reasonably wealthy. If she could but find a way to draw the two together, surely there was a chance for Miss Bates, who was generally held to be agreeable.

But no, Mr. Knightley had warned her against matchmaking. She had learned her lesson, surely. She would not meddle in others' lives.

Nevertheless, she stepped into the Crown on her way.

"Mr. Abdy, if you are not otherwise occupied, perhaps you would care to join us for tea. I am sure by now Mr. Knightley has sorted out his affairs, and will have returned. Miss Bates is to give us the benefit of her advice. You are well acquainted with Miss Bates, I believe?"

The warm expression that Mr. Abdy turned towards Miss Bates satisfied Emma that it was a good beginning.

"How is your dear father?" inquired Miss Bates. "I hope he is not suffering badly—the weather has been accommodating, to be sure—perhaps the symptoms aren't so very bad—rheumatism is so very disagreeable—especially in the winter—my mother suffers from it."

"His rheumatic gout never leaves him, though he has days when he is much improved," remarked Mr. Abdy, sadly. "I wish I could do more for him."

"You must have Mr. Perry visit him—I do not believe there is another who is his equal—we are so very fortunate to have Mr. Perry in Highbury—what would we do without him, Mr. Abdy?"

A conversation ensued about the best cures for rheumatism. Emma, satisfied that she had sowed the seeds, fell back a little, leaving the two to converse, and enjoying the sight of the short, neat, brisk-moving woman conversing animatedly with the large, rather stocky Mr. Abdy.

As they turned the corner onto the lane that led to the vicarage, who should appear before them but Mrs. Elton herself.

"Now, now, Mrs. Knightley," cried Mrs. Elton, once they had exchanged greetings. "What are you doing strolling about town at a time like this? Can it be that you are already escaping the upheaval at your home? I see that I am right, for you are looking very sly. Pray be sincere, my good friend. If you wish to consult me on anything, anything at all, I would be happy to do everything in my power. I know that I can ascertain the best arrangement for Knightley's things, for I managed the move to the vicarage very smoothly, as I am sure my *caro sposo* will testify. I have rearranged the whole place. It is now vastly superior; though of course it is nothing compared to Maple Grove."

"You are very obliging, but Mr. Knightley and I are well able to manage," said Emma.

"Your scruples do you justice, my dear Mrs. Knightley, but I assure you it would be no trouble to me at all. You are only a new bride. One cannot expect you to know everything. Besides, you have not seen as much of the world as I have."

"You need not concern yourself, Mrs. Elton, matters are perfectly in hand. I do not require any advice or assistance."

"Aye, I am quite firm in this, for I have a great deal to contribute. I would join you at Hartfield at once, were it not for the fact that Mr. E. and I are otherwise engaged—we are forever being invited somewhere or the other—I am so much in demand in Highbury society I scarcely have a moment alone. But I have it now—I will send you my housekeeper. She is extremely clever and will soon have everything in the proper order—that is, if my lord and master concurs, for I would not presume to do anything he disapproves of. You *must* accept my assistance, Mrs. Knightley; I positively insist on it, I will not let you off."

"You must not send your housekeeper, Mrs. Elton," said Emma firmly, quite beyond the limits of her patience. "We already have an excess of staff from both households, and she will be turned away. Now if you will excuse us, I must return to Hartfield. I wish you a pleasant afternoon."

Mrs. Elton looked as if she would object, but Emma signaled to Miss Bates and Mr. Abdy, who were waiting for her, and began to walk away, leaving Mrs. Elton staring after them.

As they drew close to Hartfield, Emma could make out Mr. Knightley some distance away striding towards the house. His tall figure was so familiar, so well loved, that she felt a glow of happiness just at the sight of him. Was it really possible that Mr. Knightley, always so kind and so considerate, would be discouraged by one day of difficulty with her father? He had undoubtedly returned to make amends.

He neither checked his stride, however, nor revealed in any other way that he had seen them. All her uncertainties returned. She could not tell, not unless she saw his face more closely, whether he was still angry, nor could she tell his intentions.

"Emma, is that you?" said her father, coming to the doorway. "Have you come back? Where have you been? You were gone so suddenly, and for so long, I was convinced you had met with an accident—I have never liked the corner into Vicarage Lane, you know. I was about to send the coachman in search of you, but I did not want James to put the horses to when you might return any instant."

She hurried in to reassure him, drawing Miss Bates forward. "Papa, I have brought you someone to keep you company," said Emma. "It is Miss Bates."

"Miss Bates. Oh, it is indeed good to see an old friend," said Mr. Woodhouse.

"And here is Mr. Abdy for tea as well," said Emma. "Shall we go in?"

Mr. Abdy held back, saying he would wait for Mr. Knightley, who had now passed through the garden door. Emma wanted nothing more than to run out to Mr. Knightley and ask him to set aside their differences, but she could hardly do so within Papa's earshot.

"If you will settle in the drawing room, I will ring for some tea." She watched Mr. Knightley approach with the corner of her eye.

"Tea, but not cake, Emma," said Mr. Woodhouse, preceding her into the drawing room. "Cake is far too rich. I am quite certain Miss Bates would agree with me."

"Certainly cake can be rich, Mr. Woodhouse—it depends how the cake is made. There is a way—perhaps I could tell the recipe to Cook—one can make cake so that it is much lighter—Mr. Perry himself has given me his approval—"

Emma, seeing her father move comfortably into a discussion of Mr. Perry, issued directions for tea and hurried to the doorway to meet Mr. Knightley. He was in earnest discussion with Mr. Abdy. Mr. Knightley directed a glance at her and gave her a small smile, a sign, surely, that things could not be that bad between them.

"I have invited Mr. Abdy to take tea with us," announced Emma. "Would you like to come in, Mr. Abdy? And you too, Mr. Knightley? Miss Bates is here also."

"We walked back from the village together," said Mr. Abdy.

Emma, feeling Mr. Knightley's quizzing gaze upon her, looked away, and began to chatter to Mr. Abdy of some trivial matter or the other.

"Oh, there you are, Mr. Knightley," said her father, looking up as they entered. "I was afraid you had returned to Donwell."

"I will always return to Donwell when I need to," said Mr. Knightley. "But my home is here."

"To be sure, Donwell Abbey is a wonderful place," said Miss Bates, "but home is where the heart is, as they say, do they not? And there is plenty of *heart* here." She gave a nervous laugh. "Oh, Miss Woodhouse—Mrs. Knightley—I do believe—*you* who are so clever may perhaps not find it so—but I do believe I have at last said something witty."

Everyone stared at her without understanding.

"Oh, dear—it is perhaps not as witty as I thought—no, of course not—but I had hoped—it was just that for a moment I thought—but I see I didn't explain myself—I meant heart as in '*Hart*-field.'"

Emma laughed. Then Mr. Knightley. Then Mr. Abdy.

"I am afraid I am not so very witty," said Mr. Woodhouse. "I do not quite see—"

Miss Bates leaned towards him and whispered an explanation to him, in that way old familiar friends will do.

"You have no need to be witty, Miss Bates," said Emma, "for you are among old friends. We already value your good qualities. But you *have* proved yourself to be witty. Do you not think so, Mr. Abdy?"

Mr. Abdy agreed that Miss Bates was witty, but he had by now finished his tea, and looked ready to resume work. Mr. Knightley stood up also, his tea only half finished.

"It is so fortunate, Mr. Woodhouse—Mr. Knightley's agreeing to live with you here—few men would do such a thing—to leave their homes—why, it is almost unheard of—but then Mr. Knightley has always had so much sense—he must have seen how it was—and so very considerate—I do believe you are very fortunate, Mr. Woodhouse."

"Yes," said Mr. Woodhouse, "but poor Emma did not need to marry—"

Emma rose as soon as she could. She needed desperately to speak to her husband.

She found him standing in the entrance, looking so stern her heart sank within her.

"George," she said, hoping her use of his given name would soften him towards her. He turned and looked at her, and the sternness dissolved.

"I wish I had not asked you to call me by my first name," said Mr. Knightley, coming over to her immediately. "I can deny you nothing when you do so."

"You know you cannot deny me anything in any case," said Emma, reassured enough of his affection to speak saucily.

"I can deny you a great deal, Emma, for I know you have been far too spoilt, and it has not always been in your best interest." He paused, hesitating to speak. "I have always been honest with you, Emma, and I will confess—and I am ashamed to admit it—that for a time today I believed that it was all a mistake. For you, perhaps, it is nothing, but for me living under this roof will involve a great many changes."

She, too, had been afraid. She did not wish to disclose the truth, however.

"Your papa is more impossible than anyone could have imagined. It will not be easy for Mr. Woodhouse to see you as a grown woman. He is too accustomed to seeing you as his little girl. He has been indulged by the females in the family for too long. It is too late for him to sacrifice his comfort for your sake; he is too set in his ways. I have seen you being so considerate towards him all these years, but I did not know—" He stopped, not wishing to give offence.

Emma did not know what to say. She would not defend Papa to Mr. Knightley, for she understood Mr. Knightley's difficulty. She understood all too well that the best of intentions must fail when a gentleman's pride came into play. It was women's destiny to swallow their pride to appease others, and men's to assert it.

"I have known you all my life," said Emma. "I believe I am well enough acquainted with your character to know you would never back out, once you have determined on a course of action."

"Particularly where you are concerned," he said, gazing into her eyes. "I am determined to find a way to make this work, Emma, but I do not think it will be easy." He drew her close to him. "You must be patient with me, Emma, for I will not always be good humoured."

Their exchange came to an end when two workmen entered, carrying yet another box. Emma, seeing that Mr. Knightley was occupied, and hoping that the worst was indeed over, returned to the drawing room. She discovered Miss Bates extolling Serle's apple pie.

"Miss Bates has convinced me to try a piece of Serle's apple pie," said Mr. Woodhouse. "She assures me that Mr. Perry has no objection to a tiny piece of apple pie, Emma, and I find I must agree with her."

Emma stood transfixed as her father and Miss Bates laughed in unison.

Was it possible? If Miss Bates could prevail upon her father to eat pie, what more could she do?

True, it was not cake. If Miss Bates had convinced her father to eat cake instead of gruel, that would have been a triumph indeed. Still, one could not belittle such a startling development.

It was all too soon, but perhaps *here* was the solution to their problems. It may serve, thought Emma. It *will* serve. She knew she could make it possible. A lifetime of cajoling and prompting in little ways had trained her in the art of persuasion. Not now, perhaps, but over time, Emma knew she could prevail upon Papa that Miss Bates was indispensable for his health. Gradually, in slow steps, it could be made possible.

Until then, it was to be her secret, and hers only. She would not allow anyone—no one at all, least of all Mr. Knightley—even to guess.

She was so intent on the idea that she was startled when Mr. Knightley came to stand beside her.

"You think yourself very clever, no doubt, but I am quite aware that you are up to mischief again."

"Mischief?" said Emma. "I do not understand what you mean." For a moment she thought he had hit upon her secret already.

"You understand me very well," said Mr. Knightley. "Will you never acknowledge that you are the worst matchmaker in England?"

"Indeed?" said Emma, noting from the corner of her eye that Mr. Woodhouse had noticed neither Emma's nor Mr. Knightley's presence.

"Do you think I do not know your latest plan?"

Emma tried her best not to look again in her father's direction. She did not wish to give Mr. Knightley the satisfaction of knowing himself right once again.

"I know you intend to bring Mr. Abdy and Miss Bates together," he said, "but it will not do."

She put a quick finger to his lips to silence him, trying hard to conceal her laughter from him. She must not laugh at him, but oh, how he was mistaken!

"Miss Bates and Mr. Abdy?" she said, her eyes dancing. "I would never dream of such a thing."

"I assure you, Emma, if that is your intention, it is not at all advisable. True, Mr. Abdy's fortunes have risen from the time his father was a clerk to Miss Bates's father. He is looking to open his own establishment in the near future. But Miss Bates would not do for him. He is not of the same social station. Besides, she would drive all his customers away with her incessant talk."

"Who is being unkind now?" said Emma. "It was because of you that I have come to appreciate Miss Bates. It was you who taught me to see Miss Bates's good qualities."

She was rewarded with a tender smile as he drew her hand within his and pressed it to his heart. A flutter of pleasure ran through her.

"Come," she said. "While my father is occupied with his old friend, let us determine once and for all which bedchamber is to be ours."

MONICA FAIRVIEW taught literature at university for several years, trained as an acupuncturist, and now has discovered her real vocation in writing. Fairview was introduced to Jane Austen when she was a teenager—to her books, not to that Illustrious Personage herself, though she ardently hopes such an opportunity might yet occur. Her first published novel was a Regency romance, *An Improper Suitor,* a runner-up for the Romantic Novelists' Association (U.K.) Joan Hessayan Prize. Her debut Austenesque novel, *The Other Mr. Darcy,* was chosen as Hidden Treasure of 2009 by All About Romance. Her latest novel, *The Darcy Cousins,* centers on Georgiana Darcy and was described by *Historical Novels Reviews* as "a humorous, stately romp through nineteenth-century England."

www.monicafairview.co.uk
@monica_fairview on Twitter

LOVE AND BEST WISHES, AUNT JANE

Adriana Trigiani

"Love and Best Wishes, Aunt Jane" is a story that celebrates the art of the written letter, sent person to person, in private, to impart news, feelings of love, or warnings of impending doom. One of the joys of reading Jane Austen's novels are the letters written by the characters that change the course of the action and send the plot off in new and unexpected directions. I imagined Jane as if she were alive today and, inspired by the sketchy biographical information we have of her, wrote this letter in her fictional voice. This is Jane, the good aunt, writing to her beloved niece about news of her engagement. Viva Jane!

Adriana Trigiani
New York City
September 2010

November 1, 2010

Dear Anna,

I so appreciated your call last evening to tell me of your engage-ment to Declan. I was thrilled beyond all telling; having met him, I believe he will make a wonderful husband for you and a wise father to your children. I pray they inherit your red hair and cha-risma, because ten more of you running around would make the world a better place. I am so happy that you decided to take this leap of faith, because that's what is required when you decide to commit yourself to another, to marry for life, to take a partner: it's an enormous leap.

Now, you may be wondering how your spinster aunt would know this, having stayed safely back from the precipice. The truth is I went to the edge once, and after coming to my senses, scurried back to safe ground because I knew a marriage for the sake of mar-riage would only lead to unhappiness. I could have married, and would have married, but decided that one either marries for love or doesn't, and given the choice, I would have chosen love.

I am so proud of you, my dear niece, for choosing love.

I have been described as "good and quiet," which is an apt description of a long, hot summer night, not so for the adventur-ous woman I hoped to become. I was not so much good as timid, and not so much quiet as so full of feelings, I was afraid that if I expressed them, they would pour out of me like a long note on a winded bassoon. I imagined no one would be interested in listen-ing to that kind of music. So, I instead held those feelings in, even when it meant sacrificing happiness with another. I can't explain it any more clearly than this, and even when I try, even when I winnow it down to its most basic form, the truth is always the same. It's just the way I am.

My imagination has always been full of colorful and detailed scenarios, many of which I attempted to write for the stage. Alas, the only audience who found my plays fascinating was my family, who participated as actors in the pantomimes I wrote each Christmas. I may not remember the scenes or the lines I wrote, but I remember the laughter we shared when performing them. Sometimes, it's not important for an audience to be educated by a well-structured play; sometimes a play is worth doing just for the fun of it.

I hope you will do many things in your life, not for a particular result, but just for the fun of it.

It was required of me to learn to play the piano, and it's one of the best things I ever did. I am not very good at it, but the hours I spent playing have given me a kind of peace that everyone should experience. The rote scales take me inward, to a very quiet place, and then the mastery of certain selections has given me a sense of accomplishment that I have found rarely elsewhere.

I hope you will fill your home with music.

I have the great privilege of caring for my father in his old age. Many times I have thought this a nuisance, when I would rather be off doing something to my own liking, but have found that honoring and attending to responsibility, even those foisted upon one uninvited, builds character. Often, I force myself to take the drudgery of caring for an older person as a project to complete, overlooking their cranky moods and ornery demands, to attempt to find the good in it, and make it a learning experience.

I hope you and Benjamin make a commitment to care for your aging parents.

I have learned so much from my father in his old age that it makes his raising of me almost seem beside the point. He has become an unlikely friend to me, and I to him. Your grandfather has a vivid imagination and stories to tell. I just found out that when he was young, he went to Europe, and after visiting France,

Italy, and England, went to Spain, and in Barcelona, he met a young woman and fell in love with her. Her parents refused her hand in marriage (lucky for me, it made way for my beautiful mother!) and my father returned to America brokenhearted. He thought for certain his heart would never heal, and then he met your grandmother—who put him back together again.

I hope you will travel, and not just see the world, but participate in it. I hope that when your heart breaks, you will think of your grandfather and remember that coping with loss and moving forward to love again is the cornerstone of wisdom.

You are surrounded by wisdom. My five brothers and sister have so much to share with you. Cassandra is a different sort of spinster from me, as she still hopes and longs for true love, and is certain it will find her, even at her age. I hope her dream comes true! But I am too practical for that dream any longer, and am happy that she is the guardian of it.

Your father James, and you must never tell anyone this, was my favorite brother! He and I were always simpatico from the start. We loved to go to the library and explore the fields around our home. To this day, if I have a problem, he is the first person I go to, and throughout my life, he has given me clarity. An understanding brother is a gift, and it's a relationship you can count on your whole life long.

I hope you will keep your family of origin in your life through your long and happy marriage.

And now, about writing. I know you share my fondness for reading, and my love of books. I believe that passionate readers can become good writers. If you spend every moment you possibly can, outside of duty, chores, work, and play, with your nose in a book, you will have a respite of glorious solitude that is yours and yours alone. In the noise of this world (and it gets louder every day!) a good woman needs a quiet respite for her thoughts and dreams.

Make books the furniture of your home—pile them high, wide, and deep, next to your sofa, your chairs, your bed—and when you're feeling sad, lonely or in need of inspiration, take one, open it, and let the journey begin. Just the sight of a book—its colorful binding, gold letters, and smooth leather cover—makes me happy.

I hope you will read for *pleasure* your whole life long. And I hope that your reading habit will beget writing, and that you will share your thoughts and feelings on the page. I wish every person would take the time to write down his or her life story, and what-ever small gems, conversations, and memories they might have of their grandparents and parents. Can you imagine the gift of on-going biography with chapters written by each generation? I mourn the fact that I have none to read in the Austen family.

You know your old auntie (I'm forty-one) has written a few novels. I enjoyed the process so much that when I finished one, I could not wait to start another. Writing has sustained my spirit.

Yes, your father has read my novels, and beyond that, I've sent them around. I am a *mid-list* author (so they say), but I find the term vague; it sounds a lot like *middle age* (which I am living in!). The middle is the least exciting place to be, it is safe and just enough. I want more for you. I had high hopes for my creative life. But I found I am not so much a promoter of my books as I am a writer of them. I have made peace with the fact that my novels may never reach a wide audience, and have come to realize that the only audience worth having is the audience of one.

One solitary reader can be moved by words you have written, and if a million more also get the chance, that's lovely. But the truth is, writing gives you more than it can ever give your reader. The persistence that is required to finish any project, including a novel, is a life lesson that one learns over and over again—but the end result, whether it is close to perfect or not, is always satisfy-

ing. A task completed is reward enough. I have embraced the fact
that I no longer need accolades, and the attendant recognition
that comes with a public career, because I have the satisfaction of
leaving a complete manuscript (in my case, six of them) behind, to
be stumbled upon in the years to come. The satisfaction that
comes from that potential future happy accident completes me.

I hope you will take your dreams seriously, and your writing
even more seriously, as you go through life.

I lament the loss of letter writing in our time. I cannot imagine
that a tweet or a post, an email or a text, will provide the great
thrill of receiving a letter, written by hand. There is so much to
learn about a person from their handwriting, and even more in
the depths of the words one chooses to express himself. I will miss
the ancient way of doing things until I, too, pass away.

You know, dear Anna, I've not been well. I don't like to write
the words or acknowledge the truth, because I feel they have
some magical power over my diagnosis. But I feel, within me, a
winding down, and therefore have settled my affairs. I don't want
this to cause you concern; in fact, I only tell you this because it is
my wish that you celebrate the wonderful years we have known
together, and remember the great laughs and parties, gatherings
and walks, trips and celebrations, that belong to us, and to us
alone. I could not have asked for a better niece, and I hope that I
have been a good aunt to you. You have been a great consolation
to me, in the absence of my own children, and in fact, I could not
have wished for a better daughter, had I been blessed with one.

Whether it is your good luck (and it will be!) to have children
of your own with Declan, know that there are many in the world
for you to love, who look to you for encouragement and to lead by
example. Children need to see delight in the eyes of adults, if only
to give them a sense that happiness is within reach, even when it

isn't. Adults should be full of possibility, so that children might develop a sense of adventure.

Children should live with the confidence that they are loved. Love frees them to embrace adventure, to seek truth, and to take care of one another. I know, when I remember the days of my own childhood, what it meant to me to be welcomed, named, and remembered. It's important.

I hope I have been that star point for you. And no matter what happens in the months to come, I hope to be at your wedding, and I hope to be the aunt that weaves a tiara of fresh white roses for your hair (our family tradition!). If I am not able to do so, know that not one tear should be shed, because I am with you always.

I will be with you as you sing by the piano with your children, I will be with you in summer when you picnic by the lake, and I will be with you as you open a new novel, hopeful and full of anticipation at a good and satisfying read! Take all of this with you as you go through your married life, my dear niece. You are loved in a thousand ways by your dear old aunt, and I will never forget you.

Love and all best wishes for your marriage,
Aunt Jane

ADRIANA TRIGIANI is an award-winning playwright, television writer, and documentary filmmaker. She is the author of the bestselling Big Stone Gap series and the novels *Brava; Valentine; Very Valentine; Lucia, Lucia; The Queen of the Big Time; Rococo;* and the young adult novels *Viola in Reel Life* and *Viola in the Spotlight*. Her nonfiction book *Don't Sing at the Table* was an instant *New York Times* bestseller. She lives in New York City with her family.

www.adrianatrigiani.com
@adrianatrigiani on Twitter

JANE AUSTEN AND THE MISTLETOE KISS

Jo Beverley

Elinor Carsholt was setting the final stitches in a pink linen reticule when someone knocked on the cottage door. Who could that be? In the six months they'd lived in Chawton, there'd been few visitors. She'd not tried to get to know the lower-class people of the village, and not felt comfortable about mingling with the better sort on her very low income.

She wanted to ignore the second knock, but it was Christmas Eve. Perhaps the vicar's sister felt obliged to visit.

She rose, tucking the little bag at the bottom of the mending basket. The reticule was her Christmas present to her sixteen-year-old daughter and she didn't want the surprise spoiled. Amy was upstairs helping her younger sisters with their lessons, but if she heard a visitor she might run down in hope of something to enliven her life.

Elinor smoothed her apron, tucked a stray hair back beneath her cap, and then opened the door.

"Oh! Sir Nicholas."

The handsome young baronet always described himself as their neighbor, but all that meant was that Ivy Cottage was tucked into a corner of his estate. He wasn't even their landlord, for the cottage belonged to a cousin of her dead husband's, and he lived twenty miles away. Perhaps Cousin Edwin had asked Sir Nicholas to keep an eye on them, for he was kindly attentive.

When he was at Danvers Hall he usually escorted them home from church, as their ways went together, and he sometimes stepped inside for a cup of tea. He'd generously invited them to make free of his orchards, which had been a great benefit; they were still enjoying the carefully stored apples and pears.

He smiled, bowed, and raised his beaver hat. "Mrs. Carsholt. I hope I find you and your daughters well?"

She dipped a curtsy. "Very well, Sir Nicholas. And you?"

She was always cheered by his visits, but his left arm cradled a cloth-covered basket. She deeply resented being a charity case when so recently she had been the one to dispense largesse to needy villagers.

"In excellent health," he said, "as are all my family. I think you'll have heard that my brother, Captain Danvers, is recovered from his wounds."

"Yes, it was mentioned in church, where we'd often prayed for him. I gather he's at the Hall for Christmas."

"To our great pleasure."

He wasn't passing over the basket, so she had to say, "Please come in, Sir Nicholas."

Alas, the door opened directly into the kitchen, which was disordered by Christmas preparations. On Sundays she always left it tidy.

He put the basket on the table. "A few seasonal delicacies I thought might please your daughters, Mrs. Carsholt."

"It's too kind of you, Sir Nicholas. There really is no need."

She was being ungracious, but she could smell oranges, and they made her want to weep. In happier days she'd not have thought oranges to have such an aroma, but after a year without them, it seemed pungent as a bouquet of roses.

If only she had something to offer in return, even a jar of jam, but she was not so provident. An almost-finished pink reticule would hardly serve.

She was struggling for the appropriate way to conclude the conversation when Amy ran down the stairs, all bright eyes and bouncing curls. "Oh, Sir Nicholas! How lovely to see you, sir."

He bowed again. "And you, Miss Carsholt, in such fine spirits. Are you ready for the morrow?"

"Almost, sir. My sisters and I are finishing our gifts for Mama, and later we'll be going out to gather holly and ivy for the house."

"And mistletoe?" he asked, with a mischievous smile.

He must wreck hearts in all corners, Elinor thought, with those fine blue eyes and the dimples. Astonishing that at thirty-one he was still unmarried.

"Of course we'll have mistletoe," Amy said.

"That wouldn't be appropriate, dear," Elinor said. "We are still a house of mourning."

"Only for two more weeks," Amy muttered.

Elinor chose to ignore that. Life was difficult enough without squabbles.

"Your attention to your husband's memory does you credit, Mrs. Carsholt, even though it has deprived Danvers Hall of your presence at Christmas dinner. I hold hopes of next year."

Elinor smiled, but she couldn't imagine ever dining in a place that must remind her of the home, the life, she had lost.

He turned to Amy. "If you decide you'd like a spray of mistletoe for tradition's sake, Miss Carsholt, there's ample in my apple orchard. You'll have to hurry, though. My brother plans to lead our guests on a raid."

He went to the door, but then turned. "Ah, yes. Given the

small size of your oven here, I've instructed my cook to roast an extra goose. It will arrive tomorrow at about noon. Merry Christmas, ladies!"

He made his escape before Elinor could react, and then she could hardly run after him, shouting her rejection.

She closed the door fuming. "A goose indeed. That is far beyond what is acceptable!"

"But a *goose,* Mama! Only think how delicious it will be." Amy pulled the cloth off the basket. "Oranges. And sugar plums! Now we'll have a real Christmas. Just like Fortlings." She turned to run up the narrow stairs. "I'll tell the others. They'll be so excited!"

Just like Fortlings.

This time last year she and the girls had been decorating Fortlings Hall with holly, ivy—and yes, mistletoe—while cook and her helpers labored over the lavish feast for the next day. The village children had come to sing Christmas songs and been rewarded with mince pies and pennies.

Barnie had distributed those treats. He'd thoroughly enjoyed the holiday traditions, so it had been one of their best times together.

Of course, his high spirits had also been from anticipation of the hunting season—the heart of Barnie's life. That had been how he'd met his end in January last year—leaping a hedge with an unanticipated ditch beyond and breaking his neck. It had been instantaneous, she'd been told, and she'd taken comfort from that. He'd died without pain in the midst of his greatest delight, but she could curse him for carelessly leaving his wife and daughters in such straights.

She'd had no idea. No idea how much his careless generosity and magnificent horses cost. No idea that the income of the estate had dwindled under his neglect. Gross carelessness on her part, and she was justly punished by having to live in penury. But her darling daughters had committed no sins, and they were trapped in penury with her.

Amy ran back downstairs, her sisters behind her—ten-year-old Margaret a little awkward in her coltishness, and six-year-old Maria, a wide-eyed precious angel.

"Sugar plums," Maria breathed, leaning close to the basket.

"And a goose tomorrow," said Amy, as if she feared Elinor might snatch that treat away.

"Sir Nicholas is too generous," Elinor said.

"Is there such a thing?" Amy challenged. "It's a Christian duty to be charitable, especially at Christmas."

And blessed are the poor who make it possible, Elinor thought. That was in the Bible somewhere, but it didn't say that the poor must like it.

"May we *please* go up to the Danvers Hall orchard to collect mistletoe, Mama?" Amy begged. "It won't be Christmas without a kissing bough."

"No. Even if we weren't still mourning your father, what use would a kissing bough be to us?"

Amy opened her mouth as if to argue, but she must have recognized that Elinor's patience was growing thin. "Come along," she said to her sisters. "We must finish our projects before hunting ivy and holly."

Uncomfortably aware of being the villain of the piece, Elinor unloaded the basket. She put the oranges in a china bowl, and the sugar plums on a high shelf, out of the way of small fingers. There were nuts of all kinds, some French nougat, a canister of tea and another containing chocolate, already grated. The girls could have the treat of chocolate to drink with their Christmas breakfast, and she could offer Sir Nicholas tea without being aware of how little she had left and the cost of replenishing her supply.

Of course, Sir Nicholas wouldn't escort them home after

Christmas service tomorrow. He had family and friends at the hall. He'd been away for a few weeks, and she'd missed their Sunday walks, when he'd talk about the wider world, about political and international affairs, even sometimes sharing some society gossip. They'd often chuckled like friends, but a lady couldn't have a single gentleman as friend, especially not one five years her junior. . . .

She shook away her drifting thoughts and sat to quickly finish the reticule. Once she and the girls returned with the greenery, the rest of the day would be spent in decorating the house, and she still had mince pies to make.

Elinor sighed as she worked the final stitch. When would Amy have an opportunity to use her gift? They all still wore black, because the lavenders and greys of half-mourning would have been an expense. They couldn't wear black forever, but what else?

Their Fortling gowns were packed in trunks, but what would fit? Amy had filled out in the bosom so much that Elinor had had to help her add panels to the bodices of her mourning wear. Margaret and Maria had needed extra bands at the bottom of their skirts.

Clothing was only part of it, however. Her small widow's jointure couldn't support four people, even if they continued to live rent free at Ivy Cottage. She was already eating into her modest savings.

There was nothing for it. In time, the girls were going to have to leave to find work, and for Amy, that time was now. Elinor had put it off until mourning was over, but after Christmas Amy would have to go as a governess or companion. If she could send some of her pittance of wages home, Elinor could educate the younger girls so they could find similar employment rather than go to work as kitchen maids or such.

It broke her heart. Lovely Amy, with her sparkling looks, high spirits, and generous heart, to become a spinster drudge all her days.

Elinor stared at the whitewashed wall, struggling again for a way out.

Heaven knew, she'd marry again in order to give her girls the life they deserved. She'd marry any wealthy man, no matter how unappealing, but what man wanted a woman of thirty-five with three daughters? She'd been a beauty once, very like Amy in appearance, but that was long, long ago.

Her best hope was that if she could be especially frugal she might in time be able to buy a small shop where they could all work. At least they'd be together and she could see to her girls' welfare. The world was full of dangers for pretty, penniless young ladies.

She touched one of the pink rosebuds she'd embroidered around the edge of the reticule. Perhaps Amy would go as governess to a kind family who would include her in some family activities.

Enough of this. She quickly wrapped the gift in a piece of plain white cloth and tied it with a ribbon. She'd already wrapped the slippers she'd made for Margaret and Maria. She'd give her darlings the best Christmas she could. Sir Nicholas's goose would help there, and the chocolate, oranges, nuts, and sugar plums. The house needed the traditional trimmings, however, and bringing greenery into the house on Christmas Eve was supposed to bring good fortune.

"Girls! We should go out to cut the greenery before the sun begins to set."

In moments, they poured down the stairs, already in their cloaks, cheeks rosy with excitement.

Elinor picked up the basket Sir Nicholas had brought. "This

will serve to carry our haul. Amy, find the shears." She put on her black cloak and plain bonnet, and slipped a sharp knife in her pocket in case it was needed. "We can start close to home. We have ivy on the wall here."

"Mama!" Amy protested. "That's no adventure. We most go further afield."

"And we have no holly here," Margaret said.

"Please, Mama!" Maria begged.

"It's a lovely day for late December," Amy argued. "A long walk would do us all good."

Elinor surrendered. "Very well," she said, opening the front door onto the lane. To the right lay Danvers Hall, but she turned left. "I think I remember holly near Dike's Field."

Maria ran ahead, and Margaret went after, but Amy stayed with Elinor.

"Mama, why did you refuse an invitation to eat Christmas dinner at Danvers Hall?"

"It would have been inappropriate."

"But why?"

"We're still in mourning, Amy." Before her daughter could protest, she added, "And I knew he'd have guests. There's no place for a group of black crows there."

"They wouldn't have minded." Amy dropped the argument, however, and said, "Did you hear that Captain Danvers is home, all recovered?"

"Sir Nicholas mentioned it."

"Isn't it *wonderful* to have a Waterloo hero in the village!"

"England owes much to her gallant soldiers," Elinor agreed, touched by her daughter's hero-worship, but saddened, too.

Captain Danvers was the sort of young gentleman Amy might have danced with at assemblies, or even perhaps married. Now he might as well be a Prince of Araby.

"Other gentlemen serve their country, too," Amy said. "Sir Nicholas, for example. He serves in Parliament, and that's important."

"Very important," Elinor agreed, but her mother's instincts stirred. What was Amy working up to?

"Sir Nicholas spoke so movingly of the plight of the returning soldiers. Of the lack of employment."

"That is unfortunate . . ." But then Elinor realized she'd never heard him speak on that subject. "When did Sir Nicholas speak of that?"

The roses in Amy's cheeks turned red. "A few weeks ago," she said with guilty carelessness. "I was gathering the last of the rosehips down the lane."

Elinor had sent Amy on that errand, but she'd heard nothing of this. "And you spoke together? Amy, that was improper."

"Mama! He was riding by. Were we to ignore each other?"

Elinor couldn't honestly say yes, but the situation made her uncomfortable.

"I was reaching up, and he was on horseback, so he pulled down a briar for me, and we spoke a little. I don't know why you're cross."

"I regret that you must wander the countryside alone."

"It's better than sitting at home all the time."

Amy's tone was close to impertinent, but Elinor was more concerned about other things. She knew her daughter.

"Have there been other encounters?" she asked.

"A few," Amy said, in a tone that suggested more than a few. "Margaret and Maria have been with me sometimes. He's very kind to them."

"I'm sure he is."

"You *know* he is. Remember when he came in after church and let Maria talk him into playing spillikins?"

"Claiming that it was something he liked above all," Elinor remembered with a smile.

"And when he taught us that card game."

"A gambling game." But Elinor couldn't frown. It had been fun.

"Only for beans. And he brought some spelling books for Maria."

Sir Nicholas had been consistently kind, but Amy's sparkling eyes unsettled Elinor. She'd swear that Sir Nicholas Danvers was a good man, but pretty girls were often rich men's prey.

"He said that Margaret and Maria could use the library at Danvers Hall," Amy said.

"I doubt there's anything there of interest to Maria, and Margaret isn't at all bookish."

"Very well, *I'd* like to borrow books from there. I'm starved of new reading. Please, Mama."

"No." But then Elinor sighed. "When there are no guests, perhaps. You must not go alone, however. You must take your sisters with you."

"Mama! They'll be restless and I'll have to watch them all the time."

"It simply wouldn't be proper, Amy. You're a young lady now and must consider such things."

To Elinor's surprise, Amy nodded. "You mean some men might have wicked intentions."

"Yes."

"Like Wickham in *Pride and Prejudice*."

"Yes," said Elinor, wishing she'd not allowed Amy to read that book.

Sir Nicholas had brought it to Ivy Cottage as a gift. It was an amusing representation of family life, but Elinor considered the heroine pert and one of her sisters positively wicked. Their both being rewarded with marriage—in one case, a brilliant match—was designed to put fanciful notions into young women's heads, and she'd said as much to Sir Nicholas, adding that the authoress must be a little too flighty in her ways.

He'd chuckled and said that he knew the "Lady" credited with the work. She lived here in Chawton. He'd revealed in strictest confidence that the book had been written by Miss Jane Austen, who lived with her widowed mother and older sister in a handsome house near the center of the village.

Elinor had been astonished. Miss Jane Austen, well past the age of being flighty, seemed a sensible woman, and her father had been a clergyman.

"And," Sir Nicholas had added, "their situation is a fanciful story, but true. They could be living in poverty had not one of their brothers been adopted by wealthy relatives, and now have possession of fine estates, including Chawton House."

"Not a blessing to be depended on," she'd pointed out. "Better management by their father would have been preferable."

She'd been perfectly serious, thinking of her own situation, but Sir Nicholas had laughed as if she'd been a wit.

Had that novel put notions into her daughter's head?

"Please remember, Amy, that it's only in novels that young ladies like Lydia Bennet end up married and embraced by family and friends. In reality, they fall into ruin."

"I know that, Mama. You can't imagine I'd run off with a penniless soldier."

"What's more, it's only in such novels that gentlemen of fortune offer marriage to penniless young ladies, no matter how pretty they are. Their hearts might be touched, but good sense and duty will direct them elsewhere."

"But Mr. Darcy could *afford* to marry Lizzie, Mama, and Mr. Bingley to marry Jane, so why shouldn't they?"

It was as she'd feared.

"They simply don't, Amy. But if a young lady behaves with modesty and discretion and avoids being alone with gentlemen at all times, she can't come to grief."

Amy's disgruntled face showed her warnings might have been just in time. Had she begun to spin dreams about Sir Nicholas? Her vitality earlier on seeing him had been marked, and the dangers lurking in employment seemed even greater. A governess could be prey to the brothers of her pupils, and even to their father.

Oh, Barnie, why were you so careless!

"Let's catch up to the others," she said, hurrying on as if she could outpace her problems. But one—Amy—kept up easily.

"Sir Nicholas is like Mr. Darcy and Mr. Bingley, isn't he, Mama? He's rich enough to marry whom he pleases."

Oh, Lord, could Amy have been putting herself in Sir Nicholas's way on purpose? How mortifying.

But then Elinor remembered the warm smile Sir Nicholas had bestowed on Amy today, and the increasing number of his kindnesses to the family. Was it possible? If he and Amy had been meeting, had it been by shared intent?

He was almost twice Amy's age—but mature men were attracted to youth.

It was a dazzling vision. Amy, dear, darling Amy, would have security, comfort, and the best possible husband, and the younger girls would be well provided for, too. Too dazzling.

"Sir Nicholas is in a position to marry as he wishes, Amy, but it would be very foolish for him not to marry a woman with a substantial portion, and so I would tell him if he were my son."

"Your son, Mama! He's not much younger than you are."

"Five years, which is quite enough."

"It's as if you don't like him, Mama, and I can't imagine why. He's so kind and you were so cross about the goose."

"I was a goose to be cross about it," Elinor admitted, "and I intend to enjoy every delicious morsel. I do like Sir Nicholas, Amy. If I seem sharp sometimes, it's because I resent charity in general, because I'm not used to having to be grateful for it."

"I don't think he sees it as charity, Mama. I think . . . Oh, I'm going to catch up to the others and set them to work, or we'll never gather enough."

She ran off, suddenly all girl again in her fleet-footedness, her skirts revealing a bit too much ankle.

Elinor followed, torn between hope, fear, and a strange ache. She tried to remember Sir Nicholas's visits to Ivy Cottage and whether he'd paid particular attention to Amy. She couldn't think of any such moment, but that could be because she'd been enjoying the occasions herself.

If he did marry Amy, she would sometimes have occasion to enjoy his company and hear news of politics and international affairs, as well as tid-bits of society gossip. It wouldn't be the same, however.

She wouldn't live with them at Danvers Hall. Even though that might be good for Margaret and Maria, she couldn't do that. She was sure he would provide a better house for them, however—a place similar to the Austens' house, with ample rooms and a few servants. He would increase her income so that she could mingle with local society without embarrassment.

It would all be wonderful, so the rather sick feeling in her stomach must be fear that it wouldn't come to pass. Or perhaps that Amy was intending to sacrifice herself for her family. She was capable of that. Elinor couldn't imagine Sir Nicholas being a sacrifice for any woman, not even a girl still in her teens, but if that were so . . .

Which was worse—an unhappy marriage or a life of drudgery?

Why did she want to weep?

The girls ran to meet her and put lengths of ivy and a couple of branches of holly in the basket. The best sprigs of holly were higher, so Amy and Elinor cut as the younger girls directed.

Elinor considered the haul. "I do think we'll find better ivy at home, dears. We need the younger stems and they're very high here. Time to go home."

A rattle and the sound of hooves made her look down the lane, where she saw a donkey cart carrying two women, one swathed in extra rugs. She'd heard Miss Jane Austen was not well, but she was out enjoying the warm afternoon, driven by her sister.

Elinor and her daughters stepped aside, and Elinor prepared to exchange a seasonal greeting in passing. But Miss Austen halted the cart, and Miss Jane smiled. "A merry Christmas to you, Mrs. Carsholt. And to your daughters."

They all dipped curtsies. "And to you, Miss Austen, Miss Jane. A lovely day, is it not?"

"Delightful."

Miss Jane Austen was probably in her forties and sallow with whatever plagued her. She was a most unlikely author of danger-ous novels.

"We've been gathering holly and ivy!" Maria said, making Elinor wince for her manners, but as usual, the little angel gained approval.

"An important part of the traditions, my dear. Will you add mistletoe?"

"Yes, ma'am," said Margaret.

Miss Jane's eyes twinkled. "Are you hoping for a kiss, dear?"

Margaret went pink, but said, "Amy is!"

"Probably from Sir Nicholas," said Maria, surely in complete innocence.

"What nonsense!" Amy said, turning bright red in a way that confirmed Elinor's hopes. "If he kisses anyone, he'll kiss Mama."

Elinor laughed at that, turning to share amusement with the Austen ladies. "I'm far past the age for mistletoe kisses, I fear."

Miss Jane cocked her head. "That seems a shame, for we must be older still."

Elinor hastily apologized, but Miss Jane shook her head. "I was only teasing, Mrs. Carsholt. I believe Sir Nicholas said you are thirty-six. I don't think you should refuse the mistletoe its chance."

"Chance, ma'am?"

"Do you not know that tradition?"

"Oh, sister," said Miss Austen, as if uncomfortable with the subject.

"Cassandra doesn't approve," Miss Jane said, smiling. "She thinks it has a touch of pagan magic about it. Local tradition says that if true lovers kiss beneath a mistletoe bough, they will instantly know their devotion."

"It sounds a little pagan to me, too, Miss Jane," Elinor said, but lightly. "And perhaps overly romantical."

"If by romantical you speak of men and women forming true matches based on love, does that not happen all the time?"

Maria spoke, with the disastrous honesty of a young child. "Did you never find your true love through the mistletoe bough, ma'am?"

"Maria!" Elinor chided, but Miss Austen replied.

"I did, my dear, but it was not to be. However, to experience true love is better than not, and one can always imagine a story with a different ending."

Miss Jane inclined her head; Miss Austen added a good-day and drove on, leaving Elinor to wonder if Miss Jane had encountered her own Mr. Darcy, and he had not abandoned sense in order to marry a penniless woman.

In that case, it would have been a great deal more to the point to write the truth; if Miss Elizabeth Bennet had ended up as a penny-pinched spinster along with all her sisters, and Miss Lydia Bennet had been ruined as she deserved, foolish girls might have learned by it.

"That's a wonderful legend," Amy said. "We really must get some mistletoe, Mama!"

She was already over the stile and helping the others. Elinor was suddenly drained of the energy to fight. Let them have a kissing bough if they wanted.

She climbed carefully over the stile, dearly wishing the world was like Miss Jane Austen's novel, full of happy endings.

Too late she remembered Sir Nicholas saying that his brother planned to raid the orchard. She hated to intrude. Her daughters were far ahead, so she could only pray that the Danvers Hall party had already left. When she found only some village children in the orchard, however, she felt let down.

As her girls ran around seeking the best branches, Elinor looked toward the mellow, golden manor house, trying to imagine Amy mistress there. It was larger and finer than Fortlings, and the mullioned windows glinted in the setting sun, making it seem like a fairy palace.

Indeed, it might as well be.

"Mama!" called Margaret. "Here's a tree full of mistletoe!"

Elinor turned and joined them. "Those certainly are splendid bunches, dear, but they're too high. Let's look for some that hang lower."

"But all the lower ones have gone," Amy said. "There's a ladder over there."

Elinor grabbed her cloak. "None of us are climbing a ladder."

"But what are we to do? Oh, I wish we had a man to assist us!"

"I am summoned."

Elinor turned to stare at the dark-haired young man strolling through the orchard. It must be Captain Danvers, for he was very like his brother, though more dashing, with his longer hair and a scar across his forehead.

"Captain Danvers!" said Amy in a tone that crushed all Elinor's hopes.

Oh, Amy! Miss Austen had represented that folly correctly in her novel, saying that the worth of a man of sense was nothing when put beside an ensign in regimentals. Here was not a mere ensign but a captain, wounded heroically in the service of his country. His lack of uniform didn't weaken his power.

Elinor hadn't truly feared Sir Nicholas might ruin Amy, or that Amy would allow herself to be ruined, but a man like Captain Danvers might deprive her of all good sense. Their manner was not that of strangers.

Amy must have been meeting not Sir Nicholas but Captain Danvers in the past few days.

"You are just in time to assist us, Captain Danvers," Amy was saying, with bold familiarity. "We need mistletoe. Lots of it."

"I am entirely at your service, ladies." He politely managed to address them all with especial recognition of Elinor. "Only point to the sprig you want, ma'am, and it will be yours."

Elinor had to play her part. "You're very kind, Captain. I'll let the girls each pick one."

Maria excitedly pointed to a high one, and the captain carried over the ladder. He climbed it and returned to present the sprig to her with a bow. Maria giggled, entranced.

Then Margaret demanded an even higher one and he repeated the performance, leaving sensible Margaret blushing, also with stars in her eyes.

"Shouldn't you also choose one, ma'am?"

Elinor started and turned to find Sir Nicholas close by. To her eyes his more sober manner and his neat Brutus haircut were more attractive than his brother's dashing style.

"You look lost for words," he said.

"I feel caught out ravaging your orchard, Sir Nicholas." *And what will you make of my daughter's folly over your brother?*

"I invited you to ravage my orchard, Mrs. Carsholt." He glanced up. "Are you aware that you are stationed directly below a laden sprig of mistletoe?"

Elinor quickly stepped to the side. "I'm past the age for games like that, sir."

She managed to speak lightly, but for a moment she'd wanted that kiss, hungered to be kissed by the most handsome, most admirable man she knew. Shocking, scandalous, but despite the impossible five years between them, she desperately wanted Sir Nicholas, as a woman wants a man she might marry.

"I thought you and your guests would have finished by now," she blurted, hearing the ungraciousness of it.

"We have, but my brother insisted we needed more mistletoe. An excellent idea," he added, smiling over at Amy.

Was he blind not to see the truth there?

Miss Jane Austen had urged them off to the orchard with legends of mistletoe kisses, abetting Amy and her gallant swain.

Elinor was feeling trapped in a fairy tale, like a grove in *Midsummer Night's Dream,* but it was closer to a nightmare. Could the brothers come to blows over this?

"The gentlemen pinch off a berry every time they steal a kiss," he said, "but you must know that."

"Yes."

"We must have some remaining for our Twelfth Night festivities. Can I persuade you to relax your mourning and attend them, Mrs. Carsholt? You and your daughters? There will be traditional games, and mummers from the village."

"I think not. . . ."

"Life must go on, dear lady, especially for the younger ones. Amy should be reveling in youth."

Elinor couldn't make sense of anything. He was speaking fondly of Amy. Amy was entranced by Captain Danvers, but she'd just shot a look at Sir Nicholas that implied he was the most wonderful man in the world. She couldn't be infatuated by both of them!

"You will not dance, I know," he said, "but perhaps you would permit Amy to?"

Couldn't he see his heart was going to be broken?

"And I would very much enjoy *your* company, Mrs. Carsholt. I have always enjoyed your company, and flattered myself that you enjoyed mine."

He was looking at her in an intent way, a way she was suddenly afraid to interpret. In *Midsummer's Night's Dream* people were enchanted into idiocy.

Elinor looked away. "You've always been most kind, Sir Nicholas. To all of us."

"To *you*. It's been a difficult year for you, but it's nearing its end. You will all attend my Twelfth Night party?"

Elinor looked back at him. "I . . . I don't know." It encompassed everything.

"I was speaking with Miss Jane Austen earlier," he said, "and she told me of a mistletoe legend."

"Yes, she told us, too."

"Apparently it doesn't work when the mistletoe is still attached to the tree. It must be cut and formed into a bough."

"A kissing bough."

"Do you intend to hang a mistletoe bough in Ivy Cottage?"

"The girls will insist on it."

"May I stop by this evening? I forgot to bring the bottle of port wine I had selected for you."

Did he mean . . . ?

Elinor was blushing. She couldn't control it, and suddenly didn't want to. She'd run mad to read what she did into his words and manner, but it was a madness she'd cling to as long as possible.

"Of course." But then she realized everything he'd said could apply to Amy, not herself. Of course that was what he meant. So what should she do?

"Mama, Mama!" Maria plucked at Elinor's skirts. "Can we go home and start decorating the cottage?"

Escape. "Of course. We must have all our greenery hung tonight, including our kissing bough." She dropped a curtsy and took a bold gamble. "I hope to see you this evening, Sir Nicholas. You will be very welcome."

He bowed and joined his brother. Elinor watched him for too long, allowing herself to tell a fanciful story, but then gathered her daughters and headed home.

Captain Danvers hurried after, however, insisting that they'd need help to hang the evergreens. Once back at the cottage, Amy shared that task with him while Elinor helped Margaret and Maria tie up the mistletoe with ribbons. She put aside her anxieties and joined in the Christmas Eve excitement.

Captain Danvers hung the bough in the middle of the parlor ceiling and then stole a quick, light kiss from Margaret and Maria, pinching off a berry for each as they giggled. And then he did the same with Amy. It was quick and light, but afterward the two looked into each other's eyes as if startled.

Elinor would *not* believe in mistletoe magic.

Captain Danvers turned and pulled Elinor beneath the kissing bough. If there was anything to the legend, she wasn't in love with Captain Danvers. But she already knew that.

When he left, Elinor provided a quick supper and then shooed the younger girls upstairs to bed. Amy remained to help her tidy up, still lost in a daze.

When all was done, Amy asked, "Will I have to wear mourning for Twelfth Night, Mama? It will be so close to the end. I don't want . . . But you understand!"

Elinor did. Come what may, it was time to face the future. "We'll all put on our colors. Why be crows at the feast? But we'll all have to spend some time on alterations, I fear."

Amy hugged her. "Thank you, thank you, Mama! And . . . I think Sir Nicholas is the most wonderful man in the world!"

"Amy, you can't mean that."

Amy flushed red. "Well, no. But . . . I have hopes . . . Oh, you know what I mean." She raced upstairs, doubtless to spin wondrous dreams. Elinor remembered what it felt like to be sixteen and in love, perhaps now more poignantly than ever. She returned to the parlor, looking up at the mistletoe bough, rapt in her own impossible dreams.

Men of rank and fortune didn't marry penniless young women. Even less did they marry penniless old ones. But she wanted the impossible to be true.

It wasn't a matter of wealth and station, though it would certainly be pleasant to be Lady Danvers of Danvers Hall. It was Nicholas himself. His kindness, his intelligence, his gentle humor. Everything, including his broad shoulders, vigor of movement, steady blue eyes, strong hands.

At a clench of physical longing, she moved to pace the room; Lord save her, she might be tempted on the road to ruin by such physical hungers. It had been so long. . . .

Mince pies. The small oven by the kitchen fire was ready. She would make the pies instead of sinking into lewd thoughts.

She was rolling out the pastry when someone knocked on the kitchen door, but Sir Nicholas opened it without waiting. At the sight of her, he grinned.

"Oh!" Elinor put her hands to her face, only then realizing that they were floury from the pastry. "Why did you have to come barging in here?"

"My deepest apologies," he said, putting a bottle of port on the table.

She turned to the basin of water to wash her hands, then wet a corner of her apron and scrubbed at her face.

"Allow me," he said, and turned her to gently dab at some spots. "Though flour becomes you, my dear Elinor."

Surely there was no mistaking the look in his eyes. "I'm five years older than you," she said.

"Port improves with age."

"Are you comparing me to *wine*?"

"*Shall I compare thee to a well-aged port . . .*" he misquoted. "Good wine has depth, and warmth, and gladdens the heart. As you gladden mine." He took her hand and led her into the parlor. "A very pretty bough. Now to put mistletoe to the test."

"Should we?" Elinor whispered, frightened that his kiss might feel no different to his brother's.

"We should." He drew her gently to him and put his lips to hers.

Warmth. A warmth greater than lips to lips, a warmth that spread gently through her, melting, softening. She looked at him and he looked at her, as lightning-struck as Amy and his brother.

Knowing.

There could be no doubt in that, or in the hunger that instantly ignited deep inside her. She pressed close again, opened her lips to him, savored him, sliding her arms around him in order to be even closer.

She pushed back, but stopped herself from turning it into a panicked rejection. She shook with panic of another sort. She'd never felt anything like this before.

"In my opinion," he murmured, "Miss Jane Austen knows a thing or two about mistletoe."

"And about love. I do love you, Nicholas Danvers. I don't know how I didn't realize it months ago."

"I've known for months, but you seemed such a stickler for the proprieties. When you denounced *Pride and Prejudice,* I feared I had a hard fight ahead."

She chuckled, moving back to rest against his chest, despite or because of all her wicked hungers. "By all rights and reasons, you should not marry me, you know, any more than Fitzwilliam Darcy should have married Elizabeth Bennet."

"We'll have no shoulds. The mistletoe has spoken."

She melted perfectly into another kiss, as if they'd kissed a thousand times, his strong arms around her already familiar.

Amy crept to the parlor door, squeezed into her prettiest pink gown. It just fit if she didn't breathe too deeply. It would fit perfectly by Twelfth Night with some inserts of lace.

She peered around the corner and smiled, hugging herself in delight.

Sir Nicholas Danvers was going to be the most wonderfully perfect father.

As for his brother . . . time would tell.

She crept back upstairs to dream.

Jo BEVERLEY writes bestselling historical romance set in her native England. She was born and raised in the U.K. and has a degree in history from Keele University in Staffordshire, but she lived in Canada for thirty years. Now that she's returned to England she enjoys doing even more on-the-spot research.

Her more than thirty novels have won her many awards, including five RITA, the top award in romance, and two career achievement awards from *Romantic Times*. She's a member of the Romance Writers of America Hall of Fame and Honor Roll. *Publishers Weekly* declared her "arguably today's most skillful writer of intelligent historical romance."

www.jobev.com
@jobeverley on Twitter

WHEN ONLY A DARCY WILL DO

Beth Pattillo

I stood outside the Green Park Underground station with my tour leaflet thrust high in the air, ignoring the feelings of ridiculousness that made my arm waver. The leaflet should have been unnecessary for attracting notice, given that I was wearing a plumed bonnet, an empire-waisted long dress, and a little jacket known in Jane Austen's day as a spencer. On a busy London street on a Sunday afternoon, though, few people were paying any attention to my getup. That was good news and bad news. Because when you're trying to attract tourists to your bootleg Jane Austen tour, you're shooting for notice.

After five minutes or so, my arm started to ache from holding up the leaflet and my cheeks ached from smiling, but at last a middle-aged couple was heading toward me. *Ka-ching*. That would be six pounds each, which would at least buy a few groceries or top off my Oyster card.

"Do you know where we can find a restroom?" the woman asked in a nasal American accent. Midwestern definitely. Possibly Chicago.

"If you go back in the station and follow the subway under the street, it's on the other side there." I nodded across Piccadilly and its buzz of traffic. "I'll hold the tour for you."

"Tour?" She looked at me strangely. "Oh. I see. I thought you were just . . . well, local flavor." She and her husband turned and made a beeline for the entrance to the station.

Who was I kidding? I'd thought putting together a tour of Jane Austen's London would be easy money. I'd throw up a website, get a costume, and use my grad student's knowledge of my favorite author to drum up some much-needed income. As an American studying in London, I wasn't technically supposed to hold a job. I'd managed to wheedle my way into a few hours at a local bookstore, but London was expensive. Very expensive. I was going broke just washing my clothes at the laundromat. A young single female shouldn't have to choose between eating and not smelling. And then there was the small matter of next year's tuition. . . .

My arm started to wilt and the leaflet sank along with it. Well, it had been worth a shot. This was my third Sunday morning in a row holding up my leaflet, and I still hadn't had any takers. Perhaps it was time to throw in the tea towel.

Then I spotted him emerging from the station. You couldn't miss him, really. He was tall, made even taller by the high-crowned hat of a bygone era. Jane Austen's era, to be exact. The hat matched his dark brown cutaway coat, vest, and Hessian boots. Buff-colored breeches and a white shirt, complete with cravat and high collar points, finished off the outfit of a Regency gentleman.

I shut my mouth so it wouldn't hang open. What was this guy—the competition? I could tell him not to bother. He might be a nice-looking man, swoon-worthy really in that getup if one was a Jane Austen–inclined kind of gal, but I doubted he would be any more successful as a tour leader than I had been.

He spotted me, even without the leaflet in the air, and strode toward me with purpose. When he came to a stop in front of me, I had to look way, way up to talk to him.

"Are you here for the tour?" I asked in my best fake British accent. I'd been practicing it in the mirror for weeks now. I mean, how many tourists want a Jane Austen experience in an American drawl?

He smiled. A very nice smile, if a little crooked. He had dark eyes, brown hair, and a bit of a hook to his nose. Not exactly Colin Firth, but not too shabby either.

"I am indeed here for the tour." His accent was much better than mine because it was authentic. His word choice was appropriate, too. When I'd dreamed up the tour, it never occurred to me that participants might turn up in costume as well.

"We'll just wait a few minutes for the . . . others." I looked around, aware that my optimism was misplaced.

He pulled a pocket watch from his vest, opened it, and frowned. "A quarter past." He joined me in looking around at the hordes of people passing by, all in distinctly modern clothing and none of them paying any attention to us. "Perhaps we should begin."

In all my planning, it had never occurred to me that I might end up doing the tour for one person, much less a good-looking man dressed in period clothing.

"Yes, let's begin." I paused, unsure what to say next. My plan had been to escort the group around the corner to a quiet spot and give my opening spiel. But wouldn't a guy who was dressed like Mr. Darcy already know all about Jane Austen? "This way please."

We made our way down Stratton Street and then around the corner to stand in a recess along the front of a large office complex. Once upon a time, a stately London mansion, the home of the Dukes of Devonshire, had stood upon the spot. Now it was a very posh office block.

I turned to my customer, swallowed past the lump of anxiety in my throat, and tried to keep up my accent.

"My name is Elizabeth." I held out my hand expecting a handshake, but instead he took my gloved fingers in his and raised my hand as he made a small bow. For a moment, I thought he was going to kiss the back of my hand, but he completed his bow and then let go.

I felt strangely disappointed.

"And you are . . . ?" I prompted.

A small smile played at the corner of his mouth. "Mr. Fitzwilliam Darcy."

Okay, he could be a complete weirdo. Or a serial killer. Or maybe just someone a little too into that strange role-playing or LARPing or whatever it was called. But he reached into his pocket and pulled out a twenty-pound note, which he held out to me.

"Um, thanks." My accent slipped as I accepted the money and dropped it into the small basket I carried over my arm. What could I do but play along? I rummaged for change, but he put a hand over mine.

"It's not necessary."

"But—" I looked up at him and tried to decide if he was too good to be true.

"Honestly." He flashed that crooked smile. "I'm sure it will be well worth it."

I was twenty-three. Too old to blush like I was in junior high and the cutest boy in school had just confessed to liking me.

"Thank you." I hitched the basket higher on my arm, cleared my throat, and began.

"Jane Austen was born in 1775 in Hampshire, about sixty

miles southwest of London. . . ." I'd memorized my facts so well that I said them automatically, filling him in on her family, her early years, and her preference for country life. "Jane had mixed feelings about the city, but she did enjoy the theaters and the shops when she came to London."

He nodded. "I often feel the same way." Then he smiled again. Slightly crooked but totally charming.

Oh, dear.

"When Jane visited London as a girl," I continued, "she stayed with her aunt and cousin. Later, when she was an adult, she stayed with her brother, Henry."

I started to move along the front of the building, and as I did, my erstwhile Mr. Darcy held out his arm, offering me his escort. I froze, uncertain whether to play along, but then I looked up at him and our gazes met.

I had learned over the course of the past year to read a lot in people's eyes. I'd seen the grief and sorrow in my father's after the financial markets had tumbled into oblivion. I'd seen the frustration in my mother's gaze when my father walked out, unable to deal with his failure. And I'd seen the scorn in the eyes of some of my British classmates who'd lumped me in the category of rich American whose Daddy paid her credit card bills. What I saw in my Mr. Darcy's eyes at that moment told me a lot. Maybe I should have hesitated more, but I didn't. I reached up to curl my free hand around his offered arm. Beneath my fingertips, he felt solid. Strong. Dependable. Real.

"If we turn right just ahead," I said, "we'll see the premises of John Murray, one of Jane Austen's publishers."

He nodded without saying anything and we moved along the pavement under the shelter of the building's enormous portico.

"Jane dreamed of finding success as an author, but her first effort at publication was a disaster. With her brother's help, she sold the rights to an early novel for ten pounds, but the publisher never produced the work. When her brother pressed the man, he demanded the same amount to return the manuscript. I'm sure Jane must have been heartbroken. But she then sold *Sense and Sensibility* and it was published first in 1811, followed by *Pride and Prejudice* two years later. With the help of her brother, she arranged for the publication of *Emma* by John Murray, whose offices were just here."

We came to a stop in the middle of a row of Palladian townhouses. The steps and doorway were like all the others. "We could almost imagine Jane and her brother pulling up just here, in a carriage"—I waved toward the road where a black cab whizzed by—"to pay a call on Mr. Murray to discuss business or make corrections to a manuscript."

My Mr. Darcy nodded. "She must have enjoyed the wealth that her writing brought her."

I shook my head. "Oh, no. She really earned very little on her novels. It was one of the great disappointments of her life."

We exchanged rueful smiles and my heart beat a little faster in my chest. For Mr. Darcy, he might not be terribly informed about the woman who had created him, but he was certainly sympathetic to her plight.

I would never have imagined that my two-hour tour could go so quickly. We made our way through the back streets of Mayfair, pausing here and there at a blue plaque or a pub important in Austen's day. We stopped in front of a Regency townhouse that was almost unaltered from its original state, and I gave him the complete rundown on life in the city. I had been chattering on for a while when I looked up at my companion. His eyes had glazed over.

"If you'll follow me, we'll see the only plaque in London commemorating Jane Austen." I stepped toward the curb, but he reached out to grab my arm.

"What about a cup of tea instead? There's a place just around the corner."

"But the tour—"

"We can continue it. Just a short break."

I looked up at him and hesitated. My professionalism was at stake here. Well, not that I was an actual professional guide or anything. But it was the principle of the thing.

Then he smiled. My knees went all warm and liquid, much like that cup of tea he was suggesting.

"Maybe just for a minute."

And that was how I found myself being hustled into a fancy tea shop while dressed in full Jane Austen regalia. Heads turned, of course, but we got as many admiring looks as we did headshakes. Well, my Mr. Darcy did anyway.

He settled us into an out-of-the-way corner, and I untied the ribbons of my bonnet and lifted it off with a sigh of relief. I don't know how women in Jane Austen's day managed to tolerate those torture devices.

"You have beautiful hair," Mr. Darcy said. "It's not brown, but it's not black either."

"My mother calls it 'nondescript.'" My response was automatic, but the moment I said it, I wished I hadn't. I shrugged. "She's blonde."

"It's the color of coffee," he said, and he lifted a hand, as if he were about to reach out and touch one of the ringlets I'd left on either side of my face.

"Dingy brown, then." I decided to keep my fake accent going. He might be charming. He might be handsome. He might even claim to be Mr. Darcy. But he was still a paying customer, not a suitor.

He paused and looked at me for a long moment. I fought the urge to squirm in my chair. I wasn't used to such close scrutiny. I'd kept to myself for the most part since I'd arrived in England. Classes. A sandwich and a cup of tea—Earl Gray, two sugars—in the student center every day. My few hours in the bookstore, and then there was the laundromat, of course. But as far as a social life . . . Well, I'd had too much on my mind. Too many regrets to ponder. Too many ways to devise for pinching pennies and stretching pounds.

"You look sad." This time when he reached out, he did touch me, gently, with a fingertip that barely grazed my jaw. "A damsel in distress."

I hadn't told anyone how much distress. Or was it that there hadn't been anyone to tell? My mom had all but ordered me to stay home. She'd assured me she wouldn't give me a penny to go running off to England. She thought she was teaching me the value of a dollar. I thought that she just wanted me to share her misery.

"Fine. Go, then," she'd said. "But find yourself a rich Brit. Like that Mr. Darcy. Only make sure he can hang on to his money. Make sure he's not like your father." My father had retreated to his hunting cabin in North Carolina. He hadn't even called to say good-bye before I'd left.

"I'm perfectly fine," I said to Mr. Darcy—a little briskly, so I softened the words with a smile. "Really."

He shook his head. "You are a heroine in need of a hero."

I laughed, and even though we were hidden in the corner, my laugh drew attention. It was a cross between a hen's cackle and a donkey's bray and had been the bane of my existence as long as I could remember. I quickly swallowed the sound and sipped my tea.

"What gives you that idea?"

"The worry lines. Here." He raised his hand and ran his thumb lightly across my forehead. "And the frown lines, here." He dabbed each side of my mouth.

"Gee, thanks." I abandoned the pretense of the accent altogether. "I'm too young for Botox."

He sipped his tea in a way that was well mannered without being uptight. "Perhaps I can help."

Now I wasn't sure if he was hitting on me or just being nice, but really, how was I supposed to judge, given the fact that we were sitting in a fancy London patisserie wearing Regency costumes as if it were the most ordinary thing ever?

"Not unless you really are Mr. Darcy. I could use a few of your twenty thousand pounds a year."

When I looked at him, he was smiling again. He really needed to stop doing that. Before it had made my knees weak. Now it caused my heart to thump in my chest at an alarming rate.

I glanced at the clock on the wall. "We should move on," I said. The tea hadn't soothed my nerves. "Covent Garden awaits."

"Of course." He nodded, reached in his pocket, and settled the bill with another twenty-pound note. Then he stood up.

"Don't you want to wait for your change?" I asked. I couldn't help but do the mental math. I knew exactly how many loads of laundry a tip that size could do.

He bowed again. "I wouldn't dream of imposing upon your time." He waved a hand toward the door and I led him out of the tea shop.

We finished our tour on Henrietta Street, outside the building where Jane Austen's brother had lived. Since she'd never been an official resident of London, she didn't have a blue plaque, but there was a green one here, put up by the City of Westminster.

"And that's all, I'm afraid," I said as I finished telling him how Jane Austen had died tragically young. It didn't make for a very peppy ending to the tour, but real life wasn't as conducive as a novel to a happy ending. At least, that's what I'd learned over the course of the previous few months.

"You're very well informed," he said with a wry smile. "And very charming."

"Thank you. Listen, I'm sorry about sharing my personal life with you. You were very kind to buy me a cup of tea. I didn't mean to dump on you."

He reached out and took my hand in his. "No apologies necessary. It was my pleasure."

I wanted to ask him who he really was. Why he'd turned up in that outfit. What he really wanted. But even more, I didn't want to break the spell. The afternoon had been an episode out of time. It was a memory I would always cherish. That magical day when Mr. Darcy had shown up, at least for a little while, and made the awful things in my life a little more bearable.

"Good-bye," he said. He bowed over my hand once more.

"Good-bye."

I had left little flyers about my tour all over London for the last three weeks. He could have found one anywhere. Or he might simply have stumbled over my homemade website. However he had found me, I could only be grateful. Still, as I turned toward the Tube station, my heart felt as heavy as my feet.

If only real life could be like one of Jane Austen's novels.

Class on Monday morning lacked its usual luster. Normally I would have been transported out of my worries by the vigorous discussion of Austen's use of irony in her novels. After my experience the day before, though, I wasn't quite so easily engaged. Or pleased. A dry, academic discussion wasn't enough. Not when I'd spent two hours the day before with the living, breathing embodiment of Mr. Fitzwilliam Darcy.

Why had I let him get away? I could have gone after him, when we'd parted there at the edge of Covent Garden. Instead, I'd watched him disappear into the crowd and done nothing.

Because I'd been afraid. It was so much easier to be brave in a fantasy than to be brave in real life.

Despite the costume and the role-playing, my Mr. Darcy hadn't seemed like a nutcase. No, he'd been charming and kind. Familiar, somehow, although I couldn't quite put my finger on it. Maybe he'd been an actor, preparing for a part in some "bonnet and bustle" production, as they called them over here.

Whoever he was, he was gone now.

You could show up again next Sunday, a voice whispered in my head. *He might turn up again, too.*

But if he'd wanted to see me again, he would have asked for my number. Or, if he wanted to stay in character, my address. Instead, he hadn't even asked my last name.

I found myself at the door to the student café and followed the crowd inside. Maybe a cup of tea. Or a cup of coffee. *Like my hair.* I hadn't been sure at the time that it was a compliment. Now, surrounded by the comforting smell of roasting beans, I decided that it was.

The café was comprised of several stations—hot food, sandwiches, and of course, the tea and coffee bar. I joined the queue, searching the bottom of my purse for spare change. My fingers closed around the crumpled twenty-pound note. I'd shoved it in my purse on my mad dash out the door that morning. I hadn't meant to spend it. It was a keepsake.

Who was I trying to fool? There was no Mr. Darcy in real life.

I had tuition to scrape together. Rent to pay. If I couldn't find another part-time job, I'd be walking across London every day because I couldn't come up with bus fare.

I couldn't afford to be sentimental anymore. I unfolded the note just as the customer in front of me stepped aside.

I looked across the counter. The tea and coffee guy was tall. Brown hair, brown eyes. His nose was a little hooked, but not as crooked as his smile.

"Earl Grey?" he asked. "Two sugars?"

"But—" I'd stopped here every day for weeks after class. How many times had he handed me a paper cup full of my favorite beverage?

I glanced at his nametag. *Ian.*

The guy behind me groaned. "C'mon, love. We haven't got all day."

Ian grinned. "That will be one pound fifty."

I held out the twenty-pound note without thinking. He took it, then smoothed it between his fingers. "You haven't got anything smaller?" he asked.

"No." I shook my head.

"Shame to break it." He reached into his pocket and pulled out a few coins. "Allow me."

I couldn't think of what to say, could only watch as he paid for my tea and then slid the twenty-pound note back across the counter toward me.

"You ought to keep that," he said with a wink.

"But I couldn't possibly—"

"You'll need it, when you buy me dinner." I swear his eyes actually twinkled.

I swallowed and tried to untie my tongue from its myriad knots. "My name really is Elizabeth." I had no idea where that came from.

He nodded. "I thought so." He glanced at the line of students behind me. "I'm off in twenty minutes. Maybe by then you'll be done with your tea?"

I had never known that happiness could feel like that, like the sun exploding inside of you. It should have felt corny and ridiculous, but instead it felt like Christmas, birthdays, and summer vacations all rolled into one.

"I like to walk," I said with a smile of my own. "Maybe you'd like to join me?"

"I would." He leaned across the counter to whisper in my ear. "I fancy finding out where we end up."

I resisted the urge to turn my head oh-so-slightly and kiss his cheek. "Me too," I whispered conspiratorially.

I stepped back, took one last look at him, smiled because I couldn't help myself, and turned away from the counter.

What did I know about him, really, my erstwhile Mr. Darcy? He didn't have much money, but he was generous with what he did have. He was willing to look like a fool to gain my notice. And he had listened to me in a way that no one had in a very long time.

I made my way to a table and settled in with my tea.

My mother had been right after all. Sometimes, only a Darcy will do.

BETH PATTILLO is the author of *Jane Austen Ruined My Life* and *Mr. Darcy Broke My Heart*. Her latest book, *The Dashwood Sisters Tell All* (Guideposts, Spring 2011), continues the popular series featuring The Formidables, a secret society that guards a treasure trove of "lost" Austen-related writings. Beth won the RITA award from the Romance Writers of America for her novel *Heavens to Betsy*. She is also the author of the popular Sweetgum Knit Lit Society series from WaterBrook Press. Beth lives with her husband and teenage children in Nashville, Tennessee. She enjoys travel (especially to England), reading, and hiking.

www.bethpattillo.com
@bethpattillo on Twitter

HEARD OF YOU

Margaret C. Sullivan

A steady spring rain pattered against the drawing-room windows as Sophy poured the tea. Admiral Croft passed Anne a cup with his usual courtly manners—"Tea for the bride"—and settled back with his own cup. "This is right; all of us snug by the fire here at Kellynch. This is how it should be."

Sophy looked at Anne, as if to say: what must she be feeling, a guest in her father's house? But Anne was a dutiful daughter, and would not admit to Sophy—nor even to Frederick—the intense happiness she felt at the warm welcome they had received at Kellynch; so much warmer than she could have expected from her father and sister. Kellynch was home again.

The admiral continued, his eyes on the dancing fire, "It is about time you brought home a nice little wife to Kellynch, Frederick. I wonder why you were so long about it. Miss Anne was there, waiting for you the entire time."

Captain Wentworth covered his discomfort with a sip of tea, but he could not help directing a guilty glance at Anne, who was very much inclined to laugh.

"After all," said the admiral, "you never have been behind-hand at making matches for others."

"What is this?" cried Anne. "Are you a matchmaker, Frederick?"

"Indeed not," said her husband.

"Indeed he is," said his sister, "and you know it very well." She turned to Anne. "It was Frederick who brought Admiral Croft and me together. Did you not know that?"

"No," said Anne, "and I should very much like to hear all about it."

"If I had anything to do with it," said Wentworth, "it was accidental."

"Now I *must* beg you to tell me," said Anne.

The admiral slapped his leg joyfully. "Yes, yes! This is just the kind of night for sea-stories. But this is Frederick's story, so I will let him tell it."

Wentworth might have protested further, but looked at his wife's expectant face and knew he was defeated. "It started when I was a midshipman on the *Viper.*"

April 1799
His Majesty's Sloop *Viper*
At Sea

Harville came into the midshipmen's mess clutching a handful of letters. "Mail," he said, dropping it on the table.

The mids fell voraciously upon the scattered bundles; when the table had been picked clean, Wentworth was the proud possessor of two letters, one from his uncle and one from his sister. None of the other mids had more than one letter, and several had none; and as Wentworth had only been aboard the *Viper* a little more than a month, they were inclined to grumble over it.

Wentworth ignored them and opened the letter from his uncle, who recommended in a strong, slanting hand that Frederick keep his stockings dry and his person clean, obey his captain, attend Sunday services whenever possible, and pay close attention to his studies. All but the last was unnecessary advice, but he still felt a warm rush of affection for his uncle, his guardian since his father had died the previous year. Dr. Wentworth also sent a guinea under the seal, which was appreciated more than the advice.

He opened the letter from Sophy. She knew better than to send advice to a fifteen-year-old midshipman, and instead filled her letter with gossip and amusing stories about the students and the other teachers at the school. Wentworth smiled as he read it, which attracted the attention of Bailey.

Bailey had not lessened the dignity of his position as senior officer of the mess by joining in the frenzy over the letters. There was no point in doing so, as he had no wife, no family, and no friends, and therefore no correspondents. "What have you there, Wentworth?" he asked.

Wentworth was not inclined to share Sophy's letter with Bailey, so he said, "Letter from my uncle."

"Full of good advice, no doubt." He sucked on his pipe and emitted a cloud of malodorous smoke. "Give you tuppence for it."

"Threepence," said another mid. Wentworth being new to the *Viper,* his uncle's advice would also be new, and therefore worth more. Some spirited bidding followed, which Bailey carried with a bid of one shilling. Wentworth handed over the letter, thinking that if the condition of Bailey's shirt were evidence, it was likely that the advice about personal hygiene, at least, would fall upon fallow ground.

"What else have you got?" said Bailey. "Who's the other from? Your sweetheart?" He leered at Wentworth, and the other mids leaned forward with interest.

"It is from my sister," he said.

There were groans of disappointment.

"Oh, your *sister,*" said Harville. "Never mind. I've enough sisters of my own to write to me."

Bailey was still interested. "Is she pretty?" he asked.

Wentworth thought about Sophy, about her bright eyes and curling brown hair and merry laugh. He was not accustomed to thinking of his sister as pretty, so he repeated what his uncle had said of her. "She is handsome enough."

"Hold," said Bailey, "is she the trim little piece who brought you to the dock in Portsmouth and waved her hanky as you were rowed out? I'll give you sixpence for the letter."

This occasioned surprised murmurs among the midshipmen, as letters from sisters were generally not considered worth more than a penny. Bailey was a noted connoisseur; Wentworth's sister must be pretty indeed.

"I doubt you have so much money," said Wentworth, "since you have boasted that you spent your entire leave in Portsmouth drinking wine and keeping company with doxies."

The mess erupted in a chorus of "Ooohs" and laughter, quickly choked off.

Bailey said, "Keep your letter, then," and Wentworth knew he would avenge himself in some sneaking way: a foot placed to trip him on the quarterdeck, his hammock strings cut, his shirts slashed. That was the sort of petty retribution exacted by a man like Bailey. Wentworth tucked Sophy's letter into his pocket and thought the punishment well worth it; and looking around at the admiring glances of his messmates, realized they thought it, too.

Wentworth sighted the horizon through the eyepiece of his sextant. The midshipmen of the *Viper* were taking the noon angle of the sun as practice for calculating latitude. After five years at sea,

Wentworth could take a sextant reading without thinking very much about it. Bailey, with a decade more experience, needed the practice, but instead he whispered a steady stream of abuse at the other mids.

Bailey was still angry with Wentworth for refusing to sell him Sophy's letter, and had broken into Wentworth's sea-chest and tumbled the contents looking for it. He no longer wished to read the letter, but like a small child thwarted in his desire for a toy, wanted it because it had been denied him; and he wanted to get it by cunning, so that he could taunt Wentworth with it. Wentworth kept the letter carefully in his coat pocket, and even tucked it into his shirt while he was sleeping. Bailey was universally disliked among the midshipmen, and they were inclined to help Wentworth keep his property. The more Bailey was thwarted, the more abusive he became.

"You know I will get that letter," he said now. "And when I do, I will make you all pay, by God. See if I don't."

Wentworth noted down the angle of the sun in his logbook. Bailey, irritated at being ignored, snatched at the logbook, Wentworth fought to keep it, and a struggle ensued.

"What are you about there?" cried the first lieutenant, Mr. O'Brien. "Belay that, or I will have you both at the mast-head; yes, you, too, Mr. Bailey. If you cannot behave as gentlemen on the quarterdeck, perhaps you can aloft."

Bailey would not release the logbook, and Wentworth was not about to give it up; the struggle continued, and Lieutenant O'Brien crossed the deck and said, "Give that to me."

There was no choice now, and they surrendered it. Mr. O'Brien opened the book and saw "M'man F. Wentworth, R.N." written neatly on the first leaf. "Mr. Bailey, as you are so eager to acquire what belongs to Mr. Wentworth, you may stand his watch tonight. If I see or hear of you trying to take another officer's property, there will be further consequences."

"Yes, sir," said Bailey, sending a murderous look at Wentworth as soon as the lieutenant's back was turned. Wentworth tucked his logbook back in his pocket and bent to pick up his pencil, which had been dropped in the struggle. He straightened up and touched the brim of his hat when he saw Captain Croft walking towards him.

The captain touched his own brim and nodded in response. "Good morning, Mr. Wentworth."

"Good morning, Captain," Wentworth murmured.

"A fine day for sailing, is not it? And if we are lucky, the French will stop skulking about and come out boldly to meet us, and then we shall have a fine battle."

Some of the other midshipmen, overhearing, joined in Wentworth's reply of "Aye aye, sir!" The *Viper* was part of the blockade of Brest; a week before, the admiral, Lord Bridport, had spread out the fleet off the coast of Ushant, having received intelligence that French troopships were trying to break through the blockade and invade Ireland. The *Viper* ranged back and forth along the blockade, ferrying men and information among the fleet, but the promised Frenchmen had not appeared.

Captain Croft beamed at their enthusiasm. "Ha, yes! That is right, gentlemen! That is what I like to hear. We will get our chance. In the meantime, be attentive to your duty. Remember your friends back home, for whom we fight. I hope you are writing to them regularly, and telling them of your adventures."

"Mr. Wentworth writes to his sister, Captain," said Bailey. "He gets letters from her all the time."

"Your sister!" cried the captain, turning a kindly gaze upon Wentworth. "That is right; that is well. We men come to sea to protect England, and the ladies keep our homes warm for us until we return. I am glad to hear that you are attentive to your sister, Mr. Wentworth."

"Any man would be attentive to Mr. Wentworth's sister, Captain," said Bailey. "A trim little ketch, sir; prominent in the bow, if you follow me," the last accompanied by a suggestive hand motion.

Captain Croft turned a look upon Bailey as if he were observing a curious animal in a zoo. "Mr. Bailey, I do not like to hear ladies spoken of disrespectfully, particularly a lady belonging to a brother officer. I hope I will hear no talk of that sort from you in future."

Bailey knew he had gone too far; there was nothing for him to do but touch the brim of his hat and murmur, "Yes, sir; I apologize, sir."

The captain nodded. "Very well, very well. Carry on, young gentlemen, carry on," and he walked to the wheel to consult with the sailing master.

HM Sloop *Viper*
At sea

My dearest Sophy,

I have written to my uncle, and thanked him for his kindness, and for the guinea. I write that first so that you will approve of me right off.

We continue on blockade duty, which is very much the same thing day in and day out. The captain talks of battle, but it is unlikely that a sloop will have much of a part; but we have been engaged in daily gun and sail drill, and if the French try to break the blockade, the *Viper* will not be caught napping.

You have asked about the captain. I like him very much. He is an old-fashioned kind of officer. By that I do not mean that he is behindhand in his knowledge. He is a good officer, kind and fair. His manners are old-fashioned; I suspect not the kind of manners that would be admired in high society, the kind of manners that I often have noticed hide an unpleasant nature; but he is a true gentleman, and I think, if he were a post-captain and had a frigate or a ship of the line, would distinguish himself in battle; and I do not think he would behave differently if he became as famous as Nelson.

Harville and I, along with Lieutenant O'Brien, have been invited to dine with the captain tonight. He has been inviting all the officers in turn, and has yet to invite Bailey. It is yet another excuse for Bailey to tease me, but I hear the captain keeps a fine table; so if Bailey teases me, I can tease him back with chicken pie and ham. I dare say there will be no ragouts or French kickshaws at Captain Croft's table, but one *does* tire of boiled beef and burgoo, and I dare say there will be good wine. Better than that sickly stuff Bailey obliged the mess to lay in before we sailed. My uncle says it is all very well to buy inexpensive wine, but one should never buy *cheap* wine, and he is right, as usual. I would rather drink bilge-water than Bailey's stuff. I hope to see you soon, and believe me,

> Yours affectionately,
> F. Wentworth

> *Miss Wentworth*
> *Miss Burns' Select Seminary for Young Ladies*
> *Portsmouth*

. . .

The captain welcomed Wentworth and Harville to his cabin with his usual courtly manners. Seeing that the midshipmen were nervous and inclined to remain standing, he invited them to sit down in the kindest way, and his steward—no superior *valet,* but a sailor dressed in clean slops, a gold earring in one ear and a thick queue hanging down his back, an indication of long service—brought in the steaming dishes of food.

The midshipmen sniffed at the savory scents rising from the covered dishes, and Harville's stomach rumbled audibly. The captain's eyes twinkled. "I asked Brown to make a special dish for you young gentlemen tonight; a dish I remember was very popular in the midshipmen's mess when I was a younker. Did you make the millers, Brown?"

The midshipmen exchanged a look; Wentworth could see the horror in Harville's eyes that no doubt reflected his own.

"Aye, Captain," said Brown cheerfully. "Found some good fat ones feasting in the bread-room, and caught and dressed them in a trice. Nothing like a miller fattened on ship's biscuit, I always say."

Wentworth was no stranger to the occasional roasted miller, which is what the sailors called rats; midshipmen long at sea often resorted to catching rats and cooking them, sometimes their only chance at something like fresh meat on a long voyage; but it was not what one expected to get at the captain's table.

"You roasted them?" the captain asked Brown.

"Aye, sir, with taters and onions. They'll have cooked up tender and juicy, no doubt. I made a nice thick gravy, too, Captain, that you can pour over your taters."

Lieutenant O'Brien hid his face behind his hand.

"Oh, that's excellent, excellent." The captain beamed at them, rubbing his hands together. "Nothing like a good fat roasted miller. I hope you put in plenty of herbs, Brown."

"Aye, Captain. They bring out the flavor, so to speak."

The captain regarded the midshipmen's pained expressions, exchanged a look with his steward brimful of mirth, and burst into laughter, joined by Brown and O'Brien. "Oh, gentlemen, if you could see your faces! Have no fear, there are no rats on the menu. We can give you a better dinner than that." And indeed he did: roast chicken and ham, and potatoes roasted with turnips and carrots, and even fresh rolls baked earlier in the day. Harville and Wentworth partook like the growing boys they were, encouraged by the captain and his steward, who refilled their plates as soon as they could empty them.

At last they were replete, and the captain passed round the port. Wentworth, as junior officer, made the toast to the King.

The captain lifted his glass. "To friends at home." They all echoed the toast and drank. "Speaking of friends at home," he said, "I hope Miss Wentworth is in health?"

"Yes, sir, thank you, sir. I had a letter from her in the last mailbag, and had the pleasure of hearing her well."

"Very good. Is she an unmarried lady?"

"Yes, sir. She teaches at a school in Portsmouth."

"A teacher, eh?" The captain sipped his port. "Have you no other friends with whom Miss Wentworth might find a home? Your uncle, perhaps?"

"No, sir; my uncle is a fellow at St. John's College, and my brother is up at Oxford as well. He is to take orders, sir. After my father died, Sophy lived with our cousin for a while, but they did not get on. Sophy does not like to be idle, so teaching suits her, sir."

"Of course. That speaks well for her." Wentworth did not feel that the captain's questions were impertinent; he was pleased by the attention, and it occurred to him that it was a good thing for an officer to know about his underlings' situations and obligations. The captain then turned his gentle inquiries upon Harville, and within a few moments knew all about his family, the farm his parents and older brothers tended, and the sisters who plagued him. "My sisters are not pretty like Mr. Wentworth's, Captain."

"Indeed? Miss Wentworth is a pretty girl, then?"

"I have not seen her, sir, but Mr. Bailey saw her in Portsmouth and said she is monstrous pretty."

"I hope, gentlemen," said the captain, addressing Wentworth and Harville, "that you will not model your behavior on that of those officers who are not as they should be; if I may speak plainly, between us, you should not model yourselves upon Mr. Bailey." The captain's tone was familiar; he was speaking to them as a father. "There is a reason that Mr. Bailey is thirty and still a midshipman. No captain will have him as a lieutenant, he has no interest to get on, and he has failed to take advantage of opportunities presented to him. You must always be ready to take advantage of opportunities, boys. That is how you get ahead in the Navy. Is that not so, Mr. O'Brien?"

"Aye aye, Captain."

"Very good. You've finished your port? Then go see how the wind is."

The midshipmen, knowing this to be a dismissal, made their way to their hammocks. As they undressed, Harville whispered, "The captain is a ripping 'un, ain't he?"

"Yes," said Wentworth. "He is."

HM Sloop *Viper*
Spithead

My dear Sophy,

We were ordered to Spithead with dispatches. You must not be alarmed at any rumors you hear about the *Viper*'s condition. Well, they are not really rumors as she's taken a blow, and we came in under jury-rig. We saw some action, though, and have taken a barque as prize, and there's a French frigate that won't soon forget the *Viper*'s strike.

I am writing to tell you that while the captain was at the port admiral's, he heard that there was to be a ball to-morrow. He asked me to write to you and say that you, and the other teachers, and any of the young ladies old enough for dancing, are invited. All the officers are to go, and the captain says we need plenty of pretty ladies to dance with.

If you can contrive to come to the sally port around four o'clock, I will have myself rowed in. I will look for you there, and know that if you are not there you could not leave your duties.

In haste, F.W.

> Miss Wentworth
> *Miss Burns' Select Seminary for Young Ladies*

"Freddy!" Sophy stood at the sally port, waving her handkerchief over her head. "Freddy! Over here!"

Wentworth raised a hand to acknowledge her. He could not help smiling. Sophy looked so fresh and young and, yes, pretty—he could see it now. As soon as the boat scraped against the bulkhead, he raced up the ladder and ran to meet his sister.

She embraced him for a very long moment. "How you have grown! I must look up to you now!"

"You have looked up to me for a year, Sophy." He kissed her cheek. "I am very glad to see you. I have much to tell you, but I cannot stay long."

"I am just glad you could get away." She looked him over.

"You are outgrowing that coat. If you can give it to me, I'll let down the sleeves."

"This is my old work coat. I do not care what it looks like."

"I care. I would not want anyone saying I do not look after you." She took the arm he offered, and they made their way to the ramparts, where they walked and looked out into the busy harbor, and he told her about the battle.

"The Admiralty now thinks the French sloop that was intercepted with the news of the Irish invasion was a spy sent to give false information. The French ships came out from Brest, but they turned south instead of towards Ireland, and they made it to the Med."

Sophy gasped. "Oh, no!"

"I hope the Frenchies like the Med, for they won't get out of there soon, now that we know their tricks. Bridport ordered us to Spithead with dispatches, and on the way we fell in with a French frigate escorting the barque, trying to sneak through the blockade. We took the prize and gave the frigate a tickling, to be sure, before he made a run in to Brest."

"But you were carrying dispatches, and it was a bigger ship. Should you not have run away?"

"Well—yes, but then the frigate would have got through the blockade and done who knows what mischief. No, it is better this way."

Sophy looked up at her brother solemnly. "I thought being on a sloop, I did not have to worry about you."

He smiled at her. "You do not have to worry about me, Sophy. You know I have always been lucky. Look at the prize money I shall have! I'll buy you a new gown."

"You'll do nothing of the sort; I can very well afford to buy my own gowns. You'll put your prize money in the Funds, if you please. I hope," she said, looking away from him and out to the harbor, "that the captain will not have trouble as a result of this action. I hope the Admiralty will not think he should have kept the dispatches safe, and not gone after the prize."

"Oh, Sophy," cried Wentworth, turning to her, "you should have seen him! He is so much the gentleman, you know, as I told you, but in battle so many captains start swearing and shouting, just in the moment, but he was just the same! Cool as you please, I declare—it was, 'Mr. O'Brien, if you please,' and 'Mr. Wentworth, I would be greatly obliged if,' as though he were asking us to pass his hat. And he never hesitated; as soon as they were sighted, we went after them." He stopped and said in admiring tones, "He is a ripping 'un, Sophy, I tell you."

She smiled and said, "I hope you will present your captain to me; perhaps at the ball?"

"Will you come to the ball, then?"

"Oh, yes; the ladies of Miss Burns' Select Seminary know our duty to our fighting men, and will present ourselves, beribboned and perfumed, for your dancing pleasure."

Wentworth hesitated. "I should probably tell you—Bailey saw you when I embarked, and he has told everyone that you are the prettiest girl in Portsmouth."

Sophy laughed heartily. "I hope you disabused them of that notion!"

"It was not possible," he said. "And now the officers are all wild to dance with you."

"Well, they may," she said, "but just be sure that you present your captain to me. For *my* part, I am wild to meet *him*."

The assembly room was agreeably crowded, and the *Viper*'s officers, despite the captain's apprehensions, were pleased to see there were plenty of pretty young ladies to go round. Wentworth stood on tiptoe, trying to find his sister in the crowd.

He did not know that Captain Croft was at his elbow, and was startled when he spoke. "I hope," he said, "that you will present me to Miss Wentworth."

"Yes, sir. She particularly asked to meet you."

"She did?" He looked surprised, yet pleased.

At that moment, Wentworth heard his sister's voice calling him. He turned to see her, smiling and pretty, in a new gown that seemed to his brotherly eyes cut shockingly low in the neckline. Her hair was swept up into a profusion of curls with white beads woven through them. She looked lovely and sophisticated, and he felt like a scrub in his ill-fitting dress uniform. Nonetheless, he took her hand and kissed it with what he thought was great gallantry.

She smiled and squeezed his hand. "Dear Freddy! I am glad to see you."

"And I you. May I present Captain Croft to you?"

Did she blush? Sophy *never* blushed! "Yes, of course." She lifted a hand to her hair, and then snatched it down and held it behind her back.

Wentworth brought the captain forward and put on his best formal manners. "Miss Wentworth, please allow me to present Captain Croft of His Majesty's sloop of war *Viper* to your notice. Captain, my sister, Miss Wentworth." Thinking he had carried it off rather well, he stepped back, and only then noticed that the captain had taken his sister's hand, and that they were looking into one another's eyes, their expressions all wonder and delight.

"Miss Wentworth," said the captain.

"Yes," replied Sophy breathlessly.

"Yes," said the captain, nodding and smiling broadly. "Of course you are. You could not be anyone else."

Wentworth stood by awkwardly, waiting for them to remember him. At last the captain said, "Mr. Wentworth, you will oblige me greatly if you go and dance. Spread yourself around, and dance with all the young ladies you can; it is an officer's duty."

"Aye aye, Captain." He hesitated. "Sophy, are you going to stay here?"

"Yes," she said, her eyes never moving from the captain. "I will stay here."

"I shall look after her," said the captain.

"Yes, Freddy," said Sophy. "Go and dance."

"Very well." He left them, and looked back once as he walked away. Sophy had taken the captain's arm, and they moved into the crowd, still smiling and looking at one another.

The ball was considered a particularly successful one, though several of the officers of the *Viper* were inclined to grumble that Wentworth's pretty sister was rather high in the instep, as she refused to dance with any officer under the rank of commander; though truly, she danced with no other officer than Captain Croft. When Miss Wentworth and Captain Croft were not dancing—and drawing every eye to themselves as a handsome, happy couple—they were sitting out together, taking a turn about the room together; always together.

Wentworth danced with many pretty young ladies, who did not seem at all put off by his outgrown number-one uniform. Harville had similar success, and they annoyed their messmates by talking excessively about how they had enjoyed the ball.

Two days after the ball, the captain went ashore to see the port admiral. An hour later, the boat came back to the sloop without the captain, and the boatswain conveyed the captain's compliments to Mr. Wentworth, and requested that he join him at the sally port.

Mystified, Wentworth obeyed immediately, and found the captain pacing on the pavement. "Mr. Wentworth," he said, seizing Wentworth's sleeve. "I must see your sister right away. If you would be so kind as to take me to her, I would consider myself greatly obliged."

"Of course, sir."

At the school, they rang the bell and asked for Miss Wentworth; they were shown to a small parlor, and soon Sophy joined them, looking anxiously from one to the other. "What is it?" she said. "Has something happened?"

"No, nothing is wrong, my dear," said the captain softly. "Mr. Wentworth," he added, "you will oblige me by waiting outside. I must see your sister on a private matter."

Wentworth looked his surprise. "Have I done something wrong, sir?" he cried. "I hope you will not send me away like one of the boys."

The captain smiled and said, "No, Mr. Wentworth. It is nothing about you."

Wentworth looked at Sophy, who was blushing fiercely. She said gently, "Just go outside, Freddy. I do not think we will be long." She exchanged a smile with the captain.

"No," he said. "Not long at all."

There was nothing else to do; Wentworth went outside to wait. As the door closed behind him, he overheard Captain Croft saying, "Sophy, lass, I just heard—I've got my step!"

They kept their word; he had only to wait five minutes, and the door opened. "Come in, Freddy," said Sophy. "We have something to tell you; but you must have guessed."

"Indeed, I have not," he said.

Captain Croft put out his hand. "Frederick, I have asked your sister to be my wife, and she has accepted. I hope you will welcome me to the family."

Wentworth stared from one to the other in astonishment; then he let out a whoop and shook the captain's hand energetically. "Yes! This is good news indeed! But how—when—"

Sophy and the captain looked at one another and laughed. "You must take the credit for making this match, Freddy. You told us all about each other," said Sophy.

"And then we were just waiting," said the captain. "Waiting to meet. Once we met—we knew."

"Yes," said Sophy. "We knew right away."

Wentworth waited politely, but when nothing else was forthcoming, he made them laugh by asking, "What did you know?"

As Wentworth had overheard, Captain Croft had got his step; had been promoted to post-captain. No longer merely a commander given the title "Captain" as a courtesy, his career was assured; from now on promotion would come from strict seniority, and had nothing to do with interest. He would have to leave the *Viper,* of course, and get a rated ship to command, and all the officers, except Bailey, were disappointed. Though he had lost a captain, however, Wentworth had gained a brother, and he was well pleased.

Captain Croft had asked Sophy to marry him on the strength of his promotion, though he did not yet have a ship. They did not see this as a difficulty. Captain Croft had saved a little money, and Sophy had saved a little money, and on his half-pay they would contrive; and he knew he would soon have a ship. There were no families to consult, and nothing to wait for. Captain Croft heard there might be a command soon available in the North Sea fleet, and he engaged lodgings in North Yarmouth, to which they would go immediately after the wedding breakfast.

The captain asked Wentworth to be his groomsman, an unexpected honor. Sophy had one of the teachers as her bridesmaid; a no-longer-young woman with a squint who simpered at Wentworth over her nosegay. The ceremony was over quickly, and they all signed the register and went to breakfast at the George.

After breakfast, Captain Croft said to Wentworth, "I have done what I can for you. I haven't much interest myself, you understand; but as their lordships of the Admiralty are at present kindly disposed towards me, I convinced them that you and your crony Harville have learnt all you can be taught on *Viper,* and you're to go into a frigate."

"A frigate!" He was eager to get back to the *Viper* and tell Harville. "Thank you, sir! Thank you!"

Sophy said what they were all thinking. "You will have a chance for more prize money now, Freddy. You must take care to save it, and not spend it frivolously."

"I will." He was determined to do so.

The happy couple's post-chaise was announced, and Wentworth went outside to see them off. Sophy kissed him and embraced him for a very long moment. "Remember to order some new uniforms before you go on your frigate," she said.

"Yes, Mrs. Croft." She started at the use of her married name, and then laughed.

The captain smiled at her fondly. "Someday, Frederick, you will meet a young lady and you will know that she is the one for you. When you meet her, I advise you to marry her as soon as you can. You have only yourself to please; and so I advise you."

"Yes, sir." Captain Croft had always given him good advice, so Wentworth mentally filed this useful item away for the future.

The captain handed Sophy up into the chaise, and then followed her, and they drove away, waving goodbye. Wentworth momentarily forgot he was a Royal Navy officer, and he ran after them hallooing and waving his hat in the air until he could keep up no longer.

Anne sat with her chin on her hand, her dark eyes shining. "And did you take your brother's fine advice, Captain Wentworth?"

He reached for her hand and squeezed it. "Indeed I did; eight years and a half passed between the start and the finish, but I carried it off at last." He had been dreadfully angry, and Anne wretched, when she had broken off their engagement all those years before, but now they could laugh about it. They exchanged smiles full of love and remembrance; remembrance no longer bitter, but sweetened by their present happiness.

The Crofts looked at them, the admiral's brow furrowed with confusion, and Sophy's eyes bright with dawning comprehension. "I think," she said, "there is another story to be told."

Wentworth looked at Anne, who nodded. "Tell them, Frederick," she said.

He accepted a fresh cup of tea, and said, "In the summer of the year six, you will remember, after Santo Domingo, I was promoted to commander and, not having a ship, put on the beach. . . ."

MARGARET C. SULLIVAN is the editrix of AustenBlog.com, a compendium of news and commentary about Jane Austen and her work in popular culture. She is the author of *The Jane Austen Handbook* and *There Must Be Murder.* Her favorite Jane Austen novel is *Persuasion,* which led her to a continuing enthusiasm for Age of Sail fiction.

tilneysandtrapdoors.com
@mcsullivan on Twitter

THE GHOSTWRITER

Elizabeth Aston

Darling Sara

This is to say goodbye. I've finally realized I can't ever live up to your expectations as a lover, and certainly not as a future husband. Keep the engagement ring, and this present, which I bought for your birthday. Had it been possible for me to find a lock of Mr. Darcy's hair for you, then I would have travelled the earth to find it.

I'm sorry that my love wasn't and could never be enough for you.

From my heart,
Charles

Sara stood in the hallway, the note in her hand, the front door still open behind her. She read it again, then turned it over, as though when she looked at the familiar handwriting once more, the words would have transformed into a love letter or an affectionate note.

He'd been here. The note hadn't come in the post; the envelope had been left on the table in the hall. Feeling as though she'd been punched in the stomach, she hurtled into the sitting room. Empty spaces on the walls, where pictures and photos had hung. No books lying around, no papers on his desk, no sign he had ever been there.

She shut her eyes, willing herself to turn the handle of the bedroom door. With a gulp and a violent twist of the handle, she did so and, leaning against the side of the door for support, opened her eyes.

Gone were the shirts, the jeans, the underwear, the dark suits. No shoes, no sports clothes, no squash racquet. Two steps took her into the bathroom. No toothbrush, no shaving things, no aftershave, no shampoo.

No Charles.

She went back into the bedroom and sank down on the huge double bed. Desperate thoughts raced through her head—had he met someone else? In what way was his love for her not enough? She searched the bedroom, looking for something of his, a dressing gown, a jacket, something she could bury her face in and remember the feeling and the sense of him. And then as the shock and numb bewilderment began to fade, they were replaced by anger.

She went back into the other room and felt in her bag for her cell phone. She'd call Fiona.

"He'll be back," Fiona said. "It's just a gesture."

"A gesture? When he's taken all his things?"

"Where were you today? It must have taken him awhile to pack and move out."

"I was in the Cotswolds, doing research for my new book."

"Must go," Fiona said. "I'm sure he'll be back or will get in touch. Why don't you ring him?" Click and the line went dead.

Of course, she could ring him.

No, she couldn't. His line had the buzz of a disconnected number. Email, then, and she dived into her study. She worked at home; Charles, a well-paid lawyer, didn't, so she had the study. It was a tiny room, with shelves filled with Jane Austen novels and DVDs and every empty space festooned with pictures and photos from every film or programme ever made of *Pride and Prejudice*.

She checked her email. Nothing from Charles, no one-line message, "Can you collect my dry cleaning," or "Love you to bits, see you later."

Nothing from Charles, but there was an email from her agent. "Have had thirteenth rejection of *She Walks in Beauty*. No point in sending it out to anyone else. PsychePress don't want any more books from you as your sales aren't high enough. Your two-book contract with Cocktail Dress at Cavell & Davies has been cancelled; they're dropping the list. This is the third book of yours I've been unable to place. Move on. Pick a new genre—historicals are big right now. Livia."

Sara stared at the screen. Rage was followed by dismay and then by alarm. Not just the natural hurt and despair of a rejection; all writers were familiar with rejections. Midlist was a dangerous place, but she hadn't done too badly and she'd always been able to pay towards the expenses of the flat she shared with Charles. How was she going to pay for that now if Charles had gone? She'd never afford the rent on her own; in fact, never mind the rent, she wouldn't be able to afford to eat if she couldn't sell her books.

She wrote several heartrending emails to Charles only to find they were all bounced back—he'd changed his email addresses.

Later, suffering from an excess of chocolate ice cream and tears, she was about to fall into bed when she remembered that Charles had said he'd left a present for her. She padded into the hallway and found it, wrapped in plain brown paper. On the back was a label saying Sellit & Runn, Auctioneers.

Auctioneers? Maybe a piece of old jewellery, something that he thought would be a fitting memento.

She took the package and went back to bed to open it. Inside was a box, inside the box was a locket, and within the locket, just visible, was a small twist of light brown hair. She stared at it. It wasn't a pretty locket, and certainly not the kind of thing she would ever wear.

Beneath the locket was the auctioneer's receipt. "A locket containing Jane Austen's hair. For provenance see attached." And then the staggering amount that Charles had paid for this parting gift. Five thousand pounds. She fell back against the pillows. A locket of Jane Austen's hair! An extraordinary gift from a man who knew how much she loved Jane Austen's novels.

She laid the locket on the pillow beside her before turning the light out and burying her head in her pillow to cry herself to sleep.

When she woke up, it was broad daylight and a strange woman was sitting at the end of the bed.

Shocked and startled, Sara stared at her. "Who are you? What are you doing in my bedroom?"

"I dare say you couldn't be expected to recognise me from Cassandra's portrait."

Cassandra?

She hadn't spoken out loud, but the figure, which seemed oddly insubstantial, responded, "Yes, Cassandra, my sister."

As a child, Sara had heard voices in her head and obviously, with the shock of Charles's departure, they had returned in the shape of a full-blown hallucination. This was nothing more than a projection from her imagination. She shut her eyes and shook her head and opened them again to find that the woman was still sitting there, looking a little bit more solid and less floaty.

What had the child psychologist said to her parents about her voices? Nothing to worry about, a phase imaginative children often went through, she would grow out of it. Encourage her to have conversations with the voices, then she wouldn't feel threatened or alarmed by them. The voices would disappear as she grew older.

Which they had. Until now.

Okay, she'd try a conversation with the apparition. "You're Jane Austen?"

"Of course I am."

"So why are you here?"

"You summoned me, by means of dwelling on my novels, and then acquiring a lock of my hair."

"If I throw the locket out of the window, you disappear?"

"You can try. I doubt it, not now I'm here. And the locket cost a considerable amount. Would it be wise to throw it out of the window?"

"How long have you been sitting there?"

"Some hours. When I arrived, you were sobbing, then you fell asleep. Time doesn't mean a great deal to me. Why were you crying?"

Sara's lip quivered. "Because Charles has left me."

"Charles? Your husband, or a lover?"

"We were going to be married."

"And he's abandoned you. Are you breeding, is that why he's left?"

"No. We'd planned to have children—"

"Pull yourself together. Your tears have made your complexion blotchy, and your nose is running. Do you often cry? If Charles sees you like that, I'm not surprised he's left you."

Conversations were all very well, but this one was getting out of hand. Sara swung her legs out of bed, darted into the bathroom, and locked the door. She sank down on the laundry basket, head in her hands.

"That won't help you."

The apparition was perched on the edge of the bath. No softness or twinkle in those keen eyes, just a ferocious intelligence. She'd always thought Livia had the sharpest and coldest eyes in town, but she was pure benevolence in comparison with this creature.

"I can't possibly use the bathroom with you here. Please go away."

"Very well," and the apparition vanished.

"For good, I hope," Sara muttered. She emerged cautiously from the bathroom a quarter of an hour later and breathed a sigh of relief. There was no one in the bedroom. Thank goodness. She'd make herself coffee—

No, the apparition hadn't gone. There she was, on the sofa, reading Charles's note.

"That's private correspondence," Sara said.

"Writes a neat hand, this Charles of yours. What is this reference to a lock of Mr. Darcy's hair? Is that my Mr. Darcy, the hero of *Pride and Prejudice*? The man's a fool if he thinks he could obtain a lock of hair of a man who never existed. And why would you want any such thing?"

As a child, Sara had never worried very much about the voices. They were the kind of thing that adults made a fuss about, but to her they were just invisible friends. This apparition was different. And, like a toothache or a buzz in the ear or a floater in the eye, it was going to be very irritating if she couldn't get rid of her.

Various possibilities went through her mind. Alcohol? What would happen if she drank a bottle of wine?

"You'd probably be sick. And I'd prefer it if you didn't keep on calling me an apparition. 'Miss Austen' will do nicely. I may be a ghost, but good manners reach across the centuries."

Sara realised that the ap—all right, Miss Austen—had a more definite outline, a more substantial three-dimensionality, than had been apparent first thing that morning. Coffee was what she needed. A good dose of caffeine might clear this nuisance out of her head.

"And I don't care to be called a nuisance. I'm here to help."

That, Sara didn't believe. Nothing she'd ever heard about hallucinations or ghosts ever suggested that they were there to help. From reading many lurid and scary ghost stories, she knew they usually ended unhappily. Besides, this wasn't a ghost, it was a figment of her imagination.

"You take a deal too much pride in your mind if you believe your imagination is capable of creating me."

Sara concentrated on making coffee, trying to blank everything else out of her mind.

The apparition hovered behind her and said, a trifle wistfully, "It is a sadness to me that I can no longer smell nor taste the delicious aroma and flavour of coffee."

How surprising. She'd never thought of Jane Austen as indulging in stimulants. Prim and proper in her muslins, she might take tea in the morning or perhaps a dish of chocolate. Surely nothing more exciting.

"Rubbish. I much disliked tea, and greatly enjoyed coffee, and wine, too. Your generation has a very strange idea of how things were in my time."

Sara retreated with coffee into the study. If she absorbed herself in her computer, then maybe that would switch her mind off and vanquish Miss Austen.

"Good gracious, what are all these pictures on the wall?"

"Stills and photos from television and film productions of *Pride and Prejudice*. It's my favourite book, I love it, I practically know it by heart. This one is my favourite—this is Colin Firth when he played Mr. Darcy. Mr. Darcy is my idea of a perfect man."

"Which accounts for Charles's remark about Mr. Darcy's hair. It surprises me that people are still reading my novels so long after they were written and I departed this earth, but for a young woman of your age, I suppose of moderate intelligence, to yearn for the hero of a novel seems extraordinary to me. I would have thought you had more sense. Crushes on real people are tiresome enough, and you should have grown out of any such propensity by now. No wonder Charles took himself off. Jealousy of a living man is one thing, but no man can compete with a character who never existed."

Sara turned to her emails. She had forgotten about the grim email from Livia Harkness, and as she read it again, the feeling of panic and despair returned.

Miss Austen was at her shoulder. "Who is Livia? She is hardly polite."

"My literary agent. You didn't have literary agents in your day; they work with authors and sell their books to publishers."

"Or not, in your case. Who pays for the publication? In my day the author did. Do you pay to have your books published?"

"Some people do, but I haven't." Yet, she thought.

"Each age has its own way of doing things. I used to write with a quill pen sitting at a little table, and here you are with a computer."

"How come you know about computers?"

"Do you think I've spent the last two centuries in limbo waiting for you to buy my lock of hair? I like to keep up with the times."

Sara got up and gestured towards the seat. "Why don't you use the computer? Perhaps," she added cunningly, "you would even like to write something. Just press the letters on the keyboard and the words will appear on the screen."

"They won't. It's one of the things we can't do. I can talk to people, but I can't write."

"I bet you can't," Sara said, sotto voce.

"On the other hand," Miss Austen went on, flicking her fingers across the keys, "I can play games. Where's FreeCell?"

Sara watched in astonishment as FreeCell appeared on the screen. The non-existent fingers were moving the cards to and fro with astonishing rapidity.

"I always liked card games like whist and piquet and even solitaire."

Sara tottered back to the kitchen and made herself an even stronger cup of coffee.

Miss Austen came out of the study. "You're very jumpy. I dare say you've had too much coffee. Put on your coat; a brisk walk will do you good."

As though mesmerised, Sara picked up her handbag and opened the door. Miss Austen wafted past her. She seemed to know where she wanted to go, but Sara wanted to go the other way, in the direction of the doctor's surgery.

"You don't need a physician. There's nothing wrong with your mind, except sentimentality and stupidity. Can't you walk any faster than that? In my day there were no cars and we were indefatigable walkers."

"It's different in the country. There's all this traffic and pollution in London."

"I love London. I never spent nearly enough time in town. My brothers were anxious because I liked town life so much; they thought it was unsuitable for a woman in my position. It's odd how men always try to prevent you enjoying yourself if they possibly can."

"Charles doesn't."

"Then Charles is a remarkable man, and you should have kept hold of him."

"Where are we going?"

"In here." Miss Austen floated into the Oxfam shop.

She found the secondhand book section and scanned the shelves, finally pouncing on a dreary little volume on a bottom shelf. She handed it to Sara.

Scouting for Girls?

"Open it."

With a shrug Sara opened it, expecting to find illustrations of knots and advice on knitting and all those other things beloved of the Girl Guide movement.

To her surprise, the pages inside had nothing to do with scouting. Instead, here was thick paper with the slightly brown colour of very old books and the elegant typeface of the eighteenth century. She turned to the title page.

THE ORPHAN'S PROGRESS by Clarissa Curstable.

"It's a novel!"

"Yes, and a good one. Not up to my standard of course, but it caused quite a stir in its day."

Sara had never heard of Clarissa Curstable.

"No one has. Buy it, please."

Sara obediently took the book to the till. Should she say something about it being an old volume, possibly precious? "It's not really a scouting guide for girls," she said to the assistant. "It's an old book with the wrong cover on."

"Is it, dear? I don't think so." The woman opened the book,

and to her astonishment, Sara saw a page full of old-fashioned drawings of knots. "I don't know what gave you that idea. Fifty pence, please."

"Fifty pence," said Miss Austen as they left the shop together. "A modest sum for a book. And a veritable bargain, given that it will save your career and transform your life."

"Transform my life? How?"

"First, you must read it. No doubt you're an accomplished reader, and it won't take you long. Meanwhile, I shall enjoy reading some of the novels you have written."

Not if you're really Miss Austen you won't, Sara thought.

She was right. Back at the flat, Miss Austen galloped through the books she'd plucked from Sara's shelves, emitting snorts of laughter interspersed with occasional yawns.

"You have a certain facility with words, and I think indeed you might turn into a writer of some distinction, with effort and application, but the sentimentality of these is not to my taste." She tapped the cover of *Twin Souls.* "In this volume, for instance, your heroine is a dispiriting creature and your hero is exceedingly disagreeable. Your literary agent is right to suggest a different genre for your pen."

Sara was too absorbed in Clarissa Curstable's remarkable work to argue. It was one of the raciest, most scandalous, salacious, and outrageous novels she'd ever read. It concerned the adventures of an orphaned young woman cast upon the town, who, by dint of selling her charms and a shrewd business head, achieved the distinction of marrying a marquis and ending up the possessor of several handsome properties and an enormous fortune.

It was a conventional enough story of its kind, but the breathlessness and the exciting way the story was told and the luscious lasciviousness of it were almost shocking. Sara reached the last page and put the book down with a sigh. "It's a good read. Why have I never heard of Clarissa Curstable?"

"For the very good reason that her name has been expunged from the annals of literature."

"Why, when she wrote so well, and was a published author?"

"Clarissa was widowed at an early age and left with a daughter to support. She turned to her pen and succeeded, to admiration, writing three-volume novels of the kind now called Gothic literature, in the style of Mrs. Radcliffe. However, although this made her a modest income, it barely sufficed to keep her in anything more than respectable gentility, and was not enough for the great hopes she cherished for a daughter who was both beautiful and amiable.

"By chance, she fell in with a rakish crowd, the Dilettanti, a most disreputable body of men who were up to all kinds of mischief. One of them, a wicked rake, commissioned her, on payment of a large sum of money, to write a very particular story entirely for private circulation among his circle. She did so, and because it was too scandalous for any publisher to touch, she rewrote it in a more modest vein for the general public, which is the version you now possess. Her daughter, launched into society, had the good fortune to attach the affections of a rich nobleman. He was shocked by Clarissa's literary output, and so a condition of the nuptial agreement was that she would lay down her pen and never write another word again under her own name or any other. He then went to great lengths to buy up every copy of her books and had them all burnt in a great bonfire in front of his house in the country."

"What a dreadful thing to happen to a writer."

"Yes, indeed. However, this is not why I've drawn your attention to this volume, I don't wish you to re-establish her place as a minor footnote in English literature. It is simply that, if you have any wits, you can see in the story she has written something you may adapt to your own use."

"What, plagiarize it?"

"No such thing. It's a quid pro quo. Clarissa cannot come back herself, as I have done on several occasions, since when an author's work is no longer read, or even available, the personality of the writer loses any substance and form it may have. She cannot make her presence known to others as I can."

"If I won't do it, what then?"

"You'll regret your decision for the rest of your days."

"If I agree, will you go away?"

"Certainly."

"Promise?"

"I promise."

"And otherwise?"

"No."

A life haunted by the ghost of Jane Austen? Sara gave in.

"Where will you be while I'm doing this?" The thought of working with Miss Austen at her shoulder made her shudder.

"I'll be in and out. I have a few other things to arrange while I'm here."

Why did Charles have to give me that locket? Sara asked herself the next day as she sat at her computer bleary-eyed from copying out the book, rewriting feverishly, modernising, cutting. Why not some other writer, or a scholar who would give anything to be face-to-face with the spirit of Jane Austen?

Sara was a fast worker, but two weeks later, as she printed out a copy of the manuscript, she felt as though she'd run several marathons. But she also had a sense of satisfaction, and an idea that it might be fun to write a book like this herself.

Miss Austen had returned from time to time to check on her

progress, and now, as the last sheet flew off the printer, there she was, smiling the prim little smile that hid a will of iron and an IQ Sara could only guess at.

Ten minutes later, Sara was heading out of the flat. "There's no point in you coming with me," Sara said. "I won't be able to see her; I'll leave the script with her assistant."

"I'm sure Livia Harkness will see you."

Sara was wrong, and Miss Austen was right. At reception, instead of the normal glare from the receptionist, Sara was greeted with a smile.

"I know Livia will want to say hello," the girl said. Then she frowned.

"What's the matter?" Sara asked. She knew what the matter was—the receptionist had mistaken her for one of Livia's more successful clients.

"For a moment I thought there was someone else in here, but you came alone, didn't you?"

"Just me." She went up the stairs and found Livia standing at the door. Another welcoming smile.

"Good morning, Sara. Have you something exciting for me? Did you take my advice?"

"It's something written awhile ago." At least that had the merit of being true. She handed the envelope to Livia, who sat herself down at her vast desk and pulled out the script.

"Clarissa Curstable?"

"It's an entirely different kind of book, so I thought it should be under a new name. A pseudonym."

"I generally choose the pseudonyms for my authors." Livia twirled a pen in her fingers, red nails flashing. "But this has a ring to it. A historical, by any chance?"

"Yes."

"Then the name might do. Leave it with me, I'll get back to you."

These were the most amicable minutes Sara had ever spent with Livia Harkness. She turned at the door to say goodbye, and saw a puzzled expression on Livia's face. Ha, Livia was as surprised by her mellow behaviour as Sara was. She wanted to laugh and wished she could tell Livia that she had fallen under the powerful influence of the ghost of Jane Austen. There was no point, though; Livia thought most writers were mentally deranged and this would just be further proof of it.

Out in the street, she felt a certain lightness of spirit. She was reluctant to go back to the flat, but on the other hand she'd thrown on her clothes without a shower. And she wanted to check whether Jane Austen's ghost had kept her word and taken herself off.

As she turned the key in the door she knew she hadn't.

"I'll wait until your agent confirms the book will be published."

Sara's heart sank. That could take weeks, months even, judging by past experience.

Not in this case. It took Livia twenty-four hours to get back to her. Livia was her normal terse self, but what she had to say would have been very gratifying had Sara felt she had anything to do with a novel Livia had already sent round to half a dozen editors.

By the end of the week, Livia had an auction going and Sara's financial worries were at an end.

Now, surely, Miss Austen would vanish. *"Please, please, go,"* Sara said through gritted teeth.

"All in good time. I'm glad you had the good sense to accept my offer; Clarissa will be obliged to you. While you have been engaged upon your literary endeavours, I've taken the trouble to find out about this Charles of yours. He is a most estimable young man, and you were a fool to drive him away. I've managed to make amends for you, but, before I depart, let me give you some words of advice. Were you ever to meet Mr. Darcy, you would find him a frighteningly complex and difficult man who would in no way suit you, as a lover or a husband."

Miss Austen could say whatever she liked, but Sara knew Mr. Darcy would always be her ideal man.

"You are quite mistaken. I created him; I know exactly what he is."

"Some people think you based him on the character of Tom Lefroy."

"Tom? Oh, he was a handsome fellow and most attractive, and we certainly took one another's fancy. However, we would never have suited; he was too staid for me, and would have disapproved of what I was as time went by. But he was fun and full of sparkle and playfulness. I based my delightful Lizzy Bennet on him."

"What about Mr. Darcy?"

"I myself am Mr. Darcy. Had I been born male instead of female, and in affluent circumstances, I would have been just such a man: reserved, proud, and clever. And no doubt have made some woman's life a misery. Put him out of your head, or at least leave him on the page where he belongs and, as you say today, get a life."

Suddenly she was gone. Completely and utterly. It was as though all the air had been sucked out of the flat, and Sara realised what energy her presence had brought with it. Even so, she didn't regret for a moment that the apparition had vanished and her life had returned to normal.

As normal as it could be without Charles.

At that moment, she heard a key turning in the door. And there he was, a suitcase in each hand and a squash racket under one arm. He put the bags down and held out his arms. "Sara, my love, I'm so sorry. Will you forgive me?"

Later that night, curled up with him in bed, she raised herself on one elbow and lovingly stroked his hair. "Charles, it was so generous of you to buy the locket for me, but it was terribly expensive. Do you know, I'm not interested in Jane Austen any more; I swear I never want to read *Pride and Prejudice* again or watch any of the films. I've cleared out all the photos and things from my study, and I'm turning over a new leaf. So, don't you think it would be a good idea to send the locket back to the auctioneers? Since we're planning to get married later this year, I'm sure we can do with the money."

He looked down at her, astonished. "No more Jane Austen? Are you sure? Of course, sweetheart, if that's what you want. I'll take it round to the auctioneers tomorrow."

The next morning, Charles woke up with a shout of alarm and sat up, pulling the covers up to hide his nakedness. "Sara, there's a strange woman on the end of the bed."

Oh, no, what about that promise? Sara rubbed her eyes and sat up.

It wasn't Miss Austen sitting there. This was a different woman, slightly vague in outline, as Miss Austen had been when she first arrived. A taller, more angular woman, with a humorous mouth and a firm nose.

"Good morning," she said. "You must be Sara and Charles. I am Clarissa Curstable."

ELIZABETH ASTON is a passionate Jane Austen fan who studied with Austen biographer Lord David Cecil at Oxford. The author of several novels, including *Mr. Darcy's Daughters* and *Writing Jane Austen,* she lives in Malta and Italy.

www.elizabeth-aston.com

MR. BENNET MEETS HIS MATCH

Amanda Grange

Happy for all her maternal feelings was the day on which Mrs. Bennet got rid of her two most deserving daughters. Less happy for Mr. John Bennet was the very same day, for it meant that he must part with Elizabeth and Jane. It seemed not two minutes since he himself had married, but it was in fact twenty-three years since he had first started courting Mrs. Bennet. . . .

He had lived all his life in the country of Hertfordshire, in the village of Longbourn. The village was named after Longbourn House, or so John's mother had always proclaimed, although there were rumours that the house was, in fact, named after the village. It was a fine residence, with paddocks and lawns, shrubberies and walks, a hermitage and a wilderness, and no other house in the neighbourhood could surpass it.

The house was entailed on the male line, passing from father to son in an unbroken line, unless no son was available, when the inheritance would leap over wives and daughters like a capricious frog and pass to the nearest male relative. This admirable arrangement was devised by men, who reasoned sagaciously that women had no need of a roof over their heads as they were protected from the elements by their charming bonnets.

John's mother, however, feeling that Longbourn House was a more desirable roof than a piece of straw, however elegantly contrived, preferred the idea of living out her days in her home to sleeping beneath the hedgerows. She was therefore eager for John to marry and provide the necessary heir as soon as possible.

This fact was known to every female of good family in the surrounding neighbourhood, and John was the object of their attentions from the moment he attained his majority; for who would not want to marry him and live at Longbourn House, becoming the first lady of the neighbourhood?

John took all the attention in good part. Indeed, he was not so unnatural as to object to the smiles of every pretty, and not so pretty, well-born young lady in the area. However, he was unnatural enough to tire of his parents' constant references to the subject. His mother made frequent remarks about the beauty of one young lady or the accomplishments of another, whilst his father called him into the library at least three times a month to talk about his responsibilities.

"It is time for you to take a wife, my son," he said one morning.

"I am too young to be thinking of marriage," said John.

"For many men of your age, that might be the case," said his father. "But you are in a unique position, my boy. On your shoulders rests the future of the family fortunes. Besides, marriage is a fine institution. It gives a man stability."

"I do not feel in need of stability, Papa, and as I am not yet three-and-twenty, there is no hurry, I think," said John.

"There is no hurry, no, but neither must you delay. Only think, you might go out in the carriage this afternoon and it might overturn. You might be taken up, dead."

"Then perhaps I had better ride," John said.

His father saw no humour in his remark. "Unfortunately, riding is even more perilous. Your horse might be startled by a bird and it might bolt, throwing you in the process. There are all sorts of accidents that can befall a man on horseback."

John smiled. "Then I shall go on foot."

"Even that is not without its dangers," said his father. "You could be attacked by footpads or find yourself knocked down by a cart. And even if you manage to escape an accident, then you might be taken ill with typhoid or smallpox or develop a putrid sore throat."

"Indeed, with so many dangers all around, it is a wonder I have managed to survive so far," said John.

"I am sometimes surprised at it myself. However, you have, and we must be thankful for it. We must not take it for granted, though. You must do your duty to your family, your name, and your estate without delay. I think I need not remind you that, if you die without an heir, then Longbourn will pass to Cousin Collins." A look of distaste crossed his face. "Cousin Collins is not the sort of man who belongs at Longbourn. He is a singularly unpleasant person, a man of no education and of mean intellect. He is a man I despise. Indeed, he is the kind of man to turn your mother out of the house the moment he inherits. But you can prevent him inheriting, John, by presenting us with a grandson."

"I assure you, Father, I like Cousin Collins no more than you do, but as I have every intention of staying alive, I am determined not to rush into matrimony," said John. "I will marry in the end, of course, but marriage is at all times a precarious institution, and a hasty marriage is a recipe for disaster. I prefer to look about me and take my time."

"There is no question of a hasty marriage. I am not asking you to marry tomorrow, merely to start courting one of the young ladies in the neighbourhood in the near future," said his father. "Pick a fine, healthy girl from a good family, one who will bear you many children and some good, fine sons. Anne Raistrick, now—"

John gave an involuntary shudder. "No, thank you, Papa, I have no taste for Anne Raistrick."

"I cannot think why. There is nothing to be said against her, and there is a great deal to be said in her favour. She comes from a large family full of boys, you know, and she is likely to have a great many boys herself. I advise you to get to know her. Talk to her at the next assembly; dance with her. I am sure you will find her charming. You would be welcome to invite her to the house at any time. Your mother and I would approve of her as a daughter-in-law."

John tried to hide his impatience. "I am sorry to disappoint you," he said politely, "but Anne Raistrick bores me. She can talk of nothing but her needlework and she looks like a horse."

Mr. Bennet grew irritable; John grew angry; and the interview ended with John being dismissed. He was glad to escape from the study, and he took refuge in his room. The walls were lined with books and there was a book lying open beside the bed. He picked it up and then, enticed by the sunshine, he walked out into the fields, where he could indulge his hobby without interruption.

He wished, for a moment, that there were other young men like him in the neighbourhood; men of intelligence and sense, who liked to read and learn about the world around them. He sometimes felt that he would stagnate in the small country village where all the young men of his own age spent their days riding, hunting, and drinking. Yet for all its limitations he loved Longbourn, because it was his home. He loved the house, with its cool hall and its elegant drawing-room and its airy bedrooms. He loved the gardens with their tall trees and their flower beds. But most of all he loved the library. It was a room his father seldom frequented, going there only to conduct matters of business, but John went there often. The books were, to him, old friends. They took him on journeys and showed him the places he might never see. They allowed him to know the thoughts of scholars and philosophers that he would never meet. And most of all, they offered him a retreat from the demands of his parents.

The one he was carrying was a favourite, and as he walked through the paddock to the fields beyond, he felt his spirits lift. Indeed, the day was one such as to gladden the heart of any living creature. It was March, but unseasonably warm, as happens sometimes in that month, and the world smelt of the newly awakening spring. Birds were singing and the trees were blossoming, putting forth thick pink and white flowers that filled the air with their heady scent. The sun was warm and the droning of bees was everywhere.

He swung himself into the branches of a horse chestnut tree and opened his book.

He had not been reading long when his attention was distracted by the sound of laughter and he saw the two Miss Gardiners walking down the lane that bordered the estate. Miss Gardiner was the beauty of the family, indeed the neighbourhood, for she had soft, fair hair, large blue eyes, and a good-humoured countenance which often broke into smiles and laughter. Her sister, Miss Mary Gardiner, was neither so pretty nor so good humoured, but was nevertheless a handsome girl. The two of them, walking past in their hooped skirts, brightened the lane with their brocade dresses and their large hats and their twirling parasols.

"Let us go into Meryton, Jane, and see Papa," said Mary.

"Oh, yes, we must see Papa," said Jane with a laugh. "It would never do to neglect him."

He watched them until they were out of sight, thinking that if Miss Gardiner had been the daughter of one of the landed gentry round about, instead of the daughter of a Meryton attorney, he might have been tempted to fall in with his father's wishes. But the daughter of an attorney would not be acceptable to his parents as a wife for him. Besides, he knew very little about Miss Gardiner, other than that she was pretty and good humoured, and for all he knew, she would not be acceptable as a wife to him either. So he turned back to his book and occupied himself until the sun went down.

The Miss Gardiners continued on their way. They walked the mile into Meryton, from whence they had set out earlier in the day. They had been tempted out of doors by the spring weather and by a desire to show off their new parasols, even if it was only to the cows and sheep, for they had not noticed John in the tree.

The small town of Meryton was busy with shoppers intent on their business. Some were housewives frequenting the butchers and the bakers, buying food for the family. Some were footmen making purchases for their masters, and some were young ladies, like themselves, who were intent on looking at the latest fashions.

As worn in London, ran the unlikely legend in the milliner's window.

The girls stopped to look at all the hats, praising and criticising them in turn.

"That one is not very pretty but I think I might buy it all the same," said Jane. "If I pull it to pieces when I get home, I might be able to make it up into something better. I think it might suit me if I change the brim."

"And that one is very ugly, but I am determined to have it," said Mary. "If I trim it with some ribbon, it will at least be tolerable."

They already had a house full of hats, but they shared the belief that a young lady could never have too many of them, and their mother was of their opinion. Their father could not see what all the fuss was about, but he liked to indulge them. His business was prosperous and it pleased him to see his family happy.

They went into the shop and made their purchases, and then, with only one brief stop at the general shop, they finally arrived at their father's office.

They had not really called there to see their papa, as Jane well knew, but to see his clerk, Mr. Philips.

Mr. Philips was young and handsome, and Mary was enamoured of him. She took every opportunity of calling on her father with some excuse, so that she could laugh and flirt with his clerk. Jane was happy to indulge her sister, for she liked nothing better than to laugh and flirt with her own beaux, and so she would not deny her sister that happiness.

When the two Miss Gardiners entered the office, Mr. Philips looked up and jumped to his feet. He welcomed them with easy charm, remarking on the fineness of the weather, the versatility of parasols, and the likelihood of rain.

Miss Gardiner wandered into a corner and took an interest in a painting which hung on the wall, leaving her sister to flirt to her heart's content.

At last Mr. Philips was recalled to his duties, and they left him with an invitation to dinner, which they issued in their mother's name. She, good lady, never objected to their inviting young men to the house, and it was understood by all of them that they should ask any eligible gentlemen they should happen to meet, saying that the invitation came from Mrs. Gardiner.

Then they went into the office to see their papa.

He rose from his chair with a beaming smile and opened his arms to them, for he was always pleased to see his girls. They brought laughter and brightness into his life. He made much of them, serving them canary wine and telling them how pretty they looked.

Having drunk their canary wine, the two young ladies then returned home. Their mother saw them walking down the path and jumped up, eager to greet them. She exclaimed over their purchases and agreed with them that the hats were vile but that they could be made presentable.

Their brother Edward was less agreeable and only snorted before going back to the newspaper.

"Is there any news?" asked Mrs. Gardiner.

"Well, we happened to pass Miss Long in the street and she said that George King is going to marry!" said Jane, fluffing her fair curls in front of the looking glass.

"And about time, too," said their mother. "That shop of his is flourishing and a man with a settled income ought to take a wife." She glanced significantly at Mary. "There's another man with a settled income, and prospects, too, who will soon be thinking of taking a wife, if I don't miss my guess."

"If you mean Papa's clerk, why can you not say so?" demanded Edward. "All this hinting is nothing but tomfoolery."

"And why should Mama mean Arthur?" asked Mary, tossing her head.

"Because he has a settled income and prospects, being set to take over Father's business when the time comes, and you have both of you set your sights on him joining the family," said Edward.

"And why should he not have the business?" demanded Mary. "You were offered it, but you refused it."

"He would give it to you now if you changed your mind," said Mrs. Gardiner to her son.

"Thank you, but I have no wish to be an attorney," said Edward. "I would much rather go into trade."

It had caused several family arguments so far, but Edward could be stubborn when he set his mind to something, and Mr. and Mrs. Gardiner had reconciled themselves to the idea.

Besides, it had its bright side, because then Mr. Gardiner could leave the business to Arthur and thereby provide for Mary; Jane being so pretty that neither of her parents thought they would need to provide for her.

The talk turned to the next assembly.

"You will need a new gown," said Mrs. Gardiner to her eldest daughter. "It is high time you were married, Jane, and a new gown will do the trick. You are not so pretty for nothing. Half a dozen young men in the neighbourhood would be glad to take you to wife. There is William Lucas; he is in a good line of trade and looks set to rise in the world. You could do worse."

"Oh, Mama! I cannot marry William Lucas!" said Jane, exploding into laughter.

"I cannot see why not."

"He has nothing to say for himself, and besides, he cannot dance," said Jane.

"Well, to be sure, that is a pity," said her mother, "but, after all, there is more to life than dancing."

But Jane did not think so, and young William Lucas was dismissed.

"Then there is Captain Quentin," said her mother.

"Captain Quentin?" said Jane with more interest. "Mama, is he here again? Oh, do say he is! I love a man in a red coat."

"Well, I hear that he is coming to see his cousins again shortly and that he will be here in time for the assembly."

Jane danced around the room.

"And I must have a new gown, too, Mama," said Mary.

"Oh, very well, I suppose you must, though Arthur Philips would propose to you if you were dressed in a flour sack," said Mrs. Gardiner. "We will go into Meryton tomorrow and choose some fabric, and then we will be busy until the assembly."

The following day brought a letter to Longbourn. It was from Mr. Bennet's distant and despised Cousin Collins, and in it he declared his intention of calling on the family the following week.

Mr. Bennet read the letter out to his wife and son as they took breakfast together.

"... *for my wife and I are going to Cheshire to visit her family, and would like to call upon you on the way,*" Mr. Bennet read. "*We have something to show you.*"

"With his *wife.* You see, he has married already," Mrs. Bennet said, turning to look at John. "Now, there's a man who knows his duty."

"He is five years older than I am," John said.

"That cannot be helped. I cannot now make you older than you are, nor him younger than he is," said his mama. "The fact remains that he is married and you are not."

"I wonder what he wants to show us," said Mr. Bennet.

"The only thing I want him to show us is a clean pair of heels," said Mrs. Bennet.

Talk of the Collinses' visit continued to fill the house for the following five days until Cousin Collins himself made his appearance. He arrived just after four o'clock with his wife, a vulgar creature by the name of Nancy. They had hardly descended from the trap when Nancy's voice could be heard through the window.

"Coo, William, fancy! What a big 'ouse! I never thought it'd be so grand. And it's all going to be ours, ain't it?"

And William's voice saying, "Don't get your hopes up too

high, sugar plum, it won't be ours for a while yet, not until my cousin's dead. But he looked sickly to me the last time I saw him, and I don't suppose he's got any better, living the way he does."

The door knocker announced that they had reached the door, and, as the Collinses were shown in, the Bennets reluctantly greeted their guests.

William Collins was an oily young man with an ingratiating manner. His coat and breeches were too tight and his linen was far from fresh.

His wife was worse. With her rouged cheeks and her loud cries of "Look, William, did you ever? A long case clock. I've always wanted a long case clock," she was enough to try the patience of a more patient woman than Mrs. Bennet.

"Then I must let you have the name of our clockmaker," replied that worthy woman.

William put his head on one side and looked at her roguishly. "Ah, we don't have room for one where we are. Our rooms aren't big enough, just a small apartment, you understand, but perhaps one day . . ." and his eyes drifted round the room as though assessing its worth before coming to rest on the coveted clock.

Luckily, tea was brought in. Hardly had it been poured, though, when the conversation turned to the subject of duty. William Collins, with his ingratiating smile, said that he stood ready to do his.

"You need have no fear," he said to Mr. Bennet. "I stand ready to do my duty at any time. If young John should die, Nancy and me will be here to shoulder the burden of the estate."

"I've never been one to shirk my responsibilities," said Nancy. She went over to her basket, which she had placed at the side of the room on entering, and took out a bundle of blankets. As she returned to her seat, the Bennets saw that it contained a baby.

Cousin Collins confirmed their worst fears when he said,

"This is why we've come here today, me and Nancy. We wanted to show you our son."

"Named William, after his father," said Nancy. "Just think, William," she cooed to the baby, "one day, this could all be yours." Then she turned to Mrs. Bennet and said, "Don't you worry, if anything happens to your husband and John—"

"—Carriages are always overturning these days," put in Cousin Collins, "and men keep dropping dead of diseases—"

"Then we'll be here just as soon as we learn of the sad accident, you'll see. And don't you be afraid we'll turn you out of your home. There's always something useful a woman at your time of life can do, mending tablecloths and suchlike. Me and William'll see you right. And so will little William." She had a sudden thought and said, "You can be his nursemaid."

Mrs. Bennet looked at her in horror. But she was made of stern stuff and she quickly rallied, saying, "John and his father are both hale and hearty, and as for dying in a carriage accident, why, they never travel together. Besides, there will be another heir on the way very shortly. John is determined to do his duty and fill the nursery with sons. In fact, he is courting a charming young lady at the moment, one of our neighbours, a very handsome girl with a large dowry. Oh! She is so good and so agreeable. Very genteel! We regard her as one of the family already."

Who this good and genteel girl was supposed to be, John did not know, but he suspected she was a figment of his mother's imagination, invented to foil the Collinses. Indeed, he rather began to wish that she were real, for the thought of the Collinses in his beloved home made him shiver, and for a moment he thought that, perhaps, his papa was right, he ought to marry as soon as possible. But then he remembered that he was very young and not likely to die, and so he put his efforts into helping his mama by saying that he had always had the highest respect for the married state and that it was one he had every intention of entering promptly.

Nancy continued to talk of the furniture as though it were her own, saying to the baby, "That table'd look a lot better by the window, wouldn't it, William?" or "That vase is an odd thing, ain't it? It'd be better under the stairs," whilst Mrs. Bennet continued to talk of the lovely young woman they all adored.

By the end of the visit, they were exhausted and it was with relief that the Bennets saw the Collinses depart.

"And those are the people you will have living in this house when I am gone," said John's father reproachfully.

"To think of the effrontery of the woman, to say I could do her sewing!" said Mrs. Bennet.

John knew that he would have no peace if he stayed at home and so he said that he was thinking of going to Cambridge to stay with friends for a few weeks.

"It is to be hoped there are some young ladies in Cambridge who will be prepared to put up with your freakish ways," said his mother in an ill humour.

"Do not worry, Mama," said John with a smile. "Perhaps I will come home with a wife."

He did not come home with a wife. He did, however, come home in a more sober frame of mind, for on his way home, a bird flew up in front of his horse and the animal reared and threw him. He escaped with cuts and bruises, but as he caught the reins of his horse again he shuddered to see that he had only narrowly missed hitting his head on the milestone. As he mounted he knew that, if he had fallen three inches to the right, he would have been taken home lifeless. And with his mother and father being unable to have another child at their time of life, the Collinses would have been the future owners of Longbourn.

It was in this mood that he went to the Meryton assembly. As soon as he entered the room, he saw Anne Raistrick and he wondered if she bored him quite so much, after all. Perhaps he had not taken the trouble to get to know her. And so he walked over to her and asked her to dance.

She accepted with alacrity and he led her out onto the floor.

"How boring these country assemblies are," she said. "How insipid! These people have nothing to say."

John, who was standing next to Miss Gardiner and her partner, a smart young man in regimentals, thought that Miss Gardiner, at least, had plenty to say.

"Look at them! Is there anything more depressing than provincials? The shopkeepers and attorneys and bankers, all dressed in their ill-fitting clothes, and dancing without grace or fashion. Mama has promised to take me to London for the season. Will you be going?" asked Miss Raistrick.

"No," said he shortly, being out of humour.

"A pity," she said.

She danced with a great deal of energy, stepping on his feet no less than seven times. She went the wrong way twice in the dance, and only the lively eyes of Miss Jane Gardiner, which sparkled with mischief when Miss Raistrick bumped into her, made it tolerable.

He was glad when the dance was over and he could lead Miss Raistrick back to her mama. As he did so, his eyes drifted to the other side of the room, where the Miss Gardiners were chatting away merrily to a large group of young men. To be sure, the conversation was about dancing and clothes and charades and lottery tickets, but it was lively and good humoured, and their high spirits were infectious. He could not help himself, he went over to Miss Gardiner and asked her to dance.

She looked surprised, but then gladly accepted his hand and they went onto the floor. He briefly noticed the faces of his parents, who looked as if to say, Why is he wasting his time with Miss Gardiner when Miss Raistrick is sitting down? But he took no notice.

"I am surprised you asked me," said Miss Gardiner. "I thought your feet would be too battered and bruised for another dance."

He smiled and took her to their place in the set, where she curtseyed to him without falling over, as Miss Raistrick had almost done. Her dancing, too, was good. She had none of the formal elegance of most of his other partners, but she had more ebullience, and more natural enjoyment.

Listening to her was a pleasure, for her lively nature made her a good companion. Indeed, even the most commonplace utterances sounded amusing from her lips, for they were delightfully shaped with a Cupid's bow, and as pink as the flowers she had in her hair. By the time the dance came to an end, he felt that he had never been so well entertained. Miss Gardiner was lovely to look at, her voice was sweet to listen to, and she knew everyone in Meryton. He had learned more about them in half an hour than he had in the previous year. He quit her company reluctantly, whereas he had been eager to leave Miss Raistrick.

When the evening was over and he returned to Longbourn in his parents' carriage, his father remarked on the importance of a large dowry and the folly of marrying a young lady who had only her pretty face to recommend her.

His mother, no doubt with visions of nursing the infant Collins dancing before her eyes, said that Jane Gardiner was a very pretty girl and that the Gardiners, though not genteel, were respectable.

In the Gardiner carriage, hired for the evening, the assembly was also being relived.

"What a wonderful night!" said Jane with a happy sigh.

She had danced every dance and had almost worn her slippers through.

"I think Arthur is on the point of proposing," said her sister.

Jane made some reply, but her mind was not on her sister; it was on her own affairs. She had danced with Captain Quentin, and how handsome he had looked in his regimentals! And then had come something which had surprised her. John Bennet had asked her to dance.

Her mama's thoughts were tending in the same direction, for she said, "Only think, Jane, at this time yesterday I thought that Captain Quentin would be a good match for you. But if I don't miss my guess, we will soon see you as the mistress of Longbourn."

"Oh, Mama!" said Jane. "Mr. Bennet asked me to dance once! That is hardly a proposal."

"No, indeed," said Mary.

She had seen her sister's sudden elevation with mixed emotions, for although she was happy to find that her sister was well liked, she could not help thinking that, if her sister were to marry John Bennet, it would put her own match in the shade.

"But he looked at you often," said Mrs. Gardiner. "I think you must have another new dress for the next assembly. And it would do no harm if you were to walk past Longbourn once in a while."

"Oh, Mama!" said Jane.

She had, however, been thinking exactly the same thing, for not only was John Bennet the most important young man in the neighbourhood, he was also handsome and agreeable. To be sure, some of the things he said went over her head, but that only proved how clever he was, in addition to all his other virtues.

A large estate or a red coat? Happy were Jane's deliberations as the carriage took her home. Should she marry Captain Quentin or should she marry Mr. Bennet? In her mind's eye she saw both men proposing, and pictured herself, first as the wife of an officer, established in neat lodgings, and then as the wife of a landowner, established in Longbourn, the finest house in the neighbourhood.

At that, the image began to fade. Much as he liked her—and she had not been mistaken, she was sure he did like her—and much as she liked him, he would never marry her. What, Jane Gardiner, daughter of a country attorney, to be the mistress of Longbourn? Such things only happened in fairy tales.

There was much to occupy John over the coming weeks. His father came home soaked one day, which led to a cold, which led to an inflammation of the lungs. The physician was sent for. He looked grave, but said that, with rest, he hoped for a recovery.

Whilst his father was indisposed, John took over the running of the Longbourn estate. He was young, vigorous, and intelligent, and it was no hardship to him, but he worried for his father. That once strong man was a shadow of his former self, and was confined to bed.

One morning, as John rode down the drive, he saw that the Miss Gardiners had ventured out of doors and that they were walking down the lane. Knowing it to be muddy further along because of the recent rain, he dismounted and followed them, meaning to catch up with them and warn them. But he was too late. By the time he drew close enough to make himself heard, he saw Miss Gardiner putting one foot unwarily onto a boggy patch, and she sunk in to her ankle. In an effort to extricate herself, she almost overbalanced and she was only able to save herself by putting her other foot down on an equally boggy patch, with the inevitable result.

Standing there, with her skirt held up to keep it out of the mud and in consequence revealing a shapely calf, she burst out laughing.

The joyous sound rang down the lane and John could not help laughing himself. Any other young lady would, he was sure, be crying or frowning, and he found himself thinking again that it was a pity she was only an attorney's daughter.

Her sister, meanwhile, was trying to pull her out of the mud but being afraid of getting stuck herself she soon gave up. The two young ladies suggested various methods of escape to each other between bursts of laughter.

John saw at once how it could be done, for there were some planks of wood leaning against a wall, ready for fencing. Drawing level with the ladies, he assured them he would have Miss Gardiner out of her fix in a minute.

He laid the planks across the mud, making a bridge over which he could walk without sinking into it himself. He walked across the planks and then, taking Miss Gardiner's hand, he helped her out. She stood there laughing and thanking him whilst she shook out her skirts, and then she looked dubiously at the patch of mud that still lay between her and the way she wanted to go.

John was not a great reader for nothing. Many was the time he had read of chivalrous deeds in the works of Mallory and the like. And so, begging her pardon, he scooped her into his arms and then, with his long stride, carried her safely to the other side.

She laughed and her eyes sparkled as she said good-humouredly, "What a lark!" and he thought he had never seen or heard a prettier sight.

"Thank the gentleman," her sister said.

"Thank you, Mr. Bennet," said Jane, swaying her skirts from side to side.

"I trust you have taken no hurt?" he said.

"No, none at all, thank you, though my shoes are ruined," she said, looking down at them ruefully.

"A pity. They are very pretty shoes," he said.

Jane, who had until that moment been regretting wearing her best shoes, was now grateful that she had done so.

"Never mind, I have some more at home," she said.

"The lane is impassable further along; I suggest you go around by the road," he said. He offered her his arm. "Will you allow me to escort you safely home?"

She blushed and said, "Delighted."

He offered Miss Mary his other arm. Miss Mary replied that she had dropped her handkerchief somewhere about and that she must look for it, but that they should not wait for her and that she would catch them up.

And so John Bennet and Jane Gardiner strolled along the country roads with the sun up above and the birds singing, and thought that life held no pleasures greater than this.

The combined effects of Miss Gardiner's prettiness, the loveliness of the day, his father's ill health, and his own recent accident rendered him vulnerable, and by the time he reached the Gardiners' gate he found that he had proposed.

With smiles and blushes Miss Gardiner accepted, and he was ushered inside to speak to her father.

What joy filled the Gardiners' household! Mrs. Gardiner danced round the room, crying, "Mistress of Longbourn!" whilst Mr. Gardiner cleared his throat and welcomed John to the family.

Mrs. Gardiner pressed him to stay to dinner, but John said he must go home and give his family the news.

The joy in the Bennet household was not unconfined. His parents received the news more soberly than Mr. and Mrs. Gardiner had done. There was no dancing around the room and no crows of delight.

"Well, well, she is a healthy girl and it is high time you were married; I suppose she will do," said his father with resignation. "Miss Raistrick will be disappointed, but as long as Miss Gardiner does her duty and presents the estate with a son and heir within a year of becoming Mrs. Bennet, I will have no complaint to make."

His mother said only, "I am glad it is settled. Now the Collinses will have to buy their own grandfather clock."

. . . And now the very same clock was striking, twenty-three years later, and he was no longer a young man thinking of his own marriage; instead it was his daughters' wedding day.

Where did the years go? he thought, as he watched them with pride.

There was no further time for reflection. The wedding breakfast was over and Mrs. Bingley and Mrs. Darcy were ready to depart.

"Oh, Mrs. Bingley, how happy you will be!" said Mrs. Bennet, embracing her eldest daughter. "And Lizzy," she said. "Ten thousand a year!"

Elizabeth caught her father's eye and they both smiled. Elizabeth hung back as Mrs. Bennet followed Jane and Bingley to their carriage and Mr. Bennet claimed Elizabeth's hand.

"Well, Lizzy, so you are leaving us," he said.

"Yes, Papa," she said, clasping his hand in return.

"I could not let you go to anyone who did not deserve you, but Mr. Darcy truly loves you. You will be a very happy woman."

"I know," she said with a radiant smile.

"I will miss you. You must write to me often," he said, and he even went so far as to say, "and I will endeavour to write back."

There was time for no more. Mr. Darcy, waiting by the Darcy carriage, was growing impatient. Mr. Bennet let go of Elizabeth's hand with reluctance and watched her running over to her husband with pride.

"Ah! What a wonderful morning!" said Mrs. Bennet as she joined him on the doorstep.

"Indeed," said Mr. Bennet.

They waved until their daughters' carriages were out of sight, and then Mr. Bennet offered his arm to his wife.

She had not provided him with a son and heir, but she had provided him with a handsome number of daughters and she had unwittingly provided him with a great deal of entertainment as well.

It was as much as a man could ask for, he thought. He had nothing to complain of.

And with that he led his wife back inside.

Jane Austen Award nominee AMANDA GRANGE was born in Yorkshire, England. She spent her teenage years reading Jane Austen and Georgette Heyer while also finding time to study music at Nottingham University. She has had more than twenty books published including seven Jane Austen retellings and the phenomenal *Mr. Darcy, Vampyre*. Amanda Grange now lives in Cheshire, England.

www.amandagrange.com

@HRomanceUK on Twitter

JANE AUSTEN, YEAH, YEAH, YEAH!

Janet Mullany

England, 1964

Julie Morton pushed open the door to the staff room, bracing herself for the gust of cigarette smoke that wafted into her face. Books and handbag clutched to her chest, she made her way across the room, past the women who were not quite colleagues and certainly not friends, thankful that today was Friday and that in little over an hour she would be free for the weekend and Derek.

Ah, the wonders of the English language. Not free for Derek (she wasn't supplementing her meager salary by becoming a part-time courtesan, something certainly not expected at Cleverton High School for Girls) and not free of Derek—although of course if she was thinking in Latin, a certain ambiguity would exist. How about by, with, or from Derek? She really wasn't quite sure. Yes, she would be with him, and then pleasured by him, having received attentions from him—no wonder Catullus and the rest were drawn to erotic poetry. It was really the language's fault.

And she had a whole, lovely weekend to anticipate, a special weekend, so he had promised her.

She smiled a greeting at Miss Williams, the shy History teacher whom the girls despised for her heavy Welsh accent and dark-framed glasses as much as her timidity. Julie, with the knowledge that only a few years lay between her and the girls she taught, did her best to avoid becoming the recipient of girls' confidences and opinions on the other teachers, but their contempt for Miss Williams was plain on their faces.

"These gels," Mrs. Henderson said. She was the only person Julie had met who pronounced the word to rhyme with "bells," like an Oscar Wilde character.

"Oh, I know," Miss Dickinson said.

The two of them, the queen bees of the common room, sat in their special chairs drawn close to the glowing bars of the electric fire, sipping from the china cups and saucers reserved for their exclusive use. *I hope you don't mind, dear, but that's Mrs. Henderson's chair . . . cup . . .* Julie had been saved from certain ruin by discreet whispers of reproof on her first venture into the common room.

She helped herself to a cup of instant coffee, adding milk from the bottle that stood nearby on the counter referred to as "the kitchen," and settled on a chair midway between Mrs. Henderson and Miss Dickinson, and the two art teachers, who maintained a quiet conversation about where they should go at half-term; the Cotswolds, maybe? Edinburgh? Rather too far, they thought.

"These gels," Mrs. Henderson repeated. "I don't know which is worse; first they're all mad about horses and now it's these young men, the ones with all the hair."

"And the screaming," Miss Dickinson said. "It's not nice."

"Thank goodness they don't scream in school," Mrs. Henderson said. She balanced her cigarette on her saucer. She gazed around the common room as a queen might regard her domain. "What do you think, Miss Morton? I don't see you screaming and behaving like a silly-billy."

"I think their music is rather nice, but I . . ."

"I hope you don't mind taking detention tonight," Miss Dickinson interrupted.

"Actually I—"

"You are the most junior member of the staff," Miss Dickinson said as though the matter was settled. "And since you're taking a holiday on Monday, that will give you plenty of time over the weekend."

"And drawing insects all over their exercise books," Mrs. Henderson continued. "It's quite dreadful. Saying they're going to marry Tom, Dick, or Harry, or the one with the silly name. Singing those dreadful songs."

"John, Paul, George, and Ringo," Julie said.

They both turned and stared at her.

"Those are their names. Not Tom, Dick, and Harry."

"It doesn't make any difference." Mrs. Henderson blew a dignified smoke ring. "No one will remember who they are in a few weeks."

Having got their attention, Julie continued, "I don't think I can take detention tonight, Miss Dickinson."

"It's on the blackboard."

"Oh, well, if it's on the blackboard," Julie murmured, knowing her attempt at irony would be lost.

The blackboard, along with Mrs. Henderson and Miss Dickinson, formed the three components of staff room law. What was written there was the law, and the two teachers exercised an iron control over the eraser and chalk.

Sure enough, Julie's name was written there, a partner in punishment along with those notorious outlaws of the upper fourth: Susan Castle, Catherine Brown, and Penelope Emory.

Julie glanced at her watch. If indeed her fate was sealed, she had better phone Derek, and that meant facing the Gorgon within the next seven minutes.

She slipped out of the staff room into the corridor. As she passed the cloakroom, a few girls, huddled among coats and scarves, gave her a look that was half guilt, half challenge. She wondered briefly what they were doing; rumor had it that copies of *Lady Chatterley's Lover* were circulating in the school again, well-thumbed pages destined to fall open at the dirty bits. She wished she could share with her students the irony and restless sensuality of Lesbia's sparrow, a far better introduction to the pleasures of the flesh, in her opinion, than the confused phallic mysticism of D. H. Lawrence.

And there would end her career as a teacher.

She tapped on the door of the office where Mrs. George, gate-keeper of both Miss Creegan, the headmistress, and of the school telephone, held sway.

"Hello. I'm terribly sorry, Mrs. George, but I need to ring someone up."

"Very well, Miss Morton." Mrs. George inclined her head graciously. "Please don't make a habit of it."

Good Lord, it was like visiting the Pope. How long before Mrs. George extended a hand for supplicants to kiss? But instead, Mrs. George pushed forward a box with a slot in the top, an item Julie found particularly repellent. The box, made of a cheap, splintery wood, was slathered in a sickly yellow varnish and inscribed with the words

> *Use the phone whene'er you will,*
> *But remember, please, who pays the bill!*

A nightmarish figure dressed in green and sporting ridiculous curly-toed shoes and a hideous grin pointed upward toward the slot. Since the box also bore the legend *A Souvenir from Penzance,* it was probably meant to represent a Cornish pixie.

Julie dutifully dropped a sixpence into the slot: highway robbery in her opinion. The first time she had used the phone and offered a threepenny bit, she had received another of those discreet whispered warnings in the staff room. *I do so hate to tell you, dear, but Mrs. George was rather upset about the money for your phone call. . . .*

She suspected that Mrs. George's take had nothing to do with the phone bill but more to do with the ever-increasing assortment of china figurines, mostly sickly-sweet kittens, that adorned her otherwise empty desk. Empty, that is, except for the typewriter that Mrs. George now attacked with a small brush, daring any specks of dirt on the keys to give themselves up.

Julie dialed Derek's number.

He answered, his voice low and lazy. Jazz played in the background.

"Hello, it's Julie."

"Darling. Just a mo. I'll turn this down." A brief pause and the volume of the music dropped. "How lovely to hear your voice."

"I'm afraid I'm going to be a bit late this evening. I have to take detention."

"Oh, damn."

"Yes."

"Are you ringing from that old cow's office?"

"Yes, that's right." She glanced at Mrs. George, who, her typewriter keys subdued, now flicked a soft yellow duster over the china kittens.

"How late?"

"Oh, about an hour."

"Bugger. If we're to arrive in time for dinner, it won't give us time to go to bed first. Bit of a sexual wilderness at the parental home, you know."

"The p—" she stopped herself before arousing Mrs. George's interest.

"Yes, darling. That's your surprise weekend. Mumsie can't wait to meet my fiancée."

She paused, dumbfounded. "Oh. That is a surprise."

"Well, we're sleeping together. Obviously we're going to get engaged."

"Yes, but . . ."

"Look, darling, you're not the sort of girl who expects roses and moonlight and a bloke on his bended knee and all that sort of balls, are you? I think they have Granny's diamond ring knocking around somewhere at the house, so I'll find it for you. And then you can stop working at that wretched school when we're married. Teaching Latin to silly schoolgirls—what sort of job is that?"

"Oh, absolutely," she said with a no-nonsense air, as much for Mrs. George's benefit as Derek's. "I'll see you at about six, then. Bye."

She hung up the phone, her heart pounding.

"Your young man, is it?" Mrs. George said, setting a china kitten straight.

"Oh no. My Aunty Dot. We're going to see a play tonight."

"How lovely."

At that moment, the school bell shrilled and a distant sound like murmuring thunder arose, excusing Julie from further subterfuge. When she stepped out into the corridor again, the thunder was at full volume, the sound of hundreds of girls talking and laughing, hundreds of pairs of sensible school shoes pounding on the wooden floor as they made their way to the next class. She dived into the throng like a fish joining a shoal, her green tweed skirt and pink blouse making her an exotic outsider among the navy blue gymslips and white shirts.

For the last period of the day, she took the sixth formers preparing for Oxbridge entry, serious, ambitious girls whose company she normally enjoyed. As a recent graduate of Somerville she hoped she might be able to give them some good advice. But even they, on a Friday afternoon, fidgeted and stared out of the window, longing for the final bell to ring. Julie set them a Latin passage to translate, and stared out of the window herself.

So apparently she was now engaged and they were going to Wiltshire for the weekend so she could be assessed as a future daughter-in-law.

And she'd hoped for a weekend in Paris.

Susan, Cathy, and Penny sat sprawled at desks in the front row of the classroom as Julie came in with a pile of homework to mark. She sat at the teacher's desk and read out their names, a ludicrous exercise when it was only three girls who were involved, but formalities must be observed.

Julie opened the first exercise book. The afternoon sun beamed through the tall windows full of dancing dust motes, and the room held the peculiar school end-of-day scent: female sweat, floor polish, mustiness, the lingering odor of school lunch.

She couldn't help looking up and glancing at her three charges. She'd encountered students outside of school and been surprised at how grown up, how female, they looked when wearing normal clothes and not the hideous school uniforms. The gymslip, tie, and white shirt conspired to make Susan look dumpy, Cathy skinny, and Penny awkward. Susan chewed the end of one of her pigtails, Cathy yawned, and Penny froze halfway in pushing a piece of paper across her desk.

Julie stood and held her hand out. Penny, blushing, handed the piece of paper to her.

I love Paul so much I think I will die of it. Do you love him that much?

"Thank you, Penny." She tore the piece of paper in half, dropped the pieces into the bin, and sat down again, trying to ignore the pain and embarrassment on Penny's face.

Oh for God's sake. Don't fall for it. Don't love someone that way. He'll take you to some freezing damp country house that smells of dogs and let his mother bully you when you thought he'd take you to Paris and you'd spent half the night in a panic because you thought you'd lost your passport. And because he's an English Freudian mess, he'll be too scared to have sex there and he'll drive back too fast with his hand in your knickers.

She looked up again. This was supposed to be punishment, but Julie considered it a dreadful waste of time. To make these three restless, bright girls sit in silence for an hour, doing nothing, was unforgivable. But of course you couldn't make them scrub the floor, or sew straight seams, or stand on stools with signs around their necks.

"So what have you three hardened criminals done this time?"

They fidgeted, grinned.

"We told Mrs. Henderson what we thought of *Sense and Sensibility,*" Susan said.

"Really? What do you think of *Sense and Sensibility*?"

They giggled.

"It's stupid," Cathy offered.

"Why?"

"They're such silly cows."

"All through the book?" Julie responded to Penny's comment. "Are they still silly cows at the end?"

"They don't do anything," Susan said. "Like Elinor waits around for that Edward bloke and they haven't even snogged."

"But don't you have to wait for boys to ask you out? Isn't it the same thing?" Julie said.

They looked at each other. "My mum won't let me go out with boys," Cathy said.

"My mum says I can get engaged when I'm sixteen," Penny said.

"Oh, do you have a boyfriend, then?" Julie asked.

Penny shook her head.

"And the other one—whatshername—she's daft, isn't she. I mean, she doesn't even know that bloke."

"Marianne and Willoughby? You're right, Cathy. She falls in love with a man who's her fantasy."

"Her what, miss?" Susan had produced a nail file and was attending to her nails.

"Put that away, please, Susan."

"But I don't get it," Cathy said. "Those blokes just aren't worth it."

"And then Marianne marries the old boring one. I expect they read horrible poetry to each other in bed." Penny's comment set all three of them giggling. "I mean, why do they want to get married?"

"To be honest, it's not my favorite Austen. I like *Persuasion* better," Julie said, and they all stared at her.

"You mean, you like books like that?" Susan said.

"Yes. If you're lucky, you'll like Austen too, one day."

"I don't know why anyone would want to read it if they didn't have to," Penny said.

Julie looked at them, at the marking in front of her, and weighed the odds of girls in future begging for detention with Miss Morton, who actually talked to them like human beings, talked to them about boys. Was this really a good idea? And what if word got back to Mrs. Henderson that the most junior member of staff, the lowly Latin teacher, had had the audacity to trespass upon the sacred groves of English literature?

"What if the men in the book were the Beatles?" she said.

"There's only three."

"Yes, but John's married," Susan said to Cathy. "Even though I love him best."

"Not Ringo," said Penny.

"Why?" Julie said, intrigued by the elimination process.

"He's too short. He's only an inch taller than me."

"But we don't know how tall Marianne or Elinor are," Julie said.

"He's not handsome enough either," Penny continued.

"What if something happened to John's wife and he was terribly unhappy and then we met and I—"

"That's awful!" Cathy cried at Susan's suggestion, and Penny shook her head at the terrible thought.

"So," Julie said, enjoying herself. "We have Edward Ferrars. Which Beatle do you think he is?"

"Which one's he?" Susan said.

"He's the stupid one," Cathy said. "He's the one who goes out with the stupid girl."

"Lucy Steele," Julie translated, "but he's in love with Elinor."

"Ringo," Penny said. "He lets himself get pushed around by the other three because he's short. Like Edward lets himself get pushed around by his mother, who wants him to marry the stupid girl. And he's too quiet and shy to do anything about it."

"George is the quiet, shy one," Susan said with an air of authority. "Besides, Ringo's too short for Elinor."

"That's interesting," Julie said. "Why do you think she's tall? Austen doesn't give much in the way of physical description, although she does say that although they're both very good-looking, Marianne is the prettiest."

"Of course she's tall," Susan said. "She's always telling people what to do. Even her mum."

"Like you," Penny said, "except you're short."

All three of them giggled.

"But he's a vicar," Cathy said. "None of the Beatles would ever be vicars."

"Oh, I wouldn't worry too much about that," Julie said. "It was quite a normal job for someone like Edward to have in those days."

They nodded.

"Look, they don't do anything," Susan said. "The girls. The sisters. Any of them. They just hang around waiting for someone to propose to them. And they do needlework and go to parties and stuff, but they don't have jobs."

"If you married one of the Beatles, would you have a job, Susan?" Julie asked.

"No. He'd need me at home, cooking his tea, and I expect I'd have a baby."

"So if Paul arrived in this room and dropped to one knee, holding out a big bunch of roses, you'd say yes?"

"I'm not old enough. He'd have to wait for me but I expect he'd get me a ring and all that. But I wouldn't do it before we're married."

"So you wouldn't have a job either, then. You'd leave school and get married the next day."

"But Elinor and Marianne didn't go to school," Susan said. "I don't think they did. They're older than us. And they haven't even been out with any boys until Edward turns up."

"They're posh," Penny said. "So they don't have to have jobs, and only boys went to school then. Posh schools. It was the olden times."

They all nodded in understanding.

Penny continued, "Now it's different. They keep telling us we have to do well in our O Levels so we do three A Levels and go to university, but Miss Creegan, when she talked to us about careers, said we should think about teaching as a career because we could get married and then go back after we've had children and have school holidays with them."

"So do you think it's much different?" Julie asked. "It seems like there are still the same expectations for girls, from what you're saying. What if you don't want to get married or have children?"

They all stared at her again as though she was a green thing from a spaceship.

"So we have George, the quiet, shy one, as Edward. Who's next? How about Colonel Brandon? What do you know about him?"

"He's old," Susan said in disgust.

"That's exactly what Marianne thinks of him when she first meets him. She criticizes his waistcoat."

"I think he's John," Cathy said. "He's the oldest."

"Yes, but he's quite dashing, isn't he?" Julie says. "He fights a duel, and he gallops around over the countryside to fetch Mrs. Dashwood when they think Marianne is going to die. He's a good old-fashioned hero. And he's got that lovely romantic streak, reading poetry to Marianne. Is John romantic and dashing?"

She tried not to smile as they all grimaced.

"Paul," said Penny. "I think he'd be Paul. Because he's kind. Paul has such lovely kind eyes."

"No, he's not handsome enough," Susan said. "Colonel Brandon isn't handsome. Paul's gorgeous."

"I think he's George," Cathy said.

"No, Cathy. Edward is George," Susan said.

"Wait," Julie said. "Let Cathy tell us why she thinks George is Colonel Brandon."

"Well." Cathy chewed a hangnail. "He's quiet. And I think he looks sort of brooding and mysterious sometimes. But underneath it all, you know there's all this passionate stuff. He could read you poetry and you sort of wouldn't mind too much."

"Then Ringo could be Colonel Brandon. Because he's short and he's got a funny nose but his heart's in the right place. And he's funny. John's funny too, but Ringo's funny in a nicer way," Susan said.

"I can't see Ringo galloping around on a horse like Miss Morton said," Cathy objected. "I can't really see any of them on horses."

"I've got a picture of them on bicycles," Susan said. "It's not that far off."

"Miss Morton, why doesn't Colonel Brandon marry their mum?" Penny asked. "She's old, too."

"That's a very good question, Penny, and none of the critics and academics who write about Austen have ever come up with a satisfactory answer. I suppose, simply, they didn't fall in love with each other."

Penny blushed with pleasure.

This was interesting, Julie thought. It was a ridiculous concept, but the girls were thinking and arguing, and despite their prejudices against the book and Mrs. Henderson's effectiveness as a teacher, they had managed to absorb something of what it was about. But Willoughby, she thought—Willoughby would be interesting because the girls had elevated the Beatles to some sort of romantic sainthood.

Meanwhile their conversation had deteriorated to a discussion of favorite pictures, in particular the ones that had come out just that week in *Jackie,* a magazine Julie deplored for its silliness regarding boys, but which was revered in the school.

"Willoughby," Julie said. "What do you think of him?"

"I think Marianne's really stupid," Susan said. "She doesn't even know him."

"I agree to a certain extent," Julie said. "But as you mentioned earlier, she led a very sheltered life. She didn't go to school or really do very much outside her family. So is it fair to blame her for being stupid? Everyone expects her to marry, just as Miss Creegan expects you all to marry."

Susan glanced at Julie and then at the other two girls. Julie gave her an encouraging smile.

"Willoughby's like a real boyfriend," Penny said. "He brings her flowers."

Cathy and Penny giggled.

"Well, that's what boys are supposed to do," Penny said. "It said in *Jackie* last week that if he was serious about you, he'd give you flowers. And the lock of hair thing, it was what they did in olden days, wasn't it, Miss?"

"It was," Julie said.

"I'd love to have a lock of Paul's hair," Cathy said dreamily. "It'd be so romantic. I'd sleep with it under my pillow every night."

"So Willoughby acts like a real boyfriend, but do you think he really loves Marianne?" Julie asked. "Everyone seems to think he's serious about her. Later he tells Elinor he was in love with Marianne, but by then it's too late."

"Yes, it's easy for him to say it then," Cathy said.

"Wait a mo," Penny said. "If Willoughby's not a nice person, how come everyone else thinks he is?"

"That's an excellent point, Penny," Julie said. "I really think Brandon should have had a word with Mrs. Dashwood or Sir John Middleton."

"That's what's wrong with them all," Cathy said. "All of

them! They're so prim and proper they won't tell anyone any-thing. Like Elinor won't tell Edward she likes him and he won't tell her about the other stupid girl, Lucy whatshername. And Eli-nor should have told Lucy to bugger off because Edward was hers."

"Don't swear," Julie said, trying not to laugh.

"I wouldn't tell a boy I liked him," said Penny. "What if he didn't like you back?"

"What if you were on a desert island with Paul? Or, what if you had ten seconds to live and you were with Paul?" Susan said. "You would then."

"Don't you think that's what Marianne is trying to tell him at the ball in London?" Julie said. "It's a very brave thing for her to do."

There was a short silence in which Penny scrambled under her desk for a dropped pencil and Susan studied her fingernails. Cathy hummed quietly to herself.

"I don't think any of the Beatles would do what he did," Susan said. The other two nodded agreement.

"Yes, but if Paul did—I mean, if he dumped me and I was really ill and nearly died and he came to see me and he was mar-ried, I'd . . ." Penny's voice faltered. "I think if Paul got married I'd die."

"Just like Marianne," Julie said. "Do you think you'd marry—who did we decide was Brandon?—let's say it was George—afterwards, when you got better? If he told you he was in love with you?"

"I don't know. I don't think I'd ever forget Paul," Penny said. "But I quite like George. So I suppose I'd marry him if he asked. He is one of the Beatles and I'd see quite a lot of Paul, I suppose. But I'd never be friends with his wife."

"That's true," Julie said. "Willoughby is still the Dashwoods' and Middletons' neighbor. You know, one of you—I think it was Susan—said that Marianne and Elinor were silly cows, and Marianne is certainly silly with Willoughby. But by the end of the book, do you think she's still as bad?"

"Yes," Susan said, to Julie's surprise. "But in a different sort of way. She's done what everyone has expected her to do—she's got married to the first boy who comes along when she couldn't marry Willoughby. Well, not really a boy, he's an old man. I feel sort of sorry for Willoughby. If he really loved her so much, maybe he should have asked her to run away with him. If John asked me to run away with him, I would. Even if it was George, who's my next favorite, who wanted to marry me, I'd run away with John. Marianne could get a job if he needed money. In Woolworth's or something."

All three girls laughed. "Mrs. Henderson's always saying that if we don't go to university we'll end up working in Woolworth's," Penny said, who still seemed to be brooding on the horror of Paul's marriage.

"But if Marianne did that, she'd lose her reputation. Elinor would never speak to her again and probably Elinor wouldn't be able to marry Edward. Women couldn't do things like that then," Julie said. "She probably wouldn't be able to get a job either."

"My mum would never talk to me again if I ran off with someone," Susan said, looking quite pleased at the prospect.

"And how about Elinor?" Julie asked. "What do you think of her at the end of the book?"

Susan snorted. "She's a right cold fish, miss, particularly if what you say about how she wouldn't talk to her sister if she ran off with Willoughby is true. If she really loved Edward, she should have told him and married him without waiting for his mother to say it was all right."

The others murmured assent.

"But it's not right, miss, about Marianne. What if she isn't really in love with Colonel Brandon?" Penny asked.

"That's the great thing about Austen," Julie said. "She knows when to tell us things and when not to."

The girls looked thoughtful.

Julie looked at her watch. "Girls, I think you've demonstrated that when you put your minds to it, you're capable of doing better work than you've done so far for Mrs. Henderson. I'll let you go early this once, but I don't expect to see you in detention again."

They chorused their thanks and filed out of the room.

Julie followed them out and went to the teachers' cloakroom for her coat. Now the school day was officially over, only the front entrance was open, and to her surprise she found the girls clustered there, deep in discussion.

"He's more like a dad," Cathy was saying as Julie approached.

"Perhaps she misses her dad. He's dead, isn't he? I mean, Marianne's all weepy about him at the beginning of the book but she seems to forget about him pretty quickly," Penny said, hands in the pockets of her school blazer.

They were discussing the book, Julie realized with a flush of pleasure.

And, they were waiting for her, as was evident from the beaming smiles they turned on her.

"Fab detention, miss," Susan said with a cheeky grin.

"Don't you dare tell anyone," Julie said. "I don't want to take detention five times a week, thank you very much, not even with you lot."

Cathy held the door open for her. "So why couldn't Marianne get a job, miss?"

"She's posh," Penny said. "Right, miss?"

"That's part of it. But women couldn't train for professions then, so she'd have the equivalent of a job in Woolworth's, being a servant, and it would be even worse—demeaning and poorly paid with long hours. She'd probably end up becoming a prostitute, like Eliza."

"Which one's Eliza?" Penny said as they walked down the drive to the gates.

The other two turned on her. "You know, the one Colonel Brandon fights the duel over, stupid. 'Cause she's his adopted daughter or something," Susan said.

"She never goes on the game!" Penny looked quite shocked. "I bet Jane Austen didn't even know about that sort of thing."

"She did," Julie said. "It's there, if you look for it. But it's not like *Lady Chatterley's Lover.*"

The three girls giggled.

"So do you have a boyfriend, then, miss?"

"Not really," Julie said.

"But isn't that why you became a teacher, miss?" Susan persisted. "So you could get married and have summer holiday with your kids and go back after they've started school, and all?"

"No," Julie said. "I didn't even think of it in those terms. I certainly don't now."

"This is our bus stop, miss." Cathy took off her school hat and stuffed it into a blazer pocket and dropped her satchel on the ground at her feet.

Penny took a bag of sweets out of her pocket and offered one to Julie, who shook her head with a smile.

"Bye, then, miss," Susan said.

Julie had only a short walk to the small terraced house she rented. But instead she turned the other way on the street, heading toward the center of the town. This had been the way the stages came into the town in Austen's time, descending the hill to stop at the George Inn on the way to London. Austen herself might have looked out upon these same buildings, seen the original Georgian façades now marred by modern shop windows and frontages.

She should really go home. She should repack; replace the pretty lace nightgown with a sturdy flannel one that didn't show an inch of skin and the daring strapless black evening dress—sexy, rustling taffeta—with something more innocent and suitable for a weekend in the country. But instead she turned into the coffee bar that tried so very hard to be Italian, with small replicas of famous statues in alcoves and a mural of Vesuvius surrounded by a border of vines and grapes.

Yet the owners were Italian, and the young man behind the counter, one of the sons of the family, certainly looked the part, with dark expressive eyes and a winning smile. He gave her an admiring look.

Julie knew the effect would be spoiled when he spoke in the local accent, the way Penny and Susan and Cathy spoke, but she ordered a cup of espresso and a very English bun studded with raisins and went to sit at one of the tables by the window. It was steamed up from the espresso machine but she could see a phone box on the other side of the street. Her coffee arrived, blanketed by a soft foam of froth pitted by dark sprinkles of cinnamon. She took an appreciative sip. It wasn't quite as good as coffee in Rome or in Paris, but for the moment it would have to do.

And after she had finished her bun and coffee she would ring up Derek.

Her experience today hadn't been quite that of Paul—the saint, not the Beatle—on the road to Damascus, but she knew now what she would do; about Derek, about being a teacher. Not everything in her life, but a good start.

She would invite the three girls over for tea one evening after school. She imagined showing them her books, getting them to talk about Austen, encouraging them to read more. She might even play them some records that weren't by the Beatles.

She looked again at the phone box, glowing red in the late afternoon sun, and wondered if she'd remember this day, long after Derek was a faint shadow in her memory. Even if it was true that in ten weeks, or months, or years, no one would remember those four cheeky young pop stars from Liverpool, Jane Austen would still be there.

JANET MULLANY was born in England but now lives near Washington, D.C. She's worked as an archaeologist, performing arts administrator, waitress, bookseller, and as an editor/proofreader for a small press. Her debut novel was *Dedication,* the only Signet Regency to have two bondage scenes, followed by *The Rules of Gentility* and three more Regency chicklits. Her career as a writer who does terrible things to Jane Austen began in 2010 with the publication of *Jane and the Damned,* a book about Jane as a vampire, and *Little to Hex Her,* a modern retelling of *Emma,* in the anthology *Bespelling Jane Austen,* headlined by Mary Balogh. Her most recent book is *Jane Austen: Blood Persuasion,* about a vampire invasion of Chawton (William Morrow, 2011). She also writes contemporary erotic romance for Harlequin Spice (*Tell Me More,* 2011).

www.janetmullany.com
@janet_mullany on Twitter

LETTERS TO LYDIA

Maya Slater

> *Maria, a good-humoured girl, but . . . empty-headed . . . had noth-*
> *ing to say that could be worth hearing.*
>
> —*Pride and Prejudice,* Chapter 27

To Miss Lydia Bennet
Longbourn House,
Longbourn,
Near Meryton,
Hertfordshire.
March 12th

My Dear Lydia,

Well, here I am at Hunsford Parsonage, after a Delightful Stay in London. We went to the Play, and saw *The Rivals,* in a Box! And we visited some Ware-houses, and I purchas'd a length of very pretty figured muslin, sprigg'd with forget-me-nots. 'Twill be the talk of Meryton.

How I wish we could have staid in London! Instead I am

cooped up here. I was to Write and tell you my Doings, but, alas, Doings are there none. *Every Body* here is Elderly, and they have but little Time for Me. I have try'd to confide in Hannah the Housemaid, the only other Young Person in this House, but when I ask'd her Opinion of *Otranto* she answer'd that she had never *eaten* any and, on my questioning her further, confess'd that she cannot read.

We have been here for three whole Days. Mr. Collins and Charlotte are fattening a Pig—I truly feel that the Animal is more absorbing to Charlotte than poor Me. Down with Sisters—mine and yours too: your Sister Lizzy is scarce four years older than Me, but she is as bad as the Others, censorious and teazing. She and Charlotte shut themselves away in the Back Parlour to gossip, first sending me away on ridiculous Errands. I spent an *Hour* this morning shooing the birds off the seedling Cabbages! A Scarecrow would have done the Job better.

Yesterday morning, a Chaise drew up, very grand with a Coat of Arms on the Door, and inside—Miss de Bourgh herself. She is not very old, but looks peeky-weaky, as far as Papa and I could see through the Parlour Window. She condescended to talk to Charlotte and Mr. Collins at the Gate for *twenty-three* minutes (Papa check'd on his Timepiece)! But when I asked what they had discuss'd, all Charlotte would say was "O, this and that."

Later

This evening we was invited to the Great House, which is called Rosings, to dine with Lady Catherine and Miss de Bourgh—even me! Would you believe it? Charlotte actually try'd to prevent my accompanying them because I was too young—but Mr. Collins said that I must come, so that I can tell our Neighbours in Hertfordshire about the Splendours of the Manor (only he said *ffffplen-dours,* as he is missing a Front Tooth, and speaks with the oddest Whistle).

And it is indeed *ffffplendid*! Even Papa was silenc'd, for a Change! The dining-table alone is as big as the Conservatory at Netherfield, and the Epergne is HUGE, with silver Cupids, Flowers and Fruits tumbling out. Mr. Collins says it must have cost as much as a small *Houfffe*! It completely hid those opposite. I thought I was out of Sight of Charlotte, but afterwards she scolded me, most unjustly, for helping myself three times to Whipt Sillabub. After Dinner the Tables were set up and we played at Cassino. Lizzy captured the most cards, whereat Miss De B became fatigued, and her Companion attended her Up-stairs. Lizzy picked up a Book, and I looked at an Album of pic-turesque Ruins, while the married People continued their Whist. I try'd in vain to overhear her Ladyship's Remarks, as she is a Fount of Wisdom. The Butler brought in a Magnificent Supper, but when I help'd myself to Ratafia, Charlotte privily remov'd my Glass. We dine at Rosings twice more this Week. When I grow up, I intend to wed a Titled Gentleman and live in a Great House like this one.

Her Ladyship's two Nephews are coming soon on a Visit—but I do not suppose that their Arrival will create much of a Di-version, as they are rather old, I believe.

I shall give this letter to Papa to take Home with him tomor-row—'twill save you the Postage. Please write! Last year, when I went with Mamma to Town, you sent only *five* lines, mostly about your first pair of long Gloves—*this* Time, I *must* have News of the Officers!!

Your affect. Friend,
Maria Lucas

To: The Same
April 7th

My dear Lydia,

As I feared, no Answer from you—you are the *worst* Correspondent in the World—but I have to report a TRULY *thrilling* Development, which nearly concerns You: Lady C's two Nephews have arrived to spend Easter. You may be wondering what is so particular about this, but possess yourself in Patience! One Nephew is a Colonel Fitzwilliam, and the second—none other than Mr. Darcy—yes, the very same disagreeable Gentleman who made himself so Unpopular in our District last Winter!! But that is not All. We was not expecting to see much of the Gentlemen, for Charlotte says that when her Ladyship has House Guests, she and Mr. Collins do not get invited to Rosings, unless they are needed to make up a Four at Whist. Imagine our astonishment when *on the Morning after their Arrival,* the two Gentlemen walked down from the Great House to present their Compliments! Mr. Collins *said* it was a Courtesy to Charlotte and himself, but Charlotte whisper'd that the chief Attraction was your Sister!!! Lizzy seemed unconcern'd, but Charlotte told me afterwards that Mr. Darcy was "much chang'd from the arrogant Gentleman I remember. He turn'd pale, then red, and said almost Nothing." For my part, I did not quite dare to observe him closely. But, hark to this! Charlotte tried to go off into the usual Huddle with Lizzy to talk about the Visit (they have been used to do this since our Arrival, tho' No Body has bothered to confide anything to Me). But shortly after Mr. Darcy and the Colonel had departed, Charlotte came to me in my Chamber, and told me that Lizzy positively refuses to discuss their Visit! "I must talk about it or burst!" said she. "I am persuaded that he is in Love with her, but she will not hear of it. I have been forbidden to mention it to Any One." She then urged me to be equally Discreet, so you mustn't breathe a Word to any living Soul—except for Kitty, of course.

I narrowly observ'd Lizzy's Face during dinner. Aware of our Scrutiny, she forc'd herself to partake of a hearty Meal. If *I* had but lately renewed my Tyes with my Lover, I could never have taken two Helps of Black Pudding. She is a magnificent Actress.

Your affect. Friend,
Maria Lucas

———

To: The Same
April 17th

Dear Lydia,

You must be more Careful. What you say about your Mother picking up my Letter, and you having to distract her by spilling a Basin of scalding Tea over Pug, made me almost Swoon with Horror. What will your Sister Lizzy say if she learns that her Secret is Discover'd, and by Me? Pray be more Careful in future, and Burn my Letters from this Day on!!

The Love Affair is taking a strange course. When Mr. Darcy comes to the House, he sits looking stolid, tho' Col. Fitzwilliam teazes him for his unusual Silence. Charlotte and I compare Notes after each visit. She says she never saw a man more Smitten, but, believe me, the true Passion is all on Lizzy's Side. I am daring to look at him in the Face nowadays. He is handsome, dark and smouldering like my Lord Byron, but when he fixes it on your Sister, the Look in his Eye is scarcely Languishing. If she can Hook him, 'twill be a splendid Match for her—and a Feather in their Caps for your whole Family! I daresay you will be staying in their Country Seat when they are married, meeting the Local

Gentry. Charlotte says Lizzy is playing a skilful Game, pretending complete Unconcern. Last Wednesday Mr. D came to call while Charlotte and I were out visiting the Parishioners. We arriv'd just as he was about to leave. Alone together for a whole Hour!! How did she contrive it? More of this, and she is like to catch him in her Toils. I said to Charlotte that for all we knew he might have begun to make Visits, on the Lurk outside 'til he saw us going out, then Sneaking in to be Alone with her. I suggested Enquiring of the Household if this was his Habit, but Charlotte positively refus'd to entertain such an Idea, and strictly forbade me to mention the Affair to any of the Servants. But I think she is too Particular, so I took no Notice. It would be too bad if a full-blown Love Affair were going on under our Noses without our Knowing. So when Hannah, the Housemaid, came up to lay the Fire in my Chamber, I took her into my Confidence. Hannah says Mr. D has never visited alone before To-Day. She has promis'd to tell me if he does it again. So he continues to resist your Sister's Blandishments!

Meanwhile, we have been up to the Great House twice this Week: we are needed to make up the Tables, as Lady Catherine complains that Mr. D is refusing to play. On our last Visit, both the Gentlemen stood by the Pianoforte to listen, as Lizzy played and sang, and gaz'd soulfully at Mr. D. Alas, I could not observe that Gentleman's Expression, as he had his Back to me.

I hope that poor Pug is not too badly burnt. Please kiss his dear little crumpled Nose from

Your affect. Friend,
Maria Lucas

To: The Same
May 3rd

Dear Lydia,

This MUST reach you before we meet again—it is Vital. I have held back 'til we reached yr Aunt & Uncle's House in London, whence the Postage will be cheaper for you. Would that I could have written sooner! O, why did you have to waste your Pin-Money on rose-coloured satin Slippers?

The latest Developments may Disturb you—yr Sister and Mr. D have had a Lovers' Tiff!! Yes, Lizzy and her Mr. Darcy are not speaking, and the Pity of it is, the Gentlemen left the District before a Reconciliation could take place. Is not it Pitiful—these two Loving Hearts, forever sunder'd without Hope of Happiness!!

I hope that returning to the Bosom of her Family will calm poor Lizzy. Meanwhile, when we see you next Thursday, pray PRAY breathe no word of Mr. D in her presence!!! Her Disappointment must be frightful. Perhaps there is yet Hope?

Yr Anxious Friend,
Maria Lucas

PS I have scarce had the Time to reflect upon yr News. What, you came upon Mrs. Forster and Capt. Dalby alone in the Shrubbery? I am ASTOUNDED! Tête-à-tête with a junior Officer in her Husband's own Regiment!! Mamma would call her Fast—though of course as she was looking for her Fan she can scarcely be blam'd. You are right to tell No Body but Kitty—our Parents are so old-fashion'd. And since then have you really become Mrs. F's Favourite? If so, how fortunate you are to have a mature married Lady for a Friend—and a truly modern one too!

I long to see you and hear All.

To: Miss Lydia Bennet,
Care of Colonel Forster,
9th Warwickshire Regiment,
Brighton
June 20th

Dear Lydia,

O how I Envy you! The wholesome Sea Air—and all those Officers! I still think Fondly of Capt. Dalby, Lieut. Tully, & Co, tho' Alas I fear I am quite Forgot by Them. Are there Balls, Routs and Amusements every Evening? And Mrs. Forster such a close Friend to Capt. Dalby! And O, has she really Entrusted you with the Task of carrying her Letters to him?

Here it is so DULL! Mamma STILL will not let me come Out. She says firmly that I am too young, but, after all, I am Sixteen now, and four months older than you! It is Too Bad. Worse still, yesterday afternoon I overheard her in the Parlour telling yr Aunt Philips that I was a Gadfly, but that she had no intention of bringing me Out yet. I shall be in the Schoolroom for Ever and Ever.

I am so Excited to hear that dear Mr. Wickham is now a fully-fledg'd Officer. Do you see him often? Have you danc'd with him at any of the Balls?

I took yr Letter out to the Bonfire to burn it, but Bart & Toby snatched it from the Flames and ran away with it, screaming "Maria's got a Love-letter!" I had to chase after them to get it back. In future I shall offer to fetch the Letters from the Post Office myself; then I may peruse yours on the way home without fear of Discovery.

Yr. affect. Friend,
Maria Lucas

To: The Same
July 2nd

My Dear Lydia,

Thank you for conveying Mr. Wickham's Compliments to me. I am Surpriz'd that he remembers me. I am Astonish'd at your Courage, you and Mrs. Forster meeting Capt. Dalby and Mr. Wickham in the Evenings, when you are suppos'd to be in the Assembly Rooms or at the Play. Of course Mrs. Forster says that there can be no Harm in it, as you can chaperone each other—but is this quite right? I am not sure.

   Then too I am Surpriz'd and rather Shocked to hear that the Lovers' Tiff between Lizzy and Mr. Darcy is the Talk of the Officers' Mess at Brighton. You say you have been regaling Mr. Wickham and the others with this "Tit-Bit," but that somehow you have forgot the Details. In fact I never gave them to you. I began to tell you at your Aunt Philips' Party, but you were so full of that News that Lieut. Tully was making Passionate Love to Serena Haultwick in a Butler's Pantry that you never stopt to listen to what I had to say.

   If I reveal them now, I would ask you to be Discreet, for I confess I feel sorry for your Sister Lizzy, who, as we all know, languish'd after Mr. Wickham before transferring her Affections to Mr. D, & even now may cherish the vain Hope of renewing her Tyes with the said Mr. W, since All is Over between her & Mr. D (I am persuaded that it was for this Reason that she so strongly oppos'd your going to Brighton—she must have been Desperate to make the Trip herself, and eaten up with Jealousy at your being Mrs. Forster's Preferr'd One!).

   Still, for Friendship's Sake, I shall tell you the whole Story, tho' you must make Mr. Wickham promise faithfully to say

Nothing of this to the other Officers. *Burn this when you have read it!*

It happen'd thus: the Day before the Gentlemen were due to depart, we was invited up to Rosings to drink Tea for the last time. Lizzy cry'd off—she had the Headache, she said. I was sent up with one of Hooper's Female Pills, and found her pale, heavy-eyed and ill—tho' it was a Sickness of the Heart, not the Body, as I realiz'd afterwards. Wondering what had come between the Lovers, I accompanied Charlotte and Mr. Collins through the Park to Rosings. No sooner had they arriv'd, and Charlotte made her friend's Excuses, than Mr. D, with a muttered Apology, left the room. Soon I heard the sound of horse's Hooves on the Drive. No Body else appear'd to observe it. She has cast her Net, and he has gone to her! We staid a full two Hours at Rosings, and there was still no sign of his Return when we left.

On returning to the Parsonage, the first Thing I saw was a beaver Hat on the hall Table. I was ecstatic: He is still here, alone with her: they must be Engag'd!! Mr. C noticed nothing, but Charlotte observ'd it, & straightway called for Hannah: has Miss E got a visitor? O, says Hannah, it was Mr. Darcy. He left an Hour since without his Hat, and Miss E has retir'd for the Night. I long'd for an explanation, but Charlotte stuffily refrain'd from asking for any further Details. On retiring to my Chamber I immediately call'd for Hannah to come and unbutton my Gown, hoping for News. She told me that she had let him in and shewn him into the Parlour, where Lizzy was. She then left them together, but, she said, as she had sworn to supply me with all possible Information, she did not Scruple to listen at the Door. She miss'd Much, but she did hear him say "I love you!!" Lizzy's Reply was spoken so quietly that she could not catch any of it. Then there was a long Silence, during which she conjectured that they were Embracing. But then Matters seemed to go rapidly Awry. She heard him say "Is this all the Reply I am to get?" Shortly afterwards, Mr. D rush'd out, almost knocking Hannah aside as she knelt by the Door. He left in a Whirlwind, forgetting to Tip the Boy who held his Horse!!

I woke at Dawn, and could hear a sound of muffled Weeping from Lizzy's chamber next door. I wonder'd whether to go in, but finally concluded that your Sister would be most embarrassed at her Secret's being discover'd, & so refrain'd.

Lizzy ran out alone before Breakfast, returning at least two Hours later, flushed and unhappy. She had certainly been crying. Meanwhile, her Lover had call'd to bid her Farewell, but, alack, they Miss'd each other. A few days dragg'd by, 'til we too left the County. In the carriage, Lizzy was dull & silent—I left her briefly in the Inn Parlour at Bromley, & return'd to see her quickly Stuffing a Letter into her Reticule, Tears in her Eyes.

That is all I have to tell—but it surely explains your Sister's shocking Mood since she return'd from Hunsford.

Pray tell No Body of this save Mr. Wickham—be Discretion itself!

> Your Friend,
> M. Lucas

To: Mrs. George Smith,
(*Address as yet unknown*)
July 24th

I will keep this Letter till I have a Direction for you.

I have just heard the News. Eloped! With Mr. Wickham!! I almost *fainted*!!! Our Cook met your Mrs. Hill in the Butcher's at Meryton, who told her the Awful Truth. Cook went straight to

Mamma. You cannot imagine the Turmoil here in Hertfordshire. I have not seen Kitty for a week—your Papa is away looking for you in London (are you really in the Great Metropolis?), and the rest of your Family is confin'd to the House. Cook reports that your Mother screams constantly and may have a Seizure at any moment. My Mamma whispers about you all the time. Mrs. Long and Mrs. Yates are always in the House; in fact the whole Neighbourhood is in an Uproar. Woe is me, Alas! You are Undone, and I grieve with all my Heart.

I am having the greatest Difficulty making sure I am alone on my Visits to the Post Office to see if a Letter has come. As Kitty is not allowed out of your House, I have to go with Sophy, and leave her with Jemima Morris while I pretend to visit the Library. So far I have been lucky, & No Body has seen me entering or leaving the Post Office. Also, I have had to save my Pin-Money, to pay for your Letter—if it ever comes.

Later

Your Letter finally arriv'd at the Post Office. *Still* Unmarried—can this really be true? I know not what to think. You are so Bold! To be alone with a Man, *all the Time,* Day & Night! My one Relief amid my Torment is that you are in high Spirits. I was imagining you chain'd in a Dungeon by your cruel Ravisher, and instead I find that you are enjoying the Pleasures of London! Your description of the Vauxhall Gardens makes them sound so alluring! O, how can you? When Mamma and Every Body insist that you are Lost!!!

Now that I have your Direction, I will send this Letter off to THE POST OFFICE, LONG ACRE, the moment I can escape from the House. Please write again as soon as you can & tell me that you are Married. If your Family knew that I had an Address for you, they would never forgive me for conniving with you to conceal your Whereabouts.

> Written in the greatest Perturbation,
> Your anxious Friend,
> Maria Lucas

————

To: The Same,
Care Of E. Gardiner, Esq.,
9 Gracechurch Street,
London
August 6th

My dear, dear Lydia,

You cannot imagine what a Relief it has been to receive your Letter. So you are definitely to Marry in less than two Weeks' time! It is too Good to be True. Mamma said . . . Oh, well, Mammas do have absurd Ideas. The silver tambour'd Muslin must be charming. How I wish I could be with you on the Great Day!! But it is a Comfort that we will see you in Hertfordshire shortly.

I am astonish'd to hear that Mr. Darcy has arrang'd your Wedding—and paid for it too! What a sly Puss your sister Lizzy is! The Lovers' Tiff between her and Mr. D must be over, & She communicating with him in Secret, without telling Any One! I would have expected Kitty to have found out, and to have told me how it came about—but of course I rarely get to see Kitty these Days, as she has been confin'd to the House for Weeks & Weeks. I hear that she has been knitting a little Coat to cover poor Pug's bald Patch.

You are right: it would be a great Thing for your Family if Lizzy & Mr. D were to marry, and good for you to have a very rich Sister. Let us hope that it will soon be arrang'd—but I promise faithfully to keep this News a Secret!

Your devoted Friend,
Maria Lucas

———

To: Mrs. Ensign Wickham,
The Royal Northumberland Fusiliers,
Newcastle.
September 4th

My dear Lydia,

I have to report a Catastrofe! Mamma discover'd me by the Kitchen Range, privily perusing your last Letter once more before consigning it to the Flames! She insisted on seeing it. I try'd to shew her only the last Page, but she snatch'd it from my Hands, and read the Whole, including the Passage where you recall'd how Mr. Darcy arranged your Marriage, and even paid your Marriage Portion! So Mamma now knows All! She hastened to tell Papa. They are persuaded that Mr. Darcy must have done it for Lizzy's sake, and that it is a Matter of Days before their Betrothal is announc'd. Thank Goodness, she says she will not speak of it to your Mamma. She could not endure "More of that Mrs. Bennet's Boasting. Time enough when the Deed is done." So your Mamma remains in Ignorance! But mine is writing to Charlotte to tell her the News, though I begg'd her not to.

Woe is me, alas! I have, all unwittingly, betray'd your Trust—and after you swore me to Secrecy—but I was a helpless Pawn in the cruel Fangs of Destiny—though I confess that I should have Burnt your Letter weeks ago. And the worst thing is that I cannot Burn it now, because Mamma has lock'd it away in her Desk.

When I reminded Mamma that when you were here you invited me to visit you in Newcastle, she rudely brush'd me aside, saying "I have more important Matters to attend to, Child." *Child!* It is SO unfair! Then she added, "Don't imagine that you will ever be making the Journey to Newcastle, miss. *That* Connexion is Over." When I asked her why, she had the Impertinence to say that you were Most Unsuitable! I am almost minded to escape to Meryton, catch the Stage, and make the Journey Northwards on my own!

Your contrite Friend,
Maria Lucas

———

To: Mrs. Ensign Wickham,
Royal Northumberland Regiment,
Newcastle.
September 16th

My dear Lydia,

Kitty has asked me to tell you the Great News! Mr. D's Aunt, Lady Catherine de Bourgh, came this morning to Longbourn, and sought out Lizzy. They had a long Private Talk. She must have come to arrange the Marriage—clearly it is a matter of days before the Engagement is announc'd betw. your Sister and Mr. D!! We met your Sisters outside the Milliner's at Meryton, and Kitty managed to draw me Aside to tell me. She begg'd me to write to you straight, as your Mamma reads every Letter sent to you from Longbourn, before adding a few words at the End. Kitty says she found Lady Catherine even more haughty and discourteous than her Nephew, and exclaim'd that you will be allied to a monstrous proud Dynasty. I believe however that she is Mistaken: Lady Catherine is all Condescension, and her Manner merely reflects her elevated Position in Society.

Yours in haste,
Maria Lucas

———

To: The Same
September 25th

My dear Lydia,

Alas! A most disappointing Turn of Events has plung'd your poor Sister into the most wretched Dejection.

We was still in the Dining-Parlour yesterday morning when Kitty was announc'd. She was out of Breath and red in the Face, & kept making despairing Signs at me, but Mamma notic'd Nothing, & kept her chatting for an Age, asking about Jane's Bride Clothes. When we finally made our Escape, we were scarce from the Room when Kitty hiss'd in my ear that she had lur'd them out for a Walk and then—left them ALONE!!

"Left whom?"

"Why, Mr. Darcy and Lizzy, of course! We was out on a Walk together, just the Three of us. I waited 'til we was at the bottom of your Drive, pretended I had Something important to tell you, and left them Unchaperon'd! Come on, let's go and see!"

We rac'd out—I didn't even stop to put on my Bonnet. We ran through Banfield Wood, and, when we were nearly at the Road, sure enough, there they were! And I had not even known that he was here in Hertfordshire! They had scarcely gone a hundred Paces since Kitty left them—they were standing in the Middle of the Road, she talking and he listening. I whisper'd to Kitty that it seem'd woefully Unromantic—no passionate Embrace, and she unlike to swoon into his Arms, though she did look rather pink in the Face. Finally she stopt her Chatter, and they walk'd off slowly. They were quite separate—she did not even take his Arm. Kitty had to acknowledge that their Demeanour gave no Hint of Love. What a Pity that we was too far away to catch what they said. . . .

All is hopeless. The Best that one can say for them is that they shew fewer Signs of Hostility, so the worst of the Lovers' Tiff is over. But she will never bring him up to Scratch now. No Happy Ending is in the Offing.

Is not it the saddest end to a Love Story? He, resolv'd to seek Happiness Elsewhere, she condemn'd to a lonely Life as an Old Maid! But I have just notic'd a nasty Rip in my second-best Muslin. It must have been running through the Woods.

Your devoted friend,
Maria Lucas

———

To: The Same
October 15th

My dear Lydia,

Thank you for your three Letters. I am so sorry that I have been unable to receive them all, as my Pin-Money is all gone, and Mamma gave me the choice between paying for the Postage on them and a new Pelisse for the Great Occasion; she relented only with the last one. I hope this finds you Well, and regret to hear that the Weather in Newcastle is proving so Nasty. Here we are enjoying a fine Autumn, and your Mamma plans to decorate the outside as well as the inside of the Church. She says she will use Autumn Flowers. I would prefer Blooms from the Glasshouse for *my* Marriage, though naturally I didn't say so. How I wish you could be here! But of course if Ensign Wickham cannot be spar'd from his Regiment, your Place is by his Side. You will have been told All in your Family's Letters! Do not you agree that it is the strangest Turn of Events? I can still scarcely believe it.

Mamma is in such a Flutter! She is cross and snappish, and returns from visiting Mrs. Bennet complaining of "Arrogance" & "Boastfulness." Then she fusses about her Toilette, and nothing seems good enough. She is to wear her best puce Gown, and has bought a new yellow paisley Shawl, and Mrs. Culpeper is making her a new Bonnet in a matching Hue. Mamma wishes it to be trimm'd with yellow Roses and Ears of ripe Corn—in October!—& was outrag'd when Mrs. Culpeper suggested Hops instead. Charlotte and Mr. Collins are arriving two days before the Great Day. Charlotte writes that Lady Catherine try'd to stop them coming, declaring that a Marriage between Mr. Darcy and Lizzy was an Abomination.

Yesterday, when we call'd on your Mamma, Lizzy beckon'd me out of the Room, much to my Surprize. "Was not it you who started the Rumour that Mr. Darcy and I were secretly engag'd?" says she.

I was quite frighten'd, and mumbl'd I know not what.

"When the Story first came out, I was Mortify'd. But as Time has passed, I have concluded that the Rumour was in part responsible for our Happiness. So you see I have you to thank for this joyful Outcome. When Kitty comes to visit us at Pemberley, you shall be of the Party." She kiss'd me, and gave me the prettiest gold Chain with seed Pearls woven in it. I shall wear it to the Wedding.

I always thought your Sister Lizzy was the least friendly of your oldest Sisters. She quite scared me when we staid together at

Hunsford. But now I see how wrong I was. What Fun we shall have when we visit Pemberley together—she will surely invite you and your dear Mr. W as well!

While I am there, who knows, I may meet the young Gentleman of Fortune who is destin'd to become my Husband! In fact, I am sure I will—it is written in my Stars!!

Your affectionate Friend,
Maria Lucas

MAYA SLATER gave up her career lecturing in French literature at London University to write fiction. *The Private Diary of Mr. Darcy* (published in the U.K. as *Mr Darcy's Diary*) is her first novel. As an academic, she published six books, including a verse translation of Molière's plays (Oxford World Classics), wrote many articles and papers, and lectured on four continents. She reviews for *The Times Literary Supplement*. She is married with two daughters and a tortoiseshell cat, and lives in London in a Victorian villa.

www.mayaslater.com

THE MYSTERIOUS CLOSET: A TALE

Myretta Robens

Cathy Fullerton trudged behind the tall woman in the dull black dress, wondering if people still wore bombazine. She could hear echoes of the group in the great hall and could see a glimmer of light from the end of the hallway. She'd lost count of the number of turns she'd made, following the black-clad housekeeper, and she couldn't remember when the walls had stopped being plaster covered with flocked wallpaper and turned into a dampish sort of rock. Where were the lights? And where the heck was her room?

When she had made her reservation over two months ago, staying in a converted abbey sounded like a wonderfully Gothic get-away, and a perfect escape from a life that had become unaccountably dreary after the end of her latest relationship. She hadn't expected it to be quite this Gothic.

Cathy cleared her throat. "Um, Miss . . . ?"

The figure in front of her barely broke stride. "Just call me Dorothy, ma'am."

Ma'am? Cathy was just 29 years old and this woman must be at least 104. "Just call me Catherine," she replied, feeling crankier by the minute. "And while you're calling me Catherine, can you please tell me where we're going?"

"To your room, Miss Catherine." The woman gestured vaguely toward another dimly lit corridor.

"May I ask . . . Dorothy . . . why everyone else appears to be staying in the main part of the building? You know, the part with wallpaper and electricity." *And the bar,* she added under her breath. "And I am, well, here."

"Certainly ma'am." Dorothy stopped in front of a heavy wooden door banded with iron and fumbled with a set of keys fastened at her waist that Catherine had not noticed as they were marching through the building. "You specifically reserved the Radcliffe Suite."

"I did?" Cathy peered at the plaque on the door, which definitely had something inscribed on it. Possibly *Radcliffe*. She shrugged. It had been two months. Perhaps she had, although she couldn't remember anything on the website quite like this.

Dorothy produced a heavy iron key, completely unlike the plastic cards Cathy had seen other guests receiving at the front desk, and fitted it into the equally heavy iron lock in the door.

"Is that my key?" Cathy pictured lugging eight ounces of metal around with her in a bag already weighed down by books, makeup, and various electronic gadgets.

"Strictly speaking, ma'am, it's our key." As Dorothy turned her back to unlock the door, Cathy rolled her eyes. This woman was straight out of *The Mysteries of Udolpho* or central casting. She was surprised there wasn't a raven perched on her shoulder. Dorothy turned the key, and Cathy winced as it grated against the tumblers.

"Well, yes, of course it's your key. What I meant is, will I need to carry that with me to get back into this room?" This holiday was seeming like less and less of a good idea, although perhaps it was just the room.

And then Cathy was alone in the Radcliffe Suite, the big iron key clutched in her fist, Dorothy's warning that this part of the abbey was haunted ringing in her ears. Fantastic. Just what she needed to cheer her up. She hefted the key, gauging the weight, and then tossed it onto a low chest, where it landed with a loud clang. Before she left, Dorothy had opened the heavy damask draperies shielding the mullioned window and said that dinner would be served at five o'clock.

Cathy poked at the surprisingly dust-free bed hangings on the large tester bed, checked her watch, and decided that she had time for a nap before dinner. Kicking off her shoes, she crawled onto the gigantic bed without pulling down the covers and lay gazing up at the canopy, hoping that she could sleep despite the jet lag and the time zone change.

She closed her eyes and examined the incident that had sent her to this gloomy corner of England. Broken relationships were not new. Certainly not to her. In fact, at twenty-nine, they were becoming decidedly old. Jeremy had not been the love of her life. She was pretty sure he hadn't been any sort of love. But he was kind and comfortable and easy to be around, and it had come as something of a rude awakening when he had found the love of *his* life and come home to tell her about it. Suddenly, the effort of meeting a new man, starting a new relationship, had seemed exhausting. And the idea that any new relationship, like the ones that had gone before, would be a temporary stop on an endless loop was just more than she could manage. So she had taken her hoarded holiday time and booked a room in a (mostly) renovated abbey. Apparently in the only un-renovated part. Thinking of Jeremy, and life alone, and dreary abbeys, Cathy drifted off to sleep.

Thunder cracked and a flash of lightning illuminated the room, startling Cathy from a sound sleep. She bolted from the bed, trying to figure where she was and what was happening. A second lightning flare revealed—ah yes—the Radcliffe Suite. What time was it? Cathy fumbled for the bed table and turned the light switch. Nothing.

Well, how Gothic was this? Cathy tugged at the waistband of her jeans, moving carefully across the room to the bureau on which she thought she remembered seeing a candle. Shouldn't she be floating around in a filmy nightdress, shivering her way through the rain-shrouded night, to meet her demon lover? Yes. There it was: the candle, not the demon lover. And, beside it, a box of lucifer matches. Once the candle was lit, Cathy squinted at her watch. Two-forty. And obviously A.M. So, no dinner.

She sighed and carried the candle toward the tapestry on the far wall that appeared to be moving. A breeze? The demon lover? Mice? Placing the candle on a table, Cathy drew the dingy tapestry aside. What was this? Squinting, she barely made out the outline of a door nearly as old and massive as the door to her room. An ancient padlock hung on the hasp. Well, why not? Cathy reached out and gave it a tug. It clicked open, and she pulled it free. Now what?

Now she had an unlocked door that probably did not lead to a walk-in closet. As sound sleep was obviously not one of the options open to her tonight, Cathy picked up the candle, grabbed the iron ring on the door, and tugged. It swung open with surprising ease, and she crept across the threshold into a small vaulted room containing a dusty old chest and some metal contraption about whose use she thought it best not to inquire. In the far corner was a tapestry, almost identical to the one in her room, and beside it, an identical chair.

Cathy had always had a stout heart, but for some reason, this duplicate tapestry and chair gave her goose bumps. The chair, though similar to the one in her room, looked as if it was shrouded in cobwebs. Edging closer, Cathy felt her heart give a thump as the mass of cobwebs seem to resolve itself into the shape of a man.

"Good morning."

Cathy jumped back a step and grabbed at the unidentified iron machine to her right. The cobweb had quite solidified into a rather attractive fair-haired gentleman. "What?" she gasped.

"I said, 'Good morning.' It is morning, isn't it? It's rather hard to tell in here." The man cocked his head curiously.

Cathy automatically looked at her watch. "Yes. Well, sort of. It's 2:45 A.M."

The man nodded as if she had confirmed something he had known all along, then gestured toward a chair, which Cathy could have sworn was not there when she entered this chamber. "Join me."

"Well, uh . . ." That voice: smooth, smoky, very English, very sexy. Nevertheless, Cathy continued to clutch a metal bar on the apparatus. He might sound like Patrick Stewart, but she'd never seen him before.

"Please, I insist." The gentleman gestured yet again, but this time seemed a bit more imperious.

"Okay," Cathy said. "All right. Um. Thanks." And she sat.

The man across from her raised an inquiring eyebrow and inspected her. "I rather thought you'd be in your nightgown," he said.

"What?" Cathy realized that her side of the conversation seemed to consist of one-syllable words. But, really, how did one react to this sort of thing?

"You are wearing—what are those called?—jeans?" the man observed.

Cathy looked down, strangely pleased to have her notion of

being in a filmy nightgown confirmed. She nodded. "Yes. These are called jeans." Why didn't he know that?

"And you are called?" the man prompted.

"Er, Cathy," Cathy responded.

"Ah, a lovely name. Are you Catherine, then?"

Cathy nodded.

"I once loved someone named Catherine," the man said.

"And you are?" Cathy had decided that if she were to converse with someone who had appeared to come from cobwebs, the least he could do was tell her his name.

"Here I am Henry."

"Here?" Cathy asked, emboldened by having something to call him. "Do you have other names in different places?"

Henry regarded her with a puzzled expression for several moments before answering. "Lately, I think I have only been here."

"Not precisely an answer, is it?" Cathy glanced quickly toward the iron instrument, wondering how frank she could be before she was shackled to it. As this scene was so absurd that it could only be a figment of her imagination, she decided not to worry about it.

Henry, or whoever he was in other places, had not moved, but sat staring at her in a rather flattering manner. Had it come to this? Was she flattered to be ogled by a bunch of cobwebs? Things were worse than she thought.

"Are you quite comfortable?" Henry asked.

An odd question considering the circumstances. But if she was imagining this (dreaming perhaps?), she supposed that nothing was too odd. Cathy sat back in her chair and decided to go with the flow for a change. And why not? Look where not going with the flow had landed her. "Quite comfortable," she said, wriggling into the cushions.

They sat in silence for a few moments, each examining the

other. Her host—Cathy decided that's what she would call him, as he had sort of been in the room when she got there—her host was quite appealing, if rather pale. But that could just have been the effect of candlelight or of his not being real. He had sandy hair and direct blue eyes fringed with thick lashes. Seated, he seemed tall and lean, but not soft. She imagined him on horseback or romping in a sunny garden with a litter of Newfoundland puppies. She felt a strange yearning to romp with them.

"Who are you, really," Cathy finally asked, "and what are you doing here?"

"I'm Henry," the pale gentleman repeated, looking a bit nonplussed. "And I think I'm here to meet you."

Cathy frowned, a look she knew did not enhance her own pale skin and which tended to drive her rather dramatically dark eyebrows up into her brownish bangs. "Is this part of the service?"

"Does it make a difference?" Henry asked.

Did it? Cathy's desire to frolic in the garden with Henry and his puppies immediately went to war with the suspicion that the hotel provided this little extra intrigue to amuse the guests. In that case, would Henry be flirting with the next woman to be suckered into the Radcliffe Suite?

Finally, Cathy shook her head. "At two-thirty in the morning, nothing makes much of a difference." Then she yawned. Darned jet lag. She had finally met someone interesting, if suspiciously nonexistent, and she was ready to fall asleep again.

"Come here." Henry patted the seat next to him.

Cathy blinked and shook her head. The band holding her hair back came loose, and a shiny curl fell across her face. She brushed it aside. Come here? When she had entered this—What? Room? Vault? Walk-in closet?—she could have sworn that there was one chair. Now there were obviously two and the second

seemed to have expanded into a loveseat. Well, dreams were not
to be questioned. She moved to the loveseat, beside Henry.

"You need to rest," Henry said in a soft voice, and pulled her
head down to his shoulder.

Cathy cuddled in, her eyes drifting shut. "Tell me about yourself," she murmured.

"No one who had seen me in my infancy would have supposed me born to be a hero," Henry began.

Cathy smiled. "And are you?"

"I might be," Henry said. "Much of that depends upon you."

When Cathy awoke, she was on her bed, still fully clothed and remarkably rested. After a quick shower and fresh clothes, she went
immediately to the door behind the tapestry and pulled it open.
The room was empty, except for the furniture: the chest, a medi-
eval torture rack to which she had apparently clung, a chair, and a
loveseat. An image arose in her mind of her head on Henry's shoulder, of the deep comfort she had felt as he put his arm around her,
and she experienced an unexpected pang. It hardly seemed fair.
She had met a man who made her feel completely comfortable and,
more, cherished, and he was . . . a figment of her imagination.
Didn't that just figure? How many times had she told her friends
that the only man worth having was a fictional one?

Cathy ran a comb through her hair, pulled it back with a red
ribbon, stuck a credit card and her half-pound key in her jeans
pocket, and went in search of breakfast. After several false turns,
she finally found the part of the abbey that had moved into the
current century and made her way to the dining room.

The place seemed to be full of couples happily toasting each
other with orange juice and ordering huge English breakfasts. Several groups took up the large tables in the center of the room. Cathy
stood in the doorway and scanned the room for an empty table.

"Hey!" A woman at one of the tables was waving at her. "Looking for a seat? Over here." She gestured to her right. Cathy smiled gratefully and joined the group.

"I'm Sheila," her savior said, "and I'd introduce the rest of these rapscallions, but you won't remember their names, so just ask them when you want to know. English breakfast?" she added, pouring orange juice into Cathy's glass. Cathy nodded, aware that she now had an imaginary mother and a group of all-too-real American tourists as well as an imaginary boyfriend. How weird could a holiday get?

"Just get here?" Sheila asked, passing a plate of sausages.

"Last night," Cathy said, "and it's been kind of, well, odd ever since."

"Jet lag. Know what you mean. We all arrived from New York a few days ago." Sheila speared a sausage onto Cathy's plate.

"Maybe it is jet lag." Cathy hesitated before continuing. "Where are you staying?"

"Here," Sheila said. "We're all staying here else we couldn't eat in the dining room."

"No, I mean where are your rooms?" Cathy looked around the table, including the rest of the group in her question.

They all called out room numbers and floors.

"In the refurbished part of the abbey, then?" she asked.

"Well, of course," one of the men across the table answered. "Where else?"

"Where are you staying?" Sheila asked.

Cathy colored for no reason she could identify. "I . . . I'm in the Radcliffe Suite."

"What?" "Never heard of it." "A suite? How'd you get a suite?" "Know someone in management?" The responses shot out from around the table.

"Where would that be?" Sheila asked.

"In the old part of the abbey. The part with stone walls and candles." Cathy shrugged as if to downplay the oddness of what she had just said.

"Hey. That must be part of the ghost tour. I didn't know they let people stay there. I'll have to ask for that next time I come."

"Ghosts?" Cathy gave a little shiver. Had she spent the early hours of the morning communing with a ghost? Oh, sure. That made perfect sense. Not jet lag. Not a dream. A ghost. She felt so much better.

"Sure. This is a haunted abbey. At least that's what the pamphlet says. Pick one up at the front desk." Sheila returned to her plate.

Breakfast continued with the usual chitchat. "Where are you from?" "What do you do?" "How long are you staying?" "Where do you go from here?" "Any plans for the day?"

Cathy answered them all with a minimum of elaboration. "Boston." "I'm an editor." "I'm not sure how long I'll be here." "Bath." "Nope. No plans."

"Then come with us," Sheila said in response to Cathy's last answer. "We're taking the coach to Clifton. Maybe go on to Blaise Castle. The brochure says it's the finest castle in England." Sheila waggled her eyebrows.

Cathy grinned. "So I've heard. Sure. Why not. I'd love to go."

Cathy spent the rest of breakfast examining the other diners and waitstaff, hoping to catch a glimpse of her early morning visitor. No one looked remotely like the mysterious Henry, although she did think she saw a tall fair-haired man disappear around the corner into the kitchen. She very nearly got up to follow him but was distracted by the group at her table standing in unison. Apparently it was time to leave.

Cathy boarded the coach with everyone else and found a seat by a window. She was immediately joined by a florid young man who she guessed was probably about her age. She nodded politely and returned to her perusal of the abbey.

As the coach driver closed the door, she saw him. Henry, coming out the main entrance. She was sure of it. As he passed the coach, he raised his head and looked directly at her, a quizzical expression on his face. Was it her Henry or was it her imagination?

"Wait!" She tried to rise and signal the driver that she wanted to get off, but was stymied by the man sitting next to her. He grabbed her arm and pulled her back into the seat.

"Sit down," he said in a hearty voice. "We're leaving and it's too late to change your mind now." And before she could wrestle free, they were on the road toward Clifton, and Henry or his doppelgänger was left in the courtyard staring after the departing bus. Cathy continued to gaze out the window, trying to ignore her seatmate.

"Name is Jack Thorpe," he informed the back of her head. "Been traveling with these yahoos for nearly a week. Nice to see a new face."

Relenting, Cathy turned to face Jack, suppressing a snort. John Thorpe. Just her luck.

It was all the encouragement he needed to keep talking. "What do you drive?" he asked, but did not wait for an answer. "I just picked up a vintage Corvette. Got it for a steal off of an old schoolmate. Doesn't get great mileage, but, hey, you don't expect that on a Corvette, eh?" He elbowed her in the ribs.

Cathy tried to turn back to the window, but he wasn't done. "Wish I had it with me. Be much better than tooling around in this old crate. If I had it here, I could really show you how touring in England should be done."

Cathy stifled a yawn.

After an interminable tour, during which Jack stuck to her side like Gorilla Glue, the coach deposited the group back at the

Abbey Hotel. Cathy turned down an invitation to join them for dinner and escaped to her room.

It was still daylight, and the Radcliffe Suite looked a tad less atmospheric than it had last night during the thunderstorm. There were fresh towels on the chest in the bathroom, and the tapestry had been straightened over the oak door on the far wall. Without hesitation, Cathy crossed the room and pulled it back. The door was still there and was still unlocked. She yanked it open and light from her room flooded the vaulted chamber revealing . . . a vaulted chamber . . . with shelves . . . and a clothes rack. A walk-in closet?

She backed up a step. How ridiculous could she be? Of course it was a closet, or a dressing room or another bedroom or something that would make sense in a hotel suite. Not a candlelit chamber with instruments of torture and a strangely attractive but ephemeral inhabitant. Feeling stupid, she slammed the door and went in search of the room service menu.

As she was staying in a converted abbey and not a five-star hotel, room service turned out to be tikka masala from the Indian take-away in the village. By 10:00 P.M., fed but disheartened, Cathy changed into her nightgown and crawled into bed.

A light rain had begun to tap against the window, and she pulled the covers over her head and wondered if she was losing her mind. How in God's name had she come to the conclusion that the walk-in closet held a sexy phantom? In what part of her jet-lagged brain had she conjured up Henry, and why, pray tell, did she think that the man outside the coach had been the same person? She must be missing Jeremy more than she thought, or perhaps she had narrowly escaped a nervous breakdown. Or maybe she had not escaped it at all.

It was dark when Cathy woke from a heavy sleep. The rain still pattered against the windows, and the only light in the room was a watery glow from somewhere outside. Not the moon; it was raining. Streetlamps? Fairies? Rolling to her side, Cathy snuggled into the warm form beside her in the bed.

"Mmmmm." She threw her arm over the body and nuzzled the neck, feeling the enticing rasp of a day's growth of beard and the agreeable smell of clean linen and male skin. An arm curled around her shoulders and drew her closer.

"What?!" Snapping bolt upright, Cathy snatched a pillow and held it in front of her like a shield.

"What?" A sleepy, masculine voice with a deliciously familiar accent issued from the body beside her. Henry? Fumbling on her nightstand, she flicked the light switch. Which was not working—again. Naturally. But she was prepared this time. Scrambling from the bed, she lit the candle she had placed beside the lamp and turned back to the bed.

Henry, her cobweb man, her ghost, the figment of her imagination, lay cocooned in the covers, looking up at her with a smile of gentle bemusement. "Come back to bed, Cathy." He patted the spot she had just vacated.

"Come back to bed? What are you doing here? Who are you?" Cathy looked around the room, trying to figure out what was going on. The tapestry was pulled back and the door to the walk-in closet stood ajar.

"What do you mean, 'who am I'? I'm Henry."

"You're a dream," she said, backing a little farther from the bed.

"Thank you, darling." Henry grinned. "I love you too."

She couldn't help it. He made her smile and kindled a sudden warmth within her. It made no sense. Not only did she not know who this man was, she was pretty sure that he wasn't even real. And yet, there he was in her bed, and there was that inviting niche right beside him.

Cathy moved back and sat on the edge of the bed, looking down into the face that had become oddly familiar and incredibly dear within such a short time. Sighing, she rolled back onto her pillow and turned to face him. "What the heck. Promise to tell me who you are in the morning."

"I assure you that you will know everything about me by morning," Henry said, gathering her close and just holding her.

"Did I see you this morning outside the coach?" she asked, settling into Henry's embrace.

"Did you? I wonder."

"Really. I thought I did," Cathy insisted.

"Shouldn't you have gotten off to find out?"

"Oh, I wanted to, truly, but an awful man wouldn't let me and then we were on the road." She placed her hand over his heart. "I'm sorry," she whispered.

"Nothing to be sorry about, my dear. Here you are now. That's all that matters."

"Is it really? Frankly, I don't understand any of this and, if I thought you were real, I certainly wouldn't be in this bed with you."

Henry laughed. "I'm as real as you want me to be," he said.

Oh, that voice. Cathy smiled to herself as the candle guttered.

In the morning he was gone, although Cathy could have sworn she could smell a faint whiff of his citrusy scent when she buried her head in the pillow. Which she did for several seconds, trying to remember the night. Why did he seem so real after dark and so . . . nonexistent in broad daylight? She lay looking at the velvet canopy over the bed, weighing the possibilities. Vampire? She felt her neck. No. She didn't believe in vampires. Ghost? Ditto. Visitor from another dimension? Nah. Visitor from another planet? Please! Figment of her fevered imagination?

Bingo! Cathy rolled out of bed. One more day in the abbey and then on to Bath.

Cathy loitered in the lobby, looking at ghost brochures, trying to avoid the group from yesterday's dreadful trip to Clifton. She was almost successful.

"There she is." Sheila's cheery voice rang out across the hall. Cathy's heart sank as she slowly turned around to find herself facing the argyle-clad chest of Jack Whatever-his-name-was.

"Um, hi," she said, trying to step around the bulky form invading her personal space.

"Wait," he said, taking her arm. "We're heading to Stonehenge today. You've got to see it."

Cathy was not about to be importuned twice by the same person. "No, thanks. Seen it," she said, wresting her arm from his grasp. "I've got other plans. See you." And she practically ran toward the door before anyone else could stop her. Once outside, she looked wildly around. Plans. She had plans. What were they and how could she get away before the Stonehenge contingent emerged? She looked down at the brochure still clutched in her hand. The Winchcombe Ghost Walk. Why not?

Winchcombe was an unprepossessing little town, but did have some interesting ninth-century and Neolithic sites, all apparently haunted. Cathy wandered the purported route to a Neolithic burial chamber. The lane was lined with hawthorn and primrose, but an occasional break in the hedges afforded a glimpse of the homes along the lane.

She came to a small gap and stopped, entranced by the sight: the back garden of a substantial stone house, alive with bloom and filled with the excited noise of a litter of puppies. She lingered to watch them play, wondering why they seemed so familiar, and fighting a strong urge to climb the fence and join them. The back door opened and the puppies tumbled over each other in a rush to enter the house. Cathy peered into the shadowy doorway, but couldn't tell who held the door. Nor could she figure out why she wanted to know. The door clicked shut, and she moved on in her pursuit of Neolithic ghosts.

One last night in the abbey. Cathy bolted down a sandwich from a stand in town and headed back to her room, loath to miss any possible time with her cobwebby lover. Once at her door, she fished around in her backpack for her key and thought about what a shame it was that her real life could not hold a candle to her nervous breakdown.

Having found the key settled at the very bottom of her pack, Cathy entered the Radcliffe Suite, flung her backpack onto the bed, and headed right for the closet.

What an idiot she was. Cathy stared at the empty shelves for a full minute before returning to the bed and throwing herself down in a heap of confusion. A bout of weeping led to a nap and another middle-of-the-night awakening. But this time, there was electricity and she was alone. Alone and miserable, missing someone who did not exist, wondering about her sanity and trying to decide whether she should continue with her holiday or just pack up and go home.

By morning, she had decided to continue on to Bath. Why waste those reservations at the B&B in Bathwick and why miss a chance to tread in Catherine Morland's footsteps? She packed, made one last check of the closet, and went to the lobby to check out.

It was early enough not to have to fend off the people she had come to think of as the Annoying Tourists, for which she thanked heaven as she stood on the sweep waiting for the man who was delivering the hired car. She shaded her eyes against the sun and watched an ancient Land Rover pull into the drive and swing toward the entrance. She stepped back as it pulled to a stop in front of her and the driver's door opened.

She stepped back again when she saw the driver. "Henry?"

He grinned. "Well, here they call me Hal," he said. "Hal Woodston." He gave a little bow. "But you may call me anything you like."

"What . . . what are you doing here?"

"I'm here to take you home. The puppies are anxious to meet you." He picked up her suitcase and tossed it into the back of the car.

"But . . ."

Henry leaned over and kissed her. "Don't ask questions, dearest. Everything is just as it's meant to be."

"Why not?" Cathy climbed into the passenger seat and buckled her seatbelt. She would sort out all that identity and imagination stuff later. Now, why not, indeed?

MYRETTA ROBENS is a writer of Regency Romance whose second novel, *Just Say Yes,* won the Holt Medallion and was a finalist for the Romance Writers of America RITA award. Myretta is a longtime Janeite who co-founded the Republic of Pemberley website in 1997 and still runs the site, which is now a major Jane Austen destination on the Web, drawing 150,000 unique visitors each month. A former technology director at Harvard University, when Myretta is not writing or working with her website, she blogs for Heroes and Heartbreakers.

www.pemberley.com
www.heroesandheartbreakers.com
@pemberleydotcom on Twitter

JANE AUSTEN'S CAT

Diana Birchall

"My present Elegancies have not yet made me indifferent
to such matters. I am still a Cat if I see a Mouse."

The summer of 1813 opened on Chawton, rainy at first, but soon turning into a very properly sunny July, making the rose-red bricks of the cottage glow, and the laburnum blossom shine gold as Jane Austen looked out the open window into the garden. The white syringa made a handsome display, and the shrubbery was filled with Sweet William, pinks, and columbine. But Jane's glance was unseeing, her thoughts turned inward. She was writing.

Her mother and sister were at the Great House for the afternoon, where her brother Edward, having successfully overseen the getting in of the hay, was now planning to lay out a new garden, to be enclosed by a brick wall. She could imagine, without having to hear it, the ongoing discussion with her brother James and her nephews, as to the relative merits of the garden being placed at the top of the lawn behind the House, or remaining near the Rectory. So she was in hopes of some continued quiet, a precious and rare commodity in this summer, for her brother Charles and his children had just left after a month's visit, while Edward and his long string of children were in residence at the Great House at Chawton, and James and his family were spending some weeks at the small one. Often the house was boiling with people, and Jane appreciated the silence as she deliberately brought the final threads of *Mansfield Park* toward their completion.

Both Cassandra and Henry had implored her to end the story differently, with Fanny marrying Henry Crawford and Edmund marrying Mary, but she wrote with calm and certain decision, making Mary's views on her brother's misconduct with Maria Bertram far too outrageous for her ever to become an acceptable wife to Edmund.

A scuffling of feet was heard outside the door, and a little girl precipitated herself into the room, holding a large, squirming tortoise-shell tabby cat in her arms. This was Caroline, her brother James's younger daughter of eight years old, and a favorite, though not particularly welcome at the moment. Caroline's older half-sister Anna, a lovely girl just turned twenty, with hazel eyes and a clear complexion, followed.

"Caroline! You must not disturb Aunt Jane when she is writing. I am so sorry, dear Aunt," she said.

Jane smiled, turned her paper over, put up her pen, and adjusted the white cap she wore over her dark hair, which had slipped a little while she was absorbedly composing at the small round table in the dining-parlour. "You are not disturbing me, my dears. I am come to a good stopping place. Tom will not die. But oh," she said, regarding the cat.

"Oh, Caroline, the cat. You know Aunt Jane can't bear cats . . ."

"Why do you not like cats, Aunt Jane? Tyger won't scratch you, he wouldn't."

"Cats are very well, Caroline, in the garden or in the kitchen;

but when they venture too near, they make my eyes hurt, you know, and then I catch the head-ache."

"I will take Tyger away then," said Caroline, disappointed.

"No, do not, my love. Only do not let him get up on the table. As long as I do not touch him, I believe we will do very well."

"Are you sure?"

"Quite. And what have you been doing today, young ladies? Have you gone on with your story, Anna? Have you determined what sort of a novel it is to be?"

"It will be a horrid novel, Aunt Jane," said Anna enthusiastically. "I am having a murdered ancestress haunt the castle as a spectre!"

Jane removed her spectacles and folded them away inside her writing-desk. "Anna, Anna," she said in mock sorrow, "I knew how it would be. We will have your 'Car of Falkenstein' story all over again. I never laughed so much in my life."

On a previous visit, Jane and Anna had conspired on a ridiculous tale of a neighbor, whose rides in a carriage had given rise to extravagantly imagined, horrid plots.

"A most ghastly vision, the result of reading too many novels from the circulating library. But seriously, Anna, I was half in hopes your next work would deal more in the probable."

"The horrid and the tragical are so much more striking, Aunt Jane," Anna protested. "I know you are right, however, and I must improve my taste, if I am to be an author like you."

"What, like me, and not like our esteemed Mrs. Radcliffe, or Mrs. Hunter, who so delighted us last summer with *Lady Maclairn, the Victim of Villainy*? Nearly drowning in her own tears!"

"Yes, how we did laugh at her! But I do know what you mean, Aunt Jane. It is harder to make characters who are truly lifelike, than skeletons and ghouls."

"I am glad you are so wise as to know it; but I confess a secret desire to see you work up something amusing about the excesses of your murderess. Only it might be too terrible for the public."

Caroline looked up from playing with the cat.

"What have you been writing, Aunt Jane? Is it about Jane and Elizabeth again? That is what you were writing when we were here last summer."

"No, Caroline, you know *Pride and Prejudice* has been printed," Anna told her. "Only remember, it is rather a great secret that Aunt Jane wrote it, so we are not to talk about it."

"That is very good of you, Anna. Your father has been so kind in not mentioning it everywhere; unlike your Uncle Henry. I believe he has told his entire acquaintance that the author is his sister. I do not doubt that he is now telling every one he meets in Scotland."

"Won't he be here next week? You can scold him well, then," said Anna.

Jane shook her head. "No. I would not wish to give him even a moment's pain, so soon after his loss of poor Eliza." Henry's wife had died only in April, and he had gone to Scotland for a change of scene. "And if it gives him pleasure to tell people about it, I must try to harden myself, though I dislike it being spoken of by every person one meets."

"I am sure, if I should ever be so happy as to publish a novel, I would go to London and meet all the famous!" exclaimed Anna.

"Ah, your nature is more sociable than mine, Anna. To be lionized would make me feel wild indeed. No, no, I am much better off here, where I belong."

"Well, Caroline, I must say your cat is behaving very well. He quite deserves the honour of the poem your papa wrote on him, at Christmas."

Caroline beamed. "It does not show him off as a very good cat, however. Stealing the mutton steak meant for Papa's supper."

"Can you say the poem for Aunt Jane?" Anna urged.

"No, it is too long, but you know he said that if Tyger ever did such a thing again he would have him shot through the head and hung up with the stoats and weasels as a lesson to the tabby race. But poor Tyger, I won't let that happen." She hugged the cat, which wriggled violently.

"James was always a fine versifier," said Jane, "and it is natural that the talent has descended to his son."

For James-Edward, Caroline's older brother, a schoolboy of fifteen, had lately written a humorous verse to his Aunt Jane expressing his surprise at discovering she was the authoress of two famous volumes.

"Oh, I thought his verses were so inelegant," said Anna disparagingly, "saying he was as surprised as a pig the butcher had stuck though with a knife!"

"And to have a relation whose works were dispersed through the whole of the nation. No; they are fresh, and artless, and I appreciate his sentiment—that I do."

"But you write poems that are almost as good," said Caroline critically. "The one you wrote about Anna was so fine, I wish you would write one about me."

Jane laughed. "I would call it a deliberately bad poem, Caroline, when I rhymed 'Anna' with 'savannah,' and said her wit descended like Niagara Falls. Dear me! How silly we are."

"'Caroline' would be easier to rhyme with than 'Anna,'" persisted the little girl.

"My poems are not my pride, though they are a family failing. A cat cannot steal meat without an Austen writing an ode on it. However, I will try."

She bent over her table, dipped her quill, wrote a few lines, and then handed the paper to Anna. Anna read, and laughed.

> *Merits unnumbered, has dear Caroline,*
> *As good and as fair as a goddess*
> *The Patroness of creatures feline*
> *Of curious genius, the oddest.*
>
> *Oh, where can we find, a mind of pure pearl?*
> *A heart of such tenderness, that*
> *We might search through the world, and not find a girl*
> *Who took kinder care of a cat.*

"It is very nice," said Caroline critically, "I like it being about me, but you do tell stories and write novels much better than poems."

"Who are the characters you are writing about now, Aunt Jane?" asked Anna.

"I am writing about Fanny."

"Oh, please tell about her. What does she do?"

"Fanny is a very singular girl, for she refuses to act. She thinks acting quite wicked. I am afraid she is not my most amusing heroine; but I wanted a complete change, after my last. I do not wish it to be thought that wit should be more prized than goodness."

"But acting isn't wicked—Papa says that you used to have plays, in Steventon barn," said Anna. "I wish I could have seen them."

"Did you act too, Aunt Jane? Or did you refuse, like Fanny?"

"I am sure you were the very best of the actresses! You do read so beautifully."

"Not quite," said Jane modestly. "No; our best actress was your Aunt Eliza."

"Aunt Eliza?" asked Anna thoughtfully. "I can't picture that. I only think of her as so sadly ill, and not able to leave her bed for so long."

"Yet there was a time when she was young and pretty, and quite the greatest flirt of the modern age."

Jane was silent for a moment, thinking of her sister-in-law. How the gayest spirit of all the Steventon theatricals had suffered, and been brought down to dust.

"My father once told me he was in love with her," said Anna, "and she could not decide between him and Uncle Henry. I can hardly believe it."

"Many men wanted to marry Eliza," Jane admitted. "Sometimes I thought it was only a game to her. Yet she really had a warm heart. It was her living in France so long, that gave her the airs of the world."

"It is as well Uncle Henry got her," said Anna. "He is much more fashionable than our papa."

"I admired her very much, as a girl. And she has been so much in my thoughts that one of my characters, Mary Crawford, has grown rather like her."

"Will you read us some of what you have written, Aunt?" begged Anna. "We laughed to die when you were reading about Elizabeth and Mr. Collins!"

"The work I have in hand may disappoint you, then; it is quite different. And I think it may be a little dull for . . ." She nodded at Caroline.

"Then tell us a story, Aunt Jane. Just made up for me, like your fairy tales," Caroline implored.

"But fairy tales may not amuse a young lady like Anna. I have the two of you to please equally."

"Oh, I always loved your fairy tales, Aunt Jane, and I do still. Please tell one—if you are not too tired from your writing."

"Very well. Only let us have our cold meat, first, it is time," said Jane, and summoned a maid, who shortly brought in plates of cold pie, salad from the garden, and sweet-cake, and placed them on the sideboard with the elderberry cordial. Caroline was bid to send Tyger out, and she let go the animal, which made a bee-line for the window, and after surveying the sunny scene without, jumped down into the shrubbery and was away.

When they had eaten, Jane asked Caroline what story she wanted told. "Fairies again? Command me."

"Oh, make a story about a cat!"

"Your cat? Tyger? Or a constellation of cats?"

"A constellation!"

"But I don't want to hear about cats—I want to hear more about Fanny, and acting and all," complained Anna.

Jane sipped her cordial thoughtfully, before she spoke.

"Once there lived a terrible old cat named Mrs. Norris."

"Was she a tortoise-shell cat, like Tyger?"

"Why yes, I rather think she was. A fierce, brindled creature, with jowls and a face like a monkey."

"My Tyger has a face like a pansy, *I* think."

"Well, Mrs. Norris was a stout cat, with short legs, and a propensity to direct all the household. She considered herself as the lady in charge, and gave orders very firmly, whether needful or not."

"Was she as dictatorial as Lady Catherine de Bourgh?" asked Anna.

"Quite different. She had not so much money, or rank. She was a clergyman's widow, but she did like to interfere, quite as much as Lady Catherine, and her prejudice, and her faulty judgment, made her a penance to all around. She was particularly unkind to a poor little kitten—we may call her Fanny, like my heroine."

"And what sort of kitten was Fanny?" Caroline inquired breathlessly. "Did she have brown hair, like me?"

"She was a little grey kitten, with soft, light eyes. Mrs. Norris was harsh to her, very. She would not let her play with the other cats, but kept her down, reminding her that she was not a pure bred; she would not let her have anything nice, not even to sit by the fire. Which is very cruel when you think how cold it is in Northamptonshire in winter, and how cats admire a good fire."

"The story is set in Northamptonshire, then? Not in a castle, I suppose," asked Anna, regretfully.

"No, but a very grand house, with a park five miles round. I shall call it Mans-cat Park."

"Oh! Is it like the Great House here at Chawton?"

"Very. And at Mans-cat Park, Mrs. Norris managed to get everything good for herself."

"What sort of things?"

"Oh, anything that was going. Cheese, and plants, but most of all, green baize."

"Green baize? What on earth was that for? It is ugly stuff," commented Anna. "My stepmother cuts it out for the poor to wear."

"This particular baize was intended for curtains, in the theatre. I suppose she thought the baize would come in useful, later, to line her sleeping-basket."

"Did she act—Mrs. Norris?" asked Caroline.

"No; it was the younger cats that were to act. The play was to be Puss-cats' Vows. And they wanted poor little Fanny to exhibit, but she was too modest, and shy. Mrs. Norris bullied her, and kept her working away making the costumes for all the other cats to wear."

Anna and Caroline were in fits of laughter.

"Costumes, for cats? Live cats?"

"I used to dress up my kitty in doll's clothes!"

"Certainly; one gentleman cat was to wear a cloak of pink silk, and that took a good deal of sewing, which is quite difficult for cats to achieve, with only their teeth and paws, for they cannot hold a needle. The sewing did not distress Fanny, so much as seeing the improper way the other cats behaved. Or hearing, I should say. You know what cats are; you have heard them caterwauling at night."

"Yes, and then they have kittens," said Caroline wisely.

"Yes; shocking, is not it? It would be improper to tell you of all their ways, but Mrs. Norris encouraged them in their behavior, and it was indeed a cat-astrophe."

Caroline choked with giggles, but Anna wanted to know what happened to Fanny.

"Oh, Fanny grew from a kitten into a cat and in due course became lady of the whole concern."

"And Mrs. Norris?"

"She was put right out, with the feral cats and vermin, but I believe she did take all the green baize with her, so at least she is sleeping warm of a night."

Caroline was thinking about the story.

"Why was Mrs. Norris so very bad, do you think?"

"That's the question. What makes some cats bad and others good? But I think it was, in her case, that in her litter were two especially beautiful cats, and Mrs. Norris felt quite inferior. So she spent the rest of her life attending to her own importance. Such things do happen, in nature. We all like to be important."

"What happened to the beautiful ones?" Caroline wanted to know.

"Those two cats were always excessively lazy, and they never altered. One had long lustrous silky fur, but spent her life lying on the sofa. The other was poor, with an enormous litter to keep, but you will be glad to know that they all lived happily ever after. And now I think it is Anna's turn to tell a story."

Anna rose and spun around the room restlessly.

"I shall tell you one about a heroine who is fathoms deep in love," she said.

"Fathoms? I hope it is a sincere love, otherwise such a commonplace expression as that will kill it entirely. And why do I suspect that this story is to be based on life?"

"It is, Aunt Jane . . . I have been wanting to consult you. . . ." Anna stopped spinning, flushed, and looked at her little sister.

"Offers have been flowing in, I collect?" asked Jane archly.

"Well . . . I had better tell you when we are alone. . . ."

"I am quite grown up enough to hear, Anna," exclaimed Caroline indignantly. "Indeed, I know all about Mr. Benjamin Lefroy being in love with you, and you refusing Mr. Terry, and then there's the older richer one but you won't tell me his name."

"Quite enough to puzzle a young lady, I should say, or for a three-volume novel. Have you ascertained, out of all this assemblage, which gentleman you love best?"

"Yes, I believe I have," murmured Anna, looking down.

"I hope he will be the richest one," said Caroline.

"I hope we will not be dancing at your wedding too soon," said Jane kindly. "At twenty, you need not be in a hurry, Anna, and I trust you will make no choice, until you are tolerably well acquainted with your own heart."

This kind of talking bored Caroline, and she begged for a story about another mean cat.

"Do you suppose that I have an endless supply of mean cats up my sleeve?"

"No, but will you tell us about Lady Catherine again?"

"Why, you have heard it already."

"Oh, but make her a cat."

"Well: to please you, then, I would suppose her to be another tortoise-shell, with strongly marked features and an inordinately proud tail, but she is no relation to Mrs. Norris; she is a Kent cat."

"Does she live at Godmersham, where my cousins live when they are not at the Great House?"

"She has a very fine mansion-hutch of her own, and all the cat families round there are martyrs to her interference."

"I do like your wicked cats best, Aunt Jane. What cat will you tell us about next?"

"Now, Caroline, that is more than enough of cats," said Jane firmly. "I know you love them, but I prefer to have my stories be about men and women."

"That is too bad," said Caroline wistfully, "I was going to give you Tyger as a present, if only you could love him."

"Then he would have the honour and the merit of being Jane Austen's Cat," said Anna, "but I do not think Aunt Jane would like it."

"The honour and merit are nearly the same," said Jane dryly, "but I cannot keep your cat on any account. I am very sorry."

"Please, will you tell about the people who will be in your next book?" asked Anna. "Do you know them yet?

"Oh, yes. There is a Mr. Woodhouse, who likes to sit by a warm fire in the hottest days in July, just as an old cat might, Caroline; and a silly kitten of a girl named Harriet, who collects pencil stubs belonging to the sleek cat she is in love with; and there is a Miss Bates, who never once stops mewing . . ."

"Will there be lovers in the novel?" Anna asked eagerly.

"Indeed, yes, for what is a novel without lovers in it?"

"And it all ends happily?" urged Caroline.

"Certainly."

"Aunt Jane's stories always end happily, fairy ones, and cat ones, and real ones alike," Anna observed with complacence.

"Those are the laws of literary composition, Anna," Jane answered, amused. "You would feel it a take-in, to read three volumes and find as the pages were compressing to their end, that the right people did not marry, and the wrong people did. I have been thinking of that a good deal, of late."

"And must all stories end in a wedding?"

"The best sort do."

"Aunt Jane, why did you never have a wedding, yourself?" asked Caroline.

Anna was shocked. "Caroline! You are too old to be asking such questions."

"But why? I know Aunt Cassandra was going to be married once, but the gentleman died of a fever, in the West Indies. She told us about it herself. Why may I not know about Aunt Jane?"

Anna stood. "Caroline, you are in disgrace. How can you talk to your aunt so unfeelingly, when she is so kind to you. Go out into the garden and play with your cat, if you cannot speak in a proper manner."

"I didn't mean anything, Anna," the child pleaded.

"Never mind, Anna," Jane said gently, "it is no matter, Caroline means no harm. It is very natural to want to know about people."

"But it is not right to ask such questions," said Anna, still looking angrily at her little half-sister.

"The subject need not be prohibited," said Jane cheerfully. "Do not forget that your brother has even suggested the Prince Regent as a husband for me."

Anna had to smile. "Yes, in his poem. I remember. 'And indeed if the Princess should lose her dear life, / You might have a good chance of becoming his wife.'"

"Now to me, that would be a tragical fate," said Jane. "I do not like the man, and cannot approve his treatment of his wife. Better be single than married to such a person, however high and mighty."

The girls were quiet, thinking this over, but Anna, after a moment, said, "Aunt Jane, I thought I was in love with Mr. Terry, and now I believe I really am in love with Ben. It is so easy to love, for me! It makes me worry. What if one marries the wrong man? How does one know? Your heroines all fall in love, but I do not believe one of them is as perplexed as I am."

"When you truly love," Jane advised, "it will become clear."

"Will it? How do you know . . ." Anna stopped.

Jane considered her nieces, both gazing at her across the shining mahogany dining-table, littered with the remains of their cake. She sat straight-backed in her hard chair, a woman still handsome, but in middle life, with lines forming in the fine skin by her candid hazel eyes, lightly circled with tiredness.

"I will tell you one more story," she said reluctantly, "concerning Love. Yes, a cat story, Caroline."

"What sort of cat?" asked Caroline, bouncing.

"A long, thin sort of cat, I think, with darkish fur. She came from a good litter that lived in the countryside, and was very merry, though she tended to be over satiric, and to laugh at her fellow beings."

"I did not know cats laughed."

"She is speaking metaphorically, Caroline. Now hush."

"Yes—and like any other young female cat, this cat—I shall call her Susan—had several admirers among cats of the other sex, but never quite settled on any."

"What happened to the admirers?" asked Anna, anxiously.

"One suitor was warned off because of Susan's lack of fortune; another talked of engaging himself to her, but never did; several others she ran away from before they had a chance to propose, because she saw she could not like them."

"And did she never marry, in the end?"

There was a thoughtful pause, as Jane looked out the window, at the bright summer green of the little Hampshire garden, the soft breeze lightly ruffling the shrubbery. When she resumed, her voice was low.

"One summer, she and her family went on a tour of the seaside, to a place on the south coast."

"Oh! Was it pretty? Were there bathing-machines? Did they sell cockles on the pier?"

"Yes, all of that. A fine open sea, and the town had reddish-brown cliffs that cats could leap up with ease."

Caroline was charmed. "Was it a town we know, Aunt Jane?"

"No; I do not think you have ever been to Catmouth. Well, it was there, at the seaside, Susan met a cat who was handsome, clever, and good."

"What was his profession?" asked Anna.

"He was a clergyman," said Jane, with a little sigh.

"Cats can't be Christians," pointed out Caroline logically.

"This cat was, if it is not heresy to say so," said Jane. "Well, they were there for a month, and had walks together, never to be forgotten; a visit that was only too short, yet long enough to prove that they had interests in common, and could not fail to be a happy couple together, if only . . ."

"If only, what?" asked Caroline. "Did they not marry?"

"He was obliged to go back to his parish duties, but not without earnest invitations from Susan, her mother, and her sister, to visit them at their home; invitations which he as earnestly promised to fulfil."

"And he did not?" cried Anna.

"Susan went home," Jane continued, "and letters followed; it was not thought wrong for them to correspond, and her mother knew it. The date was fixed for him to visit them for a week in the autumn, at their lodgings at Bath . . . for he lived in the North

Country. But the date passed; and then a letter came, from his rector, who had known of his proposed trip, and saying that he had died, quite suddenly, of a short illness."

The girls sat aghast.

"Aunt Jane, that is so like what happened to Aunt Cassandra," Anna whispered.

"No," said Jane, "Cassandra was engaged to Mr. Fowle. That did not happen in this story."

"That is a sad story," said Caroline meditatively. "So the cat ended up an old maid."

"I am sure she had many other chances," cried Anna.

"Other proposals? Yes," said Jane. "But Susan knew she should never meet another cat that she cared for as well; and she made up her mind not to marry."

"And was she happy?" asked Anna anxiously.

"Yes; after a time, she was, quite happy, and wished for no change. But she never would give advice to young ladies, that would not be productive of happiness. She would not counsel waiting, and the prudence that girls are so often taught to practice as a duty, once they know their own heart, and that the one they love is their own."

Anna looked at Jane feelingly, as if she could not thank her enough, but did not say anything.

Caroline jumped up to look out the window. "Oh, here is cousin Fanny," she exclaimed, "coming in at the gate."

A young woman of Anna's age, slighter, more serious and not as pretty, entered. "Aunt Jane," she said after the usual greeting, "I am come to ask you to walk back to the Great House with me. You ought not to be sitting inside this lovely day; it is quite beautiful in the meadows. The Queen Anne's lace in the pasture is quite a picture, and the wild summer roses in the hedgerows too."

"That is a very kind invitation, of a sort that I cannot resist," said Jane cordially. "Anna, Caroline, will you come?"

"Oh, yes," they said, and ran away to get their bonnets.

Fanny looked after Anna. "Has she said anything more about marrying Ben Lefroy?" she asked with a frown. "Very foolish thing."

"I confess they would seem an oddly matched couple. She, so lively and fond of company, he so inward and quiet. I do not know how it would do."

"Foolish indeed! I can never forget, none of us can, how she engaged herself at sixteen without a by-your-leave, to that Mr. Terry. Anna is so unsteady."

"Young ladies cannot all be as sober as you, my sensible Fanny," said Jane. "But there, my dear, the headship of a family has fallen heavily upon you, and made you wise beyond your years."

"Anna lost her mother, too, so I do not know why it did not have that effect on her," said Fanny disapprovingly. "She does not seem to understand how very important the question of marriage is. She does not think. I am sure I look for open scandal from her, one day to the next."

"And you? Is your heart quite fancy free?" asked Jane gently. "Is not Mr. Plumptre in the ascendant any longer?"

"Oh, no—no. He is not . . . there is somebody else . . . I cannot talk about it yet . . . ."

Fanny blushed to such a degree that Jane laughed. "I see. Well, I am sure you will open your heart in time. I expect to see you settled within a twelvemonth, and I will visit you, wherever you are."

"Oh, that can never be. My sisters are far too young to leave them, and my father needs me. Anna will be married before I am—doubtless very precipitately."

Jane sighed. "You may be right."

"She and I do not think at all alike about love and marriage," said Fanny primly.

At this, Jane laughed. "Oh, my nieces! How diverting you are, to be sure. I could never do without either of you, in the least, you are the delight of my heart. How I pray it will turn out well for you both."

Here the girls ran back into the room, bonneted, and Jane, who had tied on her own bonnet, took her shawl down from its hook. Caroline ran ahead, searching the hedgerows for Tyger, while the others more sedately started their walk toward Chawton-meadow, through the beech wood.

DIANA BIRCHALL is a story analyst at Warner Bros. Studios, reading manuscripts to see if they would make suitable movies. She is the author of two "Austenesque" books, the novel *Mrs. Darcy's Dilemma* and the story collection *Mrs. Elton in America,* both published by Sourcebooks. She has also written *Onoto Watanna,* a scholarly biography of her grandmother, the first Asian American novelist (published by the University of Illinois Press). Diana grew up and was educated in New York City but has lived for many years in Santa Monica, California, with her husband and son.

www.dianabirchall.net
@dianabirchall on Twitter

ME AND MR. DARCY, *AGAIN*...

Alexandra Potter

"Wow, this is awesome, Em."

I'm barely out of the hotel elevator before I hear Stella's voice ahead of me, whooping loudly with excitement. Lugging my suitcase, I hurry down the corridor to find the door to our room flung wide open and Stella, already lying spread-eagled on one of the twin beds, flicking through the room service menu.

"Mmmm, goat's cheese salad with tomato relish . . . porcini mushroom risotto with truffle oil . . . fish and chips with mushy peas . . ." She looks up from the menu. "What are mushy peas?"

"Are you *still* hungry? We just ate breakfast on the plane," I say, laughing, while I dump my suitcase and survey the room.

"It's not *me* that's still hungry, it's *him*." She gasps indignantly and pats her huge belly, which rises up from her tiny frame as if someone stuck a space hopper up her vintage Alexander McQueen dress. Stella is six months pregnant with her first child—a boy—but it hasn't dampened her obsession with fashion.

"I swear, he's the pig," she continues, looking pained. "All he wants to do is eat, eat, eat. It's twenty-four/seven. Gimme chocolate, gimme ice cream . . ." She rolls her eyes in indignation.

"Sounds like a nightmare," I reply, my mouth twitching in amusement. "Being forced to eat all that chocolate and ice cream."

"I know, *right?*" she says, nodding, her eyes wide with innocence. Tugging a giant-size Kit Kat out of her purse, she unwraps a finger and takes a bite. "I swear, all this eating for two is getting exhausting."

Stifling a smile, I walk over to the large window and gaze out across the busy London street, teeming with red double-decker buses, black taxi cabs, and thousands of pedestrians, to the green vista of Hyde Park beyond. It's Friday morning and Stella and I have a whole long weekend ahead of us. I haven't seen London since I was here on a Jane Austen–inspired literary tour a couple of years ago . . . no, wait a moment, it must be four years ago now.

Gosh, is it really four years?

My mind spools backwards . . . Four years since I met my English-journalist boyfriend Spike, with whom I now share a tiny apartment in Brooklyn, four years since I took over the ownership of McKenzie's bookshop, four years since I met Mr. Darcy . . .

Mr. Darcy.

My stomach gives a little leap.

Even after all these years, I don't know if I really did meet him or if it was just a mixture of jet lag, desire, and my overactive imagination. A desire so strong that I conjured him up at Chawton House, dreamt about our moonlit horse ride together, and created an entire fantasy in which I got to date him. Except—

Except I'm not sure. Part of me still wants to believe that something magical really did happen the last time I was here in England. That he really does exist. But it was a long time ago now. I'll never know for sure . . .

"You know, I've brought nothing to wear." I turn away from the window to see Stella pulling out mountains of clothes from her suitcase. Correction: *suitcases*. Their contents are spilling out all over the carpet: velvet hot pants, diaphanous skirts, floral tea dresses, feather boas . . . Meanwhile I've only brought a couple of T-shirts; the rest of my luggage is made up of books. I can't travel anywhere without a stack of paperbacks to read. And I've always got to bring with me some old classics. It's a comfort thing. Some girls reach for the Ben & Jerry's, I reach for my copy of *Pride and Prejudice*.

I'm suddenly distracted by my cellphone beeping up a text message. I dig it out of my pocket and glance at the screen.

"Is it Spike?"

Stella catches me looking at my phone. I shake my head. "No, and I didn't expect it to be," I say, trying to sound nonchalant and not show my clunking beat of disappointment as I glance at the message from T-Mobile, detailing the charges to use my phone abroad. Quickly I grab hold of myself. I'm not upset, I'm *angry*, remember? After all, he was the one being the asshole. He was the one who started it.

"It" being the huge fight we had a few days ago. It started out so innocuously, as fights always seem to do, with me asking Spike to give me a hand putting the cover on the comforter, and developed into a full-scale shouting match that dragged in every minor complaint and disagreement we'd ever had, spanning our entire relationship. It ended with lots of door slamming, me calling him an asshole, and him telling me to go to hell.

So I took his advice.

Well, *sort of*.

I didn't go to hell, I came to London instead. Well, what are air miles for? Plus I had enough for two round-trip tickets, so I suggested to Stella that she come along too, before she got too big to travel. She jumped at the chance.

"OK, so where to first?" says Stella, snapping the menu closed and hoisting herself off the bed.

"I thought you were hungry?"

"I am, but he can wait." She pats her bump affectionately. "Mommy has to go shopping."

"Shopping?" I exclaim. "But we're here. *In London.* Don't you want to go sightseeing?"

"Shopping is sightseeing!" she cries defensively. "Topshop is like the eighth wonder of the world, and London is where it all began."

Throwing her purse over her shoulder, she grins. "Coming?"

I barely manage to get to the bottom of the Topshop escalator before I change my mind. Leaving Stella to her passion, I decide to indulge in mine and make my way to the British Museum and its famous round reading room filled with millions of books.

Only when I arrive, I discover it's now used for exhibitions and most of the books have moved to the newly built British Library. "But we do still have a smaller public reference library," one of the staff informs me. "It's located in one of our older reading rooms, which was very popular in the 1800s with the novelists William Thackeray and Charles Dickens, the poet Robert Browning, and even Charles Darwin."

Not bad company to be in, I muse, making my way there. I'm not disappointed. The walls are lined with floor-to-ceiling bookshelves, the gold lettering on the leather spines catching the sunlight that filters through the large sash windows high above. The place oozes history, and imagining all the great writers and thinkers who have sat here before me, I take out a couple of volumes and find a quiet seat tucked around a corner.

As I sit down a wave of jet lag suddenly hits me, and stifling a yawn, I rub my eyes. I didn't sleep much on the plane and now it's really catching up with me. My eyelids grow heavier and I sink farther down in my chair. It's so lovely and quiet in here and the place is almost empty; surely no one will notice if I close my eyes for a moment—

"Ahem."

Snapping open my eyes, I jerk bolt upright.

"Is anyone sitting here?"

"Um . . . no, not at all," I stammer, aware of a male figure standing beside me. "Sorry . . . I'll just move my things . . ." I begin busily clearing away the pile of books I've dumped on the chair beside me, along with my bag, my jacket . . . Yet as my hands are moving my mind is slowly registering . . . hang on, something in his voice sounds familiar. If I wasn't mistaken I'd almost think it was—

I glance up and my stomach goes into free fall.

"*Mr. Darcy,*" I gasp.

"Miss Emily!" he says in astonishment; then, remembering himself, he takes off his hat and bows formally. "I thought it was you, but I couldn't be sure—"

"What are you doing here?" I'm gaping.

"I was about to ask you the same question," he replies, flicking back his tailcoat and sitting down next to me. A shiver runs down my spine. He's so close, only inches away. My eyes flick over his face, his strong cheekbones, the way his dark hair curls across his temples. This is so unreal, it can't be happening. He can't be here. I must be dreaming. Maybe if I pinch myself—

I pinch myself. Nope, it's still happening, he's still here, still sitting right next to me.

"So tell me, how are you?"

I snap back to see Mr. Darcy gazing at me.

"Oh . . . um . . . great . . ." Hastily I try collecting my thoughts while silencing the voice inside of me that's shrieking *Ohmy-godohmygod.* "Really great," I repeat firmly, for my own benefit as much as his. "And what about you? What's new?"

He looks blank at my turn of phrase.

"I mean, what has happened since I last saw you—"

"—four years ago," he says, finishing my sentence. "It's been four years."

"Yes, I know," I reply, trying to make my voice sound casual while ignoring the shivers running up and down my spine.

And did my stomach just flip over?

Sternly I flip it back again.

I am not in love with Mr. Darcy anymore, I don't even have a *crush* on him. I'm in love with Spike, remember?

Love? Did you just say *love?* What on earth are you doing talking about love, Emily?

"Did you get married to Elizabeth Bennet?" I ask, quickly reining in my feelings, which are ricocheting all over the place.

"How did you know?" He looks surprised. "Did the news travel all the way to America?"

"Um . . . yes, something like that," I reply, trying to fudge. "So are you both happy?"

"Yes, very, she stayed at home in the country while I came to London on business." He pauses, his brow furrowed. "I hope you don't think I am about to speak out of turn, but I have always wondered about you. Why you left so suddenly, without a word . . ." He looks down at his hands, interlaced on his lap, and swallows hard. "I looked for you everywhere . . ."

Raising his face, his eyes search out mine. Somewhere I feel a pulse beating.

"I had to go back to America," I manage, my voice barely a whisper.

"You left without saying goodbye."

"I know, I'm sorry."

Am I imagining it or is something happening here between us? Is something *going* to happen between us?

"Excuse me, but the library is closing."

Twirling around in my seat, I see a bespectacled attendant standing behind us. "If you'd like to make your way to the exit now, please," she says authoritatively.

"Oh . . . yes, of course," I reply quickly, before turning back to Mr. Darcy. "We have to leave—" I break off as I see his chair is empty.

Mr. Darcy has already gone.

My mind whirling, I leave the British Museum and head to the pub near our hotel to meet Stella as planned. Walking into the Fox and Grapes, I spot her perched on a barstool amid a sea of shopping bags. She greets me with a shriek. "Oh wow, Em, wait till you see what I've got!" and before I've even sat down she begins frenziedly pulling clothes out of shopping bags. "They have a rockin' maternity section, look at this awesome jumpsuit . . . and what about this T-shirt, isn't it cool?"

I stare blankly at the blur of outfits, unable to focus. I'm still reeling from my encounter with Mr. Darcy. Did I imagine it? Was it for real?

"What would you like to drink?" asks the barman, interrupting Stella's fashion show.

"Oh, just a mineral water," she says with a resigned smile, and pats her belly.

The barman glances toward me.

"Make mine a large whiskey," I say, finding my voice at last.

"*Whiskey?*" Stella turns to me, her eyes wide. "Oh jeez, Em, are you all right?" she exclaims, registering my expression for the first time. "You look like you've seen a ghost."

"You could say that . . ." I trail off.

Stella's forehead furrows in confusion. "What's happened?"

I hesitate. Should I tell her?

Tell her what? I think sharply. That I just saw a fictitious character come to life in the British Museum? "Oh, nothing . . ." I shrug.

But if I think that's going to appease Stella, I'm mistaken.

"Nothing?" she repeats suspiciously. "Right, that's it, there's definitely something up." Leaning closer, she fixes me with a hard stare. "OK, come on, spill the beans."

So I tell her everything that happened—or didn't happen.

". . . and now I don't know what to think," I finish, looking at her across the table. We've decamped outside to the beer garden and are sitting in the late afternoon sunshine. "I thought I was over Mr. Darcy, that Spike was the one, but now I don't know . . ."

"Whoa, stop right there," instructs Stella firmly. "Darcy *Schmarcy*. I've heard enough about this dude." She slams down her mineral water.

It splashes me and I jump back. To be honest, Stella can be a bit scary when she wants to be.

Leaning across the table, she fixes me with a stare. "Look, Emily, I hate to say this, but you read too many books."

I'm not sure I heard that right. *"Too many books?"* I repeat incredulously. "But—"

"But nothing," she cuts me off. "You've got to stop dreaming. This isn't one of your romance novels, this is real life. And it's full of real people. Like Spike." She raises her eyebrows. "Have you spoken to him yet?" she asks pointedly.

Abruptly brought back to reality, I shake my head. "Maybe this is a sign," I murmur.

"A sign?" Stella looks puzzled.

"That me and Spike aren't right for each other."

"Bullshit," scoffs Stella with characteristic bluntness. "You and Spike are made for each other."

"I don't think Spike feels like that," I say glumly.

"He's crazy about you!"

"We had a big fight," I continue.

"All couples have fights," she counters.

"There was a time when he couldn't wait to get me into bed, but now he falls asleep on the sofa watching soccer."

"Show me a guy who doesn't," she says, smiling ruefully. "And no, before you say it, Darcy-pants doesn't count. I mean *real* guys."

"We've been together four years and he still hasn't asked me to marry him," I blurt without thinking. It catches me by surprise.

"Aha! So *that's* what this is all about." Stella looks at me triumphantly.

I feel myself color. Gosh, where did that just come from? "No, it's not," I try backtracking. "I don't care about getting married, it's an old-fashioned concept and I like to think I'm a modern woman—"

"Cut the crap, Emily," deadpans Stella.

I feel my defiance crumble. "OK, I suppose it would be nice to be *asked,*" I confess.

"Why don't you ask him?" she suggests.

"That's not really the point," I reply—a little sulkily, I realize.

"What difference does it make?" continues Stella. "Me and Freddy got married for a green card, then we fell in love. We did everything the wrong way around, but it doesn't matter. The most important thing is we're together." She looks at me, and her expression softens. "Not everything in life happens the way you think it will, Em," she says and, reaching across the table, puts her

hand on mine. "But if you love each other, that's all that matters."
She hesitates, then asks quietly, "You do still love Spike, don't
you?"

"Yes," I answer quickly. "It's just—" I break off and heave a
deep sigh. "Oh, I don't know anything anymore." I glance up at
Stella. She looks worried. Changing the subject, I pin on a bright
smile. "OK, it's my round. Another mineral water?"

That night I can't sleep. Staring into the darkness, I listen to Stella
snoring softly in the other bed, a million thoughts going around
and around in my head. Seeing Mr. Darcy again has stirred up a
maelstrom of emotions, and I feel all churned up inside. Snippets
of our conversation filter back . . . *"I've always wondered about
you . . . I looked everywhere for you . . ."* Tossing and turning, I
bury my head under my pillow, trying to block them out.

And failing.

It's no good, I'm never going to get to sleep. Abandoning my
attempts, I reach for my phone on the beside cabinet and turn it
on. The screen lights up and I glance at the time: 3 A.M. That
means it's only 10 P.M. in New York . . . Spike would still be
awake . . . he said he was going to stay in tonight, finish up an
article he was working on.

As I think about Spike in our apartment, sitting at his tiny
desk, hunched over his laptop, surrounded by piles of papers and
his usual cup of tea that's long since gone cold, I feel a wave of
affection. And a good hard dose of reality. OK, this is ridiculous.
Stella is right. This is real life. I love Spike, not Mr. Darcy.

Quickly I text him.

Hey it's me. First night in London and can't sleep. Miss U. XOX.

I press Send and wait for a reply.

Ten minutes later I'm still waiting. I feel disappointed. Anxious. *Indignant.*

I can't believe he hasn't replied. He must be still sulking!

Annoyed that I've made the first conciliatory move only for it to be ignored, I slip out from under the covers and pad agitatedly into the bathroom. I'm wide awake now, and after fetching myself a glass of water, I walk over to the window and draw back the heavy curtains with one hand.

It's a full moon and ahead the park is bathed in silvery light. My eyes sweep across the empty expanse of grass, the small lake, the trees . . . but wait, what's that? A figure on horseback suddenly appears between the trees, then abruptly halts and gazes directly up at my window. Even from this distance, there's no mistaking who it is.

Mr. Darcy.

My heart jolts.

Why is he here? What does he want?

I pause, then turn away from the window. There's only one way to find out.

"Miss Emily," he says, and nods. Still on horseback, he tips his hat. "What an unexpected pleasure."

"Mr. Darcy," I pant, out of breath from throwing on some clothes and dashing out of the hotel and into the park. "It's nearly four o'clock in the morning, what are you doing here?"

"I'm afraid I couldn't sleep," he replies. "I had a lot on my mind."

A look passes between us and I feel myself blush.

"So I thought I would take a ride in the park to clear my head—" He pauses, and for a moment I think he's about to say something further, but then he seems to think better of it and continues, "Would you care to join me for a ride? There are stables close by . . ."

I quickly shake my head. "I think I'll pass." I smile ruefully; the memory of my last moonlight ride with Mr. Darcy hasn't faded despite the years.

He looks puzzled.

"After last time . . ." I remind him, raising my eyebrows.

"Ah yes, now I remember," he says. "It was rather eventful."

Well, that's one way of putting it, I muse, remembering shrieking as my horse bolted. That was before I hit a tree and blacked out . . .

"Perhaps we should walk instead." Dismounting, he tethers his horse to a tree, then holds out his arm so I can loop mine through his.

For a few minutes we walk arm in arm through the park. Neither of us speaks. It's a comfortable silence. Unlike the silences I've been having with Spike lately, I reflect, thinking back to the atmosphere in the apartment before I left. At the memory of Spike, I feel a sudden stab of guilt. Here I am with another man, taking a moonlight walk in the park.

But it's not like I'm doing anything wrong, is it? I tell myself quickly. And anyway, this isn't just any man. It's Mr. Darcy. He's a gentleman. Plus he's married. Nothing's going to happen.

I feel the warmth of his body next to mine.

Is it?

"So, tell me, do you have a suitor?" he asks, interrupting my thoughts.

"A suitor?" My mind snaps back to Spike. "Yes . . . I suppose you could call him that," I say, looking at my feet.

"Do you have plans to marry?"

I glance up at Mr. Darcy. He blushes. "I apologize, it's very impertinent of me, but I noticed you weren't wearing a wedding ring . . ."

"I know," I say, and then, to my complete astonishment, burst into tears.

"Miss Emily, what is wrong?" he exclaims.

Sobbing loudly, I bury my face in his chest to try to stifle my tears. But it's no good. It's as if someone just turned on a tap and they're flowing freely all over my cheeks.

And Mr. Darcy's immaculate black tailcoat.

Oh God, how embarrassing. Quickly I pull away. "I'm sorry," I hiccup, wiping my snotty nose on my sleeve. He passes me an immaculate white handkerchief, and I blow my nose loudly. "No . . ." I shake my head tearfully, ". . . we've been together for four years and he hasn't asked me . . ." I give a little sob.

"A very long courtship then," comments Mr. Darcy gravely.

". . . and a few days ago we had a huge fight, and it was awful, and now we're not speaking . . ." It's as if someone just removed a cork from a bottle, and now it's all pouring out. ". . . and it's awful, and I feel terrible, and I miss him, and I don't know what to do."

Mr. Darcy puts his arm around to comfort me. "Do not worry yourself about the argument," he soothes. "My wife, Elizabeth, and I had a terrible misunderstanding before we were married."

"I know," I sob.

"You do?" He looks shocked.

"Um . . . I mean . . . I know most couples have arguments," I say, quickly correcting myself.

"And he is in America?"

I nod, and blow my nose again. I know I look a mess, but I don't care. Whereas once I would have been horrified for Mr. Darcy to see me like this, now all I can think about is Spike.

Mr. Darcy heaves a deep sigh and furrows his brow, deep in thought.

"America, the New World, is very different to England," he

continues. "They are two very different places, of that I am sure. However, love is the same all over the world. It is universal. If his heart is true, then he will come for you, Miss Emily." He meets my gaze, and with an impassioned voice, clasps my hands in his. "Love has no bounds. And if he loves you, truly loves you, he will not let you go."

The next morning, I'm woken by an impatient Stella.

"Come on, get up, it's Saturday, we have to go to Portobello Market."

"Uh . . . what's Portobello Market?" I mumble sleepily, trying to bury my head underneath the comforter, but it's snatched away from me.

"What's Portobello Market?" repeats Stella, with the same incredulity as if I've just asked who's Obama. "Only the most world-famous market, that's supposed to be amazing for shopping."

Opening my eyes, I peer at her blearily. She's wearing a T-shirt that reads "Caution: Bump Ahead" and one of her new feather boas in bright fuchsia. "I thought you'd already been shopping," I protest weakly.

She looks aghast. "Shopping isn't something you do just once," she exclaims. "It's a daily practice. Like yoga." She grabs my jeans and T-shirt and chucks them at me. "And trust me, girlfriend, with your wardrobe, you're in serious need of practice."

Thankfully, Portobello Market turns out to be filled with an eclectic mix of stalls—including one selling antique books, I realize with a beat of pleasure.

"Ooh, I'm just going to look over here," I say to Stella, who's already dived on a vintage ball gown and is cooing loudly.

"Don't you have enough books?" she tuts, breaking from her reverie.

"I thought shopping was a daily practice," I retort. "Like yoga."

"Humph." Stella purses her lips, then turns back to the ball gown.

Grinning to myself, I wander across to the stall. Excitement buzzes as I see the faded piles of books, the burgundy leather hardbacks etched with gold stenciling, the lovingly worn paperbacks. Each one ready to transport me to a different world where I'll meet new and interesting characters. And it's all here, at my fingertips, I marvel as my gaze sweeps over the different titles.

Unexpectedly, I see an old edition of *Pride and Prejudice* propped up at the back. Excitement leaps.

"Hi, can I help you?"

I snap back to see the stallholder looking at me.

"What edition is that?" I ask, gesturing to the copy of *Pride and Prejudice*.

"Oh, crikey, I'm afraid I wouldn't know." He smiles apologetically. "I'm just covering for the woman who runs the stall. She'll be back in five minutes." He pauses, then continues. "You can have a look at it if you'd like."

"Oh no, it's fine, I'm sure I wouldn't be able to afford it—"

"It's free to look," he says, grinning.

"Well, in that case . . ." I smile as he passes it to me. Carefully I open it and look at the date. It was printed at the beginning of the last century. It's over a hundred years old, I reflect, thinking of all the people who must have held this book in their hands. As I start to turn the pages a piece of paper falls out, and I bend down to pick it up. It's probably a price ticket—actually, no, it looks like a note.

I turn it over in my hands. Written in faded ink, in old-fashioned swirly handwriting, it reads:

> *Be in Kensington Gardens at sunset. By the round pond.*
> *You have a surprise.*
> *Mr. D*

What the—?

In total astonishment, I stare at it for a moment, a million questions swirling around in my head, then glance up. The young guy minding the stall is talking on his cellphone and hasn't noticed. Quickly I slip the note into my pocket and hand the book back.

"Thanks, but it's a bit more than I can afford."

"No worries," he says. "Hope you find what you're looking for."

"Me too," I reply, and with my heart beating very fast, I hurry away.

Later that afternoon I leave Stella back at the hotel, having her afternoon nap, and make my way to Kensington Gardens at the far end of Hyde Park.

The park has emptied out. The afternoon sunbathers have already gone home, and as I reach the pond, the sun is beginning to sink slowly into the horizon, creating a pomegranate sky.

Filled with anticipation, I wait, scanning the distance for any sign of Mr. Darcy. Then I hear it—the sound of a horse's hooves—and catch a glimpse of a man on horseback between the trees.

Mr. Darcy?

But I don't have a chance to find out as all at once I'm distracted by a commotion, the sound of a horse neighing followed by a loud yell. Twirling around I catch sight of someone falling into the water, the squawking of swans as they take flight.

What the hell?

I look over to see a man pulling himself out of the pond. His hair is dripping wet, his white T-shirt is clinging to his broad frame, and I'm suddenly reminded of Colin Firth in the BBC adaptation of *Pride and Prejudice*—my heart skips a beat. I can't see his face but it must be Mr. Darcy! For a brief moment my eyes flick over his strong shoulders, the muscles in his back as he hauls himself onto dry land, and despite myself I feel a spike of desire. A connection so strong it's as if he's wrapped a piece of string around my heart and is tugging it, pulling me toward him, drawing me closer—

No, stop! cries a voice inside my head. *You love Spike. You only feel this way about Spike.* I fight the urge, determined to resist, and as I do it suddenly hits me. I don't want Mr. Darcy, I *never* wanted Mr. Darcy. I want Spike. Images of our life together flash before me: drinking coffee together in the morning, snuggling up under the covers in bed at night, laughing at each other's silly jokes, fighting over the TV remote, celebrating by eating Chinese food in our pajamas when he's made a deadline . . . I love our life together. I don't want to lose it. I *can't* lose it.

It's like a wake-up call. A sob rises in my throat and I zone back to see the sopping-wet figure brush the hair away from his face and turn toward me—

Oh my God.

It can't be. Except it is.

It's Spike!

I stand there in shocked amazement. I can't quite believe what I'm seeing. I watch as he walks over to me, muddy water squelching out of his boots.

"What are you doing here?" I gasp.

"Funny you should ask that." He's smiling ruefully.

"But how . . . when . . . ?"

He shushes me. "Hey, I'm the one that's supposed to be asking all the questions."

Wordlessly I stare at him, totally bewildered.

And then before I can say another word, he drops down to one soggy knee and, pulling out a ring, asks the most important question of all.

"Will you marry me?"

Of course I say yes. And after I've managed to stop crying tears of joy, we walk hand in hand back to the hotel to break the happy news to Stella.

"So how did you know where to find me?" I ask, looking up at Spike. "How did you know I'd be in the park?"

"Well, I went to your hotel first, so I got your note."

"What note?"

"The one you left behind reception asking me to meet you in the park." He smiles. "I have to say, I was a bit taken aback. How did you know I was even flying over? It was supposed to be a surprise."

"It was a surprise!" I protest. "I had no idea you were coming to England."

"But you left me the note," he counters.

I stare at him in confusion, trying to make sense of it all. "Do you have it?"

"Erm . . . yeah . . . hang on . . ." He tugs a crumpled piece of paper out of his wet jeans. It's all soggy, and the ink has bled, but even so I can still make out the distinctive old-fashioned hand-writing. Quickly I pull out my own note and compare. It's the same.

I open my mouth to say something, but Spike isn't paying attention. Staring fixedly ahead, he's still talking, "... and then when I got here, there was some nutter on a horse ..."

"Nutter on a horse?"

"Yeh, he was wearing some crazy costume—you know, top hat, tailcoat ..."

Mr. Darcy.

"... he was galloping so fast I had to jump out of the way, otherwise he would have knocked me over, which is how come I ended up falling in the lake, but then he disappeared and you appeared ..."

Did he set all this up? Did he send the notes? But how? It doesn't make sense. None of it makes sense—

"... and I got to propose, and you said yes."

Spike turns to me, and wrapping his arms around my waist, he pulls me close. And as he bends down to kiss me, every question disappears.

The rest of the weekend flies by. It's fun to be in London with your best friend and your fiancé. *Fiancé.* I almost can't believe it's for real. Almost. Because all I have to do is glance down at the diamond sparkling on my finger and I'm in no doubt: there's a lot of things I'm not sure about, but this is one thing I *definitely* haven't dreamt up.

"So, have we got everything?"

I look up from my ring to see Stella, laden down with souvenirs and gifts. We're at Heathrow, about to board our flight back to New York, and she's making the most of the duty-free shopping.

"Well, I need something to read on the plane ..." I reply, spotting a bookstore ahead.

"Oh, that reminds me, I got you something," says Spike, digging in his backpack. He produces a paper bag and gives it to me. "I thought you might be in need of some reading material."

It's a book. But not just any book. It's the copy of *Pride and Prejudice* that I saw in Portobello Market!

"Oh wow, how did you know?" I cry in astonishment, throwing my arms around him and giving him a big hug. Over his shoulder I catch Stella grinning.

"You could say a little birdie told me," says Spike.

"A big birdie," she corrects, patting her pregnant stomach.

Breaking away, I look back at the book. Wordlessly I trace my fingers over the cover, then carefully I look inside. And there, on the first page, is an inscription.

> *This is how it all began.*
> *Here's to a happy ending.*
> *I love you.*
> *Your Mr. D, Spike xxx*

I feel as if I've been dipped in melted happiness. It's the happy ending I've always wanted, and feeling like the luckiest girl in the world, I slip the book back into its bag. Which is when I notice the name of the shop printed on its side: *Anne Jauste Books*.

Wait a minute . . . the cogs in my head start turning . . . isn't that an anagram for *Jane Austen*? My memory flicks back to that day at Portobello Market . . . the young guy was only minding the stall for the real stallholder . . . Anne Jauste . . . *Jane Austen* . . . My mind starts whirling. Are they the same person? Did she have something to do with bringing me and Spike back together again? Just like she had something to do with me meeting Spike all those years ago on that guided book tour, only then she went under the name of Miss J. Steane and worked as a tour guide . . .

Quickly I pull myself together. Of course that's totally crazy. It's impossible.

Er yeah right, I've heard that before.

Who knows what's real and what isn't real—if I dreamt up Mr. Darcy or if he really did come back to give me some much-needed advice. But as I think about the last few days, about Mr. Darcy, about this book and how it all worked together to bring me and Spike back together again, I feel a warm glow. And smiling to myself, I give silent thanks.

To Jane Austen and the wonderful Mr. Darcy, wherever you are. Thank you.

ALEXANDRA POTTER is an award-winning author. To date she has written eight bestselling novels and is working on her ninth. Her books have been translated into more than a dozen languages and are sold worldwide. In 2007 she won the Jane Austen New Regency Award for Best New Fiction for *Me and Mr. Darcy*. Her latest novel, *You're Not the One,* is published by Plume. She is currently traveling the world researching her next book.

www.alexandrapotter.com

WHAT WOULD AUSTEN DO?

Jane Rubino and Caitlen Rubino-Bradway

It's a truth universally acknowledged that if it wasn't for vampires, werewolves, zombs, and Jane Austen, I would not be outside Principal Oakes's office right now, while he and Mom and Dad and Mrs. Pilkington, the guidance counselor, discussed my Problem.

They crack the door, thinking I overhear what's going down, I'll figure I'm busted, and take a plea deal, like a week's detention over getting suspended. But until they got DNA, the Fifth Amendment is a fourteen-year-old's best friend.

So Principal Oakes thanks Mom and Dad for coming and they go, "Is anything wrong?" and he goes, "Not wrong, *per se,*" which is his way of saying, "Yes, there is something wrong," and Mrs. Pilkington goes, "We've been a little concerned about James's behavior," which is *her* way of saying, "James is seriously freaking us out."

"What behavior?" Dad asks.

I hear the *taptaptap* of Principal Oakes's pencil on his coffee mug. "It's not any *one* thing. More like a lot of little things."

"For example?"

That was Mom. She fires off the "for example," stick a fork in it. Don't do your homework and try to float with "I had other stuff I had to do"? Mom goes, "For *example*?" and The Argument Ends There.

"For example—the way he's been coming to school. His attire," Mr. Oakes said.

"His *attire*?" Mom could go the full Lady Catherine de Bourgh in three syllables flat.

Taptaptaptaptap. "I know we don't have a dress code—*per se*—but don't you think the way he's dressing—every day a button-down shirt, slacks. A, um, tie?"

And Mom goes, "In the hall, I saw two kids with their incisors capped with fangs, a half dozen girls with Kabuki makeup and black lipstick, and someone of indeterminate gender who was sporting a tail."

That was Elton. Nobody was a hundred percent on whether Elton was a girl or a guy, and these days there's a whole buncha-lotta you Do Not Ask, or you're doing time in a Sensitivity Awareness Program. Or SAP, for short.

Mr. Oakes sighed. "And it's his language."

"His language?"

"It's not just the 'please' and 'thank you' and 'I beg your pardon' and—"

"Excuse me?"

"That too. Not just *what* he says, Mrs. Austen, it's the *way* he says it. His teachers tell me when he's called on, he stands up. He holds doors open for them. He's gotten extremely . . ."

" 'Well behaved, polite, and unassuming?' "

Pull off to the side, here comes Jane Austen. "Well behaved, polite, and unassuming" is off *Pride and Prejudice*. Mom thinks *Pride and Prejudice* is The Best Novel Ever and Jane Austen is the best writer who ever lived, who ever will live, and this is one point that You Do Not Want To Argue About. The joke in our house is that Mom married Dad for his last name, except that sometimes I don't think it's a joke. Dad told me once that Mom wanted to call me Fitzwilliam, and I don't think that's a joke, either.

Now Mrs. Pilkington jumps in, 'cause it kills her not to *have her share of the conversation.* "When we see unusual behavior like this, students getting overly careful about manners and dress, the reason is usually . . . what I'm trying to say . . ."

"You're not accustomed to your students exhibiting good manners?"

"Well . . . not *per se,*" goes Mr. O.

And Mom goes, "'Which makes his good manners the more valuable.'" That's off *Emma.* Mom goes Austen on you, she's making fun, or she's fed up. I could tell she was getting fed up.

"Mrs. Austen, there's no reason to be defensive. We all want the same thing here."

The "no reason to be defensive" line's off their playbook. They say it to put parents on the defensive.

So Dad goes, "What is it we all want?" 'cause he's all about the bottom line.

Mrs. Pilkington goes, "In our experience, when you see behavior that deviates from the norm, we have to consider the reason for it—trouble in the home, or alcohol, or drugs—"

"Drugs?" Mom could get her voice up a whole octave on one syllable. Like opera.

"And I'm sure you know that early intervention is inordinately helpful in cases like this," said Principal Oakes.

"James!" That was Dad. "Son, come in here."

So I go in and Dad goes, "James, are you using drugs?" and I go, "No, sir," and Dad gives me the laser eye, and Mrs. Pilkington gives them a look like *"Sir"? See what I mean? Kids his age don't go "Sir."*

"Then you won't mind if we search your locker, will you,

Austen?" Mr. Oakes turns to Mom and goes, "James has asked us to address him as 'Austen.'" In school they love to tell your parents stuff about you they think your parents don't know.

"You want to search my son's locker?"

"You don't have a problem with that, do you?"

I could tell that Mom had a big problem with it but she Wasn't Going To Give Them The Satisfaction. Mom's Code comes down to two regs: Read Jane Austen and Do Not Give Them The Satisfaction.

So I get perp-walked to my locker, past the zombs and the vampires and the werewolves, and they all sort of orbit in, and Mr. Oakes goes, "Don't you have somewhere you should be?" so they lurch and waft and lope off.

I open the locker and Mr. Oakes starts passing off my gear to Mrs. Pilkington. Jacket. Lunch. Gym bag. Books, he shakes out, like he expects the pages to snow coke, and then *they* fall out. My notes.

Principal Oakes unfolds them and reads off, "'Fours and eights . . . threes and sixes . . . inside hand' . . . Have you been gambling, Son?"

"Son" is what principals call you right before you get suspended.

"No, sir."

"'. . . setting up the hall . . . arming' . . . *Arming?*"

You know how they say you could hear a pin drop? Well, you could hear a pin cut through the air molecules on the way down.

"Does. James. Have. Access. To. Weapons?" goes Mrs. Pilkington, and if she wasn't seriously freaked out before, she is now.

Mom, on the other hand, is trying not to laugh and gives me a look like, *Game over, you're outed,* and goes, "Suspicion of something unpleasant is the inevitable consequence of such an alteration as you have witnessed in James."

It's off *Sense and Sensibility.*

Mr. Oakes turns over the paper and reads off, " 'ECD?' " He's churning through brain cells, you could almost get a whiff of smoke coming off the neurons. "Explosive Containment Data? Entry Control Device? Electronic Circuit Detonator? Emergency Communications Database? Do you want to tell us what this stands for?"

So I go, "ECD stands for English Country Dance."

And you never saw adults shut up so fast.

Backstory.

Summer before high school, there's one thing you know going in: you weren't a vampire, werewolf, or zomb, you were nothing. No. Thing. So summer's when you mob up because first day of school, you hit the ground at a sprint. Unless you're a zomb, then it's more like a . . . lurch.

They hung out at the library–slash–community center. The zombs, they're basically gamers without your dignity and wit. The vampires cruise the stacks, work on their wan, 'cause they don't do sunlight. Get tagged by some UV, your vamp cred's shot. The wolves were there because a lotta the vamps are girls and the pack's mostly guys, except for Elton, who's still like Switzerland, genderwise. So they all hang, hog the computer stations, tear pages outta the mags, and generally scare the bejeepers out of the Tot Timers.

I've been going (translation: Mom's been dragging me) to the library since forever. I know everything about the place: the utility closet where the kids like to make out, the storage room in the basement where the zombs crash so they can game all night, the file cabinet where Mrs. Blake keeps her stash of Oreos. There's a lock, but it's broken (or so I hear), and if you only sneak one at a time, she doesn't notice.

I was at the library–slash–community center that summer 'cause my parents, but especially my mom, are into Making A Productive Use Of Your Summer and that meant Not Having Too Much Time On Your Hands. And the library–slash–community center has a bunch of programs for kids who have Too Much Time On Their Hands. TMTOYH and you're Up To No Good because there will be Too Many Hours in the Day, which only applies to kids because once you're a grown-up there are Not Enough Hours In The Day.

So, two weeks into summer, Mom hands me the brochure for Summer Fun At The Library program and goes, "A little learning is by no means a dangerous thing," which is off Jane Austen. (If Mom says something you don't get, say it's off Jane Austen, you got a 75 percent chance of being right.) And by the time I give up trying to talk her out of Making A Productive Use Of My Time, the good stuff's gone:

Let's Talk Movies. Once a week you watch a movie and then talk about it. Twenty slots, all filled.

Werewolves, Wizards, Witches, and Vampires: What They Say About Who We Are. Thirty slots, all filled. Plus a wait list.

Are You a Poet But Don't Know It? Twenty slots, twenty empty slots and Not If You Tied Me Down On A Bed Of Red Ants And Smothered Me In Smuckers.

Let's Draw! Let's not.

What Makes Great Books "Great"? This was a trick. You go in thinking you're gonna read Harry Potter or Stephen King and you're getting dragged through *Bleak House,* and wishing you signed up for "Are You a Poet But Don't Know It?"

Let's Make Music. Twenty slots, two left. But. This is basically "Are You a Poet But Don't Know It?" for kids who own a guitar. I don't say *play* a guitar unless you use "play" in the sense that they pick at the strings and sound comes out. Mostly for girls who got dumped, and at the end of the course you got twenty songs about Why He'll Be Sorry Someday.

Country Dance for Beginners. Conducted by the Englishtown Country Dancers. Two slots left.

And that was it—except for something called "Decoupage" and I didn't like the sound of that, so country dance won out, mostly because I saw that old movie *Urban Cowboy* and the country dancing looked kind of sick, so I go up to sign up and Mrs. Blake is so "thrilled" and "delighted" and then she calls *out loud* to Mrs. Radcliffe the gloomy librarian that "Jamie Austen signed up for country dancing" and they give me that look, like they're *proud* of me for doing something *brave*. Translation: They thought it was hilarious because I just did something really dumb.

When I got home Mom's holding my baby brother, Charlie, while she's stirring something in a pot and explaining to my sister Darcy how come Charlotte marries a creet like Mr. Collins. Mom's read *Pride and Prejudice* every year since she was twelve, and now she's hardwiring Darcy.

"How'd you make out?" Mom asked.

"Country line dancing. Is that productive enough for you?"

"'Fine dancing, I believe, like virtue, must be its own reward.'"

And here's where I get her back, because you can't hear JA lobbed at you night and day without sending one back over the net, so I go, "'Every savage can dance.'"

D(ance) day, I figure I'm all in, so I dig up my western shirt with the pearl snaps and the corded yoke and a leather belt and my second-best jeans and head out.

"Where are you going, James?"

Which should have been a clue, because Mom knew where I was going—what she's saying is, "Where are you going dressed like *that*?"

"Country dance class, remember?"

Then she doesn't say anything, no pearls of Austen, nothing. Just nods and turns back to her book with this funny look on her face like she's trying not to smile, but I figure don't ask. Just go and get it over with.

They put the country dancing on the top floor by taking off the divider between the art studio and the music studio, to make one long space, and it looks like there are about thirty people, so when I walk in, that makes sixty eyes lock on, 'cause here I come, suited up for Austin, Texas, and everybody else is Austen, Jane, and you could tell the Englishtown Country Dancers from the civvies, 'cause the Dancers went all out, frills, brocade, velvet, and that was the guys.

"Jamie!" And here comes Mrs. Blake all in a shiny blue gown with peacock feathers sticking up in her hair. "Mrs. Radcliffe bet a pound of fudge that you would back out—so glad—we're so short of young men."

She got that right. Out of thirty people, eight were guys and the only one of them younger than my dad was *moi*. The women were mostly old, too—like, forty at least—but a few looked college age, and one girl my age, and she was h.o.t.

One of the ladies from the Englishtown Country Dancers asks us all to gather around and then tells us how *happy* she is to see such a great-looking group and what *fun* we're going to have and how country dancing is going to be a lot easier than we think. Translation: it's next to impossible and you're going to look like a creet for even trying.

"We're going to teach you some of the simpler country dances from the Georgian and Regency eras, and we may work in a few mentioned in Jane Austen—" And everybody lets out this sigh, like worship. I think I saw one of the guys genuflect. No kidding.

"We're going to start off with a simple cotillion. Cotillions, of course, were mentioned only in one Jane Austen work." (Everybody nods like they know what she's talking about, so I nod, too.) "Cotillions are performed in smaller groups than the long sets of the *contre danse*. Remember, in Jane Austen's day, there were very few ways unmarried ladies and gentlemen could get together, and since marriage was the only honorable provision for well-educated women of small fortune—"

(Which is why Charlotte marries the creet, Mr. Collins.)

"—dancing became the means of advancing a courtship—in fact it was one of the few occasions when a respectable young lady and gentleman could hold hands. Not all young people learned to play an instrument or to draw or to speak French, but they did all learn to dance. Dancing was, in the words of Jane Austen, 'one of the refinements of polished society.'"

"Not to mention less polished society," whispered someone behind me. "Every savage can dance, right?"

I turn around, and it was Her, and she smiles and I smile and then they tell us to pair up and she goes, "You wanna be partners?" and I say something righteously dumb like, "It doesn't mean we're engaged or anything," but she laughs.

Then the lady—her name is Mrs. Caverley—runs through a bunch of terms, and then a group of the dancers show us a few moves, and Mrs. Caverley laughs and says it's okay if we forget them because someone will yell out the steps and if we still mess up, one of the country dancers will get us back on track.

"We always begin and end each dance by honoring our partner—that means the ladies curtsey and the gentlemen bow."

So I know how to bow, but that's the first, last, and only thing I get right, because the music starts and they're going forward,

I'm going backward, I'm going left when they're going right, they're doing a one-eighty when I'm doing a three-sixty, then somebody yells "Allemande!" or "Rigaudon!" and I lose my partner and wound up grabbing on to one of the guys, but he's okay with it.

The thing is, it was almost fun. The country dance people were seriously nice when you (I) messed up, they acted like it was their fault for not showing you the right way, and when you're trying to remember the names of all the steps and forget you're dressed like Suburban Cowboy and concentrating on not looking like a total creet, time goes by pretty quick.

"So, what'd you think?" *she* asks when it's all over.

"It felt like I was apologizing instead of attending or moving wrong without being aware of it."

Which is the problem with having a mother who quotes Jane Austen day and night—the words start coming out of your mouth when you should be downing a twelve-ounce can of Shut Up.

But she's all impressed. "Wow. You read *Pride and Prejudice*?"

I shrug. When you can't lie and you don't want to cop to the truth, you can coast on the shrug. "You?"

"Yeah." She pulled the word into two syllables, and she's smiling and she's got a real nice smile. "You read Jane Austen all the time, you want to know what the dances feel like."

I was gonna say she sounded like my mom (bad idea), but I caught myself. "You sound like . . . you're not from around here."

So she tells me they just moved down from Maine three weeks ago and I go, "I'm James," and she goes, "I'm Cathy," and then she's like, "I think it's cool that you read Jane Austen. I was even named after one of her characters—Catherine, from *Northanger Abbey*? Ever read it?"

I shrugged.

"Sick, right?"

"Endstage."

"But *P'n'P*'s still my favorite."

We were down at the atrium now, and instead of heading for the exit, she heads for the library entrance, where a couple of vamp girls in black T-shirts and faces white as a character in a Tim Burton movie were on the prowl. "I'm gonna hang here awhile. I practically lived at the library back home," and she gives this wistful little shrug.

"I gotta get home." I did not need to run into the vamps and zombs with me dressed like a buckaroo. "But next week, uh, first two dances, okay?"

She gives me this little curtsey, like in class, and says, "'Mr. Darcy is all politeness.' But it doesn't mean we're engaged or anything."

When I get back, Mom's on the computer and she goes, "Did you have a good time?"

And the way she says it, the look on her face, says she knew what I set myself up for, and I sort of explode. "What the heck? Couldn't you warn a guy? It gets out I'm prancing around with guys wearing *frills. Lace!* I'll be lucky if it doesn't get out I'm gay."

"Nobody thought Mr. Darcy or Henry Tilney were gay."

I swear, sometimes it's like my parents were never teenagers, never even went to high school. If they had, they'd know it's not who you are, it's who everyone else says you are.

"So you didn't like it?"

"It was okay."

"Does that mean that you *did* like it 'against your will, against your reason, and even against your character'? Or does it mean there were a few girls your age in the class?"

So I give the shrug and I ask Mom if I can borrow one of her copies of *Northanger Abbey*—she's got a two-book minimum of everything Jane Austen wrote—and she goes, "Sure, sweetie," and looks happy about it. The thing is, even though I kind of *know* Jane Austen (you can't live in this house and not *know* Jane Austen), I never really *read* Jane Austen, so I take the one with all the underlines and notes, to clue me in to what it's about.

So before the next class, I finish *Northanger Abbey* and it's not bad. It's about this teenager, Catherine, who's hooked on Gothic novels. Ghosts, vampires, haunted houses, psychos locked in the attic, pretty much what kids are reading now. And it kind of messes with her head, like there's the story world and the real world and she can't always keep them straight. She also likes this guy, and she is not smooth at all—and believe me, I have been there.

I still think General Tilney might've killed his wife.

Next class was a little better. First off, I traded the cowboy boots for khakis and a white shirt, and I met Cathy outside class and we went in together.

We ran through the cotillion, and then Ms. Caverley lines us up for these longways dances, and she reminds us that back in the day it was not good manners to dance more than twice with the same partner. So after I danced with Cathy, I wind up with Mrs. Blake, who's wearing a Jane Austen getup again, this time with even more feathers sticking out of her head, and for all the Oreos she puts away, she could dance rings around all of us. Then I dance with some lady who's got nine kids and twenty-three grandkids, and at one point I'm next to a guy who told me how he met his wife at a country dance class and how they were in a country dance group for forty-seven years and how he's kept it up now that she died. And he said it took him a year to get the hang of some of the dances and how excellent it was I caught on so fast. And I gotta say, it's weird how interesting everybody was when you get talking to them, and how much fun they were all having, always laughing at *themselves* but never putting *you* down, and if you mostly hang with teenagers, that takes some getting used to.

I didn't get to dance with Cathy again until the last one, and I told her I read *Northanger Abbey,* and how I thought Catherine sounded like the kids around here. "They're all about werewolves or zombies, and she wants to be, like, a heroine. I mean I liked her and all, but she wasn't real sharp when it came to people."

Cathy smiled like she thought I said something smart, and said, "A lot of her characters are like that—not that they all get carried away, but they're not people smart. Except for Fanny Price. *Mansfield Park?* But the rest of them, they take someone at face value or listen to gossip and then they find out that person was totally different. In Jane Austen it's always a big deal—what people are versus what people think they are."

It's still a big deal.

We went our separate ways at the library again—she said she needs to grab a computer station because her family doesn't have the online up and running yet, and I tell her if the mob is hogging them, rat them out to Mrs. Radcliffe—and I go home and grab one of Mom's copies of *Mansfield Park*.

After *Northanger, Mansfield* was no walk in the park. At first I didn't like Fanny. I mean, it would've sucked to be shipped off to people you didn't know, and Mrs. Norris always reminding you what a nobody you were and how much you owed all of them, but still, draw the line, already.

Then I thought about it some more, and you know, Fanny was actually a lot tougher than she seems at first. She actually had more backbone than anyone in the book. She didn't let herself get talked into that stupid play; she stuck to her guns, and she wasn't a phony. *She* wouldn't spend her summer trying to figure out if she'd rather hang with the vamps or the werewolves. The more I thought about it, the more I wished I was like her.

Next class, there was one less—Mrs. Blake wasn't there, so the guy who called the steps took her place and called them from the line (set). And it was still fun and we all did pretty well, but the thing is, something was missing, and I hate admitting this, but I sort of missed Mrs. Blake. I thought her bouncing and laughing and "Jamie!" got on my nerves, but it gave us all a boost, too, and class just wasn't as fun without her.

At the break, I heard a few people whispering about "sending Lottie a card," and I knew they were talking about Mrs. Blake— around the library, the kids called her "Lotta Blake," and I wondered if she was sick. When I asked, Mrs. Caverley explained that Mrs. Blake's daughter had a baby, and she'd taken a week off to help.

I confessed to Cathy that I sort of missed Mrs. Blake, and she said she did, too. "She's kind of our Mrs. Jennings," said Cathy. "We get aggravated with *her* like Marianne does with Mrs. Jennings, and then when she's not around we're like Elinor—we start thinking of the nice things she says and does, and how people perk up when she's around."

Mrs. Caverley reminds us that these are steps we can practice at home "—because skill at the dance meant that the dancer was a person of diligence and taste."

"Like Fanny practicing her dance steps in the drawing room," I said, trying not to be all, "I READ *MANSFIELD PARK*!"

And Cathy laughs and goes, "I'm hoping that *my* awkwardnesses are as good as graces." She had a great laugh.

Cathy stayed behind at the library again, and I felt sorry for her, having to put up with the zombs and the werewolves just to log some online. I told her if she couldn't put up with the weirdness, she could come over to my place and use ours, but she says it's okay, there was a stubbornness about her that never can bear to be frightened at the will of vampires, zombies, werewolves, etc.

So I go home, and all I say is, "Mom? Marianne and Elinor."

"Sense and Sensibility."

And I have to say that after *Mansfield Park*, *Sense and Sensibility* was a coast. The girls and their mother lose their house and don't have much money, almost like when the economy takes a dive, and these two sisters, Elinor and Marianne, both fall in love with guys who can't marry them, but Elinor sucks it up while Marianne goes all emo princess and almost dies. And I think the point is, stuff happens, so do you deal or do you get all "Poor me"? Are you Team Elinor or Team Marianne?

Next class, I decide to wear a sport coat. I'm not to where I'd pike my mom's velvet blazer and try to go the full Darcy, but all the other guys wear jackets.

Mrs. Blake's back and she looks tired, but I still get a "Jamie! How nice you look!" and I go, "Thanks," and figure, okay, I'll tell her she looks nice, too, and she gives me this look, like she's grateful, like nobody's ever told her she looks nice.

By this point Cathy and I pretty much have a pact that we'll go the first and last dances and as much of the rest as we can get away with, but Mrs. Caverley says we're gonna draw for partners. Cathy gets the guy who lost his wife and I get one of the college girls and we try to stake out places next to each other in the set, but Mrs. Caverley says because I've been making so much progress me and my partner can open the dance. (I got good the way she said. I practiced at home by teaching the steps to Darcy. She thinks it's cool and she's not a bad dancer and having someone else to teach helped me get the steps down.) Opening the dance is supposed to be an honor, but the fact is, you do your moves and then you pretty much stand around and talk, but it was okay because this girl—her name was Chrissy—she spent a semester in England and made it sound cool, and then we got new partners and I'm with Mrs. Blake who said I had to thank my mom for the card and I asked how was her daughter feeling and how's the baby, and she looked so grateful that I swear I will never cop another one of her Oreos again so help me. At the end of class she cornered me and a couple others with pictures of little Tommy, and he was cute, and I tell them all the stuff Charlie's getting into, and I turn around and saw that Cathy left.

End of August, I can arm and cast and hey and allemande with the best of them, and the last class was more like a party where we just ran through all the dances and had punch and cookies and Mrs. Caverley gave out these silly prizes—Mrs. Blake got the Marianne Dashwood award for being earnest and eager in everything she did and Cathy got the Jane Fairfax award for remarkable elegance and I got the Darcy prize for being the one who improves most on acquaintance. And Mrs. Caverley reminds us that they are giving classes through the year and they have dances the first Tuesday of every month and she hopes she'll see all of us again.

So the first day of school comes and it hits me I don't have a pack, a clan, or a mob, unless you count the Jane Austen crew I hung with for six weeks, and they were all way past high school, except for Cathy. But I wasn't where I'm going all Sir John Middleton, and the dread of being alone's my prevailing anxiety 'cause I knew a couple people who hadn't turned into total creets—yet—and Cathy would be there. And because Cathy's gonna be there, I pass on the black jeans/black T-shirt and go khakis/blue shirt, and I put a tie in my pocket and buff up my shoes.

I could see Darcy revving up her "What are you *wearing*?" but

I cut her off at the knees. "Boy, Darce, your shirt is ill. Like how you did your hair, too."

Dad looks up at Mom and she goes, "'Ill' is the new 'awesome.'"

"I thought 'wicked' was the new awesome."

"'Wicked' *was* the new awesome."

"Then 'ill' is the new 'wicked,' right?" Dad sighed. "What happened to 'cool'?"

"Nothing."

"Cool."

I walk to school, and most of the time, nobody pays attention to me unless it's to give me a look like they think I'm gonna jack their yard gnomes, but now it's, "Morning, James," and "Don't you look fine today?" and I go, "Good morning, Mrs. Smith" and "Good morning, Mr. Jones" and they light up.

So I head for the sidewalk in front of the school entrance and I see the clan and the pack and the mob all hanging with their own. The zombs looked pretty much fried, and the pack, they're pulling all these creet stunts trying to get the vamp girls to notice them, and the vamp guys are trying to look wasted and cool (ill) like you-know-who, in you-know-what-book/movie.

And the wolves got their hair all gelled into points that are supposed to look like ears, and the vamps and zombs are all pasty-faced and all in black and the only way you can tell them apart is the zombs kohl up their eyes like pandas and the vamps guys wear fake fangs and the girls wear dark lipstick.

I hear someone calling my name, "James—hey, James!" and it's one of the vamp girls, but I can't tell which one because they're all Casper, black hair, black jeans, black lips.

The girl waving at me is almost my height and thin and there's something familiar about her—and I get it about a half second before she goes, "It's me."

"Cathy?" I gotta be honest, there was a moment when it sucked a little, but I can't say I didn't understand it. I knew at least a couple kids who weren't creets, but the new girl wouldn't have anybody.

And she looks me over and smiles, almost like she's embarrassed, and goes, "You look . . . nice."

"Then how come I wish I stuck with the jeans and a T-shirt?"

Jack Willoughby breaks away from his mob and plunks himself in front of me and goes, "What are you *wearing,* Austen? Parochial school's on the other side of town."

But I don't back down. I go, "Don't feel bad, lobot. I'm far from requiring that elegance of dress in *you* that becomes *me.*"

Comeback Jack couldn't do better than, "Yeah . . . well . . ." and then you could hear a leaf hit the grass.

So I go, "'You are silent, absolutely silent. At present I ask no more.'" (That's off *Emma*). And Wolfman Willoughby lurches off, straining gray matter.

Then the bell rings, and they all head for the entrance, just this one big drift of which-one's-who, and it hits me: all this stuff kids say about how they want to be individual and unique and their own person and not like everybody else, and first chance they get they gear up like they all came off the same assembly line, same date, same lot number. The only one in front of school who didn't look like everybody else was . . . me.

Cathy watches them go but she hangs with me. Maybe she's not a complete one-eighty. So I shift my pack onto my other shoulder and take hers in one hand and hold out my arm like we did in country dance class.

Then I wait for five hours. Okay, it was five seconds, it just felt like five hours.

Finally, Cathy goes, "This doesn't mean we're engaged or anything," takes my arm, and we walk up to the entrance and kids are *staring* at us, and it takes me a second to realize it's not *us,* it's not even Cathy, who, even cakefaced, is still hot—everybody's staring at *me.* And I start thinking I may be on to something here: I can start off freshman year as James the Nobody, James the Creet, James the Lunch Table Leper—or I can be James, founder and CEO of Team Austen.

JANE RUBINO and CAITLEN RUBINO-BRADWAY are the authors of *Lady Vernon and Her Daughter,* an adaptation of Jane Austen's *Lady Susan.* Jane is also the author of a contemporary mystery series set at the Jersey Shore, as well as a volume of Sherlockian novellas, and she lives in Ocean City, New Jersey. Caitlen lives and works in New York City; her first solo effort, a young adult fantasy, will be published in 2012. Jane and Caitlen are currently developing *What Would Austen Do?* into a full-length novel.

www.janetility.com
@ladyvernonbook on Twitter

THE RIDING HABIT

Pamela Aidan

There is no truth better established than that a young woman on the brink of the possession of a good fortune will become the matrimonial object of every fortune hunter and imprudent noble family from either side of the English Channel. And should that heiress be as lovely and modest as Miss Georgiana Darcy, the task of fending off plausible suitors was mightily increased. Darcy sighed and glanced at his sister riding at his side. This was especially the case when they were in Town. More so, in that London was then in the midst of paroxysms of a wild, joyous relief this April of 1814 that Bonaparte was defeated and the Treaty of Fontainebleau signed.

The sound of swift hooves behind them sent Darcy slewing around in his saddle, narrow-eyed and prickly with suspicion. The glare he bestowed upon the gentleman who approached was specially calculated to blast any tender hope the young man might have entertained that he would receive encouragement to join them. In truth, just the rigid set of Darcy's shoulders had caused the rider to think better of his manners. With a sheepish nod, he passed them and continued down the track of Hyde Park.

"Fitzwilliam! That is the third gentleman you have frightened away this hour!" Georgiana shook her head at him and then laughed. Her mount performed a little jig at the sound of her merriment. "No one will dare ask me to dance at my own ball! I shall have none to stand up with me but you and Cousin Richard."

"Frightened? Don't be ridiculous!" Darcy replied. He was only thirty, but lately he was feeling much older. The prospect of Georgiana's coming out was aging him before his time and encouraging the worst of his old habits to re-appear. His dear wife Elizabeth had said as much with the teasing candor he both prized and, truth be told, dreaded. How was a man to make good on his progress when new challenges to his hard-won equanimity were forever being flung at him? He looked over at his sister, whose wide eyes and arched brows put the lie to his claim of innocence. Darcy snorted and a grin flashed across his face. Georgiana's natural shyness was giving way to a self-confidence that was delightful to behold. Elizabeth was teaching her well.

"Shall I ride after him and—"

"No, no, you shall not!" she laughed. "Shall you leave me alone to be accosted by some other? Most improper, brother!"

"As you wish," he replied with a shrug, but the grin remained as he considered her. At eighteen, Georgiana was a beauty who, he had been warned, bid fair to exceeding the celebration that had surrounded their mother and made their father the envy of London when he won her heart and hand. But woe to any suitor who did not quickly detect the intelligence and purpose behind the lovely exterior. It would take an extraordinary man, indeed, to win his sister's respect and love, and in that fact lay Darcy's peace. That and Georgiana's confidence in Elizabeth's keen assessment of the line of hopeful swains who even now were pressing for introductions as soon as she was officially "out."

With only the natural attractions of the Park to distract him, Darcy's mind turned to the contemplation of nothing more than the satisfaction inherent in a companionable ride. He reached down and patted Nelson's neck, glad that he had gone to the trouble of bringing his favorite mount to Town for the Season, even if it was only for moments like this. Hyde Park was not his first choice for riding, but it was convenient and the favorite haunt of the fashionable for riding, driving, and . . . walking. *Walking!* He grimaced. Walking was all well and good. He liked a vigorous ramble as well as any man. But riding! *There* was challenge and mastery, the wind in your face, the melding of human will and horseflesh as the world sped past you at the rate of pounding hooves and sleek-muscled grace! *Marvelous!* Marvelous save for one thing: Elizabeth did not ride. Elizabeth walked. Her sister Jane rode. In point of fact, Jane's ride in a cold downpour was in a direct line of events that had culminated in his present, very happy matrimonial state.

Besides, if Elizabeth were here, it would not fall upon him alone to discourage the plague of locusts that now hovered in the Darcy corner of Society's otherwise fenced fields. Elsewhere in this endeavor, Elizabeth was a helpmeet indeed. Elizabeth Bennet Darcy was not a woman to whom name or rank or wealth were permitted to disguise a deficiency of character or a frivolous mind. Her quick reading of the dangerous and the foolish no longer amazed him as it had at first. Although there remained those who continued to sniff at her pedigree, he had considered Elizabeth well launched upon Society when intimations of a Blessed Event had put an end to public life. It had also put an end to his plan to teach Elizabeth to ride.

But the Blessed Event had come and gone four months ago, leaving in the nursery a lusty young son and heir to the Darcy name and estate. Little Alexander Bennet Fitzwilliam Darcy was surely the center of his mother's universe and the pride of his father. Another grin creased Darcy's face as he recalled the radiance of mother and child that morning.

"What are you smiling about, Fitzwilliam?" Georgiana asked, bringing her horse close enough to bump his leg with the tip of her well-shod foot.

"Is it so unusual for me to smile that you must ask?" he returned, unwilling to confess that tiny, bright eyes and cooing infant lips were the source of his happiness.

"No," she admitted. "You are an extraordinarily happy man, or were until we came to London." She sighed. "I know that this faradiddle has occurred at a trying time—"

"Your Coming Out? You must not think so," he interrupted. "I was thinking of Elizabeth. It is nearly four months since Alexander's birth. She should be well enough to learn to ride."

"Ride?" Georgiana gave him a startled look. "But Elizabeth does not ride."

"So she says." He frowned at his sister's lack of perception. "Yet she has arms and legs and spirit enough for any horsewoman. She must learn."

"I see." Georgiana grew thoughtful. "Who would be her instructor?" Her brother offered her an elaborate bow. "You, brother?"

"Who better?"

"As you say . . ." Her voice trailed off, then took on new life. "Oh, look! There is our Aunt Matlock and Richard! Does Richard not look splendid? And Auntie as well!"

Darcy looked up. It was true; their cousin Colonel Richard Fitzwilliam always did look to advantage on the back of a horse and the one he bestrode now appeared to be an excellent creature in all respects. His aunt also commanded attention in a very smart riding habit and on a horse on which most gentlemen would not dare to set a lady of any years, much less the mother of the soldier beside her. Darcy and Georgiana pulled up and bowed their heads in respectful greeting.

"Aunt, so good to see you. Richard, how are you?" Darcy spoke for them both.

"And you as well, my dears." Lady Matlock smiled brightly. "Georgiana, my love, has your ball gown arrived from Madame's?" Her ladyship reined her horse away from the men, turning back the way she had come, and motioned her niece to follow. The gentlemen fell in behind them.

"Well, Fitz?"

"He's magnificent to look at, I grant you."

"Look your fill, for you won't see much of either of us when the shillings are down. We've already taken Sheridan's grey, you know." Richard cocked an impish smile at him. "Fancy a little go now or are Nelson's racing days well behind him?"

"With all these people and carriages about?"

"Ha! There was a time," Richard laughed, "when you were not a stodgy old . . . no, come to think of it, you always were. Ho, there!" Richard's mount interrupted him with a sudden jump, hooves dancing a rapid tattoo against the turf. "What the devil!"

"I'm going to bring Elizabeth riding tomorrow," Darcy announced as his cousin worked to calm his beast.

"What? Riding?" he huffed, the horse now wrestled into wary compliance. "But Elizabeth doesn't ride. And what did you do to my horse?"

"I shall teach her," he replied, ignoring his cousin's very legitimate question. "It is past time that she should have learnt."

"Well, Fitz, there must be a reason. Perhaps she does not *like* horses . . . frightened her as a child, or some such a thing."

"Elizabeth? Frightened?" Darcy laughed. "It is not possible.

Besides, I have found the perfect mount for her, a sweet little mare with the calmest temperament."

Richard looked askance at him, but Darcy's pose was assured. "You, of all people, would know," he acceded finally. "Tomorrow, you say?"

Darcy nodded.

"Well, well."

Elizabeth Darcy rose from the settee in the family parlor of the Darcys' London home and firmly set the novel aside. "Abominable!" she breathed in disgust. In the next moment, she snatched the book back up and prepared to pitch it into the grate. "No, better yet, out the front door you shall go! Out to be trodden underfoot!" Such an ignominious fate seemed harsh for a tome no more ambitious than any other of the popular host of Gothic romances filled with secret passageways, ancient ruins, and vengeful ghosts. But it was neither these trappings nor the dark and ridiculously petulant hero that had roused her ire with the latest book to be pressed hand to hand among the *ton*. No, it was the heroine of the piece or, perhaps, the authoress, herself.

"Deceptive . . . insufferable . . . oh!" she exclaimed, and turned to put her impulse into action. So intent was she upon her course that she didn't hear the knock before the parlor door swung open.

"Mrs. Darcy." The housekeeper, Mrs. Whitcher, curtsied. "I was wondering if you had finished with the— Mrs. Darcy, ma'am!"

"In a moment, Whitcher," Elizabeth tossed over her shoulder as she moved with purpose into the hall and toward the front door. "Nedley!" she called to the hall footman, "the door, if you please!" The footman scrambled to attention and sprang to the door, stepping back just in time to avoid the cheaply bound missile that was hurled past his head. The paste and board hit the sidewalk and bounced into the street, bursting apart to lie in a heap that was soon torn and scattered under iron-shod hooves and carriage wheels.

"There," she sighed, wiping her hands as if they had been soiled. "Thank you, Nedley. You may close the door."

"Y-yes, ma'am!" Nedley gulped and looked questioningly at the housekeeper. Mrs. Whitcher frowned him back into the un-ruffled countenance servants were expected to display regarding the behavior of their betters. He closed the door.

"Now, what were you wondering, Whitcher?" Elizabeth smiled and motioned her to follow.

"The menu, ma'am; have you decided on the menu for Miss Darcy's ball? An' then there're the flowers. With the celebrating going on, they say lilies nor daisies are to be had."

"Yes, the ball!" Elizabeth breathed and mentally squared her shoulders against the rush of dismay that swept over her whenever she was reminded of the enormity of Georgiana's coming-out arrangements. Her experience entering Hertfordshire society at the age of eighteen and Georgiana's entrance into the *beau monde* were hardly to be compared. Lady Catherine had warned her of this before her marriage and in the bluntest fashion: *If you were sensible of your own good, you would not wish to quit the sphere in which you have been brought up.*

How quick and confident had been her reply then! Oh yes, the boundaries of gentility had lain undeniably in her favor, but lately Elizabeth had found substance to her ladyship's protest. At Longbourn, in the assembly room at Meryton, and even in the grand halls of her husband's friends in Derbyshire, she had moved with confidence, happy in herself and her choice, perfectly justi-fied in her claim to have left no sphere for another. Her husband delighted in her, and the gentry within Pemberley's sway were, to all appearances, open-minded concerning their illustrious neighbor's choice and happy that the continuance of a Darcy at Pemberley was assured.

But, London . . . London was an entirely different matter, for it was here that she had finally encountered that Society among whom Lady Catherine had been so concerned to preserve her nephew's honor and credit. Entrance into that London had never been an option for Elizabeth during visits with Aunt and Uncle Gardiner in Cheapside. Her limited experience of the city's grander inhabitants had been in public places such as the theatre, where she had observed them from a safe anonymity. The whims and inconsistencies, the ridiculous poses and airs which had amused her from afar were not so diverting when once she was plunged into their midst. It was not, as that dreadful novel's authoress had portrayed, as easy as kiss-my-hand for a girl from a village in Hertfordshire to enter into that world where name and rank were everything and her every word and action would reflect immediately upon her husband's standing among his peers.

Certainly, upon her arrival, curiosity had instantly swirled around her, the unknown woman who had captured one of England's most eligible men. But as details of her lineage were discovered and the money and influence she had brought to the match set at naught, Society's eager interest cooled, giving way to the blank stare and patronizing smile, the laughter behind unfurled fans, the furious whispers. Oh, *she* had no patience with such puffery, such self-importance and play-acting, but this was *their* world. The distance between Longbourn and London, she had come to know, was calculated in far more than miles.

And now, in exactly one month, she was giving a ball. She turned back to Mrs. Whitcher, her brows knotted in concentration. "Ah, yes, the flowers. No lilies or daisies, you say? Oh, dear . . ."

"My dearest husband, you can not mean it!" Elizabeth looked away from the horse and up into Darcy's face, her consternation plain.

"But, I do," he said, smiling down at her. "She is your very own."

Elizabeth shook her head. "No, you mistake me. I meant—"

"Come," Darcy interrupted, and took her arm, drawing her down the front steps to the street, "you must get acquainted a little. See; isn't she lovely? I have no doubt that you'll deal together perfectly."

"Fitzwilliam—"

"Here," he spoke to Harry, their groom, "give me the reins."

Harry grinned and gave them over. "She's a sweet one, Mr. Darcy. The mistress'll not be having any trouble with her, I promise." He turned to Elizabeth and tugged his forelock. "'Ad her out meself an' she's as nice a set o' manners as I've come across, ma'am."

"Hmmm," Elizabeth responded dubiously, and crossed her arms as she turned her attention to her husband's present. Darcy led the horse out into the street, first walking the little bay in a circle and then encouraging it to a trot before bringing it to a halt in front of her.

"See," he repeated, holding out the reins to her. She ignored them, but he would not be discouraged. He reached out and drew her forward. "Talk to her, love; pet her a little. Here," he murmured, releasing her, and digging his fingers into his vest pocket, he brought out a sugar lump, "make friends with this."

Elizabeth looked at the lump, then at the horse, and finally into her husband's hopeful countenance. He wanted this so much.

Why was she so recalcitrant? Slowly, she extended her hand. Darcy dropped the lump into her palm. "I am not afraid, you know," she told him archly.

"Assuredly not," he replied with an amused smile. "As I remember, any attempt to intimidate you raises your courage, and a fearsome thing that is, indeed!"

Elizabeth's response was tempered. "Now you make me to be ridiculous and a virago in the same breath! I doubt you may be successful at both." She looked again at her present. "I can assure you that I already know how to give a horse sweets." She took a deep breath and stepped forward, her palm outstretched. The petite little mare obliged her immediately, whisking away the sugar with a light, feathery motion. Elizabeth laughed, but then quickly pursed her lips. "Well, that was quickly done. I suppose I am to pet it now?" She gingerly passed her hand down the mare's face and then stepped back, only to observe her husband's crinkled brow. She raised an eyebrow. "What?"

Darcy drew a deep breath. "In Society, that would have been considered the barest show of civility, perhaps even insulting. I believe Sheba would take it as quite condescending if that is all the attention you intend to pay to her."

"Sheba?"

"'Queen of Sheba' is, I believe, the name on her registration papers; but 'Sheba' is what she responds to." Darcy ran his hand down the horse's neck in a sure stroke. "And we shall all go for your first lesson as soon as you have changed into your riding habit."

Elizabeth looked up at him in alarm, but the earnest desire in his eyes and the straight, determined line of his mouth stopped the protest that had risen to her lips. How she wanted to please him, to see the light of approbation in his eyes! If only it did not involve this and at such a time when she was already so distracted.

An infant, a ball . . . and now a horse! She offered him instead a rueful smile. "I shall be down directly," she promised, and in a whirl of skirts she skipped up the steps.

Elizabeth had barely released the bell pull before Annie Fletcher was closing the dressing room door behind her. "Oh, ma'am, is it that beast in the street?"

"Yes, a gift from Mr. Darcy." She sighed and then straightened her shoulders. "My riding habit, if you please, Annie. It appears I am to make my equestrian debut in Hyde Park this afternoon."

Annie hurried over to the wardrobe and dug back into its recesses for several minutes before withdrawing a very fetching riding habit that had yet to be displayed to the world from the back of a horse. "It's a lovely habit, ma'am," she offered in consolation as she ran her hand over the russet velvet and deep brown braid. "Lovely, indeed. You and the master will be quite the picture. Put them fine ones all to shame."

"It is Mr. Darcy, I fear, who will be put to shame," Elizabeth replied and turned the back of her morning dress to Annie's quick hands. "Horses are all very well behind a fence, but I have never been able to bring myself to trust one. Once you are upon its back, you are entirely at its mercy. I do not know how my sister . . . well, yes, of course I do." Elizabeth smiled. "Jane could tame the wildest thing with her kindness and patience, even Merrily."

"Merrily?" Annie shook out the skirt of the habit and held it wide for her mistress to step into.

"Merrily, a horrid little pony! My father had purchased it for Jane and me so that we might learn to ride. Little did he know that he had introduced a fiend into our midst. We had no groom, only an older man from the farms who would saddle him and leave him tied to a bush. It was Jane who was afraid of him in the beginning, and I was the one eager to throw myself onto his back. Strange how it ended: Jane is the rider, and I have never learnt."

Annie held up the braided jacket and slipped it up Elizabeth's arms. "A right mean one, then, if he made *you* a-feared."

"Oh, he had more tricks than a monkey and directly showed me who was in charge. Within a week I was too—well, I had too much respect for what he could do if he chose to, that I refused to go near him. I suppose that seems silly now, but as a child, I was convinced it was reasonable caution and nothing less."

"There, ma'am." Annie gave her mistress an encouraging smile as she fastened the last hook. "Now for that hat." The maid hurried to another closet and brought down a hat box from an upper shelf. Gently lifting the item from the protective tissue, she turned it this way and that for Elizabeth's inspection. "A 'quiz' is what my Mr. Fletcher calls it; says it'll set the other ladies back on their heels."

"If that is Fletcher's considered opinion, then I have no doubt of my reception among the equestrian set!" Elizabeth laughed. Her husband's valet was a man of exquisite taste whose creations in gentlemen's neck cloths were highly regarded by no less a critic than Brummel himself. With Annie's assistance, the be-plumed shako was secured at a flirtatious angle by a multitude of pins. "Well, I believe I am ready." She surveyed herself in the cheval mirror. The ensemble *was* dashing. She also took pride in having regained her figure so soon after little Alexander's birth, for the habit had been purchased hard after her marriage and had not needed to be let out. "Rather, I am dressed for the part. Whether it will make any difference remains to be seen."

Darcy's dressing room was a field under strict discipline, commanded by a valet for whom his profession was both a calling and an art. His canvas, alas, was not inclined to offer him much scope, but even within the bounds of Darcy's tolerance for Fashion, Fletcher had won the envy of the rest of his breed. Then had come his master's marriage and with it an entirely new sort of challenge to his genius.

While others might count off their days by months and years, Fletcher marked his by sartorial events. Today was such a one: the First Appearance of Mr. and Mrs. Darcy in the Park on Horseback! Fletcher had considered it from every aspect and the challenge was, indeed, exceptional. Mrs. Darcy must be the focus—how could she not be?—yet, since she was no rider, it was the better part of wisdom that attention should be tempted away from her as well. It was a summons to greatness, a new prospect for his art.

That ladies' riding dress tended toward masculine, even military cuts was vastly in Fletcher's favor. So, in anticipation of this day, he had advised his master to make a bridal present of a riding habit. Thus, it was he who had designed the habit to be perfectly complemented by several of Darcy's new riding coats and he who had tasked his wife, Annie, with properly adjusting it after the Young Master's arrival. Life's events, in Fletcher's opinion, were much too important for one's attire to be left to happenstance.

"Fletcher! Good, you are already here." Darcy entered his dressing room with an energetic stride and a pleased, excited air. "We are to ride!"

"Yes, sir, so I have heard." Fletcher bowed. "May I suggest the dark brown coat with the russet facings?"

Darcy cast another covert glance at his wife as they rode to the Park. Elizabeth appeared more relaxed than when he had first set her upon Sheba's back. Her bravado on the ground had been charming, but once atop her mount, he was surprised to see how cleanly she was out of her element. A stab of uneasiness followed close upon the heels of that surprise when they entered the environs of the Park. Instead of the peaceful byway he had anticipated in this portion of the Park, the track seethed with the horses and carriages of Treaty celebrants. Liveried drivers from all over Europe jostled for a strategic position in the flow from which their master or mistress could see and be seen by those in passing vehicles or on horseback. Equally troublesome were the drivers of sporting vehicles. Those known for their driving skill wove smartly through the crowd, but lesser lights could be heard swearing terrible oaths at a scrape of paint, the negligence of a groom, or a perceived slight offered by another whipster. Surveying the scene, Darcy feared his mistake might thoroughly discourage his wife from attempting anything more than a return to the mews behind Erewhile House. He pulled Nelson to a halt.

"Elizabeth," he shouted, leaning over to be heard above the noise, "perhaps we should—" Darcy's voice was drowned out by a sudden crescendo of savage snarls and hysterical barking. He whirled about to behold carriage dogs atop two approaching phaetons engaged in vociferous objection to each other. Caught in the crowded track, their owners were wholly engaged in guiding their fractious teams and could only roar at their animals to behave. Up and down the track, lapdogs from other carriages, excited by the sounds, strained to see the contest and, setting up their own chorus of yips and howls, added to the general confusion.

Darcy looked back at Elizabeth just as Nelson began throwing his head and backing away from the carriages that were now nearly upon them. "Elizabeth," he called, pulling the horse's head around. What he saw sent his heart into his throat. Like Nelson,

Sheba wanted none of the approaching dogfight. The little horse quivered and began a scrambled effort to back away. "Fitzwilliam!" Elizabeth cried, her eyes wide as she worked to maintain her seat and bring her mount under control.

In the next moment, the dog on the far carriage launched himself at the other, carrying both animals off the perch to land snarling in combat at Sheba's feet. The little bay started and then sprang into a run away from the track and through the trees. "Elizabeth!" Darcy shouted, but before he could get his own agitated mount turned, two riders passed him in swift pursuit of the fleeing horse and its rider. "Merciful Heavens, hold on!" Darcy prayed as, finally, he was able to turn Nelson and give him his head.

Elizabeth pulled desperately on the reins as Sheba carried her in full, terrified flight away from the dogs, but the mare paid her no heed. Trees and bushes crowded fast upon her, catching at the skirts of her new riding habit. Then, in a sudden change of direction, the mare took her straight into a cruel tangle of low-hanging branches that snatched at her sleeves and the veil of her hat. Briars ripped away a sleeve at the seam and tore the smart shako, pins and all, right off her head.

A voice behind her that was not her husband's shouted something, but Elizabeth did not dare to look over her shoulder for fear of losing her seat. Her eyes stung from the rush of wind; her hair was in her face. The voice sounded out again, nearer. A park bench arose out of nowhere. "No!" she wailed, but her protest was lost in the pound of hooves and Sheba's labored breathing. Elizabeth twined her gloved fingers into Sheba's mane and stiffened in anticipation. Why, oh why hadn't she conquered that dratted pony—

"Oh-h-h!" Elizabeth felt Sheba's gait shift and her muscles bunch. Clutching at the mane, she closed her eyes and instinctively leaned forward. Sheba's hindquarters pushed and her forequarters lifted. Up—up—and over the bench. For a moment she felt as though they were flying, but the shock of landing on the other side drove the breath from Elizabeth's lungs and nearly unseated her. Not yet satisfied that danger was not still at her very heels, Sheba resumed her flight. To her horror, Elizabeth saw that they now followed one of the footpaths that wound through the park. Any moment they could come upon some unfortunate soul!

A rider flashed past on her right, crowding Sheba so closely that Elizabeth feared the tangle of legs would trip them both and send them all crashing into the trees. Anger at the other rider lent her strength, and she hauled back on the reins again. Sheba stumbled and Elizabeth fell forward upon the mare's neck. Slowly she slid off its back, clinging to its mane and the saddle rest as the animal struggled to regain its footing. For some interminable seconds, Elizabeth was dragged along the path. Then, the saddle shifted. A second rider appeared on her left just as Elizabeth lost her grip and toppled to the ground.

"Elizabeth!" Darcy cried and swung from Nelson's back. "Elizabeth! My God, love," he choked and scooped her up to gently set her in his lap. "Easy, dearest," he murmured. "Breathe . . . slowly!" Her eyes fixed on his face, Elizabeth nodded and then fell upon his neck, trembling so violently from head to toe that she barely noticed Georgiana and Richard carefully advancing upon Sheba, blocking the path ahead.

"Ho, there!" Richard bellowed and dove for the reins, pulling the mare's head to the side as he signaled his mount to slow, then walk in a tight circle. It was not until the third time around the circle that Elizabeth recognized Richard as the rider who had crowded her. Where Georgiana had come from, she could not guess.

"Elizabeth!" cried Georgiana when she came to a stop. "Are you all right, sister?"

"So sorry to frighten you, old girl," Richard apologized, "but if your horse had taken the other path . . ."

Georgiana slid from her horse and rushed to Elizabeth's side while Richard gathered the reins from all their mounts and led the animals a short distance away. "Oh, Elizabeth! How terrible!" she said, stroking her arm. "When you are able, we shall walk back to Erewhile House. Richard can lead Sheba back to the mews." An indistinguishable sound from Elizabeth caused brother and sister to look in question at each other.

"What love?" Darcy tipped up her chin and brushed his thumb over her cheek, wiping away a tear that had started to brim over her eyelashes. "What did you say?" Shaking her head, she pushed away from him and sat up. Darcy's heart sank. Would she not allow him to comfort her? Would she not even speak to him? He observed her in helpless silence as she slowly stood and tugged her riding gloves into place and then noticed the torn sleeve hanging limply from her elbow. "My new riding habit!" she murmured. "Well, there is nothing for it, I suppose, but we must test Annie's skill with her needle."

Her eyes fixed upon Sheba, and then, with an arched brow, she looked down at her husband. "I said, I shall *ride* back to Grosvenor Square."

It was only after they had ridden home and Darcy had personally overseen Elizabeth dressed comfortably and ensconced on a divan with a soothing pot of tea that the rest of the story was told. For

Richard and Georgiana had not been at the park by happen-stance.

"Oh no!" Richard laughed as he cradled his tea. "No, I for one was not about to leave you to Fitz and his ideas of equestrian education."

"I taught Georgiana," Darcy countered. His cousin's lack of confidence in him was wounding, but how could he argue against it? He'd shown remarkably bad judgment this day.

"We both taught Georgiana to ride, if you would take the time to recall." Richard smiled at his younger cousin. "By-the-bye, that was well done, my girl. Quick thinking!" Coloring at the compliment, Georgiana turned to Elizabeth. Taking her hand, she said, "Dear sister, I hope you do not think us presumptuous. It was only that since you had not yet learnt to ride, I thought that, perhaps, the company of your family might be an encouragement to you."

"I am entirely at fault, dearest Elizabeth. Can you forgive me?" Darcy held his wife tenderly in his arms as they lay in the expanse of their bed. "It seems my cousin and sister saw what I was blind to see myself. You are not inclined to ride. And yet, I cajoled and pressed upon you a horse you did not want, a riding habit you had not asked for, and induced you to ride unprepared in a setting fraught with danger."

"Please, Fitzwilliam." Elizabeth held his face in her hands and kissed him lightly.

"No, you must allow me to lay blame where it is due. I have acted selfishly and I came very near to paying dearly for my mistake." Darcy buried his face in the sweetness of her curls and whispered, "What if you had come to harm, dear wife? What would I do?"

Both were silent, listening to the familiar sounds of Erewhile House at the close of another day. From somewhere far below came sounds from the kitchen and pantry. Soon the nurse would bring Alexander in for his nightly routine and their reverie would come to a quick end.

"It's just that you have done so very splendidly in all else. Riding seemed a small thing," Darcy mused. Elizabeth stirred, but he continued, "I should not have forced you to take a part in what is my own passion."

Elizabeth raised herself to look into her husband's eyes. "You think I have done splendidly in all things?" She gave a troubled sigh and nestled again against Darcy's chest. "It pains me to admit that Lady Catherine was right in *anything* regarding our marriage, but I fear she was."

Darcy gently rubbed her arm and back. "Aunt Catherine? What part has she in this?" He kissed the top of her head.

"Oh, the popular novels make it sound so easy." She turned to look at him earnestly. "I lost my patience and quite shocked poor Nedley by pitching a book into the street." She sighed and snuggled against his chest. "I'm sure there is scandalized talk below stairs. Sometimes I feel that I am *not* equal to the sphere in which our marriage has placed me."

Darcy tensed. "What do you mean, Elizabeth?"

"Lady Catherine accused me of having no regard for your honor and credit." Elizabeth raised her head again and searched Darcy's face. "She told me that who I am was cause enough to disgrace you in the eyes of everybody."

"That is ridiculous!" Darcy asserted vehemently.

"Yes, it is . . . in Meryton, in Hertfordshire, perhaps even in Derbyshire." She tapped a finger against his chest for each locality.

"Absolutely!" He possessed himself of her hand and kissed each finger.

"But, I have come to see there is some substance to her words. You, my beloved husband, have always lived in this world. You can move through it without thought, whereas I must consider everything I do and say, whether they may redound to your credit or end in disgrace. Here, in London, I am still finding my way." At his look of astonishment, she responded quickly, "Oh, fear not, dear husband, I am determined to rise to this challenge. As for the other, Sheba and I are destined for a long acquaintance. But," she sighed, "there is the matter of this ball."

Darcy shifted her onto her back and looked down into her troubled countenance. "Georgiana's ball? That is what has you tossing books into the street—"

"Oh, yes, Fitzwilliam! There are a thousand arrangements to be made. You have no idea! There are protocols beyond numbering. Every detail is of exceeding importance. I wish everything to be perfect for Georgiana, but I fear it is beyond me and that, in the end, your aunt will be proved right to the whole world!"

"Elizabeth! My dear, dear wife, listen to me. Recall the riding incident this very day that so nearly ended in injury and disaster. Richard and Georgiana—your family—love you and came to your aid. So it shall be with this ball." Darcy lay back and pulled her into his arms. "Send to my aunt Matlock. She knows everything worth knowing about these things. She has no daughter of her own and would move heaven and earth for Georgiana. She only waits to be asked, I assure you. Let her be your advisor." He laughed and hugged her tightly. "Even Richard may have his uses. Believe me, love! All *will* be well!"

"Truly, Fitzwilliam? As easy as that?" Elizabeth looked at him with wide eyes sparkling with that wit and humor that had first drawn his interest so long ago in Hertfordshire.

"Yes, love, as easy as that. Consult her in confidence, hear her suggestions and implement them yourself. You will not fail, and

London can go to the devil!" His finger traveled down the curve of her dimpled cheek. "You shall see, your novel had it right all along. Now, am I forgiven?" His finger traced her lips.

She smiled under his touch.

"Ahh," he whispered, "as easy as that?"

PAMELA AIDAN is the author of the Fitzwilliam Darcy, Gentleman series. She has been a librarian for over thirty-five years and a fan of Jane Austen even longer. She and her husband own and operate Wytherngate Press, Inc., which specializes in Regency fiction. Ms. Aidan lives in scenic northern Idaho, where she is at work on a continuation of the Fitzwilliam Darcy, Gentleman series and Young Master Darcy, a new series that explores Darcy's growing-up years.

wytherngatepress.com

THE LOVE LETTER

GRAND PRIZE WINNER OF THE *JANE AUSTEN MADE ME DO IT* SHORT STORY CONTEST

Brenna Aubrey

I never expected to pull a mystery out of a self-addressed stamped envelope. One yellowed page removed from a novel. In my hand, it flapped in a sudden breeze that rose up that November morning. One page. Torn from a book. Something I'd never read before. At the time I couldn't know that this page would change my life forever.

My own spidery scrawl leapt up at me from the snowy paper of the envelope: *Dr. Mark Hinton,* followed by my post office box at the medical school. As a new doctor about to finish my residency, I had sent out a stack of SASEs to medical groups around the country who were looking for physicians in my specialty. Though I'd already accepted a position to practice with a prestigious local group, I'd been curious to know what was in the envelope. It was odd, though. I thought I'd got the last of them back months ago.

The fragment came from pages 307 and 308 of some unidentified book. The top of the sheet had been torn so that I could not see the title of the work. I read it, front and back. The style of

writing was old-fashioned, as if from a classic. I felt I should recognize it, but the fact was that I only did well enough in my un-
dergraduate English courses to maintain my GPA for medical
school.

That's how I'd met Justine. She'd been my English tutor. An
unwanted memory invaded my thoughts—the slim arch of her
neck as she bent over my term papers, shaking her head in mock
horror and wielding her red pen like a scalpel. I could watch for
hours the way she twirled a long strand of her honey-colored hair
around one finger.

Wind stung my eyes but I stood glued to the spot. I shook my
head, determined to clear it of the bothersome thoughts, and concentrated on my surprising "fan mail." Or a blackmail letter,
maybe. In the movies, sometimes, threat letters were cut and
pasted from magazine pages. Was this a threat?

In the text on the page, a gentleman had entered a room to
leave a note for a lady named Anne. For some reason, they could
not speak. I assumed it was because they weren't alone.

After this man—the captain—left, Anne found the letter to
be a declaration of his love. *Unjust I may have been,* the captain
wrote, *weak and resentful I have been but never inconstant.*

The wind intensified, sending needles of ice into my uncov-
ered face. Fog billowed out from my mouth; I was still breathing
heavily from my run. I retreated to my apartment and threw the
mail aside to listen to my phone messages while I stretched.

For some crazy reason, instead of listening to my mom drone
on about the plans for Thanksgiving at my sister's, I kept thinking about lines from that mysterious page.

I am half agony, half hope. The guy had it bad. I felt sorry for
him. *I offer myself again with a heart even more your own than when
you broke it eight years and a half ago.* Don't do it, Bro. She'll only
squash it again. Like a grape.

It was impossible for me not to think of Justine. I gritted my teeth, sinking into a series of challenging squats. I'd spent six years putting her out of my mind. I was proud of myself. I had succeeded. Until last summer.

I finished my lunges and went to the kitchen of my studio, where windows overlooked the Denver skyline. The Rocky Mountains cut a jagged horizon in a partly cloudy sky that promised snow soon. I'd smelled it on the air during my run, heavy and wet.

Downing a liter of water before coming up for air, I continued to puzzle over my mystery mail. I returned to the mail pile again, in search of more pages. Nothing. Postmark? Again, nothing. I'd had the self-addressed envelopes stamped POSTAGE PAID when I'd sent them out. There wasn't even a mark of the city of origin. No clue as to who had sent it or why. Just one page. Torn from an old novel. And I didn't even know which one.

Hours later, I sat in my favorite study carrel on the fourth floor of the university library with a thick copy of *On Call: Principles and Protocols*. Medical board examinations loomed: the last great test of every doctor early in his career. Once boards were out of the way, I'd be ready to get on with my new life.

But I could not concentrate on the open book before me. My eyes slid over the highlighted page like a pedestrian on an icy sidewalk. Nothing gained purchase in my brain. I doodled. I unfolded and refolded dog-eared pages. And yet only the lines of a fictitious love letter dominated my thoughts: *You pierce my soul. Tell me not that I am too late . . .*

I sighed in frustration and nodded at my study-buddy, Eric, elbow deep in a handbook on toxicology. Then, I descended to the second floor. Literature. I'd had no further interest in reading those musty old books once I was no longer an undergrad. They were haunted by ghosts. Or, rather, just one ghost. From my past.

Was it my imagination when I heard the whisper *"Justine . . ."* as the elevator doors slid open? I willed the odd sense of foreboding away as I trod over to the desk of the librarian's aide. I mustered my best ignorant-science-guy grin and placed the page before her.

"I didn't ruin one of your books, I swear," I said in response to her raised eyebrows. "It's kind of a weird story, actually. I got this in the mail. I have no idea where it came from or what it means. Can you help me out?"

She sat up, eyes widening in interest as she took up the page. "Oooh. A mystery! A secret admirer, perhaps?"

"Do you know what it is?"

She took less than a minute to read it. "Yep. It's Jane Austen."

I raised my eyebrows. "Is that like *Jane Eyre?*" I'd been forced to read it in high school. I didn't remember much besides its weirdness—something about a madwoman locked in an attic.

The librarian's eyebrows crinkled in exasperation. "Jane Austen is an author. *Jane Eyre* is a book."

"Okay. So Jane Austen wrote this. What book is it?"

"*Persuasion*. Is that a clue, maybe? Are you being persuaded to do something?'"

I shrugged. "Do you guys have a copy of this book, maybe?"

She appeared to suppress an eye roll. "I'm sure we have several. You up to reading it?"

My doubt must have been clear on my face because she laughed. "It's not all girly stuff, you know. Men like Jane Austen, too. Besides . . . there might be a clue in the text of the novel."

I followed her down the farthest fiction aisle, skimming the books' spines and noting the names of authors whom I recognized but had read only under the duress of my English grade—Zola, Fitzgerald, Dickens, Conrad. At the A's, I scanned the brightly tagged book spines. Would this *Persuasion* be as impossible to deci-

pher as *Heart of Darkness?* And would it be worth the slog through
the archaic prose just for a clue to this little mystery?

"Here you are. This copy is annotated, coming complete with
margin notes that give definitions of word—"

"Hey now, I'm an M.D., I *do* know how to read the English
language."

"Really? So you know what a 'curricle' is?"

At my frown, she laughed and handed me the book. "I'll
check it out to you down there. It's a type of carriage, by the way."

Carriage . . . great. I scowled. Horses, carriages, people dying
of smallpox and children getting caught in soot-clogged chimneys. *This will be a fun read.*

Back in my carrel, I cracked open the novel to the first page:

*Sir Walter Elliot, of Kellynch hall, in Somersetshire, was a
man who, for his own amusement, never took up any book but the
Baronetage—*

I shot a quick glance at the margin notes, though it bruised my
pride to do so only three lines into the book. *Baronetage—an annotated list of baronets.*

I slapped the book closed and sat back in frustration, running
a hand through my hair. I had rounds at the hospital in an hour.
What I *didn't* have was the slightest clue why I was indulging
myself in two-hundred-year-old literature that didn't pertain to
any question on my board exams. Jumping up and waving to
Eric, I tapped the back of my wrist and pointed in the direction of
the hospital.

I tossed the library book and my medical tome into my locker and
changed into my greens. Pulmonology boards were in four weeks.
In addition, I'd be giving up precious study time to fly across the
country to Rhode Island tomorrow for Thanksgiving at my sis-

ter's. Was I actually contemplating making time to read a novel? No. This was why the Internet was invented. The search engine gods would guide me on my path to clues.

My smug resolve faded when I was faced with my last patient of the day.

"Hello, Mrs. Kellerman! I see the roses have returned to your cheeks. How are are you feeling today?"

Her mouth twisted in her wrinkled face; gray hair splayed out around her head against a bleached white pillow.

"Rotten. What else is new?"

I consulted her chart. "Well, the good news is that the results of your lung plethysmography were normal." Proceeding to the next test, I wheeled over the spirometer. Mrs. Kellerman eyed the machine as if it were a vicious dog about to rip off her arm.

I helped her to a sitting position. "Mrs. Kellerman, you were an English teacher before you retired, weren't you?"

"I was a professor at the community college, why?" She gave me a wary look that suggested she'd picked up on my tactic of distracting the patient during an unpleasant procedure.

"I have an honest question, actually." I took the mouthpiece of the spirometer from its resting place. "I was just loaned a novel called *Persuasion*. Have you ever heard of it?"

She looked at me as if I were an idiot. "Of course. Jane Austen. One of my favorites."

"Really? She wrote a lot of novels, then?"

She frowned. "Just six. She only lived forty-one years."

"I see. So. Can you tell me what the novel is about?"

"You should read it."

"I'll get to it eventually. I was wondering—"

Her cold stare pinned me down. I had no doubt that in her day she had been a formidable professor.

"Young man, if I can sit here all day with this blasted mask on my face, take every prodding, finger prick, and blow-in-the-tube test that you order up, then you can darn well read a masterpiece of a novel."

I twitched my eyebrows in surprise but let the subject drop. "You know the drill, ma'am. Take a deep breath." When she was ready, I pressed the tube to her lips.

Instead of returning to the library, I grabbed a quick bite at home. I opened the book again with determination—and the image of Mrs. Kellerman's stony gaze in the back of my mind.

Hours later, I glanced up at the clock and was shocked at how much time had passed. The feeling was like coming up for air after swimming underwater—like I'd been breathing in another world. With reluctance, I remembered I had physical needs to see to. I had to pee.

At two a.m., I stopped reading again, this time due to fatigue. I was nearly finished and I wanted—no, I *needed*—to know the ending. Only a few chapters into the story, I had begun to see myself in Captain Wentworth. In Anne, I read *Justine*.

Unfinished, I closed the book and rolled over, my eyes closing on the porous ceiling tiles. Memories overwhelmed me like a strong current at high tide . . .

Until the past summer, I hadn't seen Justine in six years. And at that time, seeing her was the *last* thing I'd wanted. After six years, the sting of her rejection still cut deep.

It was only once I had arrived at my sister's house for a short stay that she informed me that Justine was staying with her brother. Across the street. In their parents' old house, where she had lived when the two of us were undergraduates at Brown University.

For the next two weeks, we would be neighbors again. I

shrugged it off. It didn't matter to me. I kept busy, playing with my nephews and helping my brother-in-law with home-improvement projects.

But I ran the neighborhood tract every morning. I refused to look at the corner section of the sidewalk where Justine and I had once carved our initials into the wet cement. I had no interest to see if they had lasted longer than *we* had. I tried not to notice that the tree where I'd usually kissed her good night had grown taller. I tried not to see *her* everywhere in the neighborhood.

My luck expired after three days, though I'd chosen an early hour for my runs. I'd been rising before the birds. Like I had to do when I was on call. But one morning, sure enough, when I left the house she was standing on her brother's front lawn like a lost soul, a trowel in her hand.

At the periphery of my vision, the movement of her bending over a flower box brought me to a stop. Her brother's gardening gloves made her hands look five sizes too big for the rest of her. She straightened and our eyes met. A ghost from the past greeted me and my chest tightened. It was all I could do to keep my mouth closed despite the shock.

Justine truly looked like a ghost. "Hello, Mark," she said, a shadow of a smile crossing her pale features.

She had cut off all of her gorgeous hair and dyed what was left of it black. And she had lost so much weight that I barely recognized her. She looked terrible. As terrible as Justine could ever look.

She still had those eyes. Those haunted blue eyes.

"Um. Hi," I croaked.

"How are you?"

I clenched my jaw. "Fine. Great. *Awesome.* You?"

She nodded. "Better. I'm getting better."

I didn't ask. I burned to ask. But I didn't. I wouldn't.

My feet began to move. I made a stupid show of jogging in place. "Well. Excuse me, have to keep up the heart rate." With an exaggerated wave, I plugged in my earbuds and left.

It is over! The worst is over. They had met. They had been once more in the same room. I rolled over in my bed, my memories interrupted for the briefest of moments by an echo of the words I had just read.

"I heard you saw Justine," my sister said that same afternoon, as she loaded the dishwasher. I sank my teeth into the tuna sandwich she had fixed for me. The way I love it, with mayo and relish.

"I was running early. I didn't think she'd be out at that hour. Gardening. Since when does she *garden*?"

There was a long pause. "It's part of her therapy."

I stopped chewing and swallowed a too-large lump of sandwich. "Therapy?"

Kathy didn't hear me. Or chose not to answer, I couldn't tell which.

"So, is she back here visiting, or . . . ?"

"She's been living at her brother's for a few months. She told me she'll be looking for her own place when she gets on her feet."

"She moved back—for good? L.A. wasn't her cup of tea after all?" For some reason this news brought hot resentment burning up from my stomach. My empty fist clenched but I forced it to relax.

Kathy dried her hands on a dishcloth and turned to look at me for a minute. I feigned sudden intense interest in the quartered newspaper left on the table.

"She had a nervous breakdown, Mark."

"Hmm." I grunted without looking up so Kathy wouldn't be able to see how my heart lurched at the news. "I'm sorry to hear that."

Kathy stared at me for a long time but I refused to look up. "What did you think when you saw her?"

"I almost didn't recognize her."

I almost didn't recognize her. Those words echoed to me in the present as I contemplated the horror of them again. *She had a nervous breakdown, Mark.* I rubbed my eyes through closed lids.

Captain Wentworth is not very gallant by you, Anne. He said you were so altered, he should not have known you again.

The following day, Kathy committed me to a favor before specifying what I would have to do. With the bribe of her delicious caramel turtle cookies thrown in for good measure, she had me trudging across the street with her Rototiller to help with the garden project.

Justine stood surveying a dirt mound next to her fledgling flower box—the location of her future garden—when I got there. She held a shovel in a gloved hand and wore a sleeveless tank top. Her arms were thin and pale, like dried sticks. I forced myself not to look at them.

"So where do you want your dirt?"

"Here. Thanks, Mark."

"What are you planting?"

"Roses. I know it will be too late to see any bloom this year, but I'm going to get some grafts from the nursery. If we have a warm autumn, I might get lucky."

I spent two hours churning the dirt for her while she dug a shallow trench around the border of the lawn. Fortunately, there was little occasion to talk over the loud whirring of the machine. And when I was done, all I wanted to do was leave. But I couldn't help but notice the shoddy job she was doing with the watering trench. I suspect she tried her hardest, but there was little strength in her limbs.

I moved next to her to ask if she needed anything else. I wanted to offer to dig a proper trench, but I couldn't. Something inside me wouldn't allow it. I swallowed a spiky ball of resentment. Even then, after all those years.

She crammed the ancient shovel into the ground and yanked it back with every bit of her strength. The handle snapped at the tongue and she fell back. On instinct and reflex, I grabbed her before she fell.

Her shock prevented her from crying out. I held her for a moment too long while registering my own shock. She felt so much lighter in my arms than she once had.

What the hell had she been doing out in LaLa Land? Starving herself?

I straightened and helped her stand. Her hair brushed past my face. I caught a whiff of her familiar scent—flowers and mint. My body responded on instinct, flooding with heat. She still used the same shampoo. Memories flashed through my thoughts: holding her in my arms, tasting her lips, pressing my body to hers.

The heat turned to anger at my own subconscious reaction. I released her as if she had burned me. Preparing to retreat across the street, I moved to the tilling machine and locked the blade.

"Heya, Jus, whatcha doin'?"

We both turned. A gorgeous blonde was peeking over the fence from the neighboring yard. She was young, in her early twenties, and had enough hair and enough chest for two women.

"The usual. Working on the garden. I got a huge help thanks to Mark here," she said coolly, as if the past moments hadn't happened.

The young woman's eyes assessed me and I nodded, sporting

my best charming-guy smile. Her shirt was cut low and it was hard to take my eyes off the stretch of fabric across her breasts. When I finally looked at her face again, she had a knowing smile. My grin widened.

"Mark, this is our neighbor, Chloë," Justine said quickly, darting looks from one of us to the other. She cleared her throat and uttered the rest of the introduction as if from a great distance. "Chloë, this is Kathy's brother."

"The doctor?" Chloë immediately perked up. I got that a lot.

After making sure there was nothing further that Justine wanted for the garden, I moved over to the fence and began to chat with Chloë. To my relief, Justine faded into the background.

That was when, standing at the edge of Justine's brother's lawn, I asked Chloë out to dinner. I could hear Justine putting away the shovels and cleaning up, jobs with which I had not offered to help. I was sure she was listening to every word. I told myself that I didn't care. *She* probably didn't care either. Hadn't she once treated me the same way? And had she not just brushed me off as if there had never been a past between us at all?

So Justine was unhappy with her life. That was unfortunate, but it was the life *she* had chosen. By *her* choice, deep love had been crushed to please others and her own ambition.

No, I hadn't forgiven her. I couldn't. It hurt too much to even consider.

He had not forgiven Anne Elliot. She had used him ill, deserted and disappointed him; and worse, she had shown a feebleness of character in doing so, which his own decided, confident temper could not endure.

By my second date with Chloë, I knew we could never amount to anything serious. For one thing, I had less than a week left before

I had to return to Colorado to finish my residency. The other reasons? I couldn't really name them. Though I promised myself that they had nothing to do with Justine.

But as I brewed myself a pot of coffee after that sleepless night, I realized with surprising clarity that all of my relationships since Justine had been similarly haunted by our past.

He had been most warmly attached to her, and had never seen a woman since whom he thought her equal.

I finished the novel on the plane the next day. Then I fell against the window and slept the remaining hours. I dreamt of Justine. Of the smell of her hair. Of the first time I'd kissed her, pressed up against the stacks in the back of the library. Of the first time we made love, with fierce kisses and shaking hands. In my agitation, I awoke, shifted positions, willed my restless mind to find something different to dwell on. It didn't. I dreamt of the plans we'd made for our life after graduation. She'd applied to the law school at the University of Colorado. We'd be there, together, in the mountains. We'd start our life there, together, as husband and wife.

I dreamt of the night I'd proposed to her. The happiest night of my life. She cried when I slipped the ring on her finger.

I cried the night she gave it back. "I can't do this," she said. "I'm sorry. I've been accepted at UCLA. I'm going to live there and work in my dad's firm."

My world froze. All of our hopes, plans, our future together breaking to pieces before my eyes.

"I'm sorry," she said over and over again between sobs.

The following day, Thanksgiving dinner at my sister's was a trial. Throughout the meal, I couldn't keep my mind off the house across the street. Was Justine still living there or had she moved on? Was she still unattached? I didn't dare ask the questions hovering on my lips. What the hell had that book done to me?

Then Kathy announced that she had invited Justine and her brother's family over for dessert. A warm sense of hope washed over me. The sentiments of the novel were still fresh in my mind. I was now determined to let her know, somehow, that I still thought of her. That she was still in my heart.

When she entered the room, I was struck by her glowing skin, her hair—now honey-colored once again. She had gained weight. The wan smile had new life and now reached her eyes.

Her face lit up when she saw me and my heart missed a beat. "Mark! I'm glad you made it home." Even her voice sounded stronger. She came close to me. My throat closed and the words I wanted to say went unspoken.

What had brought about this change in me? Why, *now,* could I look past all that had happened before? I could feel the hurt and resentment fading, dissolving a barrier between us.

All that mattered was that the girl of my dreams was before me again. Damaged a little, but still there, underneath the pain and failure of the years that had separated two hearts and minds as connected as ours once were.

Before I could do anything besides ask her about her garden, Kathy hauled me into the kitchen to help her serve pie.

"She's seeing someone."

I said nothing, slicing the pies into eighths with surgical precision.

"I said—"

"I heard you." My heart was in my shoes. I swallowed. "Does her therapist approve? So soon?"

"Ah, sweetie. I think the therapist encouraged it."

I couldn't look at her as I wiped pumpkin filling off my fingers.

As dessert wound to a close, I only had one quick chance to speak with Justine again. Tomorrow, she'd be leaving on a shopping holiday with friends for the remainder of the weekend.

After informing me of this, we looked at each other in awkward silence, and then she touched me gently on the sleeve. "Mark, I was wondering . . . I'm going to Aspen in December to meet my dad for a short ski trip. I'll be passing through Denver on the sixteenth and . . . would you like to, maybe, catch up over lunch or something?"

The sixteenth. "That's the last day of my medical boards. I'll be testing all day."

The visible hope on her delicate features melted away.

"Oh. Oh, yes, of course. I'll—well, some other time then. Can I give you my cell number? In case you finish early or something?" *Not likely.*

We exchanged cards. I nodded goodbye to her, unasked questions about her new boyfriend still hanging between us. I wouldn't be jealous. I didn't have the right.

How does the story end? In *Persuasion*, of course, Anne finds the love letter that Wentworth has left for her. In it, he tells her that, in spite of his resentment, in spite of his flirting with other women right under her nose, in spite of the fact that she had crushed his heart, he still loves her. After all this time.

They exchanged again those feelings and those promises which had once before seemed to secure everything, but which had been followed by so many, many years of division and estrangement.

But my story? *Our* story, mine and Justine's? What was my persuasion? To forgive. To let go. To move forward. To never forget.

On December 16, my world swam before me. The last test of the boards—an essay test—was here. Lost in a high-vaulted, echoing testing chamber, I stared at the open blue test booklet, unable to focus on the task at hand.

An hour of stretching, clicking my pen up and down, and cracking open my water bottle had produced little beyond a page of my illegible scribble. Seven different beginnings of love letters I had written and then crossed out. Abandoned.

She was in Denver, somewhere. And I was here. And as noon grew into afternoon, my agitation increased. Where was she now?

The choice was clear. I had to see her. Before I realized what I was doing, my feet were on the floor, my legs were carrying me from the silence of the test room.

I didn't start breathing again until I was in the foyer. Leaning against the heavy wooden door, my cell phone in my hand, I pulled out the card she'd given me. She'd be on the way to the airport by now, I figured.

I typed: *Justine, I don't know if you'll get this, but I have to tell you. I need you. Always have. I've been stubborn, resentful & full of pride. But my heart never changed. I've never loved anyone else but you.*

I hit send.

I waited for a minute, heart thudding. Two. Nothing. Cold fear numbed the pulse at my throat.

My thumb hovered over the send button, unable to type the next message. *Can you? Will you?*

No answer. Maybe she had missed it? My head thudded against the brick walls of the university hall. Test-takers were now spilling out of the chamber, milling about the hallway, putting on their coats, pulling out their cell phones. It hurt to breathe. Had I walked away from my medical boards for nothing?

The entire way home, I checked my phone every two minutes. Maybe, she was in the air by now. Maybe, maybe she hadn't received my text. Or her phone was turned off. Or she was waiting, trying to figure out her answer. Or. Or.

Hours passed. No reply. I checked to see how many bars I had on my reception. I checked to see if the network was cooperating. There were no problems. There was nothing. And inevitably my mind strayed to the most believable explanation: that she hadn't meant what she had said about wanting to see me again. Or that she had changed her mind. Maybe she felt, like I once had, that the past was too painful to revisit.

Back in my apartment, I grabbed a beer and twisted the cap so viciously that it cut my palm.

My cell phone rang and I nearly dropped the bottle. I raced to answer it, my voice breathless.

"Mark! How'd you do on your test?"

My breath hitched and a pain radiated through my chest. Kathy.

"Hey, sis." I fought to keep the disappointment from my voice.

"Hey, I've been meaning to call you since Thanksgiving. I— well, I have a confession to make."

"Let me guess. You defaced one of your own books to send me a page in the mail anonymously."

Silence for two beats.

"How'd you know?"

"When I was there for Thanksgiving I saw the book in the den. Your copy is missing page 308. You pinched one of my SASEs from my job applications to send it."

She sighed. "Well, I've never been good at being sneaky, have I?"

"Not really," I said, hoping my curt reply would put her off becoming chatty. The last thing I wanted to do right now was discuss this with Kathy.

"I'm sorry, Mark. I just—I—I know how much you loved her once. That kind of love is a rare gift, you know. And the resentment over losing it was tearing you up inside. You two were so . . ."

"Sis, could we talk about this another time? I can't—can't really talk at the moment. Can I call you back later?" I was still hoping against all reason for a call from Justine. Or a text. Or a smoke signal. Or some other sign of acknowledgment whatsoever. Please don't let it be silence. I could take anything but that, though it might be what I deserved.

"I just wish . . . wish that it had all been for something."

So did I. After we said goodbye, I closed my eyes and put down the phone. I chugged the entire bottle of beer and snatched up another. I was on my third when the doorbell rang.

I suddenly remembered that I'd invited Eric over to celebrate the end of exams. I snapped open the door without looking in the peephole.

It wasn't Eric.

Justine.

Tears in her eyes, on her cheeks. Her cell phone in her hand. My heart stopped beating until she spoke.

"Mark." It was a hoarse whisper. A plea. An exultation.

I would later learn that she had gone to the airport early and checked her baggage. It had taken her time to retrieve her belongings, to fill out papers and speak with an airline official about pulling out of her flight.

I said nothing as I watched her from the doorway. Then, I took her into my arms, held her close. Her tight sobs in my ear struck arrows to the core of me.

"I always loved you," I said.

"I never stopped. But why? Why now? After everything . . ."

I backed into my apartment with her still in my arms. We kissed. She tasted the same, and different—a trace of coffee and that cinnamon gum she loved. She tasted *better*. Our lips met in quiet understanding, mutual forgiveness, passionate reunion.

When we finished, I rested my forehead against hers, her question still hanging between us: *Why now?*

I took a breath to finally respond. I hoped that she would understand my answer. "Jane Austen made me do it."

BRENNA AUBREY has always sought comfort in good books and the long, involved stories she weaves in her head. She has been in love with words and language from a young age. This led her to study her two favorite languages in college: French and English. To further her fluency in French, she was lucky enough to live in France for a year and a half.

Brenna loves reading Jane Austen, whose *Persuasion* is, of course, her favorite novel. She also loves to write historical romance and epic fantasy fiction. She is a city girl with a nature lover's heart. She therefore finds herself out in green open spaces any chance she can get.

Brenna is mommy to two little kids and teacher to many more *older* kids. She currently resides in Southern California with her family. She is in the final stages of her work-in-progress, a novel-length Regency historical romance.

www.brennaaubrey.net
@brennaaubrey on Twitter

THE CHASE

Carrie Bebris

Frank is made.— He was yesterday raised to the Rank of Commander,
& appointed to the Petterel Sloop, now at Gibraltar.

—Jane Austen, letter to her sister, Cassandra,
28 December 1798

21 March 1800

"Lieutenant Glover's greetings, Captain—and the watch has spotted sails approaching from the northwest."

Francis William Austen set down the letter he had been reading when the midshipman entered his cabin. The remains of his breakfast lay pushed aside on the small dining table, awaiting clearance by the steward. He had eaten late, having gone on deck shortly after rising to observe a French brig that had first come into their sights yesterday, and that had escaped a volley of British fire by taking refuge under the cover of a battery on shore. After assuring himself in the hazy morning light that their "chase" had not managed to sneak past them during the night, and giving orders to set a northeast-by-north course that kept their quarry in view, Austen had returned to his cabin to reread the latest dispatches over a lukewarm meal of ham and porridge. Fortunately, the coffee held its heat, and he had just poured a second cup from the pot to combat the chill of the day's early spring gales.

"How many?"

"Three, sir." The junior officer's eyes were bright, his face eager. At fourteen, he saw every foreign sail as a potential opportunity to make his fortune or distinguish himself for promotion while advancing the cause of the Crown. In truth, so did most of the Royal Navy.

"And the brig?"

"Still skulking alongshore."

"Thank you, Mr. Phillips. Tell Mr. Glover that I shall join him on the forecastle directly."

Left to himself once more, Captain Austen indulged in a last sip of coffee before rising from the table to resume his coat. It hung from a peg near one of the two cannons that dominated the cabin's sides—an ever-present reminder that despite the relative luxury of his accommodations compared to those of the rest of the ship's company, he was nevertheless aboard a sloop of war.

The *Petterel* was a fast, reliable vessel of sixteen guns—twenty-four, if one included the eight carronades mounted on the quarterdeck and forecastle. At full complement she carried one hundred twenty-one men, boys, officers, and marines, trained and disciplined to exacting standards with measurable results: last June, they had proved their merit and valor as part of a fleet action under Vice-Admiral Lord Keith in which they captured a French squadron of five ships-of-the-line near Toulon. Now on blockade duty in the western Mediterranean Sea, the *Petterel* was under general orders to intercept any vessel that came in her path—whether naval or private—thus crippling French commerce and thwarting Napoleon's attempts to supply and reinforce the army he had left behind in Egypt.

Austen hoped the *Petterel* would prove the making of him—the means by which he would rise from a mere commander addressed as "Captain" out of courtesy, to a post-captain: title, right epaulette, and all. Making post was the most significant promotion of a naval officer's career, the date from which the seniority that determined all further advancement was established. A full captain could command larger ships for better pay—frigates and ships-of-the-line; perhaps serve as flag captain to an admiral. Until that day came, however, Austen was content to command the *Petterel* to the best of his ability, to carry out his duty knowing that the smaller engagements of his sloop contributed to the greater efforts of the war that all in His Majesty's Navy strove and sacrificed to win.

As he adjusted the single epaulette on his left shoulder and smoothed dark blue lapels over his white waistcoat, his gaze strayed to the letter he had been reading when the midshipman interrupted him.

My dear Frank,

I just today rec'd your letter of July 27th, and expect this reply will be more traveled than you by the time you read it. . . .

The missive had been forwarded to him along with the dispatch packet he had received last evening, and was from Jane, his younger sister and most faithful correspondent. Separated by little more than a year in age, they shared the dark eyes and slender nose common to the Austen family, but more important, they shared a determination to stay in contact as best they could despite the obstacles of distance and war. Other family members wrote him as well, but Jane's tidings were rendered with sharp observation and wit that was uniquely hers. The letters often took months to find him and sometimes arrived out of order, but he treasured every one, for they were his connection to the people with whom he was not "Captain Austen," but "Frank," and to the home he had left when not quite twelve to enter the Naval College at Portsmouth. Now just one month shy of six-and-twenty, he had already served in the navy more than half his life.

Frank put away Jane's closely written pages, and with them, thoughts of the family he had not seen since before taking command of the *Petterel* in Gibraltar thirteen months earlier. More urgent matters demanded his attention. The letter joined others in his sea chest, which, like all of the room's furniture, would be removed to the hold if the decks were cleared for action. The dispatches he secured on his person in an inner pocket of his coat. From the windows of his cabin beneath the quarterdeck, he could not see the sails Mr. Glover had reported, but he could hear the north wind, which blew strong today. With full canvas, the unknown vessels could be within range of the *Petterel* before noon.

He reached for his hat and settled the bicorne over dark hair worn closely cropped in a futile attempt to control its curls in the Mediterranean humidity. "Captain Austen" once more, he headed for the door.

Three ships. If friendly, they and the *Petterel* would exchange news.

If not, they would exchange fire.

Upon emerging from his cabin, Austen raised his gaze to the *Petterel*'s sails before proceeding to the forecastle. The jib and driver had been set, per his earlier orders. Mr. Glover, the sloop's first lieutenant, was high up the mainmast observing the approaching ships through a telescope. Austen felt a moment of mild envy, and fleetingly entertained the notion of climbing the ratlines himself to have a look. It had been some time since he had enjoyed the view from the platform and the soaring sensation of being carried not by a ship but by the wind—the closest man could come to experiencing flight. But he resisted the impulse and instead went to confer with Mr. Thompson, the ship's master, while waiting for Mr. Glover to descend the ropes.

"Tacking again, sir," Mr. Thompson said. "West by north-west, half north."

Austen nodded. They had been tacking all night and through the morning, zigzagging to move against winds that had blown at gale force after dark and had diminished only slightly at day-break. The approaching ships, in contrast, sailed with the wind behind them and could therefore hold a steady course. Wind-ward of the *Petterel,* they also had the weather gage—an advan-tage should they bear down on the sloop to attack.

But the *Petterel* had Mr. Thompson.

The sloop's chief navigator and senior warrant officer, John Thompson possessed a gift for exploiting any ship's full capabili-ties, and his handling of the *Petterel* was truly masterful. He knew her strengths and subtleties, and could coax her to perform be-yond expectations whether assailed by wind, rain, or enemy fire. Austen looked at the sky, hoping they would not experience all three simultaneously today. Fortunately, the haze was breaking up, revealing patches of sunlight and clear blue.

"Steer us toward the approaching sails, but not too far from the brig," he said, glancing at the vessel still taunting them from under the battery's protection. "We have not finished with her yet."

An answering spark lit the master's eyes. "Aye, Captain—not if there is aught I can do to trouble her."

Austen crossed the main deck and climbed the steps to the forecastle, where Mr. Glover joined him a minute later. As first lieutenant, Mr. Glover was Austen's second-in-command, and while it was the Admiralty who had appointed him, it was John Glover who had quickly demonstrated himself worthy of the commission. He possessed intelligence, good judgment, and honor, and could be relied upon to remain steady in a crisis. A ship as small as the *Petterel* could not afford to have a first officer who was anything less, and neither could Austen. In their few months of working together in combat and out, commander and first lieutenant already had developed a rapport in which Mr. Glover often could anticipate Austen's decisions before he even voiced them.

He greeted his lieutenant and gestured toward the cluster of sails ahead. "It appears we have company approaching."

"Indeed, sir." Mr. Glover's face was reddened by the strong winds aloft and the exertion of traversing the rigging—an activity that required stamina even in calm. Though he wore his hair tied back, the cold spring wind had loosed light brown strands that now wisped round his angular countenance as the two men gazed across the bow. "Five sails."

"Five? I was told three."

"Three of them are closer than the others—the watch observed them first. They are small vessels. But I thought I saw another sail on the horizon, so I went up to have a better look. Two more ships follow in the distance."

Austen scanned the waves, and indeed spied the other two ships—tiny dots—now that Mr. Glover had advised him of their existence. At their present distance, his unaided eyes could not confirm the flag colors of any of the vessels. "French?"

"*Mais oui.*" Mr. Glover grinned. "The closest three, at least."

Austen could not help returning the smile. The *Petterel* routinely encountered merchantmen, Spanish ships, and an occasional Dutch vessel, but the only thing more satisfying than destroying a French ship was capturing it.

"And the other two?"

"I could not discern."

He took the glass from his lieutenant so that he could study the convoy for himself. The telescope caught the glare of sunlight glancing off the bay before he settled its view on the two clusters of sails. Two barques and a ketch sped along at the fore. "The farther ships appear to be a corvette and a xebec," he said.

"I thought so, as well, though I was not entirely confident at this distance."

"Keep a close watch on all five. Were I a gambling man, I would wager the corvette and xebec are French, too, perhaps part of the convoy." Austen handed the glass back to Mr. Glover. "Surely the nearest three have sighted us by now. Have they changed speed or altered course?"

"They show no signs of concern," Mr. Glover said. "We are close enough to shore that they might take us for a friendly vessel."

"Very good." That had been Austen's intent. Though the *Petterel* had spent most of the autumn and winter cruising near Minorca, presently the sloop patrolled the Bay of Marseilles with the *Mermaid,* a thirty-two-gun frigate captained by Robert Oliver. Last evening, Oliver had directed Austen to keep the *Petterel* close to shore so as to block the brig's path round Cape Croisette and deceive other enemy ships that happened along. It was a tactic Austen had used on previous occasions with great success—his record of enemy vessels captured or destroyed was already impressive—but it was not without risk. Nature guarded the coast with rocks, while Napoleon defended it with batteries.

"They might simply pass us by," Mr. Glover said.

"They might." French ships tended to concentrate on completing their missions rather than deviate to pursue unexpected opportunities—which was why Britain, not the Republic, dominated the seas. "If we allow them."

Austen studied the convoy, which grew larger as the distance between them closed. The barques would offer little, if any, resistance; they might not even be armed. When attacked, most small vessels—indeed, most French vessels in general—attempted to outrun their pursuers. If part of a convoy, they took themselves out of the way and left the fight to the larger ships assigned to protect them. The ketch was a greater source of concern. If the heavier two-masted vessel proved to be merely a cargo carrier, it might not put up much of a struggle, but that type of craft was sometimes used as a bomb-ship.

The more distant xebec and corvette would definitely mount a defense, and together might even seize the initiative and attack the *Petterel* first—especially with the weather gage to their benefit. The xebec probably carried half a dozen guns firing six-pound shot. The corvette would be armed similarly to the *Petterel,* with fourteen or more six-pounders, and perhaps a couple heavier guns.

And then there was the brig, which would also approximate the *Petterel*'s armament, and which even now cruised out of the battery's cover. If given an opportunity, would it dash past the distracted *Petterel* or join the fight?

"Do you mean to engage, sir?" Mr. Glover's question was meant not as a prompt, but as an assertion that he stood ready to execute Austen's orders the moment his commander issued them.

Austen weighed the odds. Without question, all together the French ships presented a superior force to that of the *Petterel*—particularly if the barques carried a few guns and decided to contribute shots in their own defense. However, if engaged in succession rather than at once, they might all be defeated. And with the *Mermaid*'s assistance, the two opposing forces would be more evenly matched.

"Where is the *Mermaid*?" he asked.

"There, sir." Mr. Glover directed his notice downwind. The frigate was so far to leeward that Austen could barely see it. If the *Petterel* initiated an engagement with the convoy, Captain Oliver would need considerable time to maneuver his heavier ship through the headwind to join the action.

Austen's gaze swept the main deck, where seamen performed their tasks not only with skill and efficiency that rivaled that of any ship-of-the-line's crew, but also with a palpable aura—almost an electric charge—of anticipation. Austen harbored no doubt that within minutes of the convoy's sighting, every hand on the ship had known of it, and now waited to learn their commander's intent. Engaging the enemy meant the potential for prize money if the *Petterel* captured one or more of the ships, and the hope of financial reward galvanized sailors already motivated by duty, loyalty to king and country, and a healthy disdain for the French.

Mr. Glover brought the glass to his own eye again. "The brig is adjusting her course, sir. She appears headed to join the other vessels."

"Pass the word for Mr. Thompson and Mr. Packer."

Austen would not rush into a fight he could not win. So he would have to turn it into one that he could. The *Petterel* might be a sloop, but she carried a first-rate crew. Austen had faith in his men, faith in his officers, faith in his ability to lead them. And as the son of a clergyman, he had faith in God.

"Mr. Thompson," Austen said as soon as the master and second lieutenant arrived on the forecastle, "hoist out the pinnace, take seven men, and endeavor to cut off some of the vessels coming alongshore. Mr. Packer, call all hands aft for the Prayer. As soon as we have done, Mr. Glover, clear for action, beat to quarters, and signal the *Mermaid* our intent to give chase. We will start with the brig."

Damn that brig to perdition.

Smoke and the scent of burned powder still hung about the *Petterel,* but it was nothing compared to the vexation clouding Captain Austen's mood as he stood on the quarterdeck, watching the French ship glide under the protection of another shore battery.

"Why will you not engage?" he said under his breath.

They had fired several shots at the brig—torn through a few sails, and sent one ball rolling across the deck. But instead of answering their fire, the brig had once more fled toward shore. It was not a matter of disparate firepower; from the number of gun ports and the gleam of brass on the upper deck, the brig and the *Petterel* were well matched. Indeed, the brig ought to accept the *Petterel*'s obvious challenge as a point of honor if for no other reason; its conduct thus far was akin to a gentleman declining a duel—nay, declining a duel by hiding beneath his wife's skirts.

Were Mr. Thompson at the *Petterel*'s helm, Austen would pursue the chase despite the battery, trusting the gifted master to steer them safely through the action—and through the rocks. But presently he needed Thompson commanding the pinnace, maneuvering the small boat to bedevil the barques and divert them just where Austen wanted them.

Where they finally were now.

"Do not become too comfortable," Austen muttered to the brig before turning his attention to the convoy.

The *Mermaid,* still too far leeward to assist the *Petterel* directly, would at least with her presence deter the brig from attempting to flee south while the *Petterel* neutralized as many of the other ships as possible. The convoy sailed toward land, the barques and the ketch still well ahead of the war vessels, but all were far enough away from the battery that in pursuing them the *Petterel* need not worry about the fortification's heavy guns complicating matters from shore.

He gave the order for the gun crews to remain ready, and called several of the officers to him.

"We will disable the smaller vessels before the larger two come within range." He turned to the quartermaster. "Mr. Morris, bring us close enough to fire our bow-chasers, then wear round—across all three vessels if we can, although the far barque is distant enough from the others that she might be able to divert her course and evade us once she sees what we are about."

"Aye, sir."

"Mr. Glover—pass the order to load half the guns with round shot, half with chain when we rake."

The lieutenant understood. "We want to stop them, not sink them."

"Precisely. If we can cripple their rigging and cause enough hull damage to scare them, they might surrender before the other two ships catch up to us, without our destroying the cargo."

The *Petterel* neared the ships. As they approached firing range, Mr. Glover surveyed their targets with his telescope and uttered a mild oath. "It is a bomb-ketch after all."

Austen took the glass and held it to his own eye. A chill that had nothing to do with the wind passed over him. The ketch held heavy artillery that could devastate the sloop, and at this point Austen's ship and crew were committed to an encounter. The *Petterel*'s movements this half hour had made her intention clear.

In his heart he offered a silent prayer. In his voice he projected nothing but confidence.

"We must simply make sure we hit her first. Fire the bow-chasers."

Mr. Glover left to pass the order, and the *Petterel* fired her pair of fore-facing long guns upon the ketch. One ball put a hole through its sails; the other fell into the sea. A second round tore through the shrouds of its mainmast. The sloop then tacked, turning across the path of the three oncoming ships.

It seemed to take forever to cross the bow of the ketch, to reach exactly the right position, with Austen, his officers, the men all tensely, silently waiting . . . waiting to fire, waiting to be fired upon . . . until, at last—

"Fire!" Mr. Glover cried. On the forecastle, the marine sergeant echoed him.

"Fire!"

"Fire!" Halfway down the main deck, Mr. Packer's voice took over the command. The guns exploded in succession, the force of their recoil thrusting them backwards in their carriages, as the *Petterel* moved across the path of the ketch. Two explosions issued from the forecastle carronades, six from the main deck cannons, another two—almost deafening where Austen stood—from the carronades on the quarterdeck.

As the boys known as powder monkeys scampered to deliver fresh powder, the gun crews damped down sparks, sponged the barrels, reloaded, and ran the guns back out to position. They had averaged one minute, forty-seven seconds between rounds in their last drill, and looked to be maintaining that pace. When the *Petterel* crossed the bow of the second ship, they would be ready.

Through the smoke, Austen saw that their assault on the ketch had succeeded. The chain shot had done its job, tearing through the sails, tangling the rigging and bringing it down, crippling the ship's ability to control its speed or direction. The carronades' balls had splintered its bow and rolled down the length of the ship to wreak further damage on the deck and hull.

The ketch had answered with only a single round of ineffective musket fire.

Mr. Glover returned to the quarterdeck. "No one injured," he reported.

"Very good." Though Austen was grateful for the news, his gaze remained fixed on the ketch. Its crew seemed in a state of confusion.

"Why did they not fire their artillery?" Mr. Glover asked.

Austen had been wondering the same. "I cannot speculate."

They had not time.

The *Petterel* was upon the next French vessel. At the command, the sloop's gun crews fired at the barque, raking it, too, with broadside shots that delivered as much damage to the French crew's morale as they did to the ship itself. The other barque, having seen trouble coming, had time to divert its course and now sped southwest as fast as the wind could carry her.

"Shall we pursue her, Captain?" called out Mr. Morris.

Austen looked at the fleeing barque, then back at the two damaged vessels. The crews of the impaired barque and ketch were lowering their boats—abandoning ship.

"No," Austen replied. They had captured two of the three, with the xebec and corvette still approaching. They needed time to secure the prizes already won before engaging the advancing ships—more important quarry than the barque.

As the French crewmen climbed into their boats and rowed toward shore, Austen gave the order to take possession of the prize vessels. "Lower the jollyboat," he said. "Mr. Glover, take eight men to secure the ketch. Include Mr. McAucland among your party." Perhaps the gunner could determine why the French cannons had not been employed. Austen directed the master's mate to board the barque with another seven men to the barque.

A few minutes after their departure, Mr. Thompson and the men on the pinnace, their mission achieved, returned to the *Petterel*. Austen left the quarterdeck to meet them.

"Well done, Mr. Thompson!"

"Thank you, sir."

"Are you ready for some real work now?"

Mr. Thompson laughed. "I am indeed, Captain."

For all the lightness with which he bantered with his officer, Austen was heartily glad to have the master back aboard the *Petterel* before engaging the other ships. He doubted they would be so easily won.

The pursuit of the barques and ketch had taken them northwestward, still in sight of shore but considerably distant from where they began the morning. The *Petterel* stood in the bay off Cape Couronne while the damaged vessels were assessed for seaworthiness. After receiving word from Mr. Glover that the two ships, laden with an estimated nine hundred tons of wheat between them, were yet fit to sail, Austen directed the first lieutenant and master's mate to command the prizes whilst the *Petterel* engaged the xebec and the corvette. Though they were to lend whatever assistance they could, Austen doubted it would amount to much more than simply retaining possession of the vessels, as the barque was unarmed and the ketch, by the gunner's report, depleted of both ammunition and powder.

The lull allowed the *Petterel*'s crew to clean the decks and eat a hurried midday meal following the forenoon engagement. The men were in good spirits, each calculating his share of the prize money their capture of the two vessels had likely earned. The seamen would receive little; the officers more.

"Those next ships coming—now *they* be true prizes," Austen overheard one of the yardmen say. "The captain will see that we take them, too."

Austen allowed himself a private smile at the praise—but even more, at the faith in him that the words represented. He was conscious every day—and on a day such as this, every hour—that the lives of more than one hundred men were in his care. It was a responsibility he had accepted along with his commission, and one which, at times, was heavier to bear than the weight of any anchor. He endeavored to be worthy of their trust, and to instill the same consciousness in his officers.

By two o'clock, the decks were once more cleared for action, all hands (save those manning the prize vessels) were at their stations, and the sloop was heading east—toward the corvette and xebec now cruising along the shore.

The *Petterel* sailed with the wind on the beam, at last not fighting it for every mile gained. The French ships, seeing the sloop advance, steered their courses even more toward shore. Austen had studied the charts; he knew how rocky a coastline the French vessels drew him toward, knew that the visible dangers posed by the batteries on land and the two enemy vessels in the water might prove nothing compared to unseen danger beneath the surface.

"Can you find us a fairway, Mr. Thompson?"

Mr. Thompson, too, had studied the charts, and had navigated these waters before. They posed a hazard to even the most experienced sailing master.

"Captain, 'twill be easier than plain sailing."

Even Mr. Thompson could not entirely convince Austen of that.

Moderately reassured, he went in search of Lieutenant Packer.

"The gun crews are ready, sir," Mr. Packer said. "In fact, more than ready—they can scarcely wait to fire the first broadside."

With Mr. Glover leading the prize party, Joseph Packer was now second in command, and Austen hoped that Mr. Packer was equal to the challenge ahead. He was a young man, but he showed promise; the men respected his leadership, and he had proved himself reliable in action. Moreover, he possessed courage and a quickness of both mind and person that Austen appreciated.

"Keep the men steady, Mr. Packer. We do not want an abundance of fervor to cause accidents or premature fire."

"Understood, sir."

As the *Petterel* sailed east, the French vessels moved south, closer to the protection of the battery downshore. Mr. Thompson adjusted their course. They were running free with the wind now, coming up behind the xebec, bearing down to engage the smaller of the two French ships.

"Mr. Packer!" Austen called.

The lieutenant appeared beside him. "Yes, Captain?"

"As soon as we are in range, fire the bow-chasers."

"With pleasure, sir." Though he had ample time to prepare, Mr. Packer hurried back to his station, alive to the moment and keen to execute Austen's order.

They fired the guns, striking the xebec's stern with one six-pound ball and sending another rolling a destructive path down the deck from stern to stem. A second round damaged the weakened stern further.

"Bring us alongside her!"

The xebec had but three guns on her starboard side to the *Petterel*'s larboard six guns and four carronades. On her deck, the French sailors scrambled. Although her gun crews were in position, an aura of panic emanated from the vessel. She maneuvered still closer to shore, no doubt hoping that the larger *Petterel* would strike rocks before she did.

"Mr. Thompson?"

"Not to worry, Captain."

Suddenly, with a jolt so strong that Austen seemed to feel it from his own ship, the xebec came to an abrupt stop.

She had run herself aground.

Mr. Thompson carefully slid the *Petterel,* ready and well able to deliver a powerful broadside to the motionless vessel, into position alongside her. The xebec's crew raced to strike her colors, her commander shouting *"Je cède! Je cède!"*

Austen acknowledged the French officer's surrender—then ordered Mr. Thompson to pursue the corvette ahead.

On the main deck, the men were flush with success and eager for more; they would have rowed after the corvette if Austen asked them to.

"Well done!" he called out to them, and came down from the quarterdeck. "But save your celebration until we have done with her sister ships."

He walked the length of the deck and back, exchanging words with the seamen, exhorting them to maintain their focus. As he was about to mount the steps and return to the quarterdeck, the purser approached him. Austen hoped he was not about to hear bad news from below, where Mr. Hill normally assisted the surgeon during battles.

"Yes, Mr. Hill?"

"Sir, as we are fortunate to have no injured men, and with our being short Lieutenant Glover and the others manning the prize vessels, I want to offer my services on the main deck if I can be of use."

Austen was surprised—quite pleasantly—by the suggestion from the stout, serious man most often found distributing supplies and examining his accounts. Even Mr. Hill wanted to be closer to the action today.

"That is a most handsome offer, Mr. Hill. Report to Mr. Packer and help with the guns."

The purser's face lit at the prospect. "Aye, sir!"

The corvette sailed south, trying to reach the protection of the battery before the *Petterel* caught up with her. Mr. Thompson, Austen beside him, deftly handled the wheel as they gave chase.

"She is a swift vessel, sir. I'll give her that, even if she is French."

"I would admire her speed more, Mr. Thompson, if we were not working so hard to overcome it."

The *Petterel* finally had the weather gage, but Mr. Thompson was forced to check their speed to safely negotiate the rocks. However, the corvette also slowed, and by observing her maneuvers the *Petterel* was able to gain on her. When they neared range of her stern, they fired their bow-chasers. The balls ripped through the mizzen topsail, taking down some of its rigging as well. The corvette answered with her stern-chasers, but their shots missed.

The *Petterel* came round the corvette's starboard side, swiveled the forecastle carronades, and fired at the mizzenmast. One of the twelve-pound balls smashed into the mast, sending it crashing onto the deck and scattering crewmen as they raced to escape being hit. In the confusion, the corvette struck a shoal and ran aground.

A cheer went up on the deck of the *Petterel*.

The colors came down on the deck of the corvette.

In as high regard as Austen held his officers and men, he knew luck had contributed its share to the day's success, and he wondered whether he dared test it further. But there was a brig ahead with which he had unfinished business. A brig that had been approaching from the south—to rendezvous with the vessels the *Petterel* had just defeated? A brig that now was turning round to head back toward Cape Croisette.

A brig Austen was determined to prevent from reaching it.

"Mr. Packer!"

The lieutenant came quickly, carrying his speaking trumpet. With Mr. Glover and the gunner absent, Mr. Packer was having a busy time of it, but he performed his duty with spirit and alacrity. "Captain?"

Austen gestured towards the brig. "Pass the word that we have one more ship to take this afternoon."

Mr. Packer grinned. "The men will be glad to hear it, sir."

No one aboard could match Austen's own anticipation. He loved the thrill of the chase. Let other gentlemen hunt foxes on horseback, racing across open fields amid the baying of hounds. Austen pursued his quarry on planks of oak across the open sea, amid the explosion of cannons, to an end more noble than mere sport. And this particular quarry had eluded capture long enough.

The *Mermaid* approached from leeward. If she maintained her course and speed, within half an hour she might be close enough to assist the action. But the wind yet blew so strong that he could not be confident of her participation. He was prepared, if necessary, to attempt to capture the brig alone.

"Are you ready to finish our chase, Mr. Thompson?"

"Ready indeed, sir."

The brig required time to reverse her course, and for half an hour the sloop advanced on her. By the time she was sailing south, the *Petterel* was nearly upon her.

"Mr. Packer, our bow-chasers have served us well today," Austen said. "Let us provide them more exercise."

They fired the chase-pieces, getting off several successful shots that were answered by the brig's stern-chasers. She cut closer to shore, leading the *Petterel* toward the battery. This time, Austen followed—if the battery fired upon his sloop, it also risked damaging the brig.

Fire, it did. The battery's four heavy guns launched thirty-two pound shot at the *Petterel.* The first round sailed overhead, falling to starboard.

The French ship slowed in the rocky waters.

"You know what to do, Mr. Thompson."

"I do, sir."

With the grace of the seabird for which she was named, the *Petterel* glided a-starboard of the brig.

When she reached position, the sloop released a broadside that cut the brig's sails and brought rigging raining down to its deck. The brig answered, making a few holes in the *Petterel*'s sails and dismounting one of the forecastle carronades.

The battery fired again. More shot fell over the *Petterel.*

"Report, Mr. Packer?" Austen shouted.

"No damage, sir!"

The *Mermaid,* at last near enough to use her guns, fired random shot at the brig. None, however, hit. The frigate made sail, attempting to draw closer, but the strength of the wind prevented her.

The *Petterel* would have to win this on her own. Austen could not account for his incredible fortune up to the present, but he prayed it would hold.

"Fire again!"

The *Petterel* and brig exchanged another broadside. The French ship fired mostly into—and, thankfully, mostly missed—the sloop's rigging. For some inexplicable reason, the brig was firing round shot instead of bar or chain, which would have been much more effective against the ropes and sails. Unfortunately, some of the lower shots did manage to dismount the *Petterel*'s remaining three larboard carronades.

The sloop's guns found their targets.

Shot smashed into the hull of the brig, sending deadly splinters flying across the deck. Despite the wind, smoke and the smell of powder clouded both vessels. When it cleared, the brig struck its colors.

Again, the *Petterel*'s crew cheered—then set back to work.

"Hoist out the launch," Austen ordered. "Mr. Packer, choose fourteen men to accompany you and take possession. Include our carpenter among the party, so that Mr. Robinson can assess the damage."

Two hours later, the launch returned with eleven officer prisoners. Lieutenant Packer handed Austen a sword.

"It belongs to this gentleman," the lieutenant said, indicating a short, proud-looking man.

Austen bowed in acknowledgment. *"Capitaine?"*

"Non, je suis Citizen Francis Auguste Pelabon, Lieutenant de Vaisseau. Le capitaine est mort."

"Citizen Pelabon has stated that the brig is *La Ligurienne,* and that she was traveling in company with the corvette *Le Cerf* and the xebec *Le Joiliet,*" Mr. Packer said. "The *Ligurienne*'s captain and one seaman were killed. Two others are injured."

Austen put a few questions to Citizen Pelabon—whom he speculated was a political appointee—and learned that the captain was killed by the *Petterel*'s first chaser shot. Upon his death, Pelabon had taken charge.

The marine guards took the prisoners below deck. Before returning to the brig to command the prize vessel, Mr. Packer accompanied Austen into his cabin to continue his report.

"I think you might find the prisoners happier to be in your

custody than under Pelabon's command," he said. "I received the impression that the orders he issued during the action did not demonstrate a great deal of competence."

"For which we, at least, can be grateful," Austen replied. Pelabon's failure had enabled the *Petterel* to emerge from the engagement almost untouched. "In what condition is the vessel?"

"It was fortuitous that you sent the carpenter with us, for you will hardly believe what Mr. Robinson discovered. . . ."

"Well fought, Captain," Robert Oliver greeted Austen as he boarded the *Mermaid*. "I am sorry the wind rendered me unable to offer significant assistance yesterday, but it was a glorious battle to witness."

Austen appreciated his praise. He liked Oliver, who numbered among the navy's younger post-captains.

"Thank you, sir. I have brought my official report for you to forward to the Admiralty."

"You single-handedly captured five French vessels in under five hours," Captain Oliver said. "Whatever you have written, I am certain it is too modest. Come, you must tell me the whole tale over dinner."

They entered his cabin, where Captain Oliver opened the dispatch and scanned it. "Not a single man hurt on your part—and no other damage to the ship than four carronades dismounted, and a few shots through the sails. That is extraordinary."

"We were most fortunate," Austen said.

"But here—what is this? '*La Ligurienne* . . . is built on a peculiar plan, being fastened throughout with screw bolts, so as to be taken to pieces and set up again with ease, and is said to have been intended to follow Bonaparte to Egypt.'" Incredulous, Captain Oliver looked to Austen.

"Apparently," Austen said, "Bonaparte planned to portage the ship through the desert, then launch it into the Red Sea."

"Had he succeeded, I cannot imagine the consequences. But you prevented him."

"Quite by accident."

"How it came to happen does not matter nearly so much as that it did." Captain Oliver folded the report and set it on his desk beside other papers. Then he opened a bottle of wine, poured two glasses, and handed one to Austen.

"The Admiralty is unpredictable, of course," Oliver said, "but I would not be surprised if I am about to dine with the navy's next post-captain."

In consequence of the action off Marseilles and his capture of La Ligurienne, *Francis Austen was promoted to post-captain on 13 May 1800. Due to the challenges of wartime communication, his sister Jane knew about his promotion before he did. Francis finally received the news in October, after commanding the* Petterel *through more daring engagements in Genoa and Egypt. He eventually rose to the Royal Navy's highest position, Admiral of the Fleet.*

Author's Note: Historical documents related to the *Petterel* record the name of the sloop under multiple spellings. I have chosen the one used by Captain Austen himself, penned with his own hand aboard that very ship as he recorded hour by hour the events surrounding *La Ligurienne*'s capture. For access to his logbook and other ship's records, I thank The National Archives and the Caird Library of the National Maritime Museum. For the truly extraordinary events of that day—a story that begged to be told—I thank Francis Austen.

CARRIE BEBRIS is best known as the author of the Mr. & Mrs. Darcy Mysteries. Winner of the Daphne du Maurier Award for romantic suspense, the series features the married Fitzwilliam Darcy and Elizabeth Bennet as reluctant sleuths who become entangled in intrigues with other Jane Austen characters. The Royal Navy figures prominently in the Darcys' latest adventure, *The Deception at Lyme (Or, The Peril of Persuasion)*, in which the couple allies with Captain and Anne Wentworth to solve two mysteries—one from the past and one in the present. Carrie also writes for *Jane Austen's Regency World* magazine and other publications, and has edited nonfiction books about Austen and Shakespeare. She holds an M.A. in English literature and is a life member of the Jane Austen Society of North America.

www.carriebebris.com

INTOLERABLE STUPIDITY

Laurie Viera Rigler

Well hidden from the ordinary world, in a little-known corner of jurisprudential hell considered by many to be nothing more than a myth, a relentless flow of pleadings, motions, and briefs have led to a legal drama of literary proportions.

A bailiff's high-pitched nasal voice pierced the packed courtroom. "All rise and give homage to the honorable Judge Lady Catherine de Bourgh. Draw near and you shall be chastised. Court is now in session."

"Objection!" shouted the gangly young lawyer from the defense table, Adam's apple bobbing indignantly.

"Young man," said Lady Catherine, a severe-looking older woman who nodded and waved like a queen as she entered the courtroom, scarlet robes flowing in her wake, jurors and spectators bowing and curtseying, "I am not accustomed to being interrupted. Though I have not yet deigned to speak. Are you at all familiar with the rules of this court? One does not object until I begin the proceedings. Which I most certainly have not condescended to do."

"Your Honor," persisted the young lawyer, droplets of fear

beading his forehead, "I must ask you to recuse yourself from this case."

Spectators and jurors gasped as if with one collective breath.

"How dare you!" said Lady Catherine, bringing her gavel down upon the polished surface of her bench. "Sit down this moment!"

"With all due respect," said the lawyer, voice quavering, "you must see that your own interests are directly affected by the outcome of this case, and thus it would be highly prejudicial—-"

"Let me be rightly understood," said Lady Catherine, fixing him with a death stare. "Your duty is to defend the accused—if such a thing were possible—and allow justice to take its course. In this court I am justice. Is that clear?"

"Yes, Your Honor."

"One more word, and I shall hold you in more contempt than I already do."

The young lawyer for the defense sank into his seat and, with trembling hands, wiped his sweaty brow with a handkerchief. He'd done his best. It would likely not go well for his client, but there was nothing he could do about that. No one, least of all he, would ever succeed in removing Lady Catherine from any case over which she wished to preside, especially one in which her own nephew was the plaintiff. The wheels of justice, such as they were, would turn inexorably till they reached their inevitable conclusion. Then again, he'd known what the rules were when he agreed to take this case. If rules they could be called. Most did not even believe in the existence of this court, which was hidden away so cleverly that few had ever stepped foot within its walls.

Its detractors called it the Court of Intolerable Stupidity, and perhaps he had been stupid beyond measure to have put himself in its power. Certainly he did not know anyone who had mastered its workings. Said workings were, in fact, the stuff of legend. Or nightmare, depending on whether you were crushed beneath justice's wheels or rode them to victory. But that was the lure of the challenge. And he, Fritz Williams, could never resist a challenge. A legal one, that is.

Besides, there was no accounting for the whims and inconsistencies of a jury, even one sitting under the tyrannical eye of the Honorable Lady Catherine de Bourgh. Though as Fritz ran his eyes over the knitting ladies, the bored gentlemen, and the surly youths impaneled for this case, there was little reason to believe they would act any differently than their predecessors had done.

"Is the prosecution ready?" said Lady Catherine.

Till now Fritz had not allowed himself to turn his gaze toward the prosecution table, for he would not have had the courage to stand, let alone speak. But now he indulged himself in gazing upon the perfection that was Tawny Wolfson, chief advocate for the plaintiffs.

"I am, Your Honor," said Tawny, who spent a great deal of her professional energy attempting to mask the voluptuousness of her form with the iciness of her demeanor and the buttoned-up elegance of her attire. She had never been seen by anyone in court with a hair out of place, a wrinkle in her suit, or a tear in her eye.

As was her custom at the beginning of every trial, she had starved herself down to a size 8, but it was only a matter of time before she returned to her usual 12. She was all too aware that she would never achieve the thin-hipped, waif-like style of beauty so prized by men nowadays, but there was no reason for that contemptible Fritz Williams to stare at her like a microbiologist examining a particularly rare strain of bacteria.

It was no different now than it was the first time they had met. A colleague had invited her to a holiday party at Fritz's firm, and when he introduced Fritz to her, Fritz had stared at her, barely mumbled a greeting, and whisked Tawny's colleague away, leaving her quite alone in a crowd of strangers. Finally, she retreated to the drinks table, where she overheard Fritz saying to a group of men, "Tawny Wolfson? I can't argue with that, but she's definitely not for me," at which they all had a good laugh.

Even a year later, the memory still stung. The worst part was that she had no idea what she had done to offend this man, who was unfailingly cold to her whenever their paths crossed.

She couldn't be more wrong about Fritz. What she saw as his coldness was actually shyness and embarrassment. And what he had really meant by the comment she overheard at the party was that she would never look twice at a man like him. His flippancy at the time was an attempt to mask his true feelings, for he was smitten by Tawny from the first moment he saw her, which was long before they were introduced. It wasn't just the beauty of her person that captivated him; it was the depth of her accomplishments, for her reputation as someone who fought for her clients and, most of all, for the law, was well known.

Not that her beauty was an inconsequential part of her allure. Everything about her, from the scent of her perfume as she'd walk past him in the halls of justice, to the little wisp of hair at the nape of her neck when her hair was up in a twist, which he would stare at whenever he had the good fortune to stand behind her in an elevator, made him tremble with desire. A desire that would never be fulfilled. Fritz had never been successful in love, always too timid to ask out the women he really found interesting, and unwilling to settle for the women who found him so, as they were generally enamored with the idea of a successful lawyer rather than the reality of who he was. And Fritz longed to be known, truly known, by a woman. But there was little chance of that happening with anyone, let alone Tawny. She was unfailingly icy towards him, though he had no idea why she should dislike him so.

Like now, for instance. She glared at him with her green-gold eyes, and he felt his face grow hot. He pretended to busy himself with the files on the table before him, hoping that no one would notice his discomfort.

Why was she so intent on intimidating him? As if it weren't terrifying enough to be her adversary in court—a scenario he had longed for as well as dreaded.

"Your Honor," said Tawny, fortified by her small victory over Fritz, "we will prove that the defendants' so-called literary works have caused grave and irreparable harm to the plaintiffs, who only wish to continue their lives as their Creator conceived them. Since She has long since shuffled off this mortal coil, Her creations must carry Her torch alone, a mission they are hindered from doing with every turn of the page of these heinous works.

"Your Honor, we had hoped that the conviction of the man who authored the most damaging work on record—the infamous film that dared appropriate the name of the Creator's most cherished work—would have brought relief to my clients, as there has since been an embargo of that film's sale in all the Empire. However, the State has neither the resources to do a house-to-house search of the citizenry in order to confiscate all copies, nor the means to staunch the flow of illegal downloads."

Tawny paused to run her eyes over the jurors and spectators. "The effects on one of my clients have become so severe that the State can only conclude that the screening of this illegal and offensive material has increased rather than diminished since the ruling was made."

Fritz noted that many of the spectators and jurors looked down at their laps. Were they as unable to withstand Tawny's gaze as he was, or were they motivated by guilt?

"Your Honor," said Tawny, "I call my first witness—"

Fritz rose to his feet. "Objection! I have not yet made my opening arguments."

"Silence!" said Lady Catherine.

"But Your Honor," said Fritz, "how am I to mount a defense if I cannot tell my clients' side of the story?"

"Defense? Ha!" said Lady Catherine. "Your clients not only had the effrontery to 'continue' the Creator's work and the vulgarity to peep behind the closed doors of Her creations' marital bedchamber, they had the assurance to mock the Creator's work with undead fiends and blood-sucking monsters. This shall not be borne."

"Your Honor!" said Fritz. "This is highly prejudicial to my clients. You might as well try this case yourself."

"That is the most sensible thing you have said so far, young man," said Lady Catherine. "I could save the Court a good deal of time and expense."

"Your Honor, I beg you!"

Lady Catherine bestowed a predatory smile upon Fritz's clients, a group of mostly women and a few men in their thirties, forties, and fifties, all of whom had a shell-shocked glaze in their eyes. "I have taken the liberty of preparing your lodgings in the dungeons," she said.

Then she glared at Fritz. "Now take your seat, Counselor, before I put you there as well."

Fritz knew better than to push it. He gave what he hoped was an encouraging look to his clients, but by now some of them were weeping silently.

Was there even a wisp of a chance that he could save them? All they had done was write stories inspired by the work of one of the most beloved authors of all time—Creator, he must remember to refer to her in this court.

The Creator's characters did not take kindly to the effects those new works had had on their lives. Yes, lives, for as most avid readers had long known without the benefit of so-called rational proof or the recognition of this court, the Creator breathed life into her characters and the public perpetuated that life. Those characters, in fact, had taken on lives of their own. The more people who read the Creator's works, the longer the duration of their popularity, the stronger was the life force of her creations. And thus anyone who wrote new stories that incorporated her characters tampered with their lives in a manner never intended by their Creator. Which is what led to the groundbreaking case that made watching the most infamous film of the Creator's most famous work a crime in and of itself. And which is why Fritz's clients never really had a chance, opening arguments or no opening arguments.

Fritz sighed. He would do his best for them, no matter what.

"If it please the Court," said Tawny, "I call my first witness, Mr. Fitzwilliam Darcy."

The Court was not only pleased, it exploded in a cacophony of squeals, screams, and gasps. "Darcy! Darcy! Darcy!" arose the spontaneous chant, the women in the courtroom retrieving from some heretofore hidden place placards declaring their devotion.

Lady Catherine pounded her gavel, which was barely audible above the foot-stomping and whistling. "Order! Order or I shall clear this courtroom!"

At once there was silence.

"One more sound, and I shall hold this session in closed court. Bailiff." She nodded to the stocky, uniformed woman standing guard at the courtroom doors, and everyone turned as one.

The doors opened, and through them walked a remarkably handsome man. At first glance what was most remarkable about him, aside from the rippling muscles on his torso, was that said muscles were in plain view. He was, however, fully clothed, though his shirt was thin, white, and soaking wet, rendering it transparent.

Darcy shivered as he made his way down the aisle towards the witness box, shedding droplets in his wake. The lady by his side—one noticed her almost as an afterthought—was, upon further examination, quite beautiful as well as elegantly dressed in a Chanel-like suit and large round sunglasses. Darcy continued toward the witness box, while the lady left his side to take a seat directly behind Tawny. She removed her sunglasses and, if anyone but Lady Catherine had been watching her, entranced as they were with Fitzwilliam Darcy, they would have seen that with a single cold glance of her bright eyes she did what no one had ever been seen to do before: unnerve Her Honor.

Suddenly, a large female spectator clad in loose trousers and a T-shirt proclaiming in large black letters TEAM DARCY bolted to her feet. "Take me to Pemberley, Fitzwilliam!"

"Bailiff! Remove that creature!" said Lady Catherine.

The bailiff bowed obsequiously and complied, but not before the offending woman managed to lob a rather large pair of white panties at the head of Mr. Darcy.

Fritz, who had never before laid eyes on Darcy, could, despite his prized professional demeanor, scarcely refrain from staring himself. Far more remarkable than Darcy's transparent wet shirt was the fact that the details of his face and form, while consistently handsome by any standard, were in perpetual flux. One moment he looked exactly as Fritz had pictured him from the first time he had read the Creator's work. The next moment Darcy took on the form of the actor who portrayed him in the infamous and recently criminalized film. And then he assumed the form of another actor who portrayed him in a different film. And then his visage shifted, and shifted again. It was mesmerizing.

All at once Fritz understood that Darcy's outward appearance was the result of the thousands—no, millions—of thought projections of every reader who had ever enshrined him in his or her mind, plus their collective projection of the actor who played him in the illegal film.

Which, it seemed, was the most powerful and lasting projection of all. For as Darcy settled himself into the witness stand, shivering in the chilly air of the courtroom, the image of that actor's face was the one which lingered for several seconds at a time. Or longer, depending on who the observer was.

But Fritz could not allow himself to indulge in such musings. Darcy was sworn in and, at Tawny's prompting, began to tell his story.

"No matter what I wear, no matter what I do," said he, "I end up wet and shivering. When I walk in the street, people lean out their windows and dump buckets of water upon my head. In restaurants they douse me with the contents of their water glasses. When it rains my umbrellas always break and my raincoats are inevitably stolen."

As if to punctuate his statement, an attractive lady in a business suit stood up in court and blasted Darcy with a large, double-barreled water gun.

"Bailiff Norris!" screamed Lady Catherine. "Clear this courtroom!"

Collective sobbing from the female spectators.

The bailiff hustled the struggling water-gun wielder through the doors, then looked at Lady Catherine as if to say, *How am I to eject all of these hysterical women?*

"Oh, all right," said Lady Catherine. "But one more peep and I am as good as my word."

Collective sighs and smiles all around.

"Continue," she said to Mr. Darcy.

"My health has suffered as a result," said he. "A perpetual cold, not to mention the sheer discomfort of being always wet."

"To what do you attribute this situation?" said Tawny.

"To that infernal scene in the film, of course."

"Describe it if you will, Mr. Darcy."

"The actor who plays me bathes in the lake at Pemberley and emerges dripping wet, whereupon he meets with Elizabeth Bennet, much to their mutual embarrassment."

Much sighing from the spectators. Answered by much banging of Lady Catherine's gavel.

"A scene," said Mr. Darcy, "which was not in the Creator's original work. As if I would ever bathe in my lake without first ascertaining whether Pemberley had any visitors, let alone prance about my property in a most shocking state of dishabille!"

"And is there nothing you can take to give you relief?" said Tawny, who looked as if she was about to swoon.

Mr. Darcy blushed charmingly. "At home, of course, in private moments, I do find relief in not wearing any shirt at all."

"Not wearing any shirt at all," said Tawny, her voice a thin croak. "I see."

Suddenly there was a loud thud as one lady spectator fell from her bench into a faint.

"Revive that lady!" said Lady Catherine to her bailiff.

"I would happily, Your Honor," said Bailiff Norris, a bit shamefaced, "but I forgot to have my aromatic vinegar refilled."

"Again?" Lady Catherine rolled her eyes. "Oh, just take mine." Which the bailiff did, and attended to the afflicted lady.

"Thank you, Mr. Darcy," said Lady Catherine. "I can only assure you that as soon as ever the Court gets its hands on the author of that shocking scene, we shall show him no mercy. It is only a matter of time until we flush out his hiding place."

"Nothing further from this witness at this time," said Tawny. "We call Mrs. Darcy to the stand."

"If you must," said Lady Catherine with a sneer. "We shall hear from Miss Elizabeth Bennet."

An annoyed sigh from the lady in the Chanel suit, who stood and addressed Lady Catherine. "For the record, Your Honor, my name is no longer Miss Elizabeth Bennet. It is Mrs. Elizabeth Darcy."

Lady Catherine turned red. "Miss Wolfson," she said to Tawny, "I warned your client long ago that her name would never be mentioned by any of us. Are the shades of Pemberley to be thus polluted in my own courtroom?"

"Your Honor, please," said Tawny, her hands in a supplicating gesture.

"Very well, but I am most seriously displeased!" With a chilling glare at Elizabeth, she motioned her toward the witness box. "You may approach, Miss Ben—Mrs. Darcy."

As Elizabeth Darcy was sworn in and repeated her name, Lady Catherine winced.

"Mrs. Darcy," said Tawny, "please be good enough to tell us why you are here today."

Elizabeth nodded. "As if it were not disagreeable enough for one's husband to be always drenched in water, just imagine you are at table with your husband, and suddenly he sports vampire's fangs! Or begins to joke about hunting the undead. Or attempts to perform acts that—" and here she turned a deep crimson red— "that no gentleman, let alone a gentleman married to a lady, would think of without blushing."

"That will be all!" said Lady Catherine, to which the spectators groaned their disappointment. "The Court is well aware of the prurient nature of some of the defendants' works, but we needn't dwell on their unfortunate effects." She scowled at the defendants, who cowered. "You are dismissed, Miss Ben—Mrs. Darcy. And Court is adjourned."

As the Darcys were escorted from the courtroom by Tawny, and Fritz's clients hastened home to savor their last days of freedom, the room emptied, and Fritz remained in his seat, head in hands, pondering his strategy. But what could he say that would make any difference, even if Lady Catherine would allow him to do so? His defendants were just as doomed as the screenwriter the Court had tried in absentia.

"I have to think of something," he said aloud, surprised at the echoing of his voice in the now empty courtroom. Instinctively he turned toward the prosecution table, as if Tawny were there watching him, mocking him for his outburst. But it, like the rest of the vast room, was empty. Except—what was that on the floor beneath her chair? He got up and moved toward the small rectangular object. Someone had left a wallet behind. And that someone, he saw as he picked up the wallet and opened it, was Tawny Wolfson.

As for Tawny, now opening the door to her apartment, her impending victory was Pyrrhic. For how could she continue to indulge in watching that most infamous film once the case was won? She had not allowed herself a single glance at it ever since taking on this case, but it silently beckoned to her every night from its locked drawer in her bedroom desk, just as it did tonight as she shrugged out of her jacket and kicked off her shoes, yearning for the sweet release it always delivered. If Lady Catherine or, even worse, Fritz Williams, knew that she had such contraband in her possession, it would not only throw her case, it would be nothing short of career suicide.

She reminded herself of the silent promise she had made when she took on this case: As soon as she won she would destroy her precious copy and burn every Creator-inspired book she owned. There would be no more wet-shirted Darcy emerging from the lake, no more Darcy fencing away his passion for Elizabeth, no more peeks into Pemberley's marital bedchamber, no more glimpses into the mind of its brooding, noble master.

How would she bear such unhappiness? To what would she look forward after another bone-numbing day tilting at windmills and keeping our libraries safe for future generations? How would she live in a world without sequels, continuations, or adaptations?

Could she not put off that bleak future, for just one more day?

And then, almost as if guided by some unseen force, almost as if not in her own body, almost as if she were watching herself, Tawny unlocked the drawer, carried the movie to the player, and turned it on. A glass of wine, a fire in her fake fireplace, and she was ready to forget everything. Everything except Darcy and Pemberley . . .

Fritz stood before the door to Tawny's brownstone, wondering if he'd lost his mind. He'd been relieved that there was no phone number in the wallet, relieved further when he learned that her number was unlisted. He thought of waiting till court the next day, but wouldn't she worry when she saw the wallet was missing? And wasn't he dying to see where his fair goddess lived?

But how would she greet him? Would he get a glimpse of her lair as she stood glowering her contempt in the doorway, mumbling a resentful thank-you before she slammed the door in his face? Would she be fully dressed, or clad in a robe? Would he catch her so off guard that she would beam her gratitude at him?

In your dreams, pal.

Come on. Push the buzzer, you coward. Do it.

He did. And there was no answer. He pushed it again. And again.

If he could just get inside the building, push a note under her door, lay his cheek against that door, maybe even feel the doorknob that she touched every day with her sleek, black-leather-gloved hand. O, that I were a doorknob that I might touch that glove . . .

He eyed the other buzzers. Pushed one, then the other, still another, and was about to flee down the front steps when the buzzer buzzed, long and insistently.

This was it, this was his chance. He entered the vestibule and, taking the stairs two at a time, sprinted to her door. Yes, her door. He rested his cheek against the cool wood.

Wait a minute—what was that sound inside? There were voices within. If she was home, then why hadn't she answered when he rang? And who was that in her apartment? Fritz could hear two voices—they were faint, but one was a man's, and the other a woman's:

"I remember hearing you once say, Mr. Darcy, that you hardly ever forgave, that your resentment once created was unappeasable. You are very cautious, I suppose, as to its being created."

"I am," said he.

"And never allow yourself to be blinded by prejudice?"

"I hope not."

His breath caught. Could it be? It was. There was no denying it. Tawny was inside her apartment, at this moment, watching the very film against which she had railed in court this afternoon.

Fritz stood very still, barely able to breathe as the implications of what he was hearing took hold. Tawny's watching that film not only went against every legal code of ethics, every oath she had taken as a lawyer. It also would make his case, his unwinnable, quixotic case, turn in a second.

He would report her, and his clients would win.

He would report her tomorrow, of course he would; his obligation to his clients left him no other choice.

But what would happen to Tawny? Her career, her life, would be destroyed. Perhaps she would even be consigned to the dungeons.

Then again, she could deny it. It would be his word against

hers. Still, if he, a lawyer with a spotless reputation, swore in open court to what he had heard through her door, with the wallet in his hand as a sort of proof, she would never wash off the taint of scandal. Even if Lady Catherine decided to clap him, not her, in irons.

Any way he looked at it, his disclosure would do Tawny irreparable harm.

Oh, why had he come here tonight? Why had he taken this case? Why did he, of all people, find that damned wallet?

But he did find it. He did come here tonight. And there was no turning back. He, of all men, would bring untold suffering to the woman he loved.

For his discovery was the only thing standing between his clients and prison.

Unless . . . He rummaged in his briefcase for a legal pad and scribbled a note.

And there it was, under Tawny's door the next morning as she was hurrying off to work, almost obscured by the white carpet.

She snatched it up and read it:

"Found your wallet. Will return it in court after the lunch recess." It was signed Fritz Williams, with the date and time below the name.

The date and time?

"Oh my God," she said, her legs suddenly so weak and wobbly she nearly fell against the wall. "Oh my God."

She loosened the top buttons of her blouse and collapsed onto the sofa in her entranceway. He had been outside her door last night while she was watching the film. He had heard. He knew. And he wanted her to know it.

He'd expose her, today, this morning, in open court. She'd be ruined. But why leave her a note? Why not just blindside her?

Why mention the wallet when he was about to get her disbarred? Why hadn't the damn super fixed the damn buzzer?

She was still clutching the note, which was now crumpled in her fist. She opened it and reread his words.

"Found your wallet. Will return it in court after the lunch recess."

And all at once she knew. He was giving her a chance to admit to what she had done herself. He was giving her the option to throw herself upon Lady Catherine's mercy, such as it was, in chambers. He was finding a way to delay her public humiliation.

He, Fritz Williams, the man who found her very existence an affront to his sensibilities, was being kind. To her.

As the courtroom filled, Fritz, who was the earliest to arrive, tried to steady his breathing. Any moment the floral scent of Tawny's perfume would herald her arrival. What would be her first move? He'd had all night to imagine the possibilities, from blatant denial to public confession. She'd had only the past hour or less.

There it was, that intoxicating scent. He closed his eyes, then willed himself to glance mock-casually over at the prosecution table. She looked up from arranging her files on the table and met his gaze. Gave him an almost imperceptible nod. Then looked away. There was none of her usual iciness. Finally, she was acknowledging him as a human being. And it was on this day of all days.

Lady Catherine arrived in all her scarlet glory, and Court was now in session.

"Your Honor," said Tawny, "the People request that the defense have a chance to examine my witnesses."

A collective gasp in the courtroom and much pounding of Lady Catherine's gavel. And Fritz's heart.

"What is the meaning of this?" said Lady Catherine. "The defense deserves no such attention. It has no right to examine anyone until after the prosecution finishes presenting its case."

"I am finished," said Tawny, and with a flicker of a glance toward Fritz, "Now I wish for justice to do the rest."

"Very well, Miss Wolfson," said Lady Catherine. "I hope you know what you are about."

Tawny glanced at Fritz again, giving him the merest nod. It was enough to make him flush to the roots of his hair.

He quickly riffled through the papers before him and sprang to his feet. "Your Honor, the defense calls Mr. Darcy to the stand."

A collective holding of breath as the double doors of the courtroom opened and Darcy, in all his dripping magnificence, entered with his wife and took his place in the witness box.

"Mr. Darcy," said Fritz, "we all sympathize with your plight. It must be most uncomfortable to be always wet and shivering."

Darcy nodded, his visage morphing in tune with the individual and collective projections of everyone in the courtroom. Fritz told himself to focus on his witness's words and expressions rather than get distracted by the transitory features that decorated them.

"It occurs to me that many of the most popular works on trial here," Fritz continued, "owe their popularity to the fact that they have given the public access to your state of mind as you fell in love with and pursued Miss Elizabeth Bennet, the lady who is now your wife."

Lady Catherine scowled. "Is there a question in there somewhere, Counselor?"

"There is," said Fritz. "Mr. Darcy, isn't it true that when compared to the wealth of popular new works that focus on the growth of your love for Mrs. Darcy as seen through your eyes, relatively little of your side of the story appears in the Creator's original work?"

"I suppose one could say that," said Darcy, "though not all of what the new works say about me is accurate."

"But isn't it true that almost everything in those new works has made you even more sympathetic and romantic in the public eye?"

"I could not possibly answer such a question."

"I believe you can, Mr. Darcy, and I must insist that you do."

Lady Catherine glowered at Tawny. "Miss Wolfson, are you going to object, or shall I?"

"No, Your Honor," said Tawny, the tiniest quaver in her usually well-modulated voice.

"Objection!" said Lady Catherine to Fritz. "You will cease this line of questioning."

Tawny stood up, a regal goddess in Fritz's eyes. "I beg Your Ladyship to allow Mr. Williams to present his case. I will have ample opportunity for cross-examination afterwards, if necessary."

"*If* necessary?" demanded Lady Catherine. "Have you lost your senses?"

"I am aware of what I am doing, Your Ladyship."

"I rather doubt that," said Lady Catherine, "but we shall take you at your word. For now." With an imperious wave, she motioned for Fritz to continue.

"Mr. Darcy," said Fritz, "since the release of these controversial new works, aren't you and Mrs. Darcy, and indeed the Creator Herself, more popular and beloved than ever before?"

"That is not for me to say—"

"Then tell me this: Were as many people fainting in your presence and shouting their devotion before the works here on trial existed?"

"One cannot measure such things." Mr. Darcy blushed quite charmingly, and many of the women in the courtroom began fanning themselves.

"Isn't it true that the Creator's original works are more popular today than ever before? Might that not be due to the attention focused upon them by the works of the accused?"

"That is an outrageous claim!" said Lady Catherine.

"Is it?" said Fritz. Plucking a sheaf of papers from his table, Fritz approached Lady Catherine with them. "The defense submits Exhibit A, sales figures for the Creator's original works both before and after the release of the most popular sequels, adaptations, and inspired-by's. Her works were always popular, to be sure, but there is indeed a marked increase that is directly correlated to—"

"Irrelevant," said Lady Catherine, wrinkling her nose at the proffered papers as if they were the wrappers from spoiled fish. "Only someone of your class would be so vulgar as to introduce the subject of money in my courtroom. The jury will disregard this so-called evidence."

No surprise to Fritz. Still, the jury had heard his words.

Fritz opened his mouth to continue questioning the witness, but Darcy spoke first. "All devotion and fainting aside, Counselor, what say you to the terrible indignities of being portrayed as a vampire or a zombie hunter? What possible benefit could I derive from that?"

Fritz smiled. "Surely you have not taken to draining your neighbors of their blood?" And, turning to Elizabeth, "Has he, Mrs. Darcy?"

"Certainly not," said she. "It is not in his nature."

"Exactly!" Fritz said. "None of the accused nor anything they have written can force one to do what is against his nature. Nothing can change what his Creator created."

To Fritz's surprise, Elizabeth attempted to suppress a giggle.

Lady Catherine glared at Elizabeth. "And what do you find so amusing in these proceedings, Miss Elizabeth Bennet?"

"That's Mrs. Darcy to you, Miss Bossy Corset," she said, unable to contain her mirth any longer.

Darcy frowned at her questioningly. "What is it, my love?"

"Forgive me, Darcy, but I could not help but think of the last time Lydia was at Pemberley and had once again decided to extend her visit." She giggled again. "Until, that is, you gave her a glimpse of your fangs."

"Objection!" said Lady Catherine. "My nephew is not capable of such a thing!"

"Elizabeth!" Darcy colored, but despite all his self-command he found his mouth twitching in response to his lady's arch smile.

He looked over at Lady Catherine. "For the record, I dispensed with the fangs immediately after I displayed them."

Elizabeth was by now helpless with laughter.

Darcy smiled winningly. "It was a harmless joke," he said to the rapt jury, "I assure you."

"And quite an effective one, my dear," said Elizabeth, eyes sparkling with mischief.

Fritz beamed. "So there truly *is* something useful in all these terrible indignities, am I right, Mr. Darcy?

"Objection!" said Lady Catherine. "Miss Wolfson, will you do your job or I shall hold you in contempt?"

Tawny lifted her chin defiantly and remained seated.

"Bailiff!" said Lady Catherine, pointing her gavel at Fritz. "Throw him in the dungeons for a month."

"Aunt," said Darcy as Bailiff Norris moved toward Fritz, "that is hardly necessary."

The bailiff began to pull on Fritz's arm in an attempt to lead him from the courtroom. But Fritz stood his ground. "And aren't the works which depict scenes from your bedchamber essentially harmless as well? Perhaps even beneficial?"

Darcy blushed again. "I say, sir, that is none of your affair—"

"I agree, Mr. Darcy. Nor is it anyone else's. But can you imagine a world in which no one has seen all that they have seen through your eyes? A world in which you can neither summon fangs to teach a valuable lesson nor expand the reach of lovers' bliss?"

Darcy fixed his attention on his hands, then sought out his wife's eyes for her response. She met his gaze, her look one of sweetness and concern. And then she closed her eyes and shook her head.

"I cannot imagine such a world," she said to her husband. "For some of those—developments—have been most agreeable. Not the dousing in water, of course, but that is only a recent problem—"

"And one which is directly related to the film's criminalization," said Fritz, as the stocky bailiff finally managed to drag him from the defense table. "Drop this suit, Mr. Darcy, appeal the decision against the film and its author, and I'll vow you'll be a much dryer man for it. And furthermore—"

Darcy stood up, his muscled torso rippling under his transparent shirt. "Stop, Bailiff!" He turned to Lady Catherine. "Let the man finish, Aunt."

"Very well," said Lady Catherine. "But I shall incarcerate him as soon as he does."

Bailiff Norris curtseyed to Lady Catherine and allowed Fritz to return to his table.

"Mr. Darcy," said Fritz, "I would only like to say that nothing written by the accused is carved in stone. And reiterate that no one can ever make you, or anyone, do what is not in his nature. As to your fears for your privacy, no one but you and Mrs. Darcy can ever really know what happens behind your own closed doors. After all, what happens in Pemberley, stays in Pemberley."

"Quite right," said Darcy, and with a smile for his lady he descended from the witness box and extended his hand. "What say you, Mrs. Darcy?"

"Let other plaintiffs dwell on guilt and misery," said she. "I am for dropping this case and appealing the other one."

"Order!" shouted Lady Catherine, banging her gavel over the spontaneous cheers and applause from the spectators and jurors as the Darcys stood before each other, hands clasped and eyes locked, and then, hand in hand, made their way up the aisle. "Miss Wolfson, you shall join your colleague as my guest down below. Take her, Bailiff!"

The bailiff was only too happy to comply, and, grabbing an arm of each lawyer, muscled them both towards the doors. But neither Fritz nor Tawny minded.

"Never fear," said Darcy over his shoulder to them as he and Elizabeth exited the courtroom, "I shall have you released in no time at all."

As the bailiff stopped to open the doors, Tawny reached for Fritz's hand and shook it. "Congratulations, Counselor."

The touch of her hand on his sent tingles through his body. It could have lasted a second or an eternity; he had no sense of time or even of place.

Suddenly he realized she was smiling at him.

"You may release my hand now," she said.

"I will if you allow me to buy you a celebratory dinner." The words were out before he could reckon where he got the courage to utter them.

"Is it customary for the victor to dine with the vanquished?" she asked, trying hard not to show how pleased she was by his invitation.

"No one has been vanquished," said Fritz. "Only vindicated.

After all, the gentleman or lady who has not pleasure in a good movie must be intolerably stupid. And you, Miss Wolfson, are the smartest woman I know."

Bestselling author LAURIE VIERA RIGLER's novels *Confessions of a Jane Austen Addict* and *Rude Awakenings of a Jane Austen Addict* could have been considered semiautobiographical had they not involved time travel and body switching. She would like to see her story "Intolerable Stupidity" turned into a TV pilot for a new series called *Law and Order: Special Austen Unit*. In the meantime, she is working on a third novel. She is also the creator of Sex and the Austen Girl, the Web series inspired by her Austen Addict books.

www.janeaustenaddict.com
www.babelgum.com/sexandtheaustengirl
@austen_addict on Twitter

ACKNOWLEDGMENTS

Occasionally, when the planets and stars align, something magical happens. As a debut author I have many to thank and much to be grateful for. I never dreamt that creating a blog about my favorite author would culminate into a book deal, but it did. My path to publication can be credited to passion, connections, and fate. I would like to spotlight my friends in the Jane Austen online community: Margaret Sullivan of AustenBlog, Vic Sanborn of Jane Austen's World, and Myretta Robens of The Republic of Pemberley for their geeky technical expertise and unerring advice; the affable Jeannine Harvey and Olivia Wong at PBS for generously including me in their Masterpiece Classic family; my fellow booksellers and store manager Stephanie Hare at Barnes & Noble in Lynnwood, Washington, for their encouragement and support; my inimitable literary agent, Mitchell Waters, a true gentleman in the Darcy spirit, for his foresight and patience; and my wonderful editor, Caitlin Alexander, at Ballantine Books for her expert eye and unfaltering guidance. To all who influenced and inspired, please accept my humble thanks and sincere gratitude. And lastly, my deepest appreciation to my family and friends who helped me take the road less traveled. It made all the difference.

ACKNOWLEDGMENTS

JANE AUSTEN
MADE ME DO IT

Edited by Laurel Ann Nattress

A Reader's Guide

Jane Austen's
Incomparable Words

We asked each of the contributors to *Jane Austen Made Me Do It* to select their favorite Austen quote to pair with their story—because, after all, none of these stories would exist without Austen's utterly memorable prose. We hope the following lines will inspire you to reread *your* favorite Austen novel(s) in conjunction with this anthology—and perhaps even to find some inspiration for your own novel or short story.

"He and I should not in the least agree, of course, in our ideas of novels and heroines;—pictures of perfection, as you know, make me sick and wicked." —Jane Austen, letter to her niece, Fanny Austen-Knight, 23 March 1817

(Syrie James, "Jane Austen's Nightmare")

"All the privilege I claim for my own sex (it is not a very enviable one: you need not covet it), is that of loving longest, when existence or when hope is gone!" —Anne Elliot, *Persuasion*

(Jane Odiwe, "Waiting")

"And are you prepared to encounter all the horrors that a building such as 'what one reads about' may produce? Have you a stout heart? Nerves fit for sliding panels and tapestry?" —Henry Tilney, *Northanger Abbey*

(Lauren Willig, "A Night at Northanger")

"And now here's Mr. Bennet gone away, and I know he will fight Wickham, wherever he meets him, and then he will be killed, and what is to become of us all?" —Mrs. Bennet, *Pride and Prejudice*

(Stephanie Barron, "Jane and the Gentleman Rogue")

"It is a truth universally acknowledged, that a single man in possession of a good fortune, must be in want of a wife." —*Pride and Prejudice*

(F. J. Meier, "Faux Jane")

"Poor Mr. Woodhouse trembled as he sat, and, as Emma had foreseen, would scarcely be satisfied without their promising never to go beyond the shrubbery again." —*Emma*

(Monica Fairview, "Nothing Less Than Fairy-land")

"You deserve a longer letter than this; but it is my unhappy fate seldom to treat people so well as they deserve." —Jane Austen, letter to her sister, Cassandra, 24 December 1798

(Adriana Trigiani, "Love and Best Wishes, Aunt Jane")

"I am almost afraid to tell you how my Irish friend [Tom Lefroy] and I behaved. Imagine to yourself everything most profligate and shocking in the way of dancing and sitting down together." —Jane Austen, letter to her sister, Cassandra, 9 January 1796

(Jo Beverley, "Jane Austen and the Mistletoe Kiss")

"In vain I have struggled. It will not do. My feelings will not be repressed. You must allow me to tell you how ardently I admire and love you." —Mr. Darcy, *Pride and Prejudice*

(Beth Pattillo, "When Only a Darcy Will Do")

"We sailors, Miss Elliot, cannot afford to make long courtships in time of war." —Admiral Croft, *Persuasion*

(Margaret C. Sullivan, "Heard of You")

"One half of the world cannot understand the pleasures of the other." —Emma Woodhouse, *Emma*

(Elizabeth Aston, "The Ghostwriter")

"Oh! my dear," cried his wife, "I cannot bear to hear that mentioned. Pray do not talk of that odious man. I do think it is the hardest thing in the world, that your estate should be entailed away from your own children; and I am sure, if I had been you, I should have tried long ago to do something or other about it." —Mrs. Bennet, *Pride and Prejudice*

(Amanda Grange, "Mr. Bennet Meets His Match")

". . . there is something so amiable in the prejudices of a young mind, that one is sorry to see them give way to the reception of more general opinions." —Colonel Brandon, *Sense and Sensibility*

(Janet Mullany, "Jane Austen, Yeah, Yeah, Yeah!")

"Good gracious!" cried Maria, . . . "how many things have happened! . . . How much I shall have to tell!" Elizabeth privately added, "And how much I shall have to conceal." —Maria Lucas and Elizabeth Bennet, *Pride and Prejudice*

(Maya Slater, "Letters to Lydia")

"Can you stand such a ceremony as this? Will not your mind misgive you when you find yourself in this gloomy chamber . . . Will not your heart sink within you?" —Henry Tilney, *Northanger Abbey*

(Myretta Robens, "The Mysterious Closet")

"My present elegances have not made me indifferent to such matters. I am still a Cat if I see a Mouse." —Jane Austen, letter to her sister, Cassandra, 23 September 1813

(Diana Birchall, "Jane Austen's Cat")

"To you I shall say, as I have often said before, Do not be in a hurry, the right man will come at last." —Jane Austen, letter to her niece, Fanny Austen-Knight, 17 March 1817

(Alexandra Potter, "Me and Mr. Darcy, *Again* . . .")

"Silly things do cease to be silly if they are done by sensible people in an impudent way." —Emma Woodhouse, *Emma*

(Jane Rubino and Caitlen Rubino-Bradway, "What Would Austen Do?")

". . . and as she was no horsewoman, walking was her only alternative."
—*Pride and Prejudice*

(Pamela Aidan, "The Riding Habit")

"You pierce my soul. I am half agony, half hope. Tell me not that I am too late, that such precious feelings are gone for ever." —Captain Wentworth, *Persuasion*

(Brenna Aubrey, "The Love Letter")

"Frank is made.—He was yesterday raised to the Rank of Commander, & appointed to the Petterel Sloop, now at Gibraltar." —Jane Austen, letter to her sister, Cassandra, 28 December 1798

(Carrie Bebris, "The Chase")

"From pride, ignorance, or fashion, our foes are almost as many as our readers." —*Northanger Abbey*

(Laurie Viera Rigler, "Intolerable Stupidity")

Add your favorite Austen quote here:

_____

_____

_____

Join other Jane Austen fans, get recommendations on Austen-inspired books, and look for exclusive Q&As with *Jane Austen Made Me Do It* contributors at

www.janeaustenmademedoit.com

and

www.austenprose.com

Reading Group Questions and Topics for Discussion

1. Catherine Morland of *Northanger Abbey* is obsessed with Gothic fiction famous for its ghosts and haunting, while Lauren Willig's Cate in "A Night at Northanger" is a bona fide skeptic. Why do you think Willig chose to subvert the traits Austen originally gave her character? Do you believe in ghosts?

2. Discuss the names that F. J. Meier chose for the characters in "Faux Jane." Anne Elliot is obviously a direct reference to *Persuasion,* but several others are more subtle. Why do you think Meier chose these names and how did they influence your reading of the story?

3. In what ways does F. J. Meier encapsulate the modern passion surrounding Jane Austen? Why do you think her books are of such sentimental and monetary value?

4. Jane Austen's nieces are a recurring presence throughout this anthology—particularly in Diana Birchall's "Jane Austen's Cat" and Adriana Trigiani's "Love and Best Wishes, Aunt Jane." How, if at all, do you think Austen's relationship with her nieces is portrayed differently in these two stories? What are the common themes? How do you think her nieces inspired her writing?

5. In "Intolerable Stupidity," Jane Austen's characters take legal action against writers who have used them in unauthorized sequels and spin-offs. Do you agree with the outcome of the trial? Why do you think Laurie Viera Rigler chose to put the characters on the stand instead of Jane Austen ("the Creator") herself? What do you suppose Jane Austen would think about that vast canon of work her novels have posthumously inspired?

6. In cross-examining Mr. Darcy, Fritz says, "No one can make you, or anyone, do what is not in his nature." Do you think that's true of

all literary sequels? Can you think of any examples of fiction that have completely distorted Mr. Darcy or any other of Jane Austen's characters? Can you think of examples that have helped you understand their natures better?

7. Adriana Trigiani says that she wrote her story in epistolary form to celebrate the tradition of letters in Jane Austen's novels. What are some of your favorite examples of correspondence in Austen's work? Does "Love and Best Wishes, Aunt Jane" strike a tone that reminds you of any particular Austen character?

8. In "Love and Best Wishes, Aunt Jane," Jane says that her sister, Cassandra, "is a different sort of spinster than me, as she still hopes and longs for true love, and is certain it will find her, even at her age." Do you think Jane Austen gave up on love too soon? How do you think she was able to create some of history's most memorable love stories, given that she had never been married herself?

9. In Jane Odiwe's "Waiting," Anne Elliot and Captain Wentworth's love is put to another test when he comes to meet with her father regarding their engagement. Anne is determined to marry him regardless of her family's feelings. In what ways does this scene, not included in Austen's *Persuasion,* show Anne's growth as a character? Is this how you imagined such a meeting would have gone?

10. In Syrie James's "Jane Austen's Nightmare," Jane is visited by her most significant characters—and criticized by nearly all of them. Some are resentful of their faults, some worried that they were too perfect, and some are even out for blood. Why do you think Elizabeth Bennet, Mr. Darcy, Jane, and Mr. Bingley are the only happy characters? Do you think that's an accurate assessment?

11. When Jane wakes up from her nightmare, she and her sister, Cassandra, talk about all that she has learned from her characters, and she uses this knowledge to create her final heroine, Anne Elliot. Do you think that in Anne, Jane was able to create a perfect character?

What do you think Anne would have said if she had a chance to meet Jane too?

12. In Stephanie Barron's "Jane and the Gentleman Rogue," Jane Austen finds herself the heroine of an important case of international treason. What characteristics do you think make her such an intrepid detective? How do you think the author drew inspiration from Austen's novels and letters in creating her dogged heroine?

13. Jane Austen is considered one of literature's most careful documenters of manners. But in Jane Rubino and Caitlen Rubino-Bradway's "What Would Austen Do?" a teenager who adopts them all verbatim is not only shunned but disciplined. How do you think James's experience illustrates the differences between modern society and the society of Austen's time? How do you think Jane Austen would react to the different but equally structured social mores of James's school?

14. In Pamela Aidan's "The Riding Habit," why is it so important to Mr. Darcy that Elizabeth learn how to ride? What do you think it means to him? To Elizabeth?

15. At the end of "The Riding Habit," Mr. Darcy tells Elizabeth: "Recall the riding incident this very day that so nearly ended in injury and disaster. Richard and Georgina—your family—love you and came to your aid. So it shall be with this ball." Discuss this statement, and what you think it means to Elizabeth. How does it illustrate how far the couple has come since the close of *Pride and Prejudice*?

16. Why do you think Maya Slater chose to focus on Maria's voice in "Letters to Lydia"? What did you learn from this different perspective on *Pride and Prejudice*?

17. In Jo Beverley's "Jane Austen and the Mistletoe Kiss," Elinor says that she thinks she could have liked Jane, if she was not the writer of "dangerous" books? What do you think she means by that comment? Why do you think Elinor eventually changes her mind about the mistletoe?

18. In Janet Mullany's "Jane Austen, Yeah, Yeah, Yeah!," Julie helps her students understand *Sense & Sensibility* by comparing the characters to the Beatles, emphasizing the versatility of Austen's novels. What characteristics of her novels do you think make her so appealing to different generations? Can you think of ways in which *Sense & Sensibility* or other novels are applicable to your life?

19. Later, Julie says of Austen: "She knows when to tell us things and when not to." What do you think she means by this? Can you think of some particular examples of Jane Austen's subtlety?

20. Jane Austen's ghost compares herself to Mr. Darcy in Elizabeth Aston's "The Ghostwriter," saying that had she been born a man she would have been like him: "reserved, proud, and clever." From what you know of the author, do you agree with this comparison? How do you think Jane Austen's career as a writer would have been different if she were a man?

21. In "The Ghostwriter," when Sara tells Jane Austen that Mr. Darcy is her ideal man, Austen scoffs, saying: "To yearn for the hero of a novel seems extraordinary to me." And in Alexandra Potter's "Me and Mr. Darcy, *Again* . . . ," Darcy appears in person, forcing Emily to choose between the romantic hero and her boyfriend back home. So many people have romantic fantasies about fictional characters, Mr. Darcy in particular. Why do you think that is? If you could bring one character to life (from Austen's novels or elsewhere) who would it be?

22. In Amanda Grange's "Mr. Bennet Meets His Match," John Bennet refuses to marry for money and holds out to marry for love instead. How do you think this story explains his relationship with his daughters later? What does it tell you about Mrs. Bennet?

23. In "Heard of You," Margaret C. Sullivan tells the story of how Frederick Wentworth introduced his sister, Sophy, to her husband. Why do you think the captain and Sophy's love story was so much easier than Wentworth and Anne's? What do you think this story

tells about Wentworth's character? How, if at all, would you have read *Persuasion* differently with this knowledge?

24. Several of the stories, including Myretta Robens's "The Mysterious Closet," bring up Austen's famous female predecessors, such as the Gothic writer Ann Radcliffe. Why do you think the authors thought it was important to include them? In what ways do you think Jane Austen was influenced by these writers? In what ways did she depart from their traditions? Why, out of all of them, has Austen remained the most popular over time?

25. Jane Austen famously said before writing *Emma* that she intended to create a character that no one but she would like. Do you think that's true? How, if at all, does Monica Fairview's "Nothing Less Than Fairy-land" alter your opinion of Emma Woodhouse?

26. Knightley tells Emma that she is the worst matchmaker in England. Despite all of her snafus, why do you think she is still determined to orchestrate the happiness of others? Do you think her plan for Miss Bates and her father will work?

27. In Beth Pattillo's "When Only a Darcy Will Do," a man dresses as Mr. Darcy to get the attention of a woman who has seen him every day but paid him no mind. Why do you think they are able to connect only through their literary counterparts?

28. In Brenna Aubrey's "The Love Letter," Mark's sister sends him a page from *Persuasion* to communicate her opinion about his relationship with Justine—an opinion Mark probably wouldn't have listened to if Justine had simply come out and told him. Have you ever communicated through someone else's words, whether a page from a book, a poem, a song, or something else? Why?

29. If you could sit down to tea with Jane Austen, what would you ask her?

Story Credits

"The Riding Habit" by Pamela Aidan, copyright © 2011 by Pamela Aidan

"The Ghostwriter" by Elizabeth Aston, copyright © 2011 by Elizabeth Aston

"The Love Letter" by Brenna Aubrey, copyright © 2011 by Brenna Aubrey

"Jane and the Gentleman Rogue: Being a fragment of a Jane Austen mystery" by Stephanie Barron, copyright © 2011 by Stephanie Barron

"The Chase" by Carrie Bebris, copyright © 2011 by Carrie Bebris

"Jane Austen and the Mistletoe Kiss" by Jo Beverely, copyright © 2011 by Jo Beverley

"Jane Austen's Cat" by Diana Birchall, copyright © 2011 by Diana Birchall

"Faux Jane" by F. J. Meier, copyright © 2011 by Frank Delaney and Diane Meier

"Nothing Less Than Fairy-land" by Monica Fairview, copyright © 2011 by Monica Fairview

"Mr. Bennet Meets His Match" by Amanda Grange, copyright © 2011 by Amanda Grange

"Jane Austen's Nightmare" by Syrie James, copyright © 2011 Syrie James

"Jane Austen, Yeah, Yeah, Yeah!" by Janet Mullany, copyright © 2011 by Janet Mullany

"Waiting: A story inspired by Jane Austen's *Persuasion*" by Jane Odiwe, copyright © 2011 by Jane Odiwe

"When Only a Darcy Will Do" by Beth Pattillo, copyright © 2011 by Beth Pattillo

"Me and Mr. Darcy, *Again* . . ." by Alexandra Potter, copyright © 2011 by Alexandra Potter

"What Would Austen Do?" by Jane Rubino and Caitlen Rubino-Bradway, copyright © 2011 by Jane Rubino and Caitlen Rubino-Bradway

"The Mysterious Closet: A Tale" by Myretta Robens, copyright © 2011 by Myretta Robens

"Letters to Lydia" by Maya Slater, copyright © 2011 by Maya Slater

"Heard of You" by Margaret C. Sullivan, copyright © 2011 by Margaret C. Sullivan

"Love and Best Wishes, Aunt Jane" by Adriana Trigiani, copyright © 2011 by The Glory of Everything Company

"Intolerable Stupidity" by Laurie Viera Rigler, copyright © 2011 by Laurie Viera Rigler

"A Night at Northanger" by Lauren Willig, copyright © 2011 by Lauren Willig

ABOUT THE EDITOR

A lifelong acolyte of Jane Austen, LAUREL ANN NATTRESS is the author/editor of Austenprose.com, a blog devoted to the oeuvre of her favorite author and the many books and movies that she has inspired. Nattress is a lifetime member of the Jane Austen Society of North America and a regular contributor to the PBS blog Remotely Connected. Classically trained as a landscape designer at California Polytechnic State University at San Luis Obispo, she has also worked in marketing for a Grand Opera company and at present she delights in introducing neophytes to the charms of Miss Austen's prose as a professional bookseller. An expatriate of Southern California, Laurel Ann lives in a country cottage near Seattle, Washington, where it rains a lot.

austenprose.com
@austenprose on Twitter